10/10/01

To Jack and Myrna

Love,
John

John Galligan

Red Sky, Red Dragonfly

Diversity Incorporated
Madison,WI

Art and Photo Credits
Cover: Cover art by Masami Nii; Photograph by John Galligan
Author Photograph: Ya-Ling Tsai

Text set in Garamond Light Condensed

Printed in the United States of America. Printed by QUESTprint

Advanced Reading Copy—Not for Retail Sale

Of course,

For Jinko

Red Sky, Red Dragonfly

Chapter 1

United Air flight 881 bucked hard into the outer coils of the season's sixth typhoon. Heavy clouds scoured the wings. Then the plane plunged into air thick as lard, traced a shuddering curve over rice paddies and flat gray buildings.

Tommy Morrison awoke as his stomach dropped. The portal beyond his knee showed diagonal shoreline, the other side of the Pacific beneath wing parts flapping like screen doors. He closed his eyes. With a heave in his seat, he squeezed flat a bulge of nausea. He waited for the bump of the runway, the bracing friction of arrival. Then he opened his letter once more.

Arigato gozaimasu, she had written on the back of his travel instructions, in a fine, spidery hand.

And next, *Doitashimashite*.

Thank you, this meant, and you are welcome.

Tommy stared numbly at the letter as the rush to the overhead bins began. His contact was Noriko Yamaguchi, secretary of Prince English School. Beneath these words she had added a dozen more terms of survival. Numbers and o'clocks. Please and nice to meet you. Forgive me, I will be an impediment. Please speak more slowly. I've had enough, thank you. Good night. She had also described each step of his five-train journey and provided photographs of the town (snowbound) and the Prince School staff (one blond young man, flashing a peace sign). In closing, she had wished Tommy ominous amounts of luck and instructed him to call from Takata before the final train change. The last train stopped on the mountain above Kitayama. It was too far to walk, she wrote, so she would pick him up.

And Tommy would say, *Arigato gozaimasu*.

And Noriko Yamaguchi would answer, *Doitashimashite.*

He looked away at the runway. Little silver trucks charged the plane. He tried to bring the words to his lips . . . but nothing.

He folded her note into his pocket. A stewardess cocked her head and smiled as if he might not leave the plane. He rose and straightened his bad knee slowly. Then Tommy Morrison gripped his carry-on and limped off into Japan.

The airport was drab and strictly unadorned. It could have been anywhere, could have been the old Soviet Union of Tommy's hockey-focused mind except that he felt his crushing size as he moved on and on through secure corridors. Then the stream of travelers split, Japanese to the left, giants to the right, and at passport control the clerk inquired, "Destination?"

"Kitayama."

She stalled her stamper in mid-air, faintly but potently amused, then finished her stroke.

"Have a nice visit."

On a bench in baggage claim, his right knee throbbed like a second, stunted brain. Perhaps—the Milwaukee Admirals team surgeon had told him this, five years ago—perhaps for a short time, some occasional minor *irritation.* Tommy washed down six Tylenol on a swallow of salty-sugary canned drink called Pocari Sweat. His sugar-binging teenage son, he thought, would sweat like this. That is, if the boy ever moved enough to sweat. If the boy's mother ever pushed him. If Elaine hadn't turned Gus against him. If she hadn't. . . . *Irritation.* Some. Occasional. Minor.

Perhaps.

Luggage began to spout ponderously from a fountain in the floor. Tommy watched it circulate, waiting for pain-killer to meet screws and transplanted tissue. He told himself he was among Japanese now and tried to observe them. He gazed across six hockey rinks of slick tile and human traffic. Trim, nifty people, for the most part, streamlined travelers wheeling off luggage better than his, knowing where to go. Great quantities of duty free and noisy laughter. Spike heels. Calvin Klein. NBA gear. Not a soul, it appeared, in the mood for exploitation. At least not in any new way. He didn't see why Elaine should be so disgusted.

"Tell me once more. You're *what?*"

"Going to teach English in Japan."

"You think you can go anywhere, do anything, to anyone!"

Tommy looked down at his watch. This exchange with his wife was only hours ago, en route across his ex-front lawn to his ex-garage, where he planned to pick up his skates and a few pucks.

"Well," he had told her, "practice makes perfect."

He rose and tried to shed the past. But Elaine Red Cloud stayed on him. She had appeared again to block the kitchen screen while he rummaged in a barrel of sporting goods.

"You're not one bit funny," she told him.

She allowed a long stretch of futile digging to thin Tommy's patience, then added, "Anyway, what makes you think the rest of the world needs to learn English?"

"I don't think that."

"You don't think."

She let that work.

Tommy straightened. "Where's my skates?" His search panned the garage walls, taking in fourteen years of family trophies. Between the mulcher mower and the snowblower hung Gus' hideous mountain bike, its tires starved for turf. Tommy had promised himself no anger, but suddenly the thought of his son made his head buzz.

"He hasn't touched that thing, I see. He needed it so much."

Elaine posted a tactical silence.

"What does he do now, anyway? Now that I'm gone. Does he do anything?"

Elaine lit a cigarette. "Nothing that you would recognize."

And Tommy had thrust his face back into the barrel. For an infuriating half-minute he could not recall what he was looking for. Then the phone rang in the kitchen, and Elaine locked the screen and went to answer. Tommy drove his hands toward the bottom of the barrel. There his fingers touched laces and grommets, smooth leather, a cool blade. He heaved up through the tangle of wasted games.

They were Gus' skates. Beautiful, top-dollar Bauers, begged for. Big enough for the boy's whopping Red Cloud feet, hardly used, sharp as knives.

Tommy tucked them under his arm, made haste for his car.

"Hey!" Elaine yelled. "What are you doing here anyway?"

Her last words, or so he thought, were hollered through the front screen, the phone pressed to her chest. "And what's that you're taking? Huh? Tell me! What is that?"

Tommy's old Admirals bag worked its soiled nose over the top of the baggage fountain, then flopped onto the conveyor like a huge garden slug and became stuck. An attendant climbed in to free it. One of Gus' skates had cut through the bag wall, and this sight, carried forth to customs, triggered a panic. Agents split the bag like a sausage. Tommy was appalled at his packing: a peculiar wad of clothes and paperbacks, shiny Florsheim loafers, Tums and Tylenol, ties wound up like sleeping snakes, and a half dozen hockey pucks still cold from the plane's belly.

The customs agents had a long discussion. They x-rayed the pucks. They circled him with a dog. For a moment Tommy wondered if all the dope smoke from the past still clung. But the dog sniffed his heap of possessions and was led off, quivering with disappointment. Tommy gave up his passport and waited.

He first noticed the island heat as a heaviness in his clothes. He touched his hair . . . wet to the scalp in the thin spot where a hockey helmet had rubbed his skull for fifteen years. When he thought of standing, moving his legs, he thought of Elaine's Lac Courte Oreilles relatives swimming the reservation flowage in blue jeans and then struggling around soaking wet. Then a young woman in a blue uniform brought him cold tea and bowed, hiding her eyes and murmuring. Tommy dug for his word list.

Arigato gozaimasu.

Doitashimashite.

But she was gone. He stared at his pile of clothes. *What a godawful job of packing.* He stood suddenly, as if to walk away from it all. But this brought an agent to block the cubicle door.

"I am sorry," the man pronounced carefully.

They blinked at one another.

Tommy said, "Me too."

He sat down. He had wanted to say a simple, clean goodbye, but he had swiped his kid's skates instead, and not cleanly, either. He had driven to work from Elaine's then, less than a day ago, parked his old Buick deep in the Tri-County Tech lot and ditched the plates. With Gus' skates around his bag handle he hurried inside to close out his office and call a cab. He had just boxed two years of algebra files and was swiping the last scraps from his desk with a hurried forearm when the phone rang.

"Skates," he told her, before she could ask again. "I'm taking the boy's skates."

She was on the remote phone in her basement study corner. He could hear snaps and buckles clanking in the clothes dryer.

"Fine," she said. "It's your way. I just called to read you something from my American Lit text." She was back in school, and militant this time. "Listen. This is your Robert Frost, for the inauguration of Kennedy: *The land was ours . . . vaguely realizing westward/ But still unstoried, artless, unenhanced/ Such as she was, such as she would become. . . .*"

Tommy waited, beginning his summer school grade report.

"You're going to civilize the Japanese, is that it?"

Snap. Clank. She was drying her tent.

"Great poetry they'll be reading, isn't it? So full of truth and respect for humanity."

"Elaine, if we're going to be so cozy, I'd like to talk to Gus."

"He's unavailable."

"Is he there? He's not at school. I called there. I just wanted to tell him goodbye."

"You've told him goodbye enough already."

She meant in general. A decade of hockey seasons, then a long season of self-absorbed indifference—Tommy admitted this—and then, of course, the affair.

He said, "Your problem, Elaine, is that the possibility of anything new gets buried in all your score keeping. At this moment, at every moment, the world is new and different, a whole new ball game, and I want to tell my son goodbye."

She gave his philosophizing the steam-cleaning of a good, long sigh. Finally she said: "So what are you doing with ice skates, anyway? Properly, shouldn't you be taking whiskey and blankets?"

Tommy hung up the phone with a particular snap of the wrist he had become quite good at. Repetitions. Reps, in jock talk. Do what you had to, over and over, until you didn't think about it anymore.

He finished his grade report, locked the office, tossed his keys at Swede in the mailroom. He was cutting fast across Aux Hall toward the freight elevator when his peripheral vision sent him an odd message: Gus. Tommy had spent all morning looking for his son. Now his son—his normally unfocused, chronically passive, directionally impaired teenage son—had somehow found him. *See Elaine?* he wanted to say. *Every moment, a whole new ball game.*

The customs agents returned, five of them. Tommy's pucks had been taped in a stack; the skate blades were swaddled in bubble-wrap. By committee, the agents assembled a fine English sentence.

"Mister Morrison . . . why . . . do you bring . . . these items . . . to Japan?"

"I was hoping to skate a bit. To relax."

"Relax?"

"Hoping to."

"Hoping to?"

"Yes."

"Hoping to relax?"

"Yes."

"Ah." The youngest agent emerged into comprehension. "I see. Ice skate is your hobby."

Tommy laughed. The young agent smiled uncertainly. His nametag said Sagawa. His slender hands twitched at his sides as he retrieved English words.

"Why, please, are these skates so very sharp?"

"He never used them."

"Ah."

"My son, I mean."

They had a conference. Sagawa asked him, "Please, what is your destination in Japan?"

When Tommy told them Kitayama, it was as if he had mentioned his own name to a crowd of hockey fans. Heads tilted, memories strained, eyes searched the room's corners for pathways to the obscure . . . but nobody was certain.

"Kitayama?"

"Yes."

Sagawa went for a map. He was gone a long time. The agents seemed embarrassed. It was one of those things: you never had a map of where you already were. While they re-packed his belongings into airport shopping bags, Tommy's mind festered its way back to the double take that confirmed the last-minute miracle at Tri-County Tech. It was Gus standing there in the hallway, gripping his skateboard, striving for ornery dispassion but clearly marooned and scared among the college students, Tommy's own, damn, trouble-seeking son. It was Gus.

Tommy had watched him for an uncertain moment. The kid was peering into the wrong office. Despite the heat, he wore Tommy's Red Wings jacket, the black leather one that was "stolen" after Tommy moved out. He wore this with grimy phat pants, new white Air Jordans, wanna-be rasta knots in his tortured hair.

"Gus. I'm down here."

"Oh, wow, Dad." Gus shuffled up. "Did you move?"

"No."

The boy turned a slow circle.

"Yeah, Dad. You moved."

"I've been at the same desk for five years."

"Dad——" Gus reproduced their family counselor's broad-minded leer. He laid a pen-scrawled hand on Tommy's wrist.

"It's okay to be wrong, Dad. You used to be down there, and everybody knows it. But whatever. I know you're working through some stuff."

Tommy thought a long time about what to say, watching students watch him. Finally, hoarsely, he whispered, "Gus, shut the hell up."

Then they stood paralyzed. In his mind, Tommy gave the kid the jacket, gave him amnesty for a good-bye present, but no words left his mouth. Instead he noticed the boy had painted his fingernails black to match the jacket, noticed he was pulling a rumpled paper from the pocket.

"You hitch out here?"

"Dad."

"You look stoned."

"Come on, Dad." Gus' voice was weak. "You're not supposed to hassle me, remember?"

The elevator pinged, clattered shut, went away. Tommy took the paper. It was a ninth-grade algebra handout, crumpled in private grief, re-opened and folded in some vague hope. Gus leaned in to help Tommy stare at the paper. The problem was that grains of sand were draining through an hourglass at a rate of 1,000 per second. If two-thirds of the grains were at the bottom after 30 minutes, how many grains were there in total?

"Gus," Tommy said, easing toward the elevator. "I'm in kind of a hurry. In twenty minutes my plane leaves for Chicago."

Gus followed him. "I know. Mom told me you were taking off."

"By tomorrow I'll be in Japan."

The boy sat down on a flat of textbooks, stunned. It was clear that Elaine hadn't told him taking off to *where*, but whether this was restraint or malice, it was impossible to tell. Elaine was that way now.

He gave the boy a pencil. He said, "Try this. Imagine you're hitching back to school. Cross out hourglass and write in intersection of Pine and Peterson. Cross out grains and write in cars. Now stick your thumb out."

He paused, noticing his own meaty forearms, eraser dust caught in the thatched hair.

"I'm not exactly just 'taking off.' I was asked to leave the college."

Gus hunched over the paper, flushed, scratching with the pencil. Tommy was stirred by his embarrassment. Elaine must have given him details. Tommy watched his son begin a jagged doodle. The thing looked familiar: lightning that changed its mind and became a half swastika and then something prick-like that finally began to swirl and search and gouge the paper. Tommy swallowed a bolt of heartburn and looked away, down the hall.

"I yooped a guy, Gus."

"Here? You yooped a guy? At school? Dad . . . *Jesus!*"

And then, finally, Sagawa was back. Gathered over the map, the agents leaned, squinted, exchanged grunts of dismay. One made a joke. Another glanced back at Tommy. Then they showed him the map.

"You will go to this place?"

Tommy followed Sagawa's finger. Across the island, up the Japan sea, then inland, into the map's marbled, untraveled green, to a small dot between mountains: yes, he was going there.

"Very rare!" Sagawa exclaimed, his eyes growing a bit wild. "Foreign people in this kind of town!"

Then he asked something in Japanese. Tommy's tired brain recognized the intent of the question: did he speak the language? There was a phrase in Noriko

Yamaguchi's letter for *please speak more slowly*, but he couldn't recall it. He patted his pockets. He couldn't find the letter either.

"Actually there is an American there now. A twenty-one year-old kid from Utah. They just opened an English School."

Sagawa's head very slowly tilted to the side, as though he had just heard about a golf course on the moon.

"Sooo . . . ka?"

"Prince English School. I'll be replacing the kid."

The thin young man held his gaze on Tommy an extra instant.

"Ah," he said then. "Prince School. Yes, I see."

He seemed reluctant to translate. When he did, his fellow agents found the news stimulating. A great burst of giddy talk blossomed around Tommy. A second agent, Mori, bald and avuncular, burned hot with English.

"You like hamburgers?" Mori wanted to know.

He looked pained.

"If you like hamburgers," he stammered, "you must visit Takata. Kitayama town, no hamburgers."

"Small," ventured a third agent. "Kitayama very small, small town."

He drew a barrier up and down with hands and stood behind it, looking troubled.

"I like hamburgers," declared Mori.

Then Sagawa cut them off. "Kitayama is a long way," he said. "You must start."

Quickly, the agents released Tommy into a wide corridor explosive with sound. Beyond the windows swarmed busses and taxis. The vehicles jittered in a purplish, muscular air. A sudden gust twisted hair and flattened skirts, flung car doors too far. Tommy felt Sagawa's soft hand on his shoulder. They proceeded downward, not out into the approaching storm but deeper into the airport, through checkpoints and gates and down escalators, a gradual narrowing until Sagawa stopped him on a train platform. Before them waited a sleek train, aimed into a single black hole.

Sagawa shuttled his bags inside the door.

"Good luck," he said, "in Kitayama."

Tommy dug for his note from the Prince School secretary.

A..ri..ga. . . .

Arigee. . . .

But Sagawa had slipped away into the crowd. Then the train horn sounded. Tommy stepped on, looking back. The airport exit funneled away, gates and ropes and check points, then the black pinch of the tunnel, and the sensation reminded Tommy of the old Ojibwa fish trap Grandpa Rupert had given Gus.

Having blundered in so far, that is, you could see where you came from, and you could pitch and thrash, but you could not go back.

Chapter 2

Miwa Sato made her move after calculus class. She lingered in the classroom as if to speak with Nakama-sensei. Then she sneaked past the locker room while the other girls changed into sweat suits for kendo practice. Outside Takata Girls' High School, a typhoon's shadow pressed the earth. Miwa's eyeglasses steamed over. A gust tossed hair about her face. She shouldered her heavy rucksack and her kendo stick, then ducked past the backstop, hurried across the packed-dirt ground and out the gate to the sidewalk.

There she paused. At five o'clock, main street Takata was a rolling boil of taxis and buses, shoppers and school kids. The air was pure noise, pure exhaust. As she was spun about in the rush, Miwa reminded herself that her little home town, another fifty kilometers into the mountains, was not that bad. For all its failings, for the many ways it had been difficult for its first English teacher, Kitayama remained lovely, ancient, quiet, and small. It was the entire world, after all, of her grandfather—and with this thought her breath caught. Grandfather would stop her right here. She could hear his angry voice.

Skipping school! Consorting with a white man! Treacherous granddaughter!

But it would be over soon. Mister Stuart's year had ended. He would be replaced, and he would leave Kitayama today. He would pack his big blue suitcase, attend his bye-bye party, and leave. Forever. So it was okay, she told herself. She would see him one last time.

Miwa adjusted her rucksack, then entered the stream and made two stops. At Mister Donut she waited in a long line and bought a variety dozen. She took the box and a melon soda to a tiny table in the corner. She leaned her kendo stick on the window. Bodies hurled past the glass. She composed a note. *Dear Stuart*, she wrote in calligraphy that was not her best, as she was frightened nearly senseless by what she planned to say. *I forgive you*, she wrote at last. Then she pulled her hair from her face, made way for the soda.

Her second stop was Hara's Book Store. The August comic books had come in just yesterday, so of course the narrow shop was packed. Miwa minimized her rucksack in the space between her knees. She squeezed in sideways, through the Takata Senior High boys as they fed insensate at the new *Jump Boy*, the new *Pachinko Club*, the new *No Panty Angels*. Then she burrowed among the enchanted girls in the shop's rear, reaching through skirts and rucksacks to pick up the new *Big Comic for Lady*.

Miwa's small hands had become damp. *Big Comic for Lady* was for older girls, city girls, girls who upset their grandfathers. Still, she flipped the pages with trembling fingers, checking titles. "Always Tomorrow," "The Rose of Love," "A Million Tears," "Sunset Girl," "Going Steady." Then the one she wanted: "Exotic Friend."

Miwa pushed back to the counter and paid.

The Kitayama train was an old red diesel on the last platform: three cars, smut and rust, some windows jammed open and some jammed shut. It was the worst train in the station, a wobbly, filthy shuck that Kitayama kids would suffer back and forth to Takata until such time as the town had its own high school, until Kitayama had factories, an airport, the courtesy of a high speed train. All this was coming soon, the leaders of Kitayama had promised. As soon as the likes of Grandfather were gone.

Miwa boarded early, mindful of Stuart's difficult leaving and now of all this, too. *Poor Grandfather!* Then, for a terrible moment, she could not decide where in the empty train to sit. She rushed through one whole car, a plump and guilty girl in fallen knee socks, bearing a box of donuts and a giant comic book, until at last she commanded herself to sit at the rear of the last car, beside an open window.

Grandfather, she began to herself, *I have done my best. . . .*

Then she balanced the donut box on her lap, raised *Big Comic for Lady* on top of that, and prepared a tissue. She would stop this some day, she promised herself, this searching for answers and sniveling over the pretty way it should have been.

The August issue of "Exotic Friend" began like this. It was dawn in Kyoto. A full page framed the famous hills and temples, the station, the great avenues, and the tiny visitor poised before it all with his huge suitcase. Then the artist swept in by smaller frames: from the station steps, the city spread impossibly about the blond-haired stranger; from the sidewalk, the young man's suitcase rose to his waist; through a cab driver's windshield, his first halting, mis-timed step—

BEEEEP! went the cabbie's horn. The big letters burst from the cartoon frame itself, lifted the gaijin off his feet.

BEEEEP!

Miwa studied the boy's frozen scramble for the curb. His lovely hair had become a crown of terror. His eyes were drawn wide and round. His suitcase spilled clothes about the corners of the frame.

"EH?" he gasped

How much help he needed, thought Miwa. It was only a cartoon story, nothing more than black ink on green pulp, but still her heart rose to it. The very sounds lived within her. *Grandfather,* she argued, *Stuart needed me. Truly he did.*

She turned pages quickly then, absorbing a dozen frames at a glance. *BA-TAN!* went the doors of the new school as Exotic Friend stepped in. *KIRA-KIRA!* went the eyes of love struck girls. Then came a blur of parties and outings, classes and disco dates. Miwa made the sounds with her lips. She watched with thumping heart how the artist gradually enlarged in the eyes of Exotic Friend a hollow spot that no one saw but one shy girl, the quiet girl who watched and waited until one evening after school and before another party she pushed aside the classroom door and found the stranger lonely and bereft, golden head in hands.

A noise startled Miwa. She whipped around. But it was only the sweeper, coming on to snag empty cans from under the seats. And anyway, Miwa reminded herself, she did not detect some weakness in Stuart. It was Stuart who saw some weakness in her. He sought her out. *I don't know why, Grandfather.*

Miwa buried her head again in the comic. Her lips popped and hissed and sighed along with the sound effects. The lucky girl saved Exotic Friend then. He allowed her to feed his hungry soul. On secret dates she showed him old Kyoto: the Golden Temple, the Water Temple, Nijojo Temple with the nightingale floor. The artist's clever frames explored and roamed, settled in gardens and along rivers, then zoomed away. Birds looked down on the furtive couple. At Nara, the Great Buddha himself gazed down on them. Then winter came and snow sailed. Miwa whispered, *"ZAAA!"* Through Exotic Friend's apartment window the girl sneaked imported peanut butter, corn chips, macaroni and cheese, strange and magical foods that made his eyes shine and kept him strong.

Now Miwa raised her legs for the old woman's broom. A juice can rattled along the filthy floor into the jaw of the dustbin. A hot gust wobbled the ancient train.

"Typhoon coming," muttered the old woman.

Then . . . spring! A big frame claimed both pages, a bursting hillside, all of Japan behind the couple: mountain, temple, rice field, farm. Miwa's breath snagged at a single detail: the girl stood in the foreground, her skirt blown against her thighs. Her arm stretched out, leading the eye to a small inset frame. There, a single stalk of susuki grass arced gracefully. On its furry tip balanced a dragonfly, hypnotized by the girl's circling finger . . . then deftly she caught it.

Miwa stopped breathing.

It was a trick Grandfather had taught her. And then Exotic Friend swelled into the next frame, his blonde hair askew in the breeze, his eyes aflame with desire, and with parted lips and hands like claws he reached for Miwa. . . .

She closed the book. Suddenly the typhoon pressure had forced itself inside her chest. Sweat shone on her brow. Her toes crawled inside her shoes. Then she rose and stepped around her rucksack, around the bent-backed sweeper. She carried the comic to the end of the train and shoved it through the trash slot.

She would say it aloud, she decided, strongly and plainly: *I forgive you.*

She sat back down. Then the platform whistle blew and the old diesel rumbled to life. Kitayama kids could hide from their ugly train no longer. Miwa squared the Mister Donut box on her lap, lowered her head. The boarding bells began to ring. In a moment, her classmates swarmed around her, shoving and laughing.

"Granny Miwa," shouted someone. "Sitting on the train by herself."

"Teacher knows you skipped kendo, Miwa."

"Crazy Miwa, who are the donuts for?"

Miki Ebana bounced into the seat behind her, breathing lemon candy.

"Did you hear?" Miki announced. "Last night Noriko Yamaguchi was at Stuart's apartment! And Noriko's husband was busy fishing down at Three Cedar Corner—"

Saori Endo made a long neigh of disbelief. "Ehhhhh?" she said.

"You don't believe me?"

Miki Ebana rose to her knees on the seat and poked Miwa on the shoulder. "Tell us," she said. "Granny Miwa. Who are the donuts for?"

"My friend."

"You don't have any friends," she said and turned away. "But it's true," she continued with Saori Endo. "Mother knows Stuart's every move. Missus Honda can see his apartment from the rice shop, and Mother buys her rice at Missus Honda's."

"Your mother has a crush on Stuart," said Saori Endo. "That's all. She's in love with him."

"And you're not?" Miki Ebana returned. Then again to Miwa, "What friend?" she demanded. "Prove it."

"My friend."

"Boyfriend?"

"Friend."

"What friend?"

The train bell rang, announcing its intent to bear them once more back to Kitayama. Miwa felt her courage jarred off center. *Grandfather. . . .* She watched the station trail away, the freight yard stream away, pachinko parlors, car dealers, farms. *What I mean by forgive, Grandfather, is as one human to another. . . .*

Rice whipped and whorled in the typhoon wind. Miwa's fingers stretched to the corners of the box.

"Crazy Miwa, what friend?"

"They're for Stuart," she announced at last, and closed her ears against the outcry. Her cheeks on fire, her hands sweating, she stared out at the train platform. Stared and stared, while her classmates went *baka* around her.

So it was, with her head wrenched away from the clamor, that Miwa first saw the new teacher as he rushed the train. He was a much older man, limping hard, a cloud of messy bags about him and a grimace on his whiskered face. He looked right at her, wild gray eyes, then disappeared for the moment it took him to heave aboard. She felt the car rock faintly. She felt herself shiver as the train began its wobble and screech away from the platform. As the new Prince School teacher appeared at the head of the car, Miwa closed her eyes, silently counted to ten.

Then: "Gaijin!" exploded little Kenzo Koho. "Look! Everybody look! It's a gaijin!"

The white man entered the car unsteadily, his bags jamming between the seat corners. Kenzo fled the doorway, coughing Cup-a-Noodles back into his cup.

"Hello!" he screamed. "Gaijin-san, hello!"

Now the huge man lunged in among the seats, looking for a place to hold on. Tommy, Miwa remembered. Tommy Morrison. Noriko had told her. Then, in Mister Tommy's path, Kenzo staggered, spilling soup, clutching his head in mortal dismay. Behind Miwa, girls whispered and giggled. Their Japanese was unkind. Older boys sat up and closed their comic books, shoved each other and made animal grunts.

"Hello!" Kenzo persisted, dancing in the man's path. "Hello! Hello!"

"Hi," said Mister Tommy. "How are you."

"Hello!"

"How are you."

"Hello!" Kenzo screamed back. "Hello!" And now Jun Endo was slapping himself in the face. "How are you!" he gasped. "How are you!"

The new teacher set his bristly jaw and teetered forward. Miwa tried to make a bow. *Welcome*, she tried to say. *Please ignore these stupid boys.* But she froze. Tommy Morrison was nothing like Stuart. His strange bags crowded her feet. His hip eclipsed her face. His long arm stretched above to grip the strap. He puffed, smelled of sweat. He did not smile.

"Gaijin-san!" screeched Kenzo. "Hello!"

But the new American did not blush and stammer like Stuart. He stared evenly at Kenzo through his fatigue, gnawing his lip and swaying heavily with the train, as if his strength alone could make it wobble. Miwa moved her eyes to the green blur at the window, but the new teacher was reflected there too. She kept her knees together, her fingers on the corners of the donut box. Her hair slipped over her cheeks, her shoulders hunched in. Somehow the fact of this new teacher bore down on Kitayama, she thought. There would come this strange and powerful man, she realized, then another, and another. *Grandfather*, she began, *you are right. Now, suddenly, I understand—*

Then Miki Ebana attacked over the seat back again. She made a vomiting face at the damp back of Mister Tommy. "Crazy Miwa," she resumed. "You claim Stuart likes you then? Are we supposed to believe that?"

"Yes."

"You were lovers?"

"If we were lovers, I would hide the donuts."

"Crazy Miwa. He's too cute for you. If he smiled at you, your skirt would fall off."

She grabbed a *Jump Boy* from Taka Daiwa's hands and shoved an open cartoon page into Miwa's face. "You would be like this, Miwa."

Miwa turned her head away. But she knew what was there—the boys' version of the moment beyond the first hot touch, a girl abruptly on her back, her shirt torn and her dress up, her eyes wide, just like in the books that Brother and Father read.

Miwa stared out the train window. "Soup!" brayed Kenzo Koho at Tommy Morrison. "Gaijin-san, Japanese soup!" But no, Miwa told herself. Her story was going to be different. She would deliver Stuart's donuts quickly and be done. She would pass the box into his long white fingers. *I forgive you,* she would say. *Good bye.*

Of course, Stuart would gasp and twist and reach for her. He would try to confuse her with his words. But she would be ready.

Your bye-bye party is waiting, she would remind him calmly.

And close your windows, she would advise him. *A typhoon is coming.*

And then as the dense air quivered and the sky cracked she would step back into the alley.

GORO-GORO! would come the great cartoon storm.

She would put up her umbrella. The first fat drops would strike it.

BOTA! BOTA!

Sayonara, Mister Stuart, she would say. And that would be that.

In the middle of South Tunnel, one kilometer from Kitayama, the new teacher fell asleep on his feet. Miwa watched it happen in the reflection at her shoulder. His thick arms were raised, his furry hands gripping the straps. Then as the train jerked into slow-down, his head snapped and his eyes opened. Students trampled his bags in the rush for the door. Then, as he bent to save his luggage, he staggered. His head rammed Miki Ebana square above her precious rump and she shrieked. He raised up and tried to apologize, but she had buried herself amidst the mass of black hair and blue uniforms.

"Gaijin!" bawled Kenzo, his voice gone hoarse. He waved his Cup-a-Noodles. "Happy New Year! Love me tender!"

Then the train was coasting, wobbling, its stop-bell ringing, and Mister Tommy decided to turn against the tide. Red-faced and scowling, he shoved toward the center of the car as if he meant to sit down. He raised his bags overhead. He muttered something and turned sideways. Then the train made its wretched spasm of a stop.

Miwa looked into her lap, because such moments pained her. The huge gaijin was tossed forward, then back, and then some sharpness made him wince and lift one leg from the floor. And still the train wasn't finished. A few meters more it sneaked smoothly while he wavered on one foot, and then it slammed to a dead halt that splashed supple bodies back and forth but broke the big white man into a flailing, bag-flinging lunge that brought him squarely down on Miwa's lap.

Her breath escaped in a loud squeak. The Mister Donut box flattened in her hands and his weight drove it deep between her legs.

"Sorry!" he panted.

His hair mashed her face. His shoulder choked her. Her right breast felt torn.

"I'm sorry."

He raised himself. Miwa recovered the ruined donut box. She collected her rucksack and her kendo stick. The train was suddenly empty but for them.

"I'm sorry. Are you okay?"

"Hai," she managed. "Yes, I'm okay."

And then the mob was outside, jeering, flashing peace signs, laughing. Kenzo charged the open window, waving a pen.

"Gaijin-san, hello!" he screamed. "This is a pen!"

Mister Tommy stared beyond him. She understood what he was thinking. You could not see Kitayama from here. You saw only a small, hollow station, bicycles and cars, then a deep cleft in the mountain capped by rolling gray clouds. The storm had nearly caught the train.

"This is a pen!" Kenzo howled again. His breath blasted the window. His school books spilled and blew open beside the tracks. Then his schoolmates, hanging back on the platform, grew brave. As the new teacher moved to recover his bags, they rushed the windows and danced alongside. They began to pound the windows.

"This is a pen!" the boys screamed, thrusting pens.

Then Kenzo flung his soup, noodles slid down glass, and Miwa saw rage on new teacher's face.

"Please—" she began, but she could find no English words to follow. *Please understand*, her eyes begged him. *This is such a small town. Such a small, old place. We cannot change. We cannot catch up with the rest of Japan.* But Mister Tommy turned back to the boys. He raised his right fist and thrust at them a huge and hairy middle finger.

The boys erupted. They hammered the windows, rabid with glee, thrusting middle fingers back at him. "Fuck you!" they cried happily. They skipped and tussled alongside the train.

"Gaijin-san! Fuck you!"

Miwa turned away, the ruined box in her hands. She didn't know what she would do now. The sky outside was greenly dark and rolling, obese with rain. Cars and bikes plunged away down the mountain. She didn't know what she would do. As she neared the door, the new teacher loomed behind her.

"Can you tell me," he puffed, "how much farther to Kitayama town?"

The train lights went out.

"This is Kitayama," she said, and stepped off.

Chapter 3

Where was Kitayama, he wondered. When the last of his bags hit the platform, Tommy looked up to find the station nearly deserted. One tiny white pickup truck buzzed through a U-turn, all eyes on him, then accelerated and disappeared over the rim of the mountain.

Now only the girl remained. She wedged her heavy backpack into the basket of a dirty-pink motor scooter. She covered her head with a battered helmet. She took the seat and carefully tucked the sweet-smelling box between her feet, beside the point of her long, black case. She wore saddle shoes, Tommy noticed, with pink laces. As she adjusted loose white socks about her thick ankles, the station's floodlight crackled and flickered on, charging the air with a thousand even smaller and more insistent details. But where was the town? He rested his eyes a moment. She was gone.

Tommy walked. He hung three bags on each arm and limped down the mountain. The road was steep and narrow, bent with switchbacks and crumbling at its edges. In ten minutes, resting his arms at a corner, Tommy made out a grid of rice fields in the valley below, a few weak lights on the far mountain. Wherever his destination was, it was farther than he could see. Farther than he could carry his baggage. Numbly he turned around. He struggled back uphill.

Inside the shelter that passed for a station there was a phone, a bright green plastic box with the receiver on top, but Tommy had no idea how to use it. He dug in his pocket for Noriko Yamaguchi's note. But somehow he had lost it. He fell back on a bench beside a vending machine. He would sleep here, he thought. But the bench was too narrow, too short. He sat back up. And the toilet stank.

Tommy dragged his bags outside to a trash barrel. The paperbacks, the alarm clock, the hockey pucks—as they struck the barrel bottom he felt a faint and bitter surge of energy. He hadn't been sure just how much his life would really change, and now he began to understand. It would be erased, he realized, and this sudden notion, darkly fitting, placed Elaine once more at his shoulder. He had been handed everything, Elaine liked to claim. He had been born into a favorable script, comfortable and sure of his role, but he would not survive outside of his little white man's bubble. Well, he thought grimly, dumping t-shirts into the barrel, now they would see.

Then jeans, belts, CD's, toiletries, video tapes, hats, his second suit coat, every necktie but one, the Game Boy he had carried on a thousand hockey road trips, the case of Snickers and package of new socks his mother had given him—all of this went into the trash barrel. He saved one bag of essential clothing. Then Tommy stood in the weak floodlight, typhoon wind whipping his hair, holding his son's ice skates.

He wondered if he had ever left town in his life without a pair of skates. Hockey had been his passport, the local sports hacks liked to write, but he hadn't ever seen much more than busses, hotels, hockey rinks. He had gone to Russia, lost a hockey game, gotten drunk, and come home. Same for Norway. Same for a hundred towns in the United States and Canada. Hockey had been his prison, too, hadn't it? Not that anyone would want to consider that complaint. Not that Tommy dared to make it. But he had been a good student, possessing enough of a brain for an easy math major, and still his talent on ice had defined every turn in his life. Even the job at Tri-County Tech, where the hockey coach was set to retire, was predicated on pucks into nets, or the prevention thereof. He had been a rink rat, Tommy mused sourly as he raised the skates over the trash barrel. He had been a rink rat in a cage.

Still, these were Gus' skates. The boy officially owned them. And suddenly Tommy felt baffled and sad, too exhausted to think. His mind replayed the picture of Gus staring at the buffed floor tiles at Tri-County Tech, crimson creeping between his blackheads as he thought of his father's troubles.

"I was busted, Gus. Battery. I hit a guy at school."

But what did these words mean—all these claims and charges? How real were they now? Where in his life was the proper point of focus—the right thing to feel sorry about, the right thing to change?

Tommy had to sit. He returned to the bench beside the vending machine and inhaled the smelly air. Here, after a lifetime of penalties, was his defining offense:

he had slept with a student. He had known he was wrong. He didn't need the ensuing scandal. He didn't need a colleague, Dr. Kent Minnerly, Chemistry, to "initiate a dialog on harassment" in the very hallway where Tommy had stood with Gus just hours ago. He didn't need Minnerly jabbing a knobby carbon molecule into his chest until his wires had crossed. Suddenly Tommy the rink rat had found himself thinking that Minnerly didn't know jack-shit about harassment. His colleague just couldn't get it that girls fucked the players, their choice, and somehow the good doctor had missed the idea that talk leads to action.

"I yooped him, Gus." It was a family term, to *yoop* a guy, *yoop* coming from the U.P. of Michigan's Upper Pennisula, the ancient source of Morrison stock. "I gave the man ten seconds to shut his mouth, then I busted his nose."

"Yeah," the boy mumbled. "Actually Mom told me. Just like Grandpa Bailey and Uncle Mad Dog. So they sent you to Japan?"

He must have been confused by a lifetime of his father's hockey trades.

"Nobody sent me anywhere." The words, their petty defiance, made Tommy feel stupid and small, but the boy needed an explanation. "I just hit the guy once, and then I drove him to the clinic. The school asked me to take a year off. Then we'll see."

"But, Dad." He looked forlorn. "In Japan?"

Tommy wondered how much to explain. The job market was bloated. There had been a math offer in urban Miami, another in Enid, Oklahoma, an English job in Suriname that paid in gilders.

"Your school costs a lot of money," he said finally. "Plus the house, car, credit cards. I was lucky. The Japanese school pays well. I need some time away. I'll be back in a year."

Overloaded, Gus had drifted. His pencil endlessly crossed out sand grains. As he reached for the elevator button, Tommy felt stormed by a desire to seize his child under the shoulders and drag him along. With his sunburn and pimples, his lonely mouth drooping wetly open, Gus seemed hardly more finished than the day he was born, still a vast facility for the rehabilitation of a father.

Tommy had felt his eyes blur and his stomach burn. He stuffed a knuckle into the DOWN button and said nothing. He stared glassy-eyed past the curling tiles and tall lockers, out the window at the end of the hallway, over the scattering of rust buckets and pick-up trucks in the school parking lot.

"You better go," Gus said.

He was right. Their time was up.

"You hang in there, Gusser."

"You too, Dad. And stay cool. Don't yoop any Japanese."

The elevator had shuddered up like a gulp in the old building's throat. As he stepped aboard, Tommy had felt unexpectedly lightened. It was funny, what the kid just said. *Don't yoop any Japanese.* It was gentle and warm and almost grown-up. Every moment, like had he said to Elaine, was truly a whole new ball game.

He reached out to hold the doors, to make a better parting with his son, but Gus was red-faced suddenly, stuttering.

"Hey!"

He pointed. Tommy fought the doors.

"Hey! Those are mine! Those are my skates!"

"Gus—"

"What the hell, Dad, those are my skates!"

Gus threw himself at the doors, but the opening had narrowed irretrievably. The boy's clumsy arm thrashed at Tommy, black claws grazing skin. Tommy shoved the arm out. The doors closed.

"Dad!" A wail.

Then a last thump, and Tommy had sunk slowly through the layers of Tri-County Tech to the freight dock. Now he held the skates in his lap. He wondered what to focus on at this point. What mattered? That his son had begged and wheedled for the skates? That Tommy, mired in guilt, had been desperate to satisfy him? That Gus had never used the skates? That they were in fact just one more piece of expensive name-brand property—ignored by the boy, abused, lost, forgotten? Or did it matter most that Tommy had stolen them back? Which of these was the real crime? From this sordid passage of Morrison-Red Cloud family history, what if anything should be honored?

Tommy jerked, nearly fell from the bench. He shook his head, backing away from the precipice of sleep. His dawning answer seemed desperately silly, but he had no other. The only pure thing seemed to be the skates themselves—they were good skates, and brand new.

Tommy stood weakly. He left the skates on the bench beside the vending machine. "Good luck," he mumbled to them. "You're free of us." Then he hooked the remaining bag on his arm. He looked at the darkly rolling sky. He had to move now. He would limp as fast as he could down the steep mountain road. He would run when he could. He would find the town before the storm hit. Then he would ask for her.

Tommy stopped. He would ask for her. The secretary. But he had even forgotten her name.

Chapter 4

"Noriko!"

The old woman's voice pierced the clamor. It stopped giggles, turned heads, scalded about the sweltering Prince School office. The crowd of Kitayama students had been waiting for it.

"Noriko!"

"Yes, Mother."

Mama Yama worked her way through a knot of junior high girls. She kept her mouth moving, and this marked her progress like a flag moving above the larger girls. "I can't see where you've gone, that's the problem. Kids grow so tall nowadays. These girls with their long legs and wide shoulders and useless big breasts. One can hardly move around anymore. Noriko! Eh? Where are you?"

"Here, Mother. At my desk."

If one could march in an overstuffed kimono, Noriko Yamaguchi's mother-in-law marched up. Everyone waited: the girls, the women, the committee. Mother Yamaguchi would handle pronouncement of the obvious.

"Mister Stuart is late."

Noriko tried to breathe deeply. She had coordinated Stuart's bye-bye party, sent the invitations, hung the crepe paper, cut up a hundred snapshots to make a collage of Stuart's year in Kitayama. She had made sushi and grilled chicken, bought beer, sake, soft drinks, rice crackers and shrimp crisps, arranged flowers and cut melons. She had prepared Stuart's final paycheck and removed his papers from her safe. She had arranged a surprise song, "For He's a Jolly Good Fellow," by the junior high girls. She had risen, in fact, at three-thirty in the morning. She had been trapped inside her green kimono since lunchtime. And now—

"More than one hour late."

"Thank you, Mother, for maintaining my awareness of this fact."

Noriko managed this calmly, but stress pinched her stomach. Now the girls were putting their fingers all over the collage. And old Father had become prematurely drunk and caught his head in the sagging crepe paper. And Police Chief Ebana had begun to grumble his suspicions. Stuart did not respect them, he claimed. He did not respect Kitayama.

"The new teacher didn't call either," observed Mama Yama. "And you promised he would."

"Of this too, Mother, you so kindly remind me."

"Now come here, Noriko."

Dabbing sweat with a hankie, Mother Yamaguchi pushed through the throng of girls to the table where Noriko had arranged food and drink. She pointed. The SAYONARA, STUART! banner hung crookedly. The tape had slipped.

"Thank you, Mother, for your sharp eye."

Noriko turned and started back toward her desk.

"Noriko!" Her mother-in-law pursued, shoving along, stout old Mama Yama in red kimono, not more than five feet tall, strong as a beetle prying girls aside.

"Noriko!"

"I am getting fresh tape, Mother."

"And your sushi," said Mama Yama, "is crumbling. Your rice is too hard."

"Forgive me, Mother."

"You have to form it when it's hot."

"Yes."

"Your hands are too tender."

"Your advice, Mother, is invaluable. As always."

Noriko pushed back through with the tape, pasted the banner's corner to the slippery wall. It would slip again soon. And now a picture of blond-haired Stuart fell off the collage. "Oh!" cried a girl. "May I keep it?"

"And this," said Mama Yama, "is apparently yakitori, but you've burned the skewers. And chicken is not the only thing people like. They like liver. They like pork."

"May I keep it, Noriko-san? May I keep the photo that fell?"

"Yes, you may."

Then Father pulled crepe from his head and snapped it. He had never seen such a thing. He cleared his throat. Noriko kept her head down. She waited for the fuse to reach the old man's voice box.

"Noriko!"

"Yes, Father."

"It is eight o'clock!"

"Yes, Father."

"Where is Mister Stuart?"

"I don't know, Father. This afternoon he went home to pack his—"

"He is with Ono-san again," grumbled Police Chief Ebana. "He has not respected our prohibitions, and so he has been kidnapped by crazy Ono-san again."

"Noriko!" thundered Father.

She lowered her head. "Yes, Father."

"This committee has made every effort to make Kitayama-town an international city. We have constructed our business park, our sports center. We have our own English school. We now begin a new bridge and an airstrip—"

"Airport," Mayor reminded him. For a long moment, the ugly dirt lump across south valley stuck in everyone's mind, ancient rice fields sacrificed too early, with key parcels still in enemy Sato hands and funding from the prefecture still soft.

"Airport," Mayor repeated. "Airstrip is too local-sounding. We have to say airport."

Husband came around with a beer bottle, refreshing the glasses of the committee.

"Airport," Father grunted, "and Sports Complex."

Father cleared his throat. "But we can't have a simple celebration of our progress."

"Crazy Ono," cursed Chief Ebana. "It's crazy Ono's fault."

"What will you do, Noriko?"

"Any minute, Father, I expect the phone to ring."

Then the banner slipped again. Noriko's guts cramped hard as she retreated to her desk. Mama Yama waited there, going through her desk drawers. Noriko grabbed her coin purse.

"Excuse me, Mother, but I must run to he grocery."

"The grocery? Now? With Mister Stuart one hour late for his party? With the new teacher nowhere to be found? With the committee waiting?"

"Yes, Mother. I'm sorry. Liver. And pork. And perhaps I'll see Stuart. Perhaps he is having his hair cut again. I'll take the phone with me, Mother."

And then the old woman became distracted—Father taking up the crazy Ono theme, the kidnapping idea—and Noriko tucked the cell phone in her kimono sleeve. She faded back through the classroom, through the teacher office, then fled across the pachinko parlor roof to the fire escape. There, she gripped the rail, lit a cigarette away from the wind. Her stomach pain wasn't a gas cramp after all, she thought. It was a pain that stayed there, high and tight beneath her ribs. She dug a thumb at it to no effect. Then she descended the iron steps in kimono half-steps, her bun unwinding and her free hand chasing windblown strands about her head.

"Noriko!" called Mama Yama. "Where have you gone? Get more soy sauce!"

But Noriko had no intention of going to the grocery store. She turned beneath the fire escape, pitter-pattered behind the garbage bins, and disappeared.

A few seconds later, under the blast-furnace lights of Crazy Ono's Big Play Pachinko Center, Noriko Yamaguchi appeared again, coming to a breathless stop between the upright pinball machines. Directly above, she knew, Mama Yama cursed her before the Prince School crowd. But here, in this gaudy hell beneath, Noriko's life felt distant at once. The bells and sirens, the racing-stabbing illuminations of the pachinko machines, somehow these soothed her. They blocked her thoughts, scorched away the last of her nerves, and gave her something like calm. She needed this, lately, every day.

She let her breath out, felt the pain ease. Then she moved up an aisle between the yammering machines. She touched her Uncle Nobu Gotoh on the shoulder. She saw Emiko Kawamura was having good luck on machine twelve. At the corner by the front door, Dirty Ameda swept an arm out grandly, with a rag at the end of it, showing her a free machine down the next aisle.

But Noriko went the other way. Never take the house suggestion. She knew that much by now. The game was to find the "on" machines, the ones that Ono's nail master, tapping and twisting, had made ever-so-slightly favorable. She cruised slowly down the row of pachinko-slot machines that ran beneath the classroom. Fellow gamblers slumped glassy-eyed at their machines, fingers gray from the steel balls, clothes dull with the patina of grimy seats. But at least she didn't drink, Noriko thought, coasting along. At least she didn't have affairs.

Not yet, anyway. Not since she was married.

She sat and plugged her coins. Just five minutes of play, she told herself as the small steel balls gushed down. Then, with a twist of the handle, she lobbed one ball over the painted background at the top nails. She watched it trickle over stars and planets and rockets . . . and miss the scoring slot, falling to waste. She sent another, minutely adjusted; and another, deftly establishing a simple bumping-in stroke. Soon one in ten balls dropped through the scoring slot. One in twenty drummed the crossed arms of the generator. But the machine was slow to produce. She stuck a coin in the handle to hold her stroke. She lit a second Menthol and glanced down the aisle. There was Crazy Ono, proprietor, kidnapper of gaijin, leaning over a customer's shoulder, sweet-talking. Then the phone rang in her sleeve.

She answered quickly in English. "Hello?"

But it was Mrs. Tezuka from the flower shop again, wondering if Stuart had arrived. She had just come across a special gift, a ceramic raccoon flower vase, made in Aizu Hongo, about one-half meter high, and so on.

Noriko blew smoke. "Lovely, Missus Tezuka." A ball dropped into the payout tray. "So why don't you find a nice strong box? Then carry it down to the post office and mail it to Utah?"

"But it's much too large for me to mail."

"Then it's much too large for Stuart to carry, Missus Tezuka. I'll give you the address."

"What is that I hear?" said Mrs. Tezuka. "Is that pachinko?"

"Do you have a pencil, Missus Tezuka?"

"Are those pachinko bells? Are you playing pachinko again, Noriko?"

"Do you have a pencil, Missus Tezuka? Let me give you the address. It's Stuart Norton. Bluff Utah, U.S.A."

She replaced the phone in her sleeve. She sat straight on her stool, collected hair behind her ears, rejected her cigarette. She plugged more coins, flushed a lode of balls into her tray. She teased her lob one centimeter to a more risky piercing stroke, lost it, tried again and found it. Her balls bounced about the top nails, raining down chaotically through the approach nails, missing the pinwheels and tulips and falling to waste through the bottom drain. She had picked an off machine, she thought. Then she felt human heat. Now Ono was at her elbow.

"Bad luck, Nori-chan?"

"Mmm. All kinds of bad luck."

He massaged her shoulders. "I'm so sorry."

"You don't have Stuart?" she murmured to him.

She watched his gold-toothed surprise reflect in her machine. He wore a blue bathrobe from Ono Hotel, another of his operations. He squeezed a yellow towel around his neck. His speckled head gleamed.

"Daughter!" he exclaimed, breathing sake past her ear. "You accuse me falsely!"

Noriko blew smoke. "For once you're innocent," she said, and she smiled faintly, listening to the clatter of his wooden sandals as he staggered gleefully from the insult. Then Yoichi Ono leaned closer.

"Is there trouble, Daughter?"

Noriko weighed her reply. She drew on her cigarette. There was always trouble, and she was normally blamed for it. One month ago, desperate for help no Japanese would provide, Ono had lured Stuart up West Mountain and asked him to carry a heavy box up to Kappa, the mountain demon. Stuart's asthma attack on the first curve of the steep trail had made newspapers across all of Japan. *Village Elder Endangers Foreign Guest on Primitive Hunt for Mountain Demon.* Noriko had thought Father would kill her with his big hands. She had thought Husband would kick her down the stairs. She had wished so, actually. She had wished for some change in her life.

"Yes," she told Ono finally, slipping into the gamble. "Trouble."

"Oh?"

"Your crate carriers," she said, watching the silver balls bounce and tumble to no effect. "They're both late. Missing. They're both out there somewhere. And everyone else is waiting upstairs. Even Police Chief Ebana."

Ono danced behind her as if he heard koto music. She had done it now, Noriko told herself. Trouble. As she reached in her sleeve for her cigarette pack she felt Ono's heat again. He lit her cigarette.

"Daughter," he murmured, "have you tried machine eighteen?"

She floated to the new stool, feeling oddly serene as the pachinko parlor's bells and bulbs smashed around her. She had done it now, and perhaps things would change. The colored lights of her machine danced in the still pool of her face. She established her stroke, minutely adjusted it. The nails were invisibly open. Already she was scoring.

"Nice," whispered Yoichi Ono. He squeezed her shoulder. "Nice play." He watched her another moment, murmuring various encouragements, but she didn't notice when he left. Her game had become a water cycle of balls: ground water, rain, the odds mounting toward flood. She was winning. She was sailing. She was gone.

But it was pathetic, really, pachinko. And her stomach hurt like ever as she hurried back up the iron steps.

"Noriko!"

"Yes, Mother."

"Where have you been?"

"I'm sorry, Mother. Without your guidance, I was unable to decide on the choicest cut of pork. And Mister Stuart is nowhere to be found."

Inside the lobby, the stalled party had begun to smell. Sushi and melon, beer and body heat, flowers and perfume, Noriko gasped, fanning her face with a thin hand. She shook the phone from her sleeve, holding in the Menthols. The pile of gifts on her desk had doubled. She would have to pack them, haul them to the post office, ship them to Utah.

"Where are the gaijin?" insisted the old woman, as if Noriko had them on a string.

"I don't know, Mother."

Mama Yama sighed for the crowd. Everyone stared: giddy junior high girls in sailor suits, women in kimono and party dresses, the committee with their proclamations and key to the city. Then the old woman folded a hankie into a small square. She rolled her red lips, dabbed sweat from the mole field beneath her nose. Her mouth grew back in a gold-toothed smile.

"Perhaps," she said, "your instructions were careless."

"Yes, Mother. Perhaps. If I could be always as careful as you—"

"Perhaps you failed to inform Stuart that the committee would be here at seven to make a special presentation."

"I am certain I did not fail at that instruction, Mother."

"The committee has now waited ninety minutes."

Noriko turned and bowed, to Father, Husband, Mayor Watanabe, Police Chief Ebana, and she snuck a glance at their stupid key. Mayor's wife had shaped it from clay and painted it silver. Mayor's palms were silver, as was the lap of his suit coat. He set it down and Husband grabbed it. She would have to pack the key too, she thought, haul it to the post office, ship it to Utah. And then dry clean Husband's suit.

"I beg your pardon," she told the committee. "Please forgive me."

"Stuart has always been on time," pointed out Mama Yama.

"Yes, Mother."

"So perhaps your instructions *have* been careless."

"Or perhaps, Mother, you may also mean to illustrate by this statement that my instructions have always been good."

And then the phone rang. The crowd parted. Noriko made baby steps to her desk. Through the floor she could hear Uncle Nobu hitting jackpot on the pachinko-slot.

"Hello?"

But it was Mrs. Tezuka again. Wasn't Stuart there yet? She had found, in storage, a lovely sake set that he ought to take home. Earthenware, ten cups, two flasks.

"But Stuart doesn't drink," said Noriko. "Remember?"

"Then how about a rice cooker? A Japanese rice cooker. I've got an extra."

"He won't be able to carry a rice cooker, Missus Tezuka. So if you can find a good strong box. . . ."

She put the phone down. Husband unfolded a handkerchief with paint-sticky fingers, making more laundry. And now Chief Ebana held the key, grumbling once more about Ono. Father barked, "Noriko!"

Her breath was too shallow. She tried to push it deeper.

"At exactly five o'clock, Father, Stuart went home to clean his apartment."

"You should have cleaned it yourself."

"He wanted to, Father. He insisted. I try to respect the privacy of our teachers."

"He should be here," said Father. "Not cleaning like a woman."

"Yes, Father. I will go now, and get him."

She slipped the phone back into her sleeve. A typhoon thunderclap rumbled over the school. Perhaps Stuart was frightened of the storm, she thought suddenly. That fit Stuart. Or perhaps his terrible God had struck him down by lightning. Or perhaps, anticipating this very scene, he was escaping Kitayama on his own, escaping this wretched little town, fleeing into the thrash of the storm with his big blue suitcase.

But a reckless thumping stopped Noriko at the school's front stairs. Upon the landing burst two girls in Takata Girls High School uniforms, panting and talking at once. Mama Yama hushed the crowd.

"Speak one at a time," she commanded.

The girls looked at one another. They seemed unsure how to separate.

"He's here!" they shared finally. "The new teacher! He came on the train and he's walking down the mountain!"

"Walking?"

"He was walking!"

"He must have been drunk on the train because he fell on Miwa Sato."

"He crushed her donuts."

"She said they were for Stuart."

"She said Stuart liked her but everybody laughed."

"The boys were teasing the new gaijin and—"

Noriko tried to break in. "He was walking from the station?"

"He stayed on the train like it was going someplace—"

"And we just saw Ono-san."

"Mister Tommy was walking?" insisted Noriko.

"Hush!" commanded Mama Yama, and in her excitement she slapped Noriko in the back of the head, just as Noriko's own mother had done twenty years ago. "And you saw Ono?"

"We saw Ono-san driving up the mountain."

Mama Yama turned to Noriko. Noriko tried to look surprised, hurt, concerned, anything but suddenly and utterly exhausted with her life.

"Go!" commanded the old woman. "Witless girl! Hurry!"

Chapter 5

Tommy stopped to rest a mile down the mountain road. Below, headlights flashed on a switchback. Heavy beams blinked between trees, blazed around one tight corner, then leveled on Tommy.

Puffing hard, he moved into underbrush. He covered his eyes and waited, but the car stopped beside him with a soft *toot-toot!* Tommy looked up, his tired mind slowly performing a mental flip-flop: he was in Japan, but this was an American car, a vintage Cadillac, buffed out, pale yellow, with its cream top down.

Toot-toot! went its horn.

Then a bald old man in a blue bath robe came around the long door. His wooden sandals went *klink-klonk* on the road. The wind tossed the robe about his skinny legs. He pressed his hands to his sides. "Good evening," he pronounced, making a deep bow. "Welcome to Kitayama."

Tommy was astonished to hear English from the old man. He had trouble finding breath.

"Thank you."

He came up from the underbrush. The man raised one hand. His brow furrowed in concentration. He made strokes through the heavy air as if conducting himself. Out came more English.

"Do. You. Beer?"

Tommy said, "I'm sorry?"

"Do you like. To beer?"

"Uh, I do. But right now I'm awfully tired."

"Would you drinking?" The old man grinned, made a hand gesture. "The beer?"

He looked like a hockey fan in a hotel hallway, Tommy thought: the six-Manhattan post-game wobble and chop-talk, the I'm-your-biggest-fan grin. But he was in Japan now, Tommy reminded himself. He was just minutes north of a typhoon. This man could save him.

He tried, "I'm Tommy Morrison. Who are you?"

The old man bowed again. "I am fine thank you."

Tommy let a moment pass, hoping for insight. The Caddy was from the 70's, pale yellow, mint condition, the kind of car his dad would whistle at and say, "Yessir, by golly, that one's on my list." Then a crack of lightning exposed pearlesque leather seats.

"And you?" asked the driver.

"I am fine too," Tommy said. "Thanks. My name is Tommy."

Another deep bow: "My name is Yoichi Ono."

"I am going downhill," Tommy told him.

Yoichi Ono's eyes strained in the dim light. His head tilted in question. The wind caught his bath robe and nearly shoved him over. "Eh?" he said.

Tommy did some pointing. "Down."

"Ah!"

"I am going down to Kitayama."

"Ah! Yes, yes!"

And now the old man showed a boyish agility, steering the tall wooden sandals through weeds and gravel, whisking around the tail lights, sweeping open the passenger door.

"Yes, yes!" cried Yoichi Ono. "Me too! Let's go!"

The beer was on the floor of the Caddy in a plastic sack: two big, cold silver cylinders. Yoichi Ono cracked one and pushed it foaming into Tommy's hands. *Toot!* went the Caddy's horn. Then the old man began to back the car down the mountain. He spun the wheel with his palm, hardly watching the road. He grinned at Tommy, at the beer, made drinking motions. He seemed to swallow vicariously, and Tommy drank just enough to put Yoichi Ono's eyes back on the road. Then the old man worked on a description of the weather, waving both hands around while the Caddy coasted through eerie brake light into a switchback.

"Typhoon," he managed. He said, *Tie-boon.*

Then he searched for more English. He whipped one hand around above his head, indicating rain. They barely made the corner. "We must," he said, pointing into the back seat, "to hurry."

Tommy twisted. A crate filled the broad seat. It said: *Don Shiller Auto Glass, Buena Vista, Calif.* And then, on three gulps, as the Caddy straightened and slipped backwards into a long, steep downhill, Tommy was drunk. "You'd better put the top down," he said, and he let his head flop back. He felt his grip loosen, his eyes blur. His mind gave up its striving. Let the rain come, he thought. Let the car crash. Let Elaine and Gus do whatever goddamn thing they wanted.

But the Caddy swung around suddenly. Ono grinned, floored them forward on a wider, smoother road that crossed a highway and began to flatten. Tommy watched mountain wrinkle into valley, houses clap over into storefronts. Here it was: Kitayama at last, low and cluttered, dark and maze-like. Roofs rattled in the wind. Singing leaked from tiny taverns. Fragments of neon English snatched at Tommy's eyes. SHAMPOO CUT. COFFEE SHIP. I LOVE STREET! See, he thought, they already have English. I'm just here to tidy up. *You see, Elaine—*

But then suddenly they had passed through the town. Tommy twisted on the seat. Kitayama was behind them. They coasted across a bridge on the far side of the town, then rolled into darkness behind a levee, between long greenhouses that smelled of cucumber vines. Tommy looked at Ono, who grinned back, sped up, sailed them onward between darkened rice fields. He spaced his thumb and forefinger one centimeter apart and said, "Little bit hurry, ne?"

"Wasn't that Kitayama?"

Ono narrowed his pinch of air. "Little bit, ne? Please? Little bit to help me, ne?"

Tommy sat back again. He released his neck muscles. He watched the opposite mountain approach, a great, black, roadless hump. Then his head dropped and he considered the strangeness of his watch. Breakfast in Wisconsin. Elaine and Gus at the four-leaf. Cinnamon toast. Coffee and ciggies. Gus missing first period math and she would write him an excusing note. Deconstructing the white man's time, she liked to claim lately, and yet here time was, glowing on his wrist, carried halfway around the world, eight o'clock in the night of morning and still he hadn't called the Prince School secretary. . . hadn't remembered her name . . . and he meant to ask the strange old man about that . . . began to phrase the question . . . except that suddenly, finally, he was asleep.

And then just as abruptly Tommy was jerked awake and there she was, the Prince School secretary. It had to be her. A thin young woman in a green kimono leaned over the open door, shaking his arm. "Mister Tommy?" she called. "Mister Tommy, can you wake up?"

Tommy pulled himself upright. They were somewhere on the opposite mountain now, somewhere dark and wind-whipped. A small white pickup blocked Ono's Cadillac, and a black sedan had filled the narrow road beside it. Ono stood at the end of his open door, bowing gaily into a tongue-lashing from a chorus of voices inside the sedan. The dome light glowed on four men in black suits. Then the voices stopped. For a long moment, Tommy heard only engine noise and the typhoon thrash of tree tops. Finally the young woman at Tommy's door spoke. "They are the committee for internationalization of Kitayama," she explained. "I am Noriko Yamaguchi."

She bowed. She twisted her fingers. Then she tugged the Cadillac door open.

"I am the Prince School secretary."

He followed her to the small white pickup, squeezed himself into a dusty space that smelled like clay and cigarettes and a woman's perfume.

She took a deep breath. She dug her thumb at some sore spot beneath her ribs. "Welcome to Kitayama," she said. She started the engine, lit a cigarette, and they headed back through the rice paddies. After a minute a horn blared behind her. She stopped. The black sedan pulled alongside, and a red-faced old man jabbed his finger and hollered through the window. She hung her head, acknowledging his words with whispers and bows.

When it was over, Noriko looked at Tommy and attempted a smile. "My father-in-law, who is head of the committee, says I have bad manners. He says welcome to Kitayama."

She let the sedan pass and drove on. The town appeared again, across the river, and she glanced at him, her face taut in the dash light.

"Please forgive us," she said after a while. "Ne? We are all crazy. Not just Ono-san."

"You mean the guy with the Cadillac? Where was he taking me?"

"He was taking you to West Mountain. He wants help to carry something to the top. No Japanese would go with him. Stuart was forbidden to go with him."

"That crate in the back seat?"

"I don't know a great vocabulary."

But she touched her windshield. "This kind of thing."

Tommy remembered *Don Schiller Auto Glass.* "Windshield?"

"Yes. Windshield for Kappa's car, a Cadillac like Ono's, at the top of the mountain. No one else would help him, because they are afraid of Kappa."

She gave him a helpless glance.

"Kappa is a demon," she explained.

"Demon?"

"A mountain demon."

"With a Cadillac," Tommy reviewed. He wasn't sure he got it.

She was silent for a long time. Frogs sang from the rice fields.

"Yes," she said at last. "A mountain demon with a Cadillac. Welcome to Kitayama."

They drove on. The cucumbers again, the greenhouses, the levee, the bridge. A wide, flat river sparkled below. The town crowded around. Then, mid-point on some central street, Noriko Yamaguchi slowed before a blazing game parlor and backed meticulously onto the opposite sidewalk, turning her lights off and inching back and forth into a tiny parking spot. Tommy had sunk down on his seat, nodding at the edge of sleep like a battered log on a beach. The men in dark suits had preceded them and now appeared outside the game parlor. He watched wind blow their ties around. They looked stranded. Their shadows lunged under a swaying street lamp.

Noriko sighed, wrenched the rear view mirror and checked her face. Above the game parlor, Tommy saw a corrugated tin vault, one window. Faces crowded this frame of light, calling down. Then three high school girls descended to the sidewalk. The men tried to chase them back inside, but a dozen more girls poured out, adding various stages of distress. And then the vault divulged a dozen young women in party dresses, a dozen more matrons in kimono, carefully working the stairs, and finally a chaotic old woman in red, waving and shouting. Tommy watched as the panic spread beyond the parlor in both directions. Some civic emergency, mused his tired mind. A lost child, a purse snatching, a fire inside.

Then Noriko brought him fully awake. She reached past his knee, zipped up the parking brake.

"Prince School," she announced, and killed the engine.

Inside, the names marched over him: Yoko, Yuko, Yuki, Yukiko, Yumiko, Kumiko, Keiko, Kazuko, Kazuo. Then the stout woman in red kimono charged and poked him in the ribs. Noriko translated. "My mother-in-law says you don't look like a teacher."

Tommy made a poor smile. Words came from his mouth. "Tell her I'm the Zen type. See? My whole life in a shopping bag."

Noriko returned a puzzled face and tried to translate, but the old woman cut her off. Noriko repeated her words.

"You don't look like Stuart, she says." Noriko twisted her hands, looked at the floor. She began, "Please understand—"

But now the red-faced old man cut her off. Her father-in-law. He exploded into question, thundering at Tommy as if a river stood between them.

"He asks you, Didn't you see Mister Stuart at the train station?"

The old woman pushed a snapshot: the lanky blond kid, the pale blue eyes, the peace sign.

"No."

"At Takata train station?"

"No."

"Why did you go with Ono-san?"

Tommy explained.

"Didn't Ono-san also carry Mister Stuart?"

"No."

The old man raised and shook heavy, work-mashed hands. He orated. His suit became twisted beneath his arms. Then a younger and milder man beside him, a tall man with combed black hair and large glasses, put it a milder way. Noriko translated carefully.

"Mayor says, This is an international city. We are very proud. Welcome to Kitayama."

"Thanks," Tommy said. He fought a yawn. "But I was told I would have to send out for hamburgers."

Noriko's face went blank. Tommy stared into his strange luggage through a long, dead silence. Fatigue made his skin burn. Things would get better, he told himself, but the idea did a U-turn on the flight deck of his brain. His cheeks flared out. He wavered.

"I don't really like hamburgers anyway," he mumbled, looking up at Noriko.

She put him in a squeaky-wheeled chair beside her desk. On the wall, behind a heap of presents, there were more pictures: Mister Stuart arm-in-arm with girls and women, cuddled in groups, smiling huge white teeth and flashing peace signs with his long pink fingers. Clean. Stable. Appropriate. The universal opposite of Gus, Tommy thought. The universal opposite of *him*.

"He looks like the kind of kid who would come to the party on time."

Noriko seemed to hear this acutely. She was moving away, but she returned. "Do you think so?"

"I mean, he seems like a polite young man. Eager to please."

She hesitated anxiously. The party was lurching into flux now, struggling to re-start itself as a welcome party for Tommy. Then her eyes were back on him.

"Do you need to sleep?" she asked.

"Yes."

Five minutes later, Noriko led Tommy down the front stairs. As they reached the sidewalk, the typhoon burst on Kitayama at last. Dense rain pounded the awnings. It poured onto the street, jingling wind-strewn bicycles on the sidewalk, swirling and foaming and steaming at the curbs.

Red Kimono had followed them down, a relentless voice beneath an umbrella. Noriko turned, her jaw set angrily. Their words made no sense to Tommy. He picked a newspaper from the trash, held it above his head, leaned out from the game parlor awning. The paper went soggy in an instant, and he stepped back as a taxi splashed past. He had never seen such a rain. The rain of rains. He looked up and down the street. Only the game parlor was open, its multi-colored reflection on the asphalt smashed by the taxi and reforming, sudsy and liquid, as rain reclaimed the street. He felt an ocean stirred above him. Or two oceans, crashing together over a narrow spine of rock and timber, rice paddies and scabby buildings. Maybe this Stuart kid was swept away, he thought.

When he turned, the sayonara party had become a search party. Umbrellas shot up around him. Noriko's mother-in-law led the way. They splashed through dark and crooked streets, girls and women, Tommy, the whole party sloshing and bumping umbrellas down one cobble-stone jag, down another, past a gas stand and a mini-market, past taverns leaking song and dark shops with their grates rolled down. Then at last they crowded into the stairwell of a two-story apartment building.

Noriko unlocked a first-floor door. She turned on lights. Two small rooms blazed empty. No Stuart. But still the searchers poured into the rooms, leaving wet shoes and umbrellas in the entry, searching the toilet, the tub room, closets, beneath the sink, searching the very air for traces of Stuart, giggling and sobbing and gossiping until Noriko chased them out. She stood fast in a conflict with her mother-in-law, finally closing the door on the old woman in mid-sentence.

Then, muttering crossly in Japanese, she raked shut the drapes. She unrolled a futon and laid a blanket. She lit the bath boiler and started water. She stepped into her shoes and bowed. She lifted her umbrella.

"Thank you," Tommy said.

"Doitashimashite."

Alone after the door closed, Tommy turned once around. The lights were too bright. The ceilings were too low. Bath water drummed the miniature tub, rain drummed the thin walls.

The door popped open. "Lock it," Noriko Yamaguchi said. She was a green blur, breathing mad red lipstick, scalding Tommy once with tear-slick eyes. Then she was gone.

Chapter 6

They blamed him, Yoichi Ono reflected happily. As always, they blamed him.

In the hurling rain he puttered contentedly beneath a vast umbrella. He wore yellow farmer boots with cheap pants snagged around the tops. He wore a golf shirt, a turquoise string tie. He carried a plastic sack out to the big Caddy. Its splendid white top beat off the typhoon. "Oy!" he called, and a desk clerk hurried out between the glass doors of Ono Hot Springs Hotel.

"Sir?"

Ono grinned. "Towels, ne? Lots of towels."

"Yes, sir."

"And slippers, a bath robe, and a room key."

"A room key, sir?"

"Any room near the bath."

"Yes, sir."

"And magazines."

"Magazines, sir?"

"Suzuki, you know what I mean."

"Yes, sir."

The clerk brought these items. Into the sack they went. Ono danced in his yellow rubber boots, performed his ancient steps to the music of rain cascading down the hotel roof. The red clay roof tiles gleamed prettily. Rainwater spun exquisitely down through the brass chains at the corners. Great orange and black carp frolicked in the rising ponds. The fountains spouted. Rain!

"Mister Ono, sir?"

"Yes, Suzuki?"

"Police Chief Ebana was here while you were bathing. He was looking for you. I switched the banners, and thus he searched for you in the women's area, which of course was empty. He was quite angry, sir."

"Wonderful."

"But what shall I tell him, sir, when he returns?"

Ono found a deep puddle and pranced through it, forward and back. His splashing made the clerk step back.

"Tell him to smile!" Ono beamed gold teeth at his clerk. "Tell him to enjoy!"

Then with a deft trimming of his umbrella, the wealthiest man in Kitayama slipped in behind the wheel—*Toot! Toot!*—and the big Caddy coasted slowly down the mountain, spreading a wake across the flooded road. So Ebana had come for him, Ono reflected. How fine. So the rumor must be true that Mister Stuart had never shown up for his sayonara party. Ono grinned and squinted into the rain. And now they blamed him! How pleasant! How proud Kappa must be!

Yoichi Ono had a habit, a tap of the horn at every familiar object, and every new one, a wave and a grin. *Toot! Toot!* He saluted the empty cucumber stand on the highway. He toasted the police box, where perhaps Chief Ebana saw him slide by. He startled the Naganuma crone as she stood in a slicker over her burn barrel, dropping in garbage. *Toot! Toot!* Then a stray dog limped across the street, soaking wet. Ono played the brake. He had just the thing. He rattled in his bag and ran down his window, tossed out a long hank of squid jerky. The dog limped beneath a mud-spattered hydrangea bush and sprawled to eat.

Toot! Toot! The big Caddy tilted down into Kitayama town. The car filled alleys, tipped bonsai with its mirrors, then rounded onto Shinmei Street and cruised amidst the festival preparations. Today was meant to be the *obon* carnival, the big parade. But the booths and floats and carnival workers remained under plastic, waiting with numb expressions on their faces, as if the rain were some kind of tiresome insult, as if their lives, their schedules, were fixed to some much greater purpose than the watering of the forests and the filling of the rivers. How Kappa, for this very reason, loved a good rain! How pleased the imp must be!

Ono pumped to a near stop beside the international phone booth, peering in, hoping. But the booth was empty. He passed the pachinko parlor and Prince English School. Beyond Mrs. Tezuka's flower shop—*Toot! Toot!*—he twisted to see who followed him. But he was not followed after all. So perhaps Chief Ebana had been in the smelly police box toilet again, the poor man. The imp could be anywhere, Ono mused, reviewing the empty street behind him. Even in the bowels. It was those who fought Kappa, who warred with him, who suffered most.

Ono feathered the brake. And now, as if to make an example of himself, here came the young Yamaguchi, the festival director, the one who married Noriko, stomping out from beneath a tent of blue plastic to wave the big Cadillac off the street.

"Oy!" he hollered. He pointed at a barrier of stanchions and rope. "Fool! The street is closed!"

Toot! Toot!

"It's a fine day, Yamaguchi-san. Finer than you think."

Yamaguchi glared fiercely at Ono, his long cigarette ash somehow typhoon proof. "Bastard!" the young husband cursed, and he flung a kick at the Cadillac. When that didn't ruin Ono's grin or move the big car, Yamaguchi looked about him in a fit of rage. Then he raised a heavy stanchion and staggered forward with it. Ono, startled and suddenly cold, could not find reverse. Yamaguchi slammed the concrete footing down on the hood of the Cadillac.

"Bastard! Idiot! Where is Mister Stuart?"

Shakily, Ono backed away. He found an alley. He parked. He splashed out, forgetting his umbrella, and touched the damage. He shivered as he ran his fingers over the ugly dent, across the ruined paint. Then the old man wept. He was blamed! He was blamed for everything!

And why? How much capacity would Mister Tommy have for listening? More than Mister Stuart, Ono hoped. He put the car in gear. With Mister Tommy, he imagined, the sake would flow, his English would blossom, and he would tell the story. Mister Tommy, do you know the Edo Period in Japan? Long ago? While you, in America, were having your Civil War? Yes? No?

This time he would beg forgiveness for the slow start. But certainly Mister Tommy would be a better listener than Mister Stuart. He would have to reach back, after all, into the late dusk of Edo and establish the fact that his great-grandfather was the last of his family who had been trusted in Kitayama. He would have to begin with brave old Nobutaka Ono, prospecting on East Mountain with a team of bearded Ainu slaves and finding the gold-flecked black granite. This granite, he would explain, was a great treasure. And Yamaguchis had taken it.

But no one liked a bitter story, Ono reminded himself, backing from the alley. Perhaps this is why Mister Stuart's eyelids had fluttered and his fingers had twisted. "Arigato!" he blurted whenever Ono paused. Or "Gomen nasai!" So perhaps, anyway, he should skip Great-Grandfather's impregnation of the poor Yamaguchi girl, omit the bribery, the atrocious price of silence.

Ono paused here, his tail lights jutting into Shinmei Street, and he considered the sudden and uncomfortable realization that young Yamaguchi should have dropped the heavy stanchion on his own foot. That was Kappa's way, was it not? Why was he, Ono, the one damaged? Could it be a sign, in the fiend, of dissatisfaction?

Ono swung the Cadillac around. He aimed it at young Yamaguchi, who now supervised the construction of a tower for the singers and the obon princess. *Toot! Toot!* he warned, and then proceeded head on, at low speed but quite steadily, and soon enough he had spilled young Yamaguchi from his stepladder. Ono looked back in his mirror. An egg blue hard hat spun on the pavement. Precisely half of the unkind young man was darkened with the juices of an oily puddle. His cigarette was bent and cold. Ono grinned. *Toot! Toot!* That was more like it.

Now: where was he? The wayward old man. The pregnant Yamaguchi girl. The leverage. And in no time at all, as it happened, the Yamaguchi clan took over the mountain. Ono's great-grandfather had died with his carnal sin in suppression, but his grandfather Tsutomu fell into shameful debt, and then to preserve the continued good name of his family he agreed that upon his death his interest in the mountain would pass in total to the Yamaguchi brothers; and forthwith, beneath a precision avalanche, shunt-blast, Tsutomu Ono died.

"Gomen nasai!" piped Mister Stuart at this point. He was apologizing. But surely Mister Tommy would have more sense. From that point on, he would surely understand, to be an Ono was to be a non-person. Ono's father, the dead man's son, cleaned trains, played pachinko, and married a slow girl from elsewhere. Their child—*the man before you now, Mister Tommy!*—was ugly and restless. The boy's right eye wandered. He laughed too loud. He ran everywhere. He loved to steal. Any man who caught him, beat him, and he deserved it. Little Kappa, they called him. Little Yoichi Ono, so dirty he was green. Kappa's son, people said. Son of Kappa. And in time he had embraced the title.

Ono hit the end of Shinmei Street and backtracked along the river road, squinting through the rain-spattered windshield and lost now in precious memory. When he turned fourteen, he had begun to use his dead father's lifetime train pass to leave Kitayama and roam the big town of Takata, then two hours south. American GI's camped there. Black markets boomed. He had moved joyfully among these elements, and in spring of 1947, on a slow morning, the Reverend Sergeant Ronald Brown, chaplain of the Takata Occupation Force, had lent him a Holy Bible and offered him a pencil payment to recite one page of it.

"In the beginning of Creation," he pronounced on the train home that evening. English had made him sound like a wounded animal, a spastic madman colliding with dangerous thoughts. The seats around him emptied.

But that night he had eaten with the book beside his rice bowl. By midnight, as his mother stared open-mouthed and frightened, he uttered, "God said, 'Let there be lights in the vault of heaven to separate day from night.'" Then he fell asleep with the word of God upon his chest. His dictionary fluttered at the end of his arm. His head swam with *abyss* and *vault* and fruit-trees bearing fruit, and by the next afternoon, Ono had earned his pencil from Reverend Sergeant Brown. It was long and shiny yellow, with a pink eraser and perfect black point. He wore it behind his ear. Back in Kitayama, boys glared in envy.

"Arigato! Arigato!" Stuart had blurted, his strange blue eyes lunging and batting. Thank you! Thank you! Ono chuckled. By week's end, long ago, he had accumulated six more pencils. He had toured the barracks, chattering in a strange new language about Ham and Shem and Noah, and the GI's had laughed and slapped his back and given him candies. Back in Kitayama, boys chased him for these treats, but he was too quick. Then they begged him. He bartered. Yohei Yamaguchi, the boy who would inherit the mountain, gave up a whole ripe melon for just one pencil and Ono had rushed home that night, filled with joy, gripping the fruit's rough, fragrant skin and comprehending wealth.

Arigato indeed. Ono stopped at a vending machine and bought two cartons of sake, one for Mister Tommy. Mister Stuart would not drink, he recalled, not even in the presence of a good story. *Because, Mister Tommy, Kappa found me then.* Along a black curve of East Mountain road, the night air had wrinkled and a stench had come down through the leaves and the shadows of leaves. Ono had stopped. After a long wait came the noise of smacking jowls, sighs and gasses, a laugh.

"Ah!" gasped a voice from the unseeable region beyond the last moonlit trunks. "Melon!"

Ono had taken a step back, shaking with fright. Brush crackled. A rabbit streaked across the road. Then silence, darkness, stench. A faint sigh. The deep, deep quiet of assumption. *Feed me*, breathed the quiet. He had set the melon down and fled. In the morning he had found the rind beside the road, its pieces arranged in a kanji character, open boxes atop one another, with single shreds inside. The kanji meant *MORE*. Ono had rushed onward toward his train, terrified and enlightened. That day in Takata, he had begun the fiendish prank of getting rich, and he had packed one of every treasure up to Kappa. He hauled wristwatches and televisions, coffee pots and rice cookers, leather shoes, chewing gum, chocolate, scotch and gin across the valley and up the steep West Mountain trail, to the shrine where Kappa was said to dwell.

"Do you know City of Angels?" Ono had asked Mister Stuart.

"Gomen nasai!"

"Hollywood?"

"Arigato!"

But perhaps it was his English. Perhaps in forty years it had unraveled a bit, but it had worked sufficiently then, in 1975, when he had finished construction of a massive spa over the hot spring on East Mountain and boarded an ocean liner to Los Angeles. He had toured Universal Pictures. He had ordered Bloody Marys in his Old Testament English. "Lo!" he hailed his cabs. And then, one smoggy morning while the movie stars slept, he glimpsed upon a Beverly Hills car lot a long yellow Cadillac that made his heart race. Sailing back across the Pacific, two cars in the cargo hold, he had shivered with new anxieties, his mind aswim with thoughts of rope and winch, lever and fulcrum, block and tackle. How would he do it? Then for twenty years—alone, as no Japanese would help, not for any price—he had delivered the second car, piece by piece, up the trail to Kappa. All but the huge and fragile windshield.

Now at last Yoichi Ono motored over the splashing grate and into the lot of Mister Tommy's apartment. His great vehicle consumed seven spaces, each one receiving a *toot!* of apology. The old man wobbled out with his cartons of sake and his sack of gifts. He put up his umbrella, and then again, freshly, he beheld his horrible injury. Rain collected in the dent. Cracked paint spidered outward. Ugly and ruined—this mess that should have been young Yamaguchi's foot. *But please have patience, Kappa! My endeavors . . . they are delicate!*

Ono rapped on Mister Tommy's door. He listened. He opened his carton and dumped a swallow down upon his poor scorched belly. He rapped a second time.

No reply. He peeped in the window. There slept the gaijin, a great motionless heap, immune to all manner of tapping and window-rattling.

Kappa, Ono begged. *He rests, my muscular friend, and gains his strength.*

Ono hung his gifts on the doorknob. He turned out into the rain. He finished his carton and tossed it in the weeds. He danced hopefully through a puddle, forward and back.

Smile, Kappa! Enjoy!

Chapter 7

"Now Noriko," began Father at breakfast. Slowly, he trapped a yellow daikon pickle with red chopsticks, wrapped it around a bite of white rice. "Let us hear that Mister Stuart called last evening."

"No, Father, I'm sorry. He didn't."

Father crunched the pickle. Rain lashed the cluttered yard beyond the window, made strange music on the cat pans. Husband was hung over, breathing through his nose. He had just returned from Shinmei Street, where the rain had postponed everything. "Bakayaro," he cursed.

"Husband, please."

"He makes fools of us."

"Daughter didn't handle him properly."

"Thank you, Mother, for—"

"Kimura-san saw a red car going into the tunnel," Mama Yama reported. "Stuart must have a girlfriend in Takata, with a red car."

"Takata," fumed Husband. "Always Takata."

"Takata girls," said Mama Yama, "come cheap."

"It was Ono," asserted Husband. "I saw Ono. He acted guilty. The idiot drove his car down Shinmei. I chased him off."

For a long moment no one spoke. But Noriko knew their thinking. If Ono had taken Stuart for his shrine business, then a proper search would include the climb up Kappa's trail, in a typhoon rain, on a festival day. Not that any of them believed in Kappa. Of course not. Not that Husband and Father were afraid. No, of course not. Impossible. Noriko waited a long time, head down, using her chopsticks to line up rice kernels on the edge of her bowl. Her stomach hurt.

"Yes," retreated Husband finally. "You are right, Father. Takata again, stealing our efforts, our people, our history. Stuart was lured away to Takata."

"Plenty of whores in Takata," confirmed Mama Yama, as if she had studied the subject from her garden in Kitayama, and thus the subject was closed.

Father grunted, pointed. Noriko brought the sake bottle and poured. Father and Husband had two quick cups. Noriko poured a third. She watched their faces turn red as they ate her rice and miso soup. Then "Ah!" she cried suddenly, and she jumped up. She had forgotten the ginger green beans. She hurried them to the table in a round white dish. "Overdone," muttered Mama Yama.

Father finished his third cup of sake. Husband quickly caught up.

"Now," said Father. "The rain will stop before lunch time. Thus we will still carry out the Samurai Parade. And to show that we are not disgraced, the new gaijin will ride with us."

Husband put his chopsticks down and cleared his throat. He took a long but shallow breath. *He* was the festival director.

"But Father," he said, "we have only four samurai uniforms. You, me, Ebana, and Mayor. Someone would have to miss the parade."

Father simply stared at Husband through his ruined old eyes.

"Father," pleaded Husband, "we have only four horses."

Noriko refilled their cups. Father sipped. Husband gulped. With no further words, the issue was settled. Husband would give up his place in the Samurai Parade.

Now Husband rose noisily to re-fill his rice bowl. He threw ginger beans over the rice and stabbed them down into it. He glared at Noriko.

"My stomach was full," he said, "and now you serve the beans."

By lunchtime, as Father decreed, the rain had stopped. The sun burned hot over the southern mountains. Starlings strutted on steaming roads. Dragonflies lifted on glittering wings from the flooded rice fields. The mountain breeze smelled of mud and worms and cucumber leaves, but as Noriko drove down toward Kitayama the air was gradually claimed by the gassy diesel trucks hauling in tents and platforms, by the burnt-miso aromas of roasted squid and chicken and the sickly-sweet smells of bean cakes and cotton candy. Then there was the snarl of traffic, all of Husband's drunken little old men with sticks and helmets yelling at her to go this way and that, and on top of that all the looks she was getting—*there goes Noriko Yamaguchi, and did you know that Mister Stuart never even showed up for his bye-bye party?* By the time she reached Mister Tommy's apartment, Noriko had to pass it by and hurry to the riverbank. She gagged over a dark hole in the riprap, but nothing came out.

She had to use her key on his apartment door. She brought in a bag of Ono Hotel towels, plus sake, a room key, slippers and robe, and two copies of *Score Man Club*, the same cartoon that Husband read. She flipped its pages briefly, numbly, making a stale and pulpy breeze of cartoon body parts, reeling women and exploding men. Then she had to shake the new man's heavy leg. "I'm sorry," she said as he came awake. "We have a parade today, and you are expected to join."

Mister Tommy struggled. His limbs moved like bags of sand, haphazardly attached.

"Today?"

"It is Sunday now. Today is the festival for the obon holiday. They want you to ride in the Samurai Parade, which displays the great history of Kitayama."

He sat up, looked groggily around. He was still wearing his clothes. There was nothing to see in the apartment. Just his one shopping bag and the futon he had slept on. She had worked with Stuart to pack up his hundreds of gifts. Beyond that, Stuart's life had been curiously blank.

Mister Tommy said, "They?"

"My father-in-law," she said. "He is head of the committee. Their purpose is to make Kitayama an international city."

He yawned. "Oh yeah. I remember." He used his toilet. He splashed for a minute at the kitchen sink. When he returned he asked, "Ride what?"

In ancient Kitayama, Noriko explained, the samurai rode horses.

He rubbed his face. "Horses?" he said.

He was silent as she navigated the mess around Shinmei. There was a lot to look at, she imagined. When they reached the police box above the town she paused her pickup to wait for a bus and she told him, "Today is one great day in Kitayama. During the o-bon holiday, many people return to Kitayama to respect their families and their ancestors. Today is a big celebration."

Then she wondered. What else should she tell him? That Father and Husband had been drunk since breakfast? That the committee as a unit had been celebrating since mid-morning? That the horses tied to the police box eave were Motoki's, and thus ill-trained? That the samurai uniform would not be sized for a twentieth-century white man? She had spent so much time advising Stuart, explaining, preparing, apologizing, watching his contact lenses slip around his strange blue eyes as he nodded and said, "Hai, hai. Wakarimatshita. Arigato." *Yes, I understand. Thank you.* But in the end, it seemed Stuart had understood nothing. If he had grasped the first thing about Kitayama life, she thought, the first thing about *her* life, he would have come to his party.

She stopped the engine and turned greenly to Mister Tommy. There were so many things to say, but what she said to him finally was, "Excuse me." The she ran into the bamboo behind the police box. She leaned over the steep edge. She coughed. Her stomach cramped. But nothing. It was empty, she realized. Her stomach. She hadn't eaten in two days.

Inside the police box, the men of the committee wore breastplates and leggings of straw and leather. They sat around a low table on the floor, steel helmets at their sides. Did Mister Tommy like Japanese food? Noriko clamped her jaw. *How could he?* How about the heat? *What about it?* Would he like some sake? *Did he have any choice?* What, perhaps, explained the actions of Mister Stuart Norton?

Tommy swallowed his sake. She watched alcohol collide with jet lag at high noon. His skin flushed and he yawned. At the first sound of his English, Ebana's German Shephard awoke and came out from beneath a desk to growl at Tommy. Ebana shoved the dog away. Mister Stuart Norton had gone home, Tommy guessed. To Utah.

Noriko translated with her head bowed. Father scowled and corrected.

"Our call this morning to Narita Airport," she explained to Mister Tommy, "was not successful. Mister Stuart had not arrived there. The committee believes he has accepted another job in Japan, Takata perhaps, even though this is against his agreement with the committee. They want to know what you think."

"I'm sorry?"

"You may understand the behavior of Mister Stuart, they believe, whereas they cannot. And now my father-in-law is requesting your idea. Why, perhaps, did Mister Stuart choose to insult the people of Kitayama?"

Mister Tommy bit off a second yawn. He closed one eye, then the other. He sniffed as if to clear his breathing. Noriko recalled something from her conversation with the broker. Something about Mister Tommy and ice hockey. Was this how his nose had been broken?

"Perhaps," he said, glancing at her, "yes, Mister Stuart may have felt awkward about accepting another job and so he didn't show up for the party."

Noriko translated. The ensuing silence allowed a flatbed truck loaded with outhouses to air its brakes at the tunnel mouth and grind gears for the turn down into Kitayama. Police Chief Ebana rose in vigilance, twisting inside his breastplate to watch the tight corner. Then Mayor spoke patiently.

"Mayor tells you that Kitayama is a good town, worthy of respect. People here will be nice to you and say hello to you on the street. We welcome you—"

Then Father interrupted. His voice exploded in a loud, breathless squeak. His hands jabbed and pawed. Then he laid them down beside his horned helmet. He drained his cup and returned to his cigarette.

"My father-in-law is very drunk. He says, There is no better town in Japan. He says, Kitayama sake is the best sake in Japan. And also Kitayama potatoes. He recommends you to try ginger and potato, with sake. It is a famous dish from Kitayama since Edo period."

Her gut cramped as she poured. She wanted to run outside, try again to throw up. But Husband shuffled the petals of his mail skirt and made a long statement, punctuating with bows and puffs of smoke. Then he drained his cup.

"My husband, who is also very drunk, says, yes, what Father mentions is very famous dish of Kitayama. He also recommends you to try mountain rhubarb. A few years ago, he says, Kitayama contributed mountain rhubarb to the wedding dinner when Prince Akihito was married."

Tommy nodded. Police Chief Ebana broke in with a growl. His dog sat up, ears flat, ready to defend.

"However, as Mister Ebana adds, the mountain rhubarb was misplaced in Takata, by Takata officials, and never arrived. And, as Husband is now saying, this committee traveled to the Imperial Palace to make apology, but they could not be received. Their intention to contribute was not respected. Still, mountain rhubarb is an excellent dish. It is hoped that someday you will—" She was interrupted again by Father. "It is hoped that someday you will try both these dishes."

"I will."

Mister Tommy pushed himself back from the table. He winced as he straightened his right leg. Ebana shoved the dog back.

Then Mayor leaned in, his eyes wide and patient. He was a weak but kind man. He put his hand on Noriko's in an effort to stop the sake pouring. "Mayor says, Welcome to Kitayama. We are very proud. We are sometimes too proud, of course, but we hope you are happy here."

Father grunted. They sat quietly for a moment, sipping sake. Police Chief Ebana suffered another truck around the tight corner. Mayor adjusted his straw leggings. Outside, a horse reared and stamped. Mister Tommy looked startled as the police box shook.

Then Husband grumbled. Noriko lowered her head.

"My Husband, who is very injured in his feelings, tells you that Kitayama has the best fishing in Japan. Stuart should have learned the hobby of fishing. And Mayor is now saying that perhaps fishing is not for everyone but Husband is answering that in Kitayama fishing is for everyone. Fishing *is* Kitayama. And Father—" the old man wheezed fervently "—says put a Kitayama char with sea salt into a bottle of sake and soak for two months. That is the best way."

Police Chief Ebana returned to the table. He took a fierce bolt of sake. He stared at Mister Tommy's chest. Mayor laid a hand on Ebana's armored shoulder, but the chief spoke anyway.

"Mister Ebana says to you, though Mayor tries to stop him, that he caught seven fish, this morning, under the bridge. Seven fish."

Their new teacher nodded dully. He massaged his knee. Husband grabbed the bottle from Noriko and filled Mister Tommy's cup. Mister Tommy laughed strangely and looked at Husband. Husband looked away. Outside the police box, Officer Wada was arriving in his little black-and-white patrol car. Noriko felt a small measure of relief when the huge deputy came through the door grinning at her and said, "Gotoh—" that was her high school name, Noriko Gotoh "—you're parked illegally. I'll have to write you a ticket."

"Wada," snapped Police Chief Ebana, "shut your fat mouth. Go back outside and clean up the horse shit."

Wada shrugged. He went back outside. After a moment they heard a shovel scraping the cinders. Then Mayor tugged her sleeve and spoke.

"Mayor hopes you will meet the nice people of Kitayama."

"I'm sure I will," said Mister Tommy.

Police Chief Ebana snorted. He held out his cup.

"Perhaps you have many fish in America, Mister Ebana says. Perhaps this is true. But he questions if you can catch seven fish under one bridge. And if so, he questions if they would be good to eat."

"That depends," Tommy said.

"Perhaps they would be the kind of fish that is bony, with weak flesh."

"Perhaps."

"In the Prince School system, says Mayor . . . and Husband says the Yamaguchi family is a successful maker of stone goods for many years . . . and now Mister Ebana is saying that perhaps people make a gossip that he cannot fish as well as Mister Ono, but this is a lie, that Ono cheats . . . and Husband says for five generations they are making stone goods . . . and Mayor—"

Suddenly Father's hands thumped the table. Harsh words tore from his mouth. His square face turned purple. He pulled his stiff white hair. He thrust his arms. Then he stopped and rubbed his chest.

Noriko glanced at Mayor.

"Father says, catch a char no bigger than twenty centimeters. Roast the fish with salt. Roast it by fire, not oven. When the fish becomes cool, put it in the sake bottle. You must use Kitayama sake. After one year, drink the sake. Perhaps Mister Stuart prefers some ladies' drink, perhaps he does not respect the famous history of Kitayama and prefers some kind of Takata cocktail, but this is the best liquor in the world."

Then Husband thrust his finger at Mister Tommy, spluttering and fumbling a cigarette. Vehemently he spoke, at even greater length than Father. Then, red-faced, nearly tipping in his armor, he sparked his lighter. He took a deep drag and sat.

Noriko's shoulders sagged and her gut cramped. She could not raise her head.

"My husband," she reported, "says the same."

Another long silence passed. Once more Ebana's ratty Shepherd ventured out to sniff and growl at Mister Tommy. Husband splashed sake in the teacher's cup, waved impatiently for him to drink it. Mister Tommy did so. He leaned toward Noriko then and said quietly, "I feel sick."

Her heart leapt suddenly. She wanted to weep. She wanted to hold this huge, sleepy stranger, shake him and cry out, *Let's go!* She wanted to pull at him suddenly. *Let's run!*

But she kept her head down, her eyes averted. She pointed through the window, toward the spot outside where she had failed before and said one word: "Bamboo."

Chapter 8

.

But he looked confused out there. After a moment, Noriko rose shakily from her knees and went to the window. The glass was grimed with horse slobber and she stopped short of it. She kept her hand out, pointing toward the bamboo grove at the roadside. *There*, she meant. *Just there*. It was neither her plan nor her fault, of course, that crazy Ono's car appeared *just there*, at just that moment. In fact her stomach heaved at the sight of it. She glanced back. Police Chief Ebana had risen from the table. Then came Husband on his heels.

"No," she protested. "He only means to throw up in the bamboo. Husband," she begged, "he has simply had too much sake."

But Husband threw open the police box door. His first step was a misplaced one, forgetful of the step down, and he plunged to one knee in the cinders.

"Bakayaro!" he howled in the direction of Ono and Mister Tommy. He rose, his samurai costume skewed, and he shook his fist. Beside him, Chief Ebana had made the step cleanly. His sword was drawn. "Fiend!" he hollered, staggering forth. "I will cut your arms off."

Meanwhile Officer Wada just stood there, his shovel full of horse shit and cinders, grinning. Noriko flew through the door and slugged his massive shoulder. "Stop them!" she cried. "You big goof! Why don't you stop them?"

Wada shrugged. He put down his shovel. "Okay, Gotoh. If you say so."

But it was too late. Up and over the side of the Cadillac went Mister Tommy. *Clang!* sounded Ebana's sword as the big car pulled away. *Toot! Toot!*

"Bakayaro!" howled Husband.

And—Ebana. He was going for his horse.

By the time Wada caught them in his squad car, she could not bear to look. She stared at her peeling hands as the siren whooped and the little police car pried through the crowd on Shinmei Street. But Wada kept jabbing her in the shoulder, saying, "Look, Gotoh! Look at them now!"

Maybe the sight of idiots would help her throw up, she thought, and so finally she looked. Ono was a block ahead of them, motoring south, serenely parting the crowd with little toots of his horn. Close behind came Husband and Ebana, drunken samurai on bad horses, skidding sideways, colliding, turning in circles, scattering the Kendo Club and the Boshin War drama, tipping over squid roast and turtle dip, driving Kitayama's visitors in screams against the storefronts. Noriko returned her gaze to her hands. She was ready now. She would fill the cup of her palms.

"Gotoh," said Wada, "watch this."

"Just catch them. Stop them."

"Gotoh, do you want me to run someone over?"

Then he nearly did. The car stopped with a jolt. A camera burst from the glove box into Noriko's hands. She looked up in time to see Husband ride his horse into the ropes of the beer tent. The horse wheeled on hind legs, the tent came down, and then Husband bailed off. He grabbed a light pole and slid down in a cursing heap of armor. Noriko stared in paralytic horror as he sprang to his feet and tipped over backwards, then sprang up again and began to shove and berate Ueno-san, manager of the ruined beer tent. Wada surged the car forward, tight now behind Police Chief Ebana as he galloped straight through the Kimono Club singing contest and the junior high school reconstruction of the Boshin War. Then, cornering onto the river road, Ebana's horse saw the swollen current and stopped. With a murderous howl the chief was slung to the end of his reins, then dashed to the stones between the horse's hooves. He rose, his left arm dangling badly, and kicked the horse twice in the belly.

"Bakayaro!" the chief screamed at the escaping car. "You devil! I will cut your hands off!"

Wada's big finger nudged Noriko's shoulder. "Gotoh, did you see that?"

"Catch them!"

He clucked his tongue, returned his hand to the wheel. He was in the clear now and he shifted up, accelerated, and caught the Cadillac easily. He drew alongside, then stopped the patrol car and got out. He jogged easily alongside the open Cadillac, one hand on the door, explaining something, gesturing. The south bridge was under water, Noriko saw suddenly. A high brown froth covered the ancient tracks of the low-slung bridge. Still the big car maundered toward it. Wada jogged along, waving, explaining. He was ordering Ono to stop, she imagined. But at the river's edge, the Cadillac spun to the right and splashed in. Ono found the bridge treads, and the car began to ford the river as surely as a motorboat.

Wada let go, up to his ankles in the brown current.

Toot! Toot!

"Uncle!" she cursed when he returned. She slugged him again. "Why didn't you stop the car?"

"Gotoh," he laughed, "I'm not that strong."

"Then what's the point of being so big? Chiyonofuji would have stopped the car."

"Gotoh. . . ."

She shoved him. He didn't budge one centimeter. "Stupid uncle. Why didn't you just tell Mister Tommy to jump out?"

Wada shrugged. "I don't speak English."

She gave him a glare. Her guts hurt.

"None?"

"I tried. Nothing came out."

"You sat beside me for three years in English class, stealing my answers, and you remember nothing?"

Wada just shrugged.

"Why didn't you pull him out by the arm? Why don't you follow?"

"Gotoh," he said, "be sensible. You saw Ebana. A man's arm is fragile. And this little car would be swept away."

"Not with you in it."

Wada smiled. "Gotoh," he said, backing down the river road, reversing for the long trip back through town to the main bridge. "Chances are that Ono will stop for sake and snacks. We can still catch them before they reach West Mountain."

She glared at him. "Uncle." This was the worst name a young woman could call a young man. But Wada only eyed her calmly.

"Take it easy, Gotoh. Something is wrong with you. You need to take it easy."

He picked his way once more through the undone festival. Noriko sat rigidly beside him, her head down, her stomach grinding. She had forgotten how she hated Wada. He was so impossibly dense, as if the size of him reflected the millstone of his mind.

"Why don't you tell me what's wrong?" he asked when they had crossed the bridge.

Noriko huffed. As if her situation could be a mystery to anybody. As if she wouldn't be blamed all over again. She would puke in his car if she could. She would puke through her hands onto his floor.

"Gotoh, what's wrong?"

"You're stupid, for one thing."

"Gotoh, that hurts!"

"And I'm not Gotoh anymore for another. Did you miss something? I'm married now. I'm property of Yamaguchi."

He clucked, "Ara!"

"Ara? That's what old people say. Ara! You sound like a big, fat uncle."

Wada shrugged. Among rice fields the heat stunned. Dragonflies peeled away before the windshield. Wada left the main road to take a short cut through the paddies. The little car hammered over potholes and humps of old weeds. Noriko felt the pain in her stomach shake loose and rise like a bubble in her throat. She clenched her jaw, packed her tongue back tight. But as stupid Wada hit every bump along the sun-scorched levee, the pain burst into her mouth and she parted her lips with a dry moan.

"Stop," she gasped.

"Eh? Gotoh, what's wrong?"

"Just stop, you fool!"

He slammed the brake and the car stalled. Noriko pushed from the car, fell to her knees in the slash of wilted weeds at the edge of a rice paddy. Frogs leapt and splashed. She leaned after them and wretched so hard her stomach felt torn. But nothing.

"Gotoh," said Wada as she crawled back in, "now I'm sure something's wrong." He looked at her. "Let me see your tongue," he said.

"Shut up."

"Your tongue, Gotoh."

"Shut up and drive."

"No tongue," said Wada, crossing his massive arms, "no drive."

She stuck it out at him.

"Thank you," he said, and started the engine. He drove another kilometer to the Yamazaki store at the base of West Mountain. He stopped the car and reached through her knees to grab his purse from the glove box. His purse! Then he levered himself out of the car.

"Where are you going?"

He wouldn't answer.

"Stupid Wada, where are you going?"

Noriko slammed back against the seat. The Yamazaki clerk had come out to gawk at them—*and then a police car pulled up outside, and she was in there, red-faced, wiping tears, Noriko Yamaguchi!* God, she hated this town, Noriko thought. And it hated her. So lucky to be Brother, she thought, far off in Gifu. Lucky Mother, to be with him. Lucky Father, to be dead and done with. Lucky Stuart, she thought suddenly, to escape.

She watched Wada return with a sack. "What," she demanded.

He took a bottle from the sack. "Pocari Sweat."

"You took all that time to get Pocari Sweat?"

"You need fluids, Gotoh. You're dehydrated."

He reached into the sack again. Rice balls. Egg sandwiches. Grilled octopus. Pickled radish.

"And you need food. Your tongue is white. You're digesting yourself."

"Stupid Wada. I'm fine."

But he reached in the sack a third time.

"And chocolate," he told her. "To make you happy. You need to smile."

"Wada—"

"Your body needs it. It's the best thing, next to making love."

She couldn't speak. She could only glare at him, his orangutan face and placid eyes, his sumo-crinkled ears, the awful, stupid, hulking stillness of him.

Stupid Wada!

He would never change!

They drove up the mountain. West Mountain Village was deserted. Everyone had gone to the parade in Kitayama. Wada drove slowly between the stucco storage barns and the old straw-roofed houses. The Shinto shrine was at the dead end of the road, guarded by stone lion-demons. Just outside the red wooden arch waited Ono's yellow Cadillac, empty. Wada coasted to a stop.

"Just drive in." Noriko felt her guts cramp again. "You're a cop."

"Gotoh, you want me to drive on sacred shrine ground?"

"You are such an old man," she accused. "You believe in this ancient spirit stuff, don't you?"

"No."

"You do."

He shrugged. He drove the little car on its tiptoes past the dead iris garden, around the flat green pond, along the statuary to the head of Kappa's trail. He parked. They sat in silence a long time. Nothing but flies moved in the hot shade.

"Uncle," Noriko said finally. "Why don't you go up there?"

"Not me," said Wada.

"Coward. You have a gun. Why don't you go up there?"

"And shoot Kappa? Gotoh, you're confused. Kappa is a spirit. I can't shoot a spirit."

"Then you believe in him, don't you?"

"No, Gotoh, you do. If you think I could shoot him, then you must think he's real. He is not real."

"Then why don't you go up there?"

"Why don't you?"

So they sat. Noriko's stomach grumbled. She picked up a rice ball, put it back. Then Wada got out, took ten steps up Kappa's dark, rocky trail. "Now you're going up there?" Noriko called after him, startled. She sat a moment, then hurried after, rather than be left behind. But when she caught up, Wada was peeing on a tree trunk.

"I told you, Gotoh. I'm not going up there."

She stomped back to the car. Stupid! She threw herself inside and felt Wada all around her. His stupid little space was all tidy, a picture of his wife and babies on the sun flap, lamb's wool seat cover, tea thermos tucked beside the hand brake. Inside the glove box: a heavy camera, a toothbrush, a sumo comic book. The car tipped as he got back in. They sat in silence another ten minutes.

Finally Wada said, "Aren't you going to eat?"

She was silent. She wouldn't talk to him anymore.

"Okay," he said. "Do you want to hear my theory about Mister Stuart?"

She glared at him. No. She didn't. Wada grinned at her and shrugged. He wouldn't tell her then. They sat another half hour. Then Wada reached into the sack and opened a chocolate bar. He broke off a square and held it out to her. She turned her face away. He put it in her hand. After a minute she ate it.

"What?" she demanded finally. "Now you flirt with me?"

"I'm not flirting, Gotoh."

"Don't say I'm too ugly for you. That's impossible"

"Gotoh, I'm not flirting."

"Why not?" She slugged him. "You wouldn't make love to me?"

Wada laughed. His big voice echoed across the empty shrine ground, across the pond where blue hydrangeas glowed like a second, cooler sky within the deep shade of pines. "A married man doesn't discuss such things," he said.

"Uncle," she cursed. "Plenty of married men discuss such things. You don't know how many times I've been dragged halfway to the love hotel by one married man or another. I tell them, you want a whore, go to Thailand."

Wada's eyes narrowed. "Eh? Thailand? Gotoh, you're stealing my theory."

"What theory?"

"Mister Stuart went to Thailand."

She blew at her bangs. She didn't want to hear it.

"You see, Gotoh, he was afraid of women. Such men go to whores. In America perhaps Mister Stuart was not a noticeable person. But in Kitayama, he was suddenly a cute, blonde boy. Suddenly he was exotic, surrounded by women, attacked by them, overwhelmed by them. But he could not act. He was terrified. In the meantime, Kitayama men tell him their Thailand stories, beautiful whores, as many as he wants, for the change out of his pocket. There is a tension in this, Gotoh. His manhood must be proven."

Noriko ate another square of chocolate. "So now you're a psychologist."

Wada shrugged. "It makes more sense than blaming Takata," he said.

"Well for your information, Uncle, he never arrived at Narita Airport. He never boarded his flight. So he never left Japan."

Wada shook his head as though he pitied her. "And how about Haneda Airport, Osaka Airport, Sapporo Airport? How about another airline? How about a boat? Gotoh, you'd make a lousy cop."

They sat in silence another long time. Amidst her anger Noriko now felt what seemed like hunger. She found her fingers unwrapping the rest of the chocolate, breaking the squares, pushing them between her lips. And she found herself admitting that Wada could be right—not about Thailand, of course, but about the fact that Stuart could have taken any of several routes home. It was unlike Stuart. He was timid, afraid to be alone. His "girlfriends" took him everywhere, did everything for him. But it was possible. Suddenly the chocolate bar was gone, and Wada was watching her.

"Gotoh," he said, "I know your problem, too. You were too fussy. No boy in Kitayama was good enough for you. You frightened us. You acted better, studying your English, reading your books. You waited too long, and then. . . ."

Wada trailed off under Noriko's glare.

"Shut up," she said. "Uncle. Leave me alone."

Wada shrugged again. He reached over, his big elbow sinking between her knees. He popped the glove box once more and took out his camera. Then he stepped out onto the shrine ground.

"Where are you going?"

"There's good light on the hydrangea. I'm going to take some pictures."

"Again you're going to leave me?"

"See?" He smiled. "Gotoh, you're the one who's afraid of Kappa."

She watched him go, shaking her head, chewing her lip. The pond bridge creaked beneath his massive body. His camera whirred. He leaned over a hydrangea bush, looking just like a huge bear dressed up in club and pistol; he leaned over slowly and smoothly with perfect balance and stared through his lens for what to Noriko was one eternity and then another. And another. What kind of person was this?

Click! went his camera.

Her gut ached for food now, and she reached into the bag. She ate the rice balls, both of them, and felt her hunger doubled by the salty salmon in the center. She ate three egg sandwiches and then the entire leg of the octopus. She drank the bottle of Pocari Sweat. She paused a moment.

Her head buzzed.

She felt almost good.

She ate the last egg sandwich and then the second chocolate bar. Then, feeling dazed, feeling calm and controlled and yet enormously sick, she rose from the car. She crossed the pond bridge and parted two hydrangea bushes and climbed up through the pines until she couldn't see Wada any more. This was Kappa's forest, she told herself, and through her mind whirled her grandmother's stories of fox gods and owl gods, lost and captured children. She could lose herself in Kappa's forest, she imagined, and she could be taken. She walked on a bit farther. Then gave up the thought and knelt, shoved her finger deep down the back of her throat, and up came everything. She fell onto her palms. She coughed and drooled. She felt wonderful.

But as she sat back on her heels a moment later, she felt her sense of well being drain away. She felt cold suddenly. The pines had begun to sway above her. The earth stank. She heard a snap behind her, a faint squeak, then heavy breathing. She shivered. She remembered now: Kappa was limp and wet and fetid, her grandfather had told her, with webbed hands and feet and a leering grin. He was drunk, always, and he loved trouble. Vomit drew him in. She let her smock drop, wet where she had bitten it.

"Kappa?" she called.

"Boo," said Wada plainly behind her, and when she wheeled he stood there grinning, proud of himself, just like a fat old uncle, and she would have flown at him then in her rage and smashed his balls and clawed his eyes out, but suddenly she was darkening, slipping, falling through the pines, she was weightless . . . and then she was riding out over the pond bridge across Wada's fantastic shoulders.

He put her down on the car seat. He dropped a single stem of blue hydrangea in her lap. "Gotoh," he said, "you wait too long. Not just for love. For everything. You should have eaten hours ago."

Chapter 9

What happened, Tommy was trying to explain to Ono, is that Elaine—yes, his wife, her name was Elaine, Elaine Red Cloud, yes she was Indian, and no she didn't have a horse already—but what he was trying to say was that Elaine had suddenly wanted a horse so badly that she hadn't checked the animal's background, and right away, with Tommy watching, the beast had bitten her, taken a chunk out of his wife's thigh the size of a small pot roast—

Ono's eyes swam. "Pot roast?"

"A piece of meat."

"Ah! Mister Tommy is hungry?" The old man was worried again. "I have food. I have meat of the squid." He set down his end of the crate. "Thou shalt chotto matte," he said, and he dug in the plastic sack that had banged and thrashed from the crook of his arm for the last hour.

Tommy put the crate down and wiped his forehead. He had been trying to explain his fear of horses, his abruptly visceral decision outside the police box that he would not, under any circumstances, ride in a samurai parade. But now, once again, they were linguistically lost.

"Squid meat," Ono announced, passing him something that looked like the liner of an old hockey skate. Tommy took a bite and Ono beamed, slapped him heartily on the shoulder. "Mister Stuart," the old man began, "Mister Stuart no—" But again his English failed to flow as he seemed to hope. "Mister Stuart . . . very . . . not," he said. "Not help," he said, and then he did his pantomime again: he held his breath and staggered clumsily, all elbows and knees, his face turning purple and his eyes bugging crazily, and then he spun around and collapsed upon the trail.

"Ne?" he said as he rose. He was dusty on one side, grinning and hustling over to massage Tommy's shoulders again. "Mister Tommy . . . very . . . help, ne? Mister Tommy very big strong man."

He offered sake again. Tommy declined.

"Ja," said Ono. "Thou shalt ikimashoo."

And off they went again, hauling the awkward crate up over the next tangle of pine and chestnut roots. Tommy puffed along on the down side, stumbling to get beneath the entire load every time Ono lifted his hands to supplement his constant chatter. What was he saying? That he was a happy man? That he was crazy? Or that people thought he was? That he had no friends—except Mister Tommy? He took a bath every day, that seemed certain. He seemed to say that he had no stomach. He dropped his end and made a scissoring motion, tossed an imaginary organ off a steep ledge toward Kitayama valley. "Money," he said, and he danced in a circle, waving his hands in the air. "No problem," he sang, and somehow this led to Hollywood, a trip there maybe, and then talk of engine parts, and demonstrations of old gashes and injuries to trees along the trail. Tommy's head spun and he tripped. The crate slammed down.

"Chotto!" Ono cried, rushing to the wooden box. He pressed his ear to it, wagged it gently back and forth. "Thou shalt very, very kiotsukette," he begged. "Ne? Not to break firmament, ne?"

"I'll just take it," Tommy told him. "I'll just take the whole thing. Go ahead."

Tommy put the crate up on his shoulder. Ono cringed, hustled up the trail to guide a corner. Now what was he saying? Kappa this, Kappa that. Cigars. Whiskey. A fishing rod. But no car. A very long time. Waiting. Kappa had been waiting a long time. Then, suddenly, "Utah?"

Tommy puffed. "I'm sorry?"

"Mister Tommy, Utah?"

"No. Wisconsin."

Ono backpedaled along a level stretch, pondering. "Demon? Wisconsin demon?"

"No. No Wisconsin demon."

"Mister Tommy . . . believe? Demons? Mountain spirits?"

"No," Tommy puffed, "not believe," and then he stopped short, nearly toppled. His knee. One of the screws had touched a nerve. His knee was on fire. He leaned the crate and sank to a rock. "No," he told Ono. "I'm fine. Just give me a minute," he said, and then he sat there working his patella back and forth, wondering at the long reach of Elaine—as if she had just heard his careless surety—*not believe*—and taken a sledge hammer to his sorest point. *Her* mountains were full of spirits, she would have reminded him. It was only *his* people, she claimed, who denied that, as a preface to tearing the mountains down. As for demons—he could hear her voice, the new, angry Elaine—one day they would catch him. She hoped. For his sake. And so on. But what about Gus, Tommy wondered suddenly. What was Gus doing now? Was he in school? What was he thinking? Would Gus even miss him?

"Mister Tommy?"

Ono seemed worried now as he looked up the trail. He lifted a dry branch that lay snapped in two ahead of them. He turned toward Tommy, the pieces in his hand. "My Kappa," he said, and he tried to smile. Tommy worked his knee around. He felt the sudden intensity of the forest around them. Leaves baked in the sun. Cicadas buzzed. Flies swarmed. Unfamiliar bird calls sawed and screeched and moaned through the heavy brush. When Tommy stood for relief he could see, framed in fans of rust-red sumac, the Kitayama valley far below, deep and hot, a thousand dragonfly specks dotting the rice paddies; and then, against the opposite mountain, he found Kitayama town, blue and red rooftops packed in the curve of a wide and shallow river. Smoke rose faintly, dissolving toward the cloudless blue sky.

Ono came nervously to his elbow. "You like?"

"Yes."

"I want you like."

"I do."

Ono dropped the sticks.

"Please tell Kappa."

Then Ono scrambled up ahead of him and waved him on, trying to steer the crate away from tree roots and rocks. But Tommy felt clumsy now, unnerved by new urgency and the need to protect his knee. On a steeper stretch they cornered quickly into heavy brush, nearly fell. Ono ransacked for words.

"Chotto . . . abyss!" he cried, indicating the edge over which Tommy had nearly dumped his precious windshield. The old man's voice came out as a pained yelp. Tommy panted at him. And then, more slowly, they continued.

But Ono's energy was fouled now. He picked up more sticks from the trail. He fingered leaves and the broken wisps of spider's webs and glanced darkly about. The crate bumped and dragged, slammed down once more as Tommy stumbled.

Ono scolded him in Japanese, then apologized, raced ahead, raced back, seemed by his urgent hand motions as if he wished to sweep Tommy up the trail.

"Thou shalt giddy-up," he begged. "Ne? Please?"

Then at last the ground flattened. The trail widened. They arrived gasping among twisted pines on the summit, where earth and sky divided cleanly and cool air rushed along their boundary.

Tommy filled his aching lungs. He stooped and massaged his knee. Ono spun slowly, strangely. The breeze carried an odd, sweet smell. Ono cried out, "Kappa?"

Following him, Tommy carried the crate through a small timbered arch. The old man paused, touched the heavy broken spider webs.

"Kappa?" he whispered.

No sound but sweet breeze in the scrawling red pines.

"Thou shalt once more chotto matte," he told Tommy. And then in speechless desperation Ono paddled away into queer, sky-lit shadows down a footpath between shaggy cedars.

The air stunk, Tommy decided. After five minutes he followed, finding Ono on his knees at a small wooden shrine. Long braids of hair hung from the lattice door. About the steps and sides of the shrine lay a thousand objects in rust and decay, televisions and microwave ovens, golf clubs, faded whiskeys, moldering shoes, books and magazines, clothing and china and pillaged boxes of food. Tommy held the crate over his head as he stared. Most amazingly of all, beside the shrine was parked a yellow Cadillac, bird-spattered and flat-tired, but somehow proud yet, all assembled and still awaiting the windshield. The sun wove among the weeds and saplings that had sprung from her broad, damp floor. A bare stripe of earth extended toward Tommy, dots of green in it where grass had grown through what must have been a chain. And Ono was searching now, coming around the shrine, his face damp and pale.

"Ono!" Tommy cried. "Fantastic!"

But Ono shuddered. He paddled toward Tommy, his eyes closed. "My Kappa," he whispered, "very . . . not . . . happy." He shushed Tommy, seemed to listen to the underbrush. Then Tommy swung the crate down and Ono leapt to it, his ear cocked. And Tommy heard it too. As the battered wood touched earth, the window glass inside surrendered with a delicate crinkle. A thousand cracks, then a brisk and final tumbling into slush.

"Go!" Ono whispered. "Mister Tommy, we must go now!"

Chapter 10

"I'm sorry," Tommy told Father Yamaguchi, and he waited as Noriko translated. The old stone-blaster glowered back at him, red and bent as an old salmon. His bottom lip hung wetly open. Then he spoke.

"Father says that all of Kitayama feels this injury. He says for generations we have struggled for respect and—" she checked her dictionary "—for prosperity. He says it is his purpose in his life to bring prosperity to Kitayama."

Tommy looked about the room. Noriko and the big cop had delivered him to the ancient Yamaguchi house on East Mountain, and now he sat with the committee for green tea and cigarettes around the family table. He had no sense of Japanese wealth. Perhaps this vast fortress of a house was not prosperity. He had no sense of Japanese time yet either, but it was clearly too late for Mayor, who snored on a pillow beneath the window. Police Chief Ebana wore a cast on his right arm. He sipped his tea and he shifted painfully, mumbling something in the direction of Husband, who nodded dully. Only Mama Yama, at the foot of the table, was bright-eyed. She spoke sharply to Noriko, who rose and tiptoed across the ancient mats. She opened a cabinet, laid a quilt over Mayor's stomach. Then she re-filled the teacups. She did all this with the stem of a blue flower clenched in the fist of her left hand. Tommy followed the flower.

"I made a bad decision," he said, "and I'm sorry." Noriko settled back down, the flower in her lap. She transformed his words. "I'm afraid of horses," Tommy added.

Police Chief Ebana snorted. He made Noriko speak. "Mister Ebana informs you that in his case, it is horses who are afraid of him."

Tommy met the chief's narrowed eyes. He was red in the face and Tommy knew the look. His arm hurt like hell. Two fingers and a thumb stuck out of the cast, gingerly gripping a cigarette lighter.

"Mister Ebana tells you that it is also the yamame, the mountain trout, who fear him. And now Husband warns him that a man cannot fish with one arm, but Mister Ebana says that he can fish better than Husband by only using his feet. And now my father-in-law wishes to know why you went with Ono."

"Mostly because I'm afraid of horses," Tommy repeated. "I saw one take a bite out of my wife."

Noriko reported this and now Husband bore down on Tommy. Smoke gushed from his nose. "Husband demands where is your wife?"

"She's in Wisconsin."

"Why she is not with you?"

"We're not together right now."

Husband scowled and snapped his cigarette as if he had no patience for more foreign evasions. He cut to the quick.

"Husband asks you how you plan to eat without a wife. How you plan to have clean clothes."

"I can take care of myself."

Husband's response made Noriko blush deeply and twist the flower in her lap. It was a hundred tiny flowers actually, bunched together in a dense cloud, improbably blue.

"I am sorry for my husband," she said, her head lowered. "Please forgive him. He asks are you a lady man, like he hears of in America?"

Tommy laughed and suddenly Mayor sat up. He rubbed his eyes as apparently Ebana gave him the news: Mister Tommy was a lady man. Mayor located his big eyeglasses, put them on, and spoke at some length. Then he removed his glasses and lay back down.

"Mayor points out that Mister Stuart also did not come here with a wife, and yet we did not consider him a lady man, even though, perhaps, there may have been some more reasons to do so, as Mister Stuart was unable to catch a fish and did not always walk properly. Mister Stuart had many girlfriends, Mayor points out, to feed him and do things for him, yet he took no Kitayama woman to his bed. Still, we did not call him a lady man. And now my mother-in-law punches me and demands to know the name of your wife."

Tommy told her.

"Family name please."

"Red Cloud."

Noriko frowned. The flower stirred in her lap. "Mother has read in a magazine that American women refuse to take the name of their husbands. They even refuse to cook. Then—" she listened to Mama Yama a while longer "—when their husbands find girlfriends they kick their husbands out of the house and take everything for themselves."

Tommy nodded at the old woman. That about summed it up. Minus the few hundred years of American history that Elaine had recently discovered.

"What kind of name is Red Cloud?"

"Her mother is Ojibwa. Her father is Winnebago."

"American Indian?"

"Yes."

Now Mama Yama spoke directly to Tommy while Noriko bowed her head and twisted the flower. Tommy glanced as small blue petals fell upon her lap.

"Mother says that in Japan, we don't marry Koreans, Chinese, or Thai. We marry Japanese. We keep the energy of Japanese within Japanese people. This is why we are strong. And Father interrupts to ask why we were not informed of these matters by the—" she thumbed her dictionary "—broker of English teachers. Perhaps, Father says, there was something also in the information of Mister Stuart which we should have known. And now Mister Ebana says that perhaps Mister Stuart *was* a lady man. And my husband charges that Ebana, after all, cannot fish with his feet. No one can fish with his feet, my husband says."

Noriko drooped at the end of this. She stared down and twisted the flower. Then she spoke quietly, flinching as if she might be hit. At the end of her speech, Mama Yama snatched the flower away, dropped it an empty teacup, and ordered Noriko toward the kitchen. Noriko said as she rose, "I have explained that of course the broker of English teachers does not share every information about a teacher, only information important to teaching of English, and I have assured them that it is also the first time that I as well have learned that Mister Tommy has a wife. My surprise, also, is very great."

Noriko returned with a vase. She moved the flower into it.

"Is there another thing about you," she translated, "that the committee should know?"

Tommy wondered. His endless string of hockey trades? His penalty minutes? The nightmare in Canada, and his abiding anguish and guilt? But no. Nothing deep or subtle about himself could be shared here. He felt suddenly exhausted. He wanted to lie down like Mayor, except alone and very far away. Already, he thought, he was tired of Kitayama. "I have a son," he said finally. "Gus."

More red-faced consternation. More hoarse discussion. More cigarettes. Husband demanded: "What is your son—Indian or American?"

Tommy shook his head and shrugged. Husband could take his pick. He wasn't going to answer. Instead he would watch the flower Noriko had reclaimed to her lap. Her brown fingers probed the blue cloud as if searching for something. Then Mama Yama snatched the bloom away again and replaced it in the vase. About them the old house seemed to slump into deep night, its smoke-grimed timbers descending heavily toward the ancient straw mats. From across the room an ivory Buddha stared without pupils. A small, green frog had climbed up the window to hunt.

"My husband has a question."

Tommy looked at the man. Husband stared shrewdly at his cigarette as he coned it on the edge of the ashtray.

"Why did you come to Kitayama town?"

Noriko rose behind Tommy. Moving away, she delivered his answer from beneath the beam of the doorway.

"Because I need the money."

Police Chief Ebana sat up sharply. "Ha!" he cried.

The chief looked eagerly about him. But Father was asleep now too, his head nodding into his chest. Mayor stirred, gasped, and rolled over. Mama Yama rubbed Husband's shoulders. The flower was gone, its brilliant blue cloud gone like life itself from the room.

Tommy rose. He could hardly walk, his knee was so stiff. He could hardly think, his mind felt so dark and exhausted. He limped across the straw mats and down the plank hallway. His steps rattled windows and doors. A narrow door shut quickly ahead of him, and Tommy smelled the toilet as he passed. He heard Noriko cough. There, in the entry, inside his shoe, she had placed the flower.

Chapter 11

Yet she greeted him flatly, without eye contact, as he arrived to teach on the next Monday afternoon. She met him in front of the pachinko parlor. She kept her head down, kept her hands sweeping at her navy skirt, and she led him up the stairs and showed him the classroom, the teacher office, the lavatory. The phone rang and she left him for a moment at the desk where Stuart had sat. The kid was neat. The bookshelves were ordered with textbooks and playing cards, plastic fruit and toy money. Even Stuart's garbage was neat: the can beside the desk was densely, perfectly packed.

Noriko returned. "Your first class is cancelled," she told him.

Tommy looked at the schedule taped above Stuart's desk. The student was a Mrs. Tezuka, for a one-hour private lesson.

"She's sick?" Tommy wondered.

Noriko crossed the class off the schedule. "No. She's finished. No more English."

Tommy didn't feel encouraged to ask. Noriko carried the trashcan away and he sat down. He flipped through a text book called *Side-by-Side,* page after page of cartoon people standing in front, behind, beside, near, under, buying apples and hats and pets, turning left and right, reading books and eating and sleeping, telling one another their heights and weights and ages and hobbies. "Hello!" they beamed. "How are you? I am fine, thank you. And you? What time did you wake up this morning?"

In an hour Noriko introduced him to his next class, a group of middle-aged housewives gathered at two p.m. for an hour and a half of English. Tommy stood before them, suddenly in a full game sweat. He got their names, and, after a great giddy turmoil, some version of their ages that made them all laugh and chatter and argue for a good ten minutes. Then Tommy established, by opening it, that Stuart never used the textbook. He had made the room abruptly quiet.

"What do you usually do?" he wondered.

After some Japanese discussion the plump woman who was the bravest put together five English words in perfect order. "Please," she said, "where is Mister Stuart?"

"Home," Tommy answered. "By now I'm sure he's home."

Then the plump woman spoke again. This question took time, discussion, dictionaries, multiple misunderstandings and revisions. Finally Tommy got it: Could they please, with the rest of their time, write Stuart letters?

He felt more ready for his next class, a group of older women united by their membership in a flower arrangement class. Before he could speak they presented him with a delicate arrangement of mums, berries, and sumac twigs, centered around a big blue cloud-flower like the one Noriko had given him. Then Tommy introduced himself and cut to the quick. Stuart was certainly home now. Would they like to write him letters?

They applauded his excellent idea.

And so it went through the day, until his last class, a group of thirteen exhausted high school girls just off the train from Takata. They scuffed in, all platform shoes and baggy socks, heavy backpacks and Sony earphones. They flopped at the table, stared down at it. He had them prepare nametags.

"You more or less met me last week on the train," he tried to joke.

Nothing.

"So how about we all write letters to Stuart?"

They issued sighs of exasperation, flopped over their notebooks, and began to write. All but one of them, and Tommy recognized her as the girl he had crushed on the train. Miwa Sato was her name. She had leaned her kendo stick on the wall behind her. She opened what looked like a somber English text book, written in Japanese, and read for several minutes. In the quiet, Tommy noticed that pachinko bells rang up through the floor.

"Miwa," he said finally. "Don't you want to write a letter to Stuart?"

She looked up at him. She pulled long strands of black hair from the wire rims of her glasses. Tommy realized the other girls had looked up too.

"I am not interested in Stuart," she told him in English, and then one of the girls who understood this passed it to the others in Japanese and there was an outcry of jeering voices. But Miwa Sato had returned to her study. Mutely, she turned page after page until her classmates gave up. Then she looked up again.

"Teacher," she said. "Please. What is the difference between *that* and *which*?"

"They were all girls and women," Tommy noted to Noriko as she locked the door behind them at the end of the night.

"Of course," she said, and started down the stairs. The pachinko bells grew louder as they descended.

"Why of course?"

She started a cigarette on the sidewalk, under the bright neon of the pachinko marquee. All afternoon Tommy had been thinking about what she wore: a navy blue business suit that hung almost crookedly on her thin frame, plus white nylon stockings and black buckle shoes with thin high heels. She was tall this way, and her manner fell somewhere between severe and bereft. She pulled hard on the cigarette and shivered at the sudden autumn air. Her hair was pulled up, anchored with a glittery clip. She wore makeup in an effort to hide the blemishes on her cheekbones. She carried her keys and other items on a long, messy chain that now hung about her neck. She didn't answer his question. Instead, she pointed across the street and said, "From that phone, you can call international."

"Thank you."

"Do you call home?"

"Not yet."

His answer felt strange. She was sure to ask him why. Because his family didn't want him too? Because he didn't know what to say? He could imagine the conversation. *Hey, Elaine. I made it.* A long silence. Then finally: *So?*

But Noriko surprised him. She dropped her cigarette in the street. She released a long jet of smoke.

"Do you love your wife?"

"Yes." Tommy felt no hesitation. "Yes, I do."

She turned the chain around her neck, found her coin purse and squeezed it. Seeming preoccupied suddenly, she said good night in Japanese and turned away as if to see more clearly under the light. Tommy crossed the street. When he looked back she still stood there. Then she rubbed her arms and moved back inside, into the blast-furnace glare of the parlor.

A week more of cold nights turned the trees. The mountains around Kitayama glowed with golds and reds that made Tommy homesick for Wisconsin, and the chill in his apartment made him rise at dawn, escape his featureless quarters and walk. He walked away the mornings across the farm roads and up the obscure trails that branched across the mountains. He staunched his leaking spirit with the thousand thrills of newness, noting how the apple farmers had wrapped each fruit in its own tiny paper bag, noting the inside-out look of the houses and the way all the dogs looked related, wondering at the forgotten shrines swathed in spider webs and moss at the trail ends and backing away quietly, wondering at the notes tied to the trees, the hair tied to the doors. Some day, he vowed, when his knee was stronger, he would climb again to Kappa's shrine. Then, as the hour for his strange English classes approached, he returned on low ground, hopping along the giant jacks that rip-rapped the river, which now ran clear and shallow, sparkling over gravel and garbage within its concrete jacket. Yes, Tommy determined. It was more than habit to say so. He did love Elaine. But here were the new mysteries: *Why?* he asked himself. *And so what?*

In one week more the rice was cut and hung on poles to dry. Farmers stockpiled, hung long white radishes from the eaves, heaped squash at the field corners, spread chestnuts and ginko nuts and persimmons across their steps in the fading sun. Tommy, exhausted and unspooled at the end of a hike to the far end of the valley, concluded two things. First: his love, his way of loving, had been a bad thing for Elaine. His love had damaged her. From its murky origins to its fabulous consequences, the idea sapped him. He could hardly move his feet. And this second conclusion too, this parallel intuition that arrived like a stick in the gut: winter came hard and fast in Kitayama.

Then, that Wednesday night, when the Stuart letters had gone three weeks without reply, Noriko finally answered his question. She had just taken another class off his schedule. He had no classes at all now on Wednesday afternoons, and only Miwa Sato remained in his evening girls class. Tommy waited for her.

"Of course Prince School is only girls and woman," Noriko said, "because in this town there is no experience with foreign people, except by TV and movies. When Stuart arrived, it was like a kind of dream. Every woman was in love with him. Every man felt," she said and paused, needing her dictionary, "the feeling of to covet Stuart. It was a very strange situation. Every day was soap opera. Women fed him and flirted with him and looked in his windows and cried about him when he walked down the street. Men ignored him and talked about him and raced their cars at him. Now," she said, "the excitement is finished. Now it is a kind of, how do you say it? After you drink too much alcohol?"

Tommy sat down hard on the office sofa.

"Hangover."

"Yes. This is Kitayama hangover."

Tommy stared dully at his shoes for a minute. Already, they were worn out. He had a flash of an old hockey feeling: after the knee slowed him he had become a skilled enforcer, a wet blanket, a squelcher of offense and a burster of bubbles. He had gotten better, actually. More useful to a team, at least. Now, in far-away Kitayama, he was still Tommy Morrison, the official end of the party, and doing his usual fine job of it. Noriko seemed to read his mind.

"It's not your fault," she said. "It has nothing to do with you, really."

"It had nothing to do with Stuart either."

"Yes. Nothing. He was not any kind of movie star. Not at all."

"What was he like?"

The question clouded her face. She frowned a long time, and Tommy studied her. Today she wore her beige suit with the big black lapels. It hung away from her collarbones and her blue bra showed. Her complexion was raw at the cheekbones and her make-up strained to draw attention upward, to her plucked black eyebrows, and downward, to her small mouth, rimmed in lavender. Her hands were raw and chewed. She read magazines while he was in the classroom and today she had left a dog-eared *Cosmo* open on her desk. A flawless blonde supermodel smoldered up, as if from a magic mirror.

"He changed," Noriko said at last. "At first he was very bashful but also very cheerful. He went to every tea party, every karaoke sing-along. He never said no. He was always dating with some woman, eating cake, or eating noodles or sushi or some woman's special homemade soup. They were always feeding him. There was so much gossip, so much talk and fighting, because no woman could capture him. A woman would get close, and he would become frightened and move on to the next woman. Unless she was old, like a grandmother, and then he seemed more comfortable."

"But he changed?"

Noriko paused. The door downstairs had opened, letting up a small riot of pachinko sounds. Then shoes scuffed slowly up the steps.

"Yes," said Noriko, distantly now. "Sometime in spring, he changed."

Miwa Sato bowed as she entered the school. Hair hung through her glasses and Tommy couldn't meet her eyes.

"Hi, Miwa."

"Konban wa."

The girl trudged through the lobby and into the classroom. She put down her rucksack, leaned her kendo stick against the wall, and sat at the table. *Changed how*, Tommy wanted to know, but the phone rang. Noriko talked for a moment and sighed as she hung up. She crossed another class off his schedule. Then she gathered a breath and looked him in the eye.

"You are free tomorrow," she told him. "All day tomorrow."

"It's supposed to snow tomorrow."

"Yes. But you are free. Aren't you?"

Tommy nodded. He felt heavy, guilty, confused. He glanced back from the classroom door. She was heading out, her coin purse in hand. But she must have known he would look back. From the doorway she did an odd thing. She smiled.

Chapter 12

"Elaine?" He pushed his sorry greeting into the green plastic phone outside the Kitayama main branch post office.

"It's me. Finally."

She extended the remote antenna. Music played, a drum circle, and the tv droned talk show. She must have been praying, one eye on Oprah.

"Say that again."

"It's me."

"You're drunk."

"It's still me. I didn't want to interrupt your morning study, so I killed a little time on the bench beside the vending machine."

"The bench beside the vending machine?"

"Never mind."

Her footsteps: out of the living room, onto the kitchen tile, the flimsy lattice door closing her in. A crowd of drinkers staggered passed the phone booth, pointing at Tommy and working their five words of English.

"So," Elaine began, "have you laid your little Yoko in the raked gravel garden yet?"

He let her taste that. It was late now in Kitayama. Across the street at Big Delicious Dumpling House the lights went out. The big delicious dumplings were calling it a night.

"I called to see if Gus was okay."

"He's fine."

"He's at school?"

"No."

This threw Tommy. His mind had already traveled up to the bedroom and pushed the door into the tangle of clothes and made the boy's bed. Now suddenly Gus lay there, sprawled there, in full-blown adolescent ennui, fiddling with his Sega set at ten-thirty on a school day.

"What did you say?"

"He's not in school."

"Jesus, Elaine! The kid is supposed to be in algebra or something. What do you mean he's not in school? Is he sick?"

She was putting something in the microwave. Probably a half-cup of coffee. "Public school wasn't working out too well."

"Wasn't *working out?*"

Elaine allowed a seven-thousand-mile silence to highlight the shrillness in his voice. Lately, she loved to upset him. It seemed to fortify her.

"He needs alternatives," Elaine said.

Tommy's ill-timed beer welled up. He felt exhausted and sad and cold. He wanted to fall down inside the booth.

"Elaine, I'm gone now. The problem has been removed. Now leave Gus alone. Let him live a normal life. No more alternatives."

Her answer ripped back and stood him up: "Normal? You call this life normal?"

He drifted, searching for an answer. Outside the booth now, a pair of tipsy young women were pointing at him, covering their giggles with slender, red-nailed hands. He knew enough Japanese now. They said: *Look. He must be Stuart's uncle.*

"Huh?" Elaine insisted. "Tell me, All-American Normal Tommy. Why are you calling?"

There had been no special reason. It was time. He needed to know if she could ever be happy again. During his class with Miwa Sato his mind had flashed way back, years ago, to a hard-partying Indian girl in Zena jeans and Tommy's letter jacket, trusting everything and thinking as little as possible. She had been fun. She had been happy. He thought.

He said, "I just called to let you know that you should check the bank balance because I wired money today. And how's your studying? And how's Grandpa Rupert? And back in '85 I did, in fact, sleep with that puck-fucker from Calgary."

Elaine said nothing. Tommy thought he heard his son's heavy tread on the stairs.

"And also with that big-haired young woman from TriCounty Tech who came to our front door last spring."

Elaine's coffee cup hit the counter. "Of course you did. You made me your squaw. You called to tell me that? Why?"

"I don't know. I guess I just wanted to move things along a little between us."

He took a desperate breath of the booth's cold and grimy air. Neon hung on him like grease.

"Okay then. Let's talk about our son. What alternatives? May I know?"

"Of course you may know."

He heard a can crack.

"Elaine, what are you doing?"

"Having a beer with you."

The silence between them replayed the past.

"It's morning there," he said at last. "Right?"

"Don't tell me what to do," she warned him, and Tommy watched the red numbers gallop, his telephone card running down.

"Your son skipped half of the first month of high school," she said. "He stole some kid's jacket. He punched the phys-ed teacher. Just like you taught him."

Tommy stared down the gaudy emptiness of Shinmei Street. *Just like you taught him!* "Right, Elaine. The theme of my fatherhood exactly. So where are you sending him?"

"He's sent himself. A camp for Indian kids in Arizona."

"He what?"

"Black Mesa Pottery Camp."

"Good God, Elaine. Pottery camp?"

She said nothing. The two women lingered under their umbrellas, waiting for a cab.

"So he's going?"

She cleared her throat, lit a match.
"No," she said. "He's gone."

In the morning, frost rimed the rooftops. Then clouds moved in and rain dissolved the frost. Tommy wondered how Stuart had kept warm. The apartment had come furnished with less than a Morrison would take camping. He put his hand to a seam between straw tatami mats: winter, rising steady as a tide. The mailman knocked. A postcard.

Dear Corn Dog,

   Big news here! Katelyn is walking, and Traci's PG again! Mom can't believe it. She never thought any of us would have more kids than her, and I guess us having a fourth kind of takes away her position as woman-in-the-trenches. Donna is a lot like you, Corn Dog. She hates getting beat at anything. Isn't it funny when you can look at your own mom and think, Man, there goes one hell of an outside linebacker! I guess Dad's still going to the rink all Saturday, and Mom says he ducked out of church last Sunday to watch a couple of "blue chip" 7-year-olds. Good old Bailey. David says he's going to get his GED and enroll at your college for some new program in electron microscopes, so Bailey gave him money and Mom's teed off. Then David gets this "great" job selling stereos and decides to wait another year, up his workouts, and try to make the Admirals one more time. Traci thinks he does coke. I wouldn't know. What do you think? By the way, Corn Dog, it must be hard on you to leave Gus. You want me to check in when I pass through Madison? Would Elaine tolerate that? I'd keep my mouth shut, just drop by, pass the ball a little, chat. Maybe not. Anyway, you're in some small town, Mom said, but nobody really knows where, since it's not on the map. What's it like over there? How's the teaching? Yours, Big Dog.

So what was it like? Was it time to consider that? Did he dare? Warming corn soup on the heater, Big Dog. Wiring money home. Dreaming of bratwurst and hockey. Stuffing newspaper in the cracks between my floor mats. Launching postcards to Bailey and Donna, you and Mad Dog. Freezing, starving, purifying myself. But then Elaine would bust me for spiritual theft.

Wouldn't she?

Apotheosis. She once sneered this up from a book on some poet, as though Tommy had written the lines himself and forced her to read them. Because he had once played hockey for the university that made her read English poems to know literature, when her Winnebago and her Ojibwa had sung for millennia to the very soil the school bricks were made of—

Let go, Tommy commanded himself.

But he could not let go. Gobby rain struck the glass now, and the thought of snow made his mind skip. He shifted and coughed, brought his arms up, and then he was moving in the past suddenly, in a Canadian hospital, shoving open snow-spattered doors for his father, who stomped in yakking about Tommy's shots-on-goal and knocking the snow off his Rangers cap, and then Tommy was holding the doors open eternally for his mother, who straggled feebly along the salt-crusted walk as though the long drive up from Milwaukee had turned her hips to jelly.

"Tell us what happened," she gasped when they had settled in a corner of the hospital lobby.

Bailey snapped at her, "He paid the bastard back, that's what happened."

Tommy was tired of them already. He had asked them not to come. Not on a fifteen-hour drive to Thunder Bay. He remembered staring at the hospital chairs: metal frames holding orange foam tablets at right angles. The weight of a body contorted the foam so that it bent against his mother's neck and pushed up between Bailey's bowed legs. They sat strangely still because Tommy hadn't answered. To him, every sound from the corridor behind them invoked the image of Rennard Dombrowski, his massive body motionless in the intensive care bed. The big jerk had creamed Tommy two years earlier, before the knee, and Tommy, a stride slower and meaner on account of it, sick to death of the minor leagues, had abruptly creamed him back.

"The doctors want to fly him to Detroit," Tommy answered finally. "It's a big risk, I guess. But they can't help him here."

"But what happened?"

"Mother!" Tommy's father sprang from his chair and began to pace. "You've seen a million hockey games!"

Tommy went to get coffee. When he returned, his father was still standing, inspecting the wildlife paintings on the wall. He looked like a little boy, a little gray-haired boy stirred by the sight of game animals moored in the wide-open, just begging to be shot. Tommy cleared what felt like sawdust from his throat.

"I, uh, called Elaine this morning."

His mother sighed. "Is she sympathetic? She's not going to turn this into some kind of Indian thing, is she? Saying you've done this just because you're a white and. . . ."

She glanced at Bailey, who was rigid. She did the talking on the subject of Elaine. Tommy had long ago warned Bailey to keep his mouth shut.

"Yes, Mom. She's sympathetic. But what I mean is that she said the team called. You know, the front office guys."

"Hell," said his father to an elk posing in Manitoban heather. "It's a business. We know that."

Tommy sipped his coffee, scooted up to the hard edge of the chair and laid his forearms across his knees. He was on the fifth day of a three-week suspension. The Admirals were back in Milwaukee on a home stand. He had stayed behind at the hospital. He remembered staring at the mop swirls on the tile floor, which were wider than the day before.

"The team said the Mounties were in touch. They're going to file felony assault charges. If Dombrowski dies it's murder."

He couldn't recall why he had told them this, but it made sense as an urge to drive a wedge through his own confused feelings, to split the shock he felt from the sense that he deserved punishment. His loyal parents would carry the burden of outrage, leaving him to focus on the nightmare of Dombrowski's impossibly shallow breathing.

His mother sputtered, struggling in her chair. "But, you're supposed to hit people, aren't you? I mean—" She fell back. "Assault? Did you try to hurt him?"

Bailey broke from the landscapes and told her harshly, "Of course he did. That's what they pay him for."

He stared at his wife and by bowed head she acknowledged something discussed in the car: the righteousness of their son's mayhem, his proximity to the National Hockey League, their hopes he would fuse Big Dog's grace with Mad Dog's madness, their unflinching support.

Bailey wandered away and said almost mystically, "It's our only shot. We haven't been that cute on skates, Mother, since the knee."

Then he planted himself and four-squared his attitude. "Well, son," he said, swinging his arms as if to pump up hope from the hospital floor. "I'm sure the team will stand behind you. You're the tough guy of tough guys now." He made a grimacing attempt to smile. "They'll have to call you up now."

"We're behind you," his mother said.

And then Bailey fumed, "Jesus," unable to draw another atom of cheer. "Assault? Murder? The hell with that. I'll get you a lawyer."

As they walked down the corridor to Dombrowski's room, Tommy felt grateful for their outrage, but the balance of his emotion was bitter estrangement. Their belief in him was absurd, maniacal. He watched his mother balance a Walgreen's get-well card on Dombrowski's window ledge, heard his father recite with gee-whiz respect some goony statistics about Dombrowski's penalty minutes and times traded. But admitting the actual pain of the man had been beyond them, diverted and denied and buried inside Tommy. He was alone with it. He had crushed the man's windpipe with his knee, raised his elbow and clocked Dombrowski's head so hard against the ice his neck had gone limp. Then he had risen and skated a wide, defiant arc to the penalty box. Fans threw beer on him. But as he sat in his own steam he had felt a strange severance from the commotion around him. His hockey life had reached some kind of awful surprise climax. He had understood what he was doing. He was quitting. He was forcing his life into the unknown. And now, at his window in Kitayama, here he was.

He had the feeling back now, the immense, branching guilt that had consumed him that afternoon in the fluttering snow outside the hospital. He felt omnipotent, terrified. As his mother valiantly leaned into the door of a Hardee's and his father jogged to the corner booth to phone an old lawyer friend, Tommy had severed himself from them and anyone else who tried to help. Arriving home the next week, seeing in Elaine's eyes the frail scaffolding of her support, he had kicked it down.

"You're happy," he accused her. "Finally I'm the misguided violent asshole you need me to be. Now you can get on with your life."

And she had gotten on with her life. She was nearing her bachelor's degree. She was a fancy dancer for the campus Wunk Sheek tribal drum. She was re-connecting herself to ancient spirits, to the turtle, the coyote, the spider. At the same time, she was applying to master's programs in literature. And Tommy was a misguided, violent, and *handsomely rewarded* asshole, she reminded him when the front office called again, offering him ninety thousand American to kill penalties and start fights with the Detroit Red Wings for the rest of the NHL season. And throughout this time the Canadian court case slowly evolved. Dombrowski lay still and white as a turnip in his hospital bed. And the conflict – *just like you taught him!* – began its slow, inexorable escape from hockey.

Tommy lit the heater. He ran a bath. He hunkered down to his armpits and turned up the boiler until it stormed like a blow torch under his feet. Ninety thousand bucks to shove people around. He had let Elaine have the whole wad and she had bought the house that she now had all to herself. So, now his son was at pottery camp instead of high school? What the hell?

Tommy dropped down a hand into the bath water and stirred. Let go, he commanded himself, and he worked on a simple fantasy. He imagined a kettle with sliced onions floating in three bottles of bubbling Old Style. He sank a raft of bratwurst. Elaine would be gone at school. Gus would be at . . . pottery camp? Stop it. Let it go. Now by force of will Tommy found his battered lawn chair in the garage, found his *Sports Illustrated* under Gus' bed, and then . . . and then a horn beeped outside the bath vent.

He knelt in the tub. Noriko's small white pickup idled below the window.

"Tommy-san?"

She rattled the door handle.

"Oy!" she called, sounding frustrated. "You're not here?"

Then she must have smelled the heater. "It's too smoky," she called. "Are you dead?"

She let herself in. Her sandals dropped, her feet squeaked up. She moved urgently into his toilet room, his kitchen. She was at the bath door when he announced himself with a splash. Her feet stopped. She stepped back into her sandals.

"I'm sorry. I thought you were dead."

"Only half dead."

He heard her panting beyond the door. "Stuart closed all the windows once," she said, "and he turned up his heater and went to sleep. . . ." She stopped. "Today, snow will come," she said finally, and he heard her moving about to his sleeping room, cracking the window.

"Yes, I thought so."

"Actually," she said and paused a longer time, "you know, my father is ill and my husband is fishing. Prince School is closed and I've just dropped Mother at the cut and perm. It feels so nice to be free time." She paused. "Doesn't it?"

Tommy rose into the chilly air of the apartment. His towel was in the kitchen. Then she was thrusting it through the door. She had painted her fingernails red.

"So don't you want to go with me—" he heard the *zip* of her dictionary "—to make an excursion?"

"An excursion?"

"A picnic?"

She squinted into the frigid deluge, driving fast. She wore a kitchen smock and thongs. Her wet toes squeaked as she burst the truck down the river road, then across the bridge and south along the levee.

"That apartment has a lousy bath," she said, "ne?"

"Ne."

"I can't take a good bath either," she said. "Always the young wife is last, in the dirty cold water."

Kitayama passed by the other way. Simon and Garfunkel pined like long lost cousins from the door speakers. Tommy noticed that the downpour had already sullied the river. It flowed high and off-color. He rolled his wrist slightly. It was just before ten. But she caught him.

"Don't you want to make a picnic?"

"Well, the weather sure is right."

She looked perplexed. Tommy laughed thinly. "Sorry," he said. "I was joking."

"I'm sorry," she returned. "My English."

"No," Tommy said. "My Japanese."

She frowned and drove on. Simon and Garfunkel sang of Richard Cory as they splashed abreast of the business park. Beyond Tommy's window slipped the earthmoving project for the airport: a rain-strafed platform of dissolving dirt that stretched back to West Mountain. The surviving paddies brimmed with brown runoff. All ditches led to the river. Then Noriko bounced the truck abruptly left. For a bone-jarring moment, the truck skidded and pitched across wet stones, finally stopping on a sand spit beside a tangle of scrub birch.

Ahead, the river braided around a wide curve. Fisherman shifted long poles in the downpour. She left the motor running.

"Do you fish?"

"No."

"Good."

She lifted a heavy bag from behind her seat and opened a lacquered box on her lap. With chopsticks, she arranged rice balls, a neat Japanese omelet, a small fish, a stack of yellow pickles. As she reached into the bag once more, the rain let go around them, drawing down a curtain. Simon and Garfunkel started in *coo-coo-ka-choo*-ing Mrs. Robinson and Tommy closed his eyes on a familiar slide of images he was helpless to stop. First came *The Graduate,* Dustin Hoffman and Anne Bancroft, a black nylon stocking, and then Bailey Morrison, the old business hack, telling Mad Dog "insurance" and then, of course, Elaine.

Elaine! Elaine!

And forthwith came Tommy's own Elaine, nineteen, in her big white wedding dress, every Indian relative from Milwaukee to Nebraska standing around mutely in new blue jeans and string ties, wondering what in hell possessed her, while Tommy's relatives, missing a Packers pre-season game, hogtied to the half-barrel, were thinking, What the hey, a Redskin?

Noriko balanced the lacquered box on the dash and began to fill another with bean cakes and sweet rice.

"Last night," she said. "My friend Tomo was out to drink and she saw you in the phone box."

"Sure. Calling home."

"Everyone is okay?"

"Okay enough."

"Everyone misses you?"

Tommy felt a thickness.

"She said you looked angry."

"Well . . . that's just the way we are."

She fixed him with a sudden bright smile. "Same at my house," she said.

She sat up then, squinted through the fogged window and blew the truck's tinny horn. Tommy jumped. In the river, fishermen stirred vaguely. She flashed the lights and finally one man turned in mid-stream and waded slowly toward shore.

"Lately, always Husband is fishing. Every day. It's last chance before winter."

"Too much water for good fishing."

"So," she mused. She balanced the boxes and thermos on her lap. Her right hand anxiously gripped the door handle. She punched the horn again and the sound reached the river like a slippery rock that Husband hadn't seen. He twisted, flung an arm toward them. Then her door sprang open. She shoved her umbrella into the downpour and dashed beneath it across the slippery rocks to a rough hut of plywood. Husband had staggered halfway there and now he was telescoping his long pole down to a thick black cudgel. Rain coursed off his round straw hat.

Noriko placed the boxes and thermos inside the hut. She bowed through the rainy distance. Then she ran back. She shoved the wet umbrella between them.

"Now," she panted, and she looked at him, "can we make our picnic?"

No jokes, Tommy told himself. "Okay."

She bore south, away from town around the river's curve, until the fishermen were out of sight. Then she coasted a minute, squinting. When she saw what she wanted, she punched the truck left again, down a muddy access to the water.

Tommy put his hands on the dash. It was the low bridge where Ono had driven across. But the water was higher now, suddenly brown and frothing through the bridge rails.

"Don't worry," she said. "I have grave stones in the back."

And then they were skidding down the muddy bank and plunging into the river. The truck sank a moment, then touched the bridge bottom and advanced slowly. Soon, though, the water deepened and the front end slipped. They swung around to face a downstream rapid.

Noriko lost ground to shift.

"Chotto," she murmured, biting the hair in her face.

But then in reverse the tires gripped the bridge planks and she swung her head around, her hair whipped Tommy, and with her lip crushed between small gray teeth she plowed them backwards to the opposite shore. She stopped there, pulled the hair from her face.

"In English you say, No sweat?"

"No sweat."

"Piece of pie?"

"Piece of cake."

She laughed like Tommy had never heard. It was a bursting, high-pressure laugh, a bolt of joy escaping. Then she sang something in Japanese as they passed the fishing tackle shop and the lumber yard. Then a quick right put them on rain-pink asphalt between tall concrete walls. A sign beside Tommy's window sparked pink hearts into the downpour: Miss Pretty Love Hotel.

Tommy shifted, peered through his window. He had heard about it. Slit-windowed rooms above, discrete parking below. A recorded voice asked them to take a ticket. As she rolled down her window, Noriko smiled at him, touched his knee.

"Ne?" she said.

Tommy said, "I don't think so."

She laughed. "Don't worry. I drove from the back. Nobody takes that bridge. And in this weather, nobody sees us."

"Still no."

She plucked the ticket, rolled up her window. "They have a bath in every room," she went on, as though they were just exchanging manners, as though he hadn't really refused her. "A big, hot bath. And I have food and sake. Survival picnic," she said.

Tommy looked out at the rain pounding neon pink hearts. They were cute hearts, linked and blinking like a giggle in the deluge. Survival, she said, but somehow he had been here before, and there were no survivors.

"I made tuna rice balls, broiled squid, mountain vegetable and ginger potatoes, ham-ketchup omelet. . . ."

He took her hand, shaped it around the hard ball of the gear stick. He traced slender fingers and chipped red nails. "No," he said. "I'm sorry."

Now her eyes burned on him like hot coffee. He was unsurprised to want her suddenly, having understood that he shouldn't. This is how it was for him. His mouth had gone dry, his head fuzzy. She sensed his surge of desire. He would need to say it again.

"Arigato gozaimasu," he said. "But no."

His glance caught her lips rolling inward, tugging down her broad nose so that it whitened at the ridges. She pulled her hand free and with a small, tight shriek, she slammed her fist into his chest. Then she reversed the truck.

"Noriko, I'm sorry. It's not you."

"I don't see anyone else in this truck."

"It's not you. Really. I have a whole life following me around."

She backed out in dangerous swerves. Then she was silent along the river road. The truck smashed milky puddles outside the sake brewery. Garfunkel claimed he'd rather be a forest than a street.

Tommy said, "I'm just confused right now. I'm not feeling well."

As if this made her suddenly exhausted, Noriko lifted her foot and the life went out of the engine. She refused to drive him another meter. She let the truck run down beyond his apartment without turning in.

"Why don't we talk?"

"Talk?" She seethed. "Like Stuart? Talk and talk and talk, like a barking dog?"

"Come in, Noriko. I'll make some tea."

"Tea." She laughed bitterly. "Do you think I want tea? Do you think I want to hear about how difficult is your life?"

Tommy tried to take her hand.

"No," she replied. "I will play pachinko. Then I will pick up Husband's dishes, and then pick up Mother at the cut and perm. Then I will make supper."

She pushed a ragged umbrella at him. He got out and stood beneath it. He watched her speed away toward Shinmei, the truck bursting gray puddles against storefronts.

Then around Tommy the rain fell thick as lead. For a moment, unbidden, he entertained a bizarre image of Stuart, the kind of cornball scene where a frail kid opens an umbrella to help himself and gets blown completely away.

"Samui na?" blurted a neighbor, huddling past to his car. Cold, huh?

Inside the apartment, frigid air fizzed through loose window seals, seeped up beneath Tommy's feet. He had to stop the cold, he thought, do something to insulate himself. He chose the leakiest tatami mat, the mold-stained mat in the center, and he pried it up to see what could be done. He leaned it into the pale flash of the neighbor's daytime headlights. The rain had suddenly softened into snow.

Then over the cold hole, Tommy saw the smooth dark shape. It had been there all along, beneath his pacing at the window, beneath his guilt and worry, beneath Kitayama's pains and denials, shoved through a broken rib of the sub-floor and wedged between the building's frame and the dirt where the wind rushed in.

He saw it now. He saw the square blue shape of Stuart's suitcase.

Chapter 13

The Kitayama train squealed and swayed through the long East Mountain tunnel, its windows jammed with the leering reflections of Miwa Sato's classmates. She kept her head down. Shuichi Kawai had tried to grab her kendo stick, but she had lashed the handle of its long cotton sack through one strap of her rucksack, and the whole clumsy package had proven unworthy of his trouble.

"Bah!" he cursed. "Auntie Miwa. So much luggage." He tried to yank away her Civics book but she clung to the corners. "Crazy Miwa," he said. "Always studying. What good will it do you? Anyway, you'll just be a wife."

"Ehhhh?" put in Miki Ebana. "Who would marry Miwa?"

She kept her head down. She would finish her lesson. Mother worked until seven, but grandfather, as always, would demand his bath and supper at sundown. Each day, as the sun set earlier, the tension increased. Already Grandfather was ranting about the empty bath tub and the cold rice pot, scuffing about the house in search of his sake bottle.

Miwa leaned over her textbook beneath a screen of limp black hair. Sphere and orbit, she read. Sphere and orbit. From Tokyo outward constellated Japan's forty-seven prefectures. Within each of these small worlds radiated a dominant urban star, a Sendai, a Niigata, and about these revolved the flatland centers, the Koriyamas and Takatas, and deep within surrounding mountains winked the ancient castle towns . . . like *Kitayama*, Miwa put in, as Kitayama was always left out of such descriptions. And then the book stopped there, as if smaller places like West Mountain Village, and ancient people such as Grandfather, did not exist at all.

Miwa paused to think about this. The book, with its glossy pages and its clean, concise explanations, had stopped far short of the ancient and slow-moving world in which she lived, as if someone somewhere, speaking for the rest of Japan, had simply decided to move on. This was exactly Grandfather's complaint, wasn't it? That new Japan was tromping over the old? With textbooks like this in the hands of the next generation, could she really blame him? And who else was there to bear his anger, who else but the granddaughter who ran his bath and cooked his fish?

The train rattled and squeaked and lumbered onward into the black center of the mountain. Miwa continued on her own, taking the textbook where it should have gone. Sphere and orbit, she recited, sphere and orbit, and within this system of shrinking spheres, the smallest, dimmest body was the person, she decided; and among people, the farmer; and among farmers, the old-fashioned, hand-planting, scythe and sickle rice farmer. And so—now she imagined herself emboldened, standing in class and speaking aloud, hushing Moto-sensei with the force of her example—and so the great, unacknowledged conflict of old Japan versus new Japan had made its way into her life by the following path. In the matter of local airports, Tokyo handed down regulations about runway length. She had heard as much a hundred times during the fights between Grandfather and the neighbors. In turn, the prefecture engaged in selective interpretation and the granting of exceptions. In their capacities, Takata officials advised the prefecture on the merit of projects within their sphere, and in keeping with an ancient pattern, Kitayama was denied its airport. *Fine*, Grandfather had responded. *Let them deny us.* Planes couldn't properly decelerate while clearing such high mountains, counseled Takata officials. *Correct*, argued Grandfather. The air in Kitayama was exceptionally dense and turbulent, officials said, and could not conform to general expectations. Not to mention, added Grandfather, the inadvisability of a flight pattern passing over the shrine of Kappa, who was sure to cause mischief. *Bah!* scoffed the neighbors. But Takata officials had ruled and Grandfather had celebrated. Barring an additional three hundred meters of runway—and tragically, the neighbors thought, given Kitayama's efforts to modernize—an airport was not feasible.

Miwa looked at her watch. It was nearly five. She felt Grandfather stirring through the empty house, looking for the sake bottle. She had put it behind the umbrellas. But perhaps he would try to go outside. Perhaps he would find it.

Miwa hunched deeper in her seat. The Takata decision had pleased Grandfather, and it had seemed secure until secret payments—Yamaguchi stone money, Grandfather charged—had begun to travel to and fro across the bureaucratic universe. Three hundred meters shrank to two hundred meters. Then, upon the West Mountain farmers who held this vital two hundred meters of rice paddy, briberies were enacted. Old Yuki Bando's lifelong fishing offenses were forgiven. Uncle Wada's huge son, Miwa's cousin, the one who failed at sumo, became a Police Division deputy. And Takayuki Takahashi was promised a supervisory job in airport baggage, plus a uniform, and a helmet. In this manner, the problem of two hundred meters shrank to a problem of one hundred meters. But this mere hectare of paddy land—Miwa would speak smoothly, forcefully, not bungling her words for once—this land remained in the possession of a citizen of old Edo, an ancient one who believed in Kappa and had never so much as ridden in a car, who was opposed to modernization in all its manifestations, and who, for all his rage, froth, and spittle, was still a person whose existence had to be acknowledged and respected. *He is my grandfather,* concluded Miwa— whispering beneath her bangs but imagining she had spoken out, at long last, with the full force of her busy mind—and then, feeling a warm wetness on her scalp, she looked up. Kenzo Koho was leaning over the seat back, dangling a string of ramen over the top of her head. She felt her hair: *noodles.*

"Jerk," she said quietly. Her classmates jeered. Miwa brushed her head off and grabbed her rucksack and her kendo stick and pushed her way to the head of the car where the driver sat within his dirty booth. She stood at the very nose of the train as it groped its way through the mountain. She turned her lips in and bit them.

"Almost there," the driver told her. He was a thin man, more than sixty. He slept in Kitayama, drove the train back in the morning. He smelled like cigarettes and dirty clothes and alcohol. He glanced at her, checked his watch, his timetable, chucked his throttle, shifted uncomfortably in his seat. "Almost there, little sister."

And now Miwa's exhausted heart felt close to breaking. They were used up, old men like this. Wrung out and shoved aside, useless and confused and angry. Who could blame Grandfather? He was acting as a man of his time, in defense of his history. Even at his worst, she thought, he deserved respect. And now she shuddered and squeezed her eyes shut. "Never!" he had snarled that morning, long before sunrise. "Never cross this door again!"

Miwa had sat up quickly, yanked out of sleep into the chilly air. She had heard rain but smelled snow. The old house held no heat. She had found her glasses beside the futon and put them on. She had yawned, trying to convince herself that all was well. Then she heard the old man thump and curse in the toilet.

"Out, traitors! Out of my house!"

Miwa rose and tied her house jacket. Her feet found slippers. Mother stirred: "Eh?"

"Grandfather."

Mother fell back with a gasp of exhaustion. "Ah!"

"I'm up," said Miwa. "I'll watch him."

She collected damp newspapers from the toilet floor and set down fresh ones.

"Out!" Grandfather snarled again, now from his cushion before the television. Miwa hurried. She found his sweater and his slippers. She lit the heaters, started rice, brewed tea. She plugged in the thermal mat beneath his cushion. She put a quilt on his shoulders. For a moment, re-balanced, he sat quietly.

She laid a cautious stone on the side of hope. "I smell snow today," she said. "The first snow is always so pretty."

"It's too early for snow."

"But they never ask you, do they Grandfather?"

"Ask me what?"

"Would you like radish pickles, or plums? It's always so pretty on the mountain, first snow, the way it sticks to just one side of everything, like shadow."

He blinked at her. There. She had leveled his mind. He lit a cigarette, turned on the tv, stared at the weather report: snow. He accepted this. But a minute later something in the news disturbed him and he shouted, "Oy!"

She hurried from the kitchen with pickles and plums.

"Yes, Grandfather?"

"You like hakujin, do you?"

Miwa's body had tensed. Hakujin. The word meant white man to Grandfather, as in enemy. Every day he accused her, and every day she labored for balance: "We call them foreign people now, Grandfather."

"You like kinpatsu?"

"His name is not Golden Hair, Grandfather. His name is Mister Stuart. But as I've told you, he's gone. He left nearly three months ago."

"Nn," replied the old man. He opened his mouth to let smoke out. He stared through the plume.

"Open the screen."

"Yes, Grandfather."

Gray light lurked beyond the window. Rain misted through the cedars on the shrine ground. No snow yet. Miwa began to sing her grandfather an old song as she carried dishes to the table. She sang the red dragonfly song:

Red sky, red dragonfly
I chased you with my net . . . when was that?

Mountain field, mulberries
Into my basket I picked . . . was it a dream?

Big sister, husband's house
A distant letter. . . .

"You lie," Grandfather interrupted. "The hakujin is not gone."

Startled, Miwa stopped in stride. Her pose was awkward: toes turned in, shoulders rounded, glasses slipped down her nose and black hair snagged through them.

"Eh?"

"Yesterday I saw the hakujin. Walking in the rice fields."

"That is a different man, Grandfather. The new teacher."

"He is the same."

"Mister Stuart left at o-bon, Grandfather. More than three months ago."

"He is the same."

Miwa stood straighter. She took a deeper breath. She spread both feet evenly, righted her shoulders, freed her hair.

"Grandfather," she said, "are your eyes so bad?"

She paused to see how far this would tilt him. Some mornings, if lucky, she could put down enough gentle teasing against his anger to keep him quiet through breakfast.

"We'll have to take your musket away, Grandfather, if you can't tell the difference between a deer and a bear. Because that is the difference between Mister Stuart and the new man." A door slid open. Footsteps thumped the plank hallway. A moment later Father and Brother sleepwalked out in their blue-and-gold uniforms. They did factory work in the winter. Mother clerked at the Yamazaki store. She came out last, shivering, carrying her orange smock on a hanger. "Ne, Grandfather?" Miwa continued carefully. "You can still see well enough, can't you?

That's a different foreigner. His name is Mister Tommy. And it's deer season now, remember? You want to keep things straight."

Grandfather smoked, staring out the window. Silently, the Sato family had taken their places at the table. Miwa poured tea. Mother brought rice and natto from the kitchen. Reaching for pickles, Brother jarred the table with his knee. Then Father coughed. Miwa felt Grandfather's balance break, felt his thoughts tip and slide.

"Where is my musket?" he accused Father.

Father said nothing. He hunched over his rice bowl.

"You took my musket. Answer me. You are not my son. You are a thief. Where is my musket?"

Under the table, Brother drove his foot into Miwa's thigh. "Why don't you leave him alone?" he fumed. "You always upset him with your crazy talk."

"Grandfather," she began.

"Hush," said Mother. "Both of you."

Then they waited. Grandfather ate nothing. He lit a cigarette and blew smoke over the table. As he stared at Father, Miwa felt the struggle overwhelm them all. Love, harmony, common sense, the beauty of a first snowfall, these things weighed nothing against Grandfather's rage.

"You'll sell," the old man accused Father finally. "The moment I'm dead, you'll sell my fields."

Father did not answer. He ate his rice quickly, his bowl raised to his chin.

"You'll sell like Bando," Grandfather said. "And Wada and Takahasi. And look at the heap of dirt they made. Airplanes. As if we need airplanes."

Miwa pushed the fish toward Father. Mother had candied it last night with soy and brown sugar; the over-cooked bones were soft enough to eat.

Brother reached.

"Look at you," Grandfather addressed him. "In your fancy suit. You don't like farming? You like sitting on a stool making radios for fat hakujin? Eh, fancy-suit grandson?"

Brother looked wounded. He glanced at Father. But no response.

"They'll put big holes in the mountains," the old man continued. "They'll name one tunnel South Yamaguchi Tunnel and the other tunnel North Yamaguchi Tunnel and they'll run the train right through the farmland in the valley. You'll eat rice from California and it will taste like dung. There will be hakujin everywhere, noisy, filthy, pink-faced hakujin."

He poured himself sake.

"You don't remember the soldiers. None of you. They ate on the streets and pissed in the shrine grounds. They grabbed our sisters and our girlfriends and sneaked around with our wives. If you had any love for Japan you'd dig pits and sharpen sticks." He poured again. "Instead of wearing your silly radio-making uniforms."

Father put his bowl down empty.

"Look at you, Grandson. You look like a trombone player."

Miwa re-filled Father's bowl. She put a curl of fish on the rice.

"Miwa!"

She started, dropping her chopsticks. "Yes, Grandfather?"

"You like hakujin? Is that it? You like to be grabbed by noisy, filthy hakujin?"

She felt blood pound in her face.

"No, Grandfather."

"You will meet him today, won't you?"

"I told you no, Grandfather."

"You lie." He pounded a fist on the table. "You always lie! All of you!"

Father rose. Brother tried to eat everything at once. Miwa made a ball of her unfinished rice and dropped it in her skirt pocket. She clattered the sake bottle down behind the umbrellas. Grandfather hobbled after them to the genkan.

"Out!" he commanded as they tilted into their shoes. "Out of my house!"

Mother hurried with the lunches.

"Out!" he berated her. "I disown you!"

She struggled into her Yamazaki store smock. "Your lunch is on the table," she puffed. "And if the heater smokes, shut it off and call Mister Fukui."

"Out!" he raged, waving his thin arms from the genkan step. He tilted down into slippers and shuffled to the door.

"My house will be locked," he promised, "when you return, and all the garbage of your lives will be in the snow."

Father had to warm the truck's cold engine. Miwa sat on Mother's lap, between Brother and the door. With her head bowed, through heavy black bangs, she watched Grandfather seize and pull the door . . . and pull, and pull with all his fury, until at last he inched it shut.

Now, as the train wobbled from the tunnel at last, a cry went up behind Miwa. Snow! It was snowing in Kitayama—big, puffy flakes, clean as the soul of Buddha himself, spreading at the train's blunt nose, sweeping past its grimy windows, covering over the track-side trash and rounding the aluminum and concrete edges of Kitayama Station. At the rubble-strewn terminus where the tracks stopped, nothing but a field of fresh white dissolved up East Mountain into snow-laden cedars. The train bumped and squealed and shuddered to a standstill.

Miwa was the last off. With her kendo stick separated from her rucksack at last, with the heavy sack on her back, with the stick over one shoulder and her mittens and cap on, she stepped out to see the last taxi pulling away from the station, and, having no one to call, she began to slip and slide in her saddle shoes down the mountainside. Her shoes and socks were wet before a hundred meters. Her toes were frozen. She would be late.

Grandfather, she began in her head. *I was slow on the train. Everyone pushed past me and then my knot was difficult, and then you know, for walking, how short my legs are, you say so yourself, how bowlegged and clumsy, and you should know, please Grandfather, that I did not chase Stuart like some whore. He followed me. I don't know why, Grandfather.*

She slogged on. This was true: Stuart had pursued her, and she didn't know why. Still, a half-year after their first encounter, she was reviewing events, looking for ways to blame herself, finding a few, knowing she had made mistakes, but wondering still, and daily, *Why me?*

A kilometer down the mountain she heard a horn and looked up. It was Officer Wada, her cousin, in his police car. He grinned at her through the snow.

"Again, Miwa-chan. Again you are left behind. I knew it."

She used her mitten to brush snow from her shoes. Her kendo stick jammed in the doorway. Finally she laid it in the back seat and sat in front. Wada laughed as he turned his car around, the car leaning as if he turned it with his weight alone, like a boat or a sled. "You're wonderful," he told her. "My kind of girl. You take your time. You're polite. You never want to trouble anyone. Anytime the weather is bad, I know who will be left without a taxi down the mountain."

"I'm just slow," she told him.

He shook his head. His wheels spun and they slid through a corner. "No," he said. "You practice kendo, so I know you can't be slow. You can move when you want to. But maybe you're sad." He pumped the brakes softly at the next switchback. "Cousin, are you sad?"

She wouldn't answer that. She hung her head behind a screen of hair. She checked her watch. It was nearly five-thirty. Grandfather might reach for an umbrella, find the sake, and then—

"Maybe you need love," Wada told her. "And don't think it's impossible, Cousin. Don't ever think you're too short or too fat or too ugly." He laughed. "Look at me."

Stupid Cousin Wada, suddenly he was singing in terrible English, absurdly off-key, *All you need is love* . . . and Miwa burrowed deeper into her review of the past. When Stuart had first approached her, she had been startled, taken utterly by surprise. She had been sitting in the Prince School classroom, and once again Miki Ebana had been telling a raunchy story in Japanese. Miwa had glanced up at Stuart. His white skin, from his temples to his chin, was aflame in deep red blotches the shape of upside-down Africa. His eyes were stiffly wide, his long golden lashes blinking rapidly over odd blue pupils. His straight white teeth were bared in the grimace that he hoped was a smile. So he knew, Miwa concluded, that the story was about him.

Miki Ebana was saying her mother had been drunk. Her aunt too. They had gone to the castle ground for a picnic under the cherry blossoms and by evening they were sloppy-drunk and on a mission to do what most Kitayama women had by then concluded was impossible. They were going to seduce Mister Stuart.

Shut up, Miwa had raged silently at this point. *Shut your cheap and stupid mouth.* But Miki Ebana had pressed on through the gasps and giggles. Stuart, half-understanding, had nervously spindled his long white fingers. He had grinned harder. Her mother, Miki said, had gone down on her knees beneath the window over Stuart's bath tub. Her aunt removed her shoes and climbed on top. And there was Mister Stuart in his bath. Miki Ebana paused slyly. *Washing*, she said, *very carefully*.

Miwa pushed her voice through the hoots and moans. "Please be quiet," she said in Japanese. "This is an English class. We should talk in English. And we should respect our teacher."

The girls were silent for a moment. Stuart blinked and grimaced at her, only half-sure what she said. His hands were fists now, his knuckles white.

"Please be quiet," she repeated.

"Crazy Miwa," Miki Ebana retorted. "You're just as curious as anyone. Don't lie. You've probably never seen a man's ding-dong. Unless you've been sucking your brother's."

The girls gasped and hooted. Miwa hung her head, stunned, deaf with rage and forgetting about Stuart. She remembered the rest of the story only vaguely now. Miki Ebana's mother had grown ill beneath her aunt's heels and vomited amongst the bicycles. Then the two sisters had gone to the door, found it unlocked, and they had entered. They had burst singing into Stuart's bathroom to find him gone. More practiced tellers than Miki Ebana had taken the story from there, and Miwa had since heard it a dozen times. Poor Stuart had gone out the window in a towel and taken refuge in old Mrs. Honda's rice shop next door. Mrs. Honda, hearing a commotion, had hobbled out from her supper to find a mostly naked white man stammering among her fifty-kilo rice bags. The old widow had smiled hugely and toothlessly, reached her weary arms out of ragged sleeves and cried, "Oh, so thin! Come, young man, and eat!" And Stuart had obeyed. He had sat down in his towel and eaten.

But Miwa's giant cousin had stopped his singing and they were on Shinmei Street now, nearly to the bus stop. Snow caked the awnings and the phone booths and the seats of bicycles left out on the sidewalk. Wada slowed the patrol car.

"Are you hungry, Cousin?" he asked. "I'll buy you dumplings."

Miwa shook her head, no. *Come, young man, and eat. . . .* She was remembering how Stuart had remained in his chair long after the class had ended and the girls had rushed out to giggle in the lobby. Miwa had been slow as always, packing up her English text, her workbook, her pencil case, untangling her kendo stick from the mess of chair legs. She was reaching for a mitten under the table when suddenly Stuart spoke to her.

"You're slow," he said.

Miwa's brain had frozen. It had taken her several seconds to process the English words she had just heard, to integrate them with the oddly cold tone and to guess that she had somehow offended him. She glanced at Stuart. His teeth were still bared. His hands unclenched on the tabletop. She said, "I'm sorry."

"Slow," he repeated, with an odd huff, like he was trying to laugh, "and clumsy."

Miwa rushed her mittens on. She yanked her rucksack off the tabletop. She slung her kendo stick over one shoulder. She moved quickly for the door. But Stuart jumped up. His chair fell back as he took two quick steps toward her. He could have pushed her. She saw his hands trembling at his sides. She heard him puffing through his teeth.

"I'm sorry."

He gulped air. "You should be."

She took a step. "Bitch," he whispered hotly, his eyes wide, as if thrilled, and he closed the door behind her.

Cousin Wada dropped her off at the bus stop, hustling his huge bulk around the patrol car to sweep her door open like she was some kind of royalty.

"Miwa-chan," he said gravely after her. "Hold your head up. You're going to bump into something."

She stood at the bus stop, her umbrella growing heavy with snow. She had looked the word up—*bitch: female dog; derogatory for woman*—and found herself bewildered. She had lain awake that night, sweating on her futon, the endless hours measured by her mother's snores as she wondered: *why?*

By the next week, the rainy season had started. Miwa had left her rucksack and her kendo stick neatly arranged, umbrella on top, at the side of Noriko's desk, and she had rushed from the class the moment it had ended. Earlier, she had dozed on the train and dreamed about Grandfather, that he would slip in the rain, slash himself with his weed cutter, and bleed to death in a rice paddy. After class she had hurried to the bus stop. But on her first glance back toward Prince School she had glimpsed Stuart coming after her, his golden head bobbing above the crowd, carried in long strides past the heaps of eggplant and daikon at the grocery store, and then the whole man, wet and distraught, had emerged at the curb and skittishly crossed the street, finally arriving out of breath at the dripping brim of her umbrella.

Miwa had hung her head as Stuart loomed over her. There had been another story during class: someone's wise-ass uncle, at dusk on the river road, had blown a truck horn at Stuart's back and he had jumped into the gutter, landing up to his knees in laundry suds and backwash from the sake brewery.

"Why didn't you tell them to shut up?" he puffed.

"Please leave me alone," Miwa murmured.

Stuart laughed. "Why don't you leave me alone? You keep coming to my class," he said. "I don't ask for it."

"I'm sorry."

Stuart let out a gust of foul-smelling breath. "Sorry. Yeah. I shouldn't have called you a bitch," he said. "I don't know why I did. It just jumped out."

Miwa kept her head down as he paced around her. She felt cars slowing to watch them. A scooter honked. A boy yelled, "Hey baby! This is a pen!" After a moment Miwa heard a lighter click. "I don't even smoke," Stuart said, gushing smoke, coughing. "I don't even know how. But look at me."

Miwa didn't know how to respond.

"It would have been nice if you'd said something. It would have meant a lot to me. But what the hell. Two more months, anyway, and I'm out of here."

Miwa's mind scrambled to keep up with his English. She thought she understood his statement, but then he was off again. "I mean for one thing," he said, "nobody learns anything. That's not what I'm here for. The last thing anybody wants from me is English."

That wasn't true, Miwa had thought, not for her, and she had just begun to form the words when he wheeled away and fed a vending machine. A Cup Sake thumped to the bottom. When she turned back, the bus was pulling up.

Stuart had climbed on behind her. He sat in the seat to the rear, leaning toward her ear as the bus rumbled away. "So I figure," he said, "maybe give them what they want." He peeled off the aluminum top of his sake cup. "I know," he said. "I don't drink. I'm supposed to be some kind of big-time Christian. You know what a Mormon is? Well watch this."

In the driver's mirror she saw him drain the whole cup. Then he sat back, made a long sigh. He fanned his face with his red necktie. He leaned up. "Okay," he said. She could see his face in the mirror. He was smiling.

"Please leave me alone," she murmured again.

He didn't seem to hear her. He leaned closer. He said, "You want to hear what it's like for me? You think this is a big bunch of fun? Shit." Then he spoke sharply for a long time using words Miwa understood, names and events she knew, but in combinations and patterns she could not decipher. She hunched inside her hair, knowing that every passenger on the bus was riveted by the strange sounds of English. Even the driver stared in his mirror. Then somewhere, halfway up West Mountain, Stuart had swerved from Kitayama to his family: a mother, a father, many brothers, some kind of problem. His long white fingers gnawed the seat back.

"Cute!" croaked an old farm wife finally, tone deaf to the torment in Stuart's voice. "Such blue eyes and golden hair! Cute, cute, cute!" she croaked. She had huge warts on her face. She touched his hand as she waddled past at her stop.

Stuart hunched closer to Miwa. Rain fell in sheets, and West Mountain Village was in clouds. Miwa's mind was painfully split, half-worried again about Grandfather and his whirling, screaming saw blade, slashing weeds in the rain, half trying to understand Stuart. She was looking for Grandfather through the steamed window, looking for a wet shape in the paddies.

"Hey," Stuart whispered into her ear. "I'm talking to you."

She bent her neck.

"I'm talking to you."

"I'm sorry."

He made a kind of breathy laugh through his teeth. As he muttered to himself, Miwa had collected her things, hoping for a quick exit. But suddenly he gripped the collar of her school uniform in his fingers. Miwa became totally still.

"You're not sorry," he told her.

It was nearly her stop.

"You just say that. You all do."

She twisted out of his grip. Her collar tore as she lurched up. She bounced painfully between the sharp seat backs before the bus was fully still. "See you next week," he called as the doors flapped shut.

Miwa had crossed the road and glanced back. Stuart was wiping the window's steam away with his big pink palm. Then her teacher's face appeared as the bus pulled away. He wore a kabuki grin, a grotesque mask of anguish.

Now the same bus came groaning through new snow and Miwa struggled on and sat behind the driver. She held her rucksack on her lap, her kendo stick and umbrella between her knees. She took up her position again: shoulders hunched, head down, her face behind a screen of hair. That rainy night last summer had produced a treacherous revelation that she still wanted to believe. She had carried her July *Exotic Friend* to bed, and she had studied the comic while Mother combed her hair, then did her stretches and fell asleep. Miwa studied the cartoon frames. The love between a boy and a girl was always some act of fantastic astronomy: two lonely souls adrift in the vast human universe, pining and wasting, then suddenly finding one another, rushing into one another, colliding, reckless and fatal, as if driven by some dire chemical incompleteness. But surely Stuart didn't love her. Still, what explained his sudden, passionate attention? And what was this new heat in her face, in her breast, when she thought of him? Could it be? Impossible, Miwa had told herself, because here was Mother, snoring beside her. Patient Mother, who had joined Father not on a miracle from the universe but on the advice of a matchmaker and on orders from her family. Patient, selfless Mother, who absorbed Father's moody silences and Grandfather's wild harangues, who cleaned and cooked and shopped and worked, who had taught Miwa in every moment that duty was love and sacrifice was passion. Mother, who humbly took what her men dished out and quietly served them.

Miwa had stopped her thoughts right there. She had fumbled her way in some kind of a circle, she realized. She let go of the comic book, and her hands came away sweaty and trembling. *Exotic Friend* was a only comic, she told herself. And she was a real person, living a real life. And real men and women could find each other, by chance, by miracle, but there were all kinds of love, and one could do worse than Mother, who was needed, and therefore loved.

Miwa had trembled on her futon. She had curled against Mother and held on to the soft folds of Mother's belly. But still she was unable to sleep. Somehow, however strangely, Stuart needed her. And this need was love itself, she decided. This was the life of a woman.

Through the next hot month she had attended him. She brought him donuts from Takata, hidden in her rucksack. She neglected Grandfather, instead hanging around Kitayama until Stuart's classes were done. Then she met him at the dark shrine behind the grocery store.

"You're late," he would say to her usually, even though she had been there waiting. His words would freeze her and then he would laugh to show he was kidding. "I see you dressed up for me again." She would hunch on the shrine step in her school uniform. She would line up her saddle shoes until the bi-colored panels were exactly parallel. She would line up her ankle socks. She would grip her knees. He would drink his sake. He would poke her like a piece of fish through a package. "Miwa," he would whisper. "You're scared of me, aren't you?" Then he would laugh. "Oh, God. I don't know what I'm doing. This is so weird. I'm sorry, Miwa. Trust me, I'm sorry. I'm really sorry. I don't know why I'm doing this. It's not me." And then would come the flood of talk. On and on he would go, too fast for Miwa, but she would nod *yes* and murmur *yes* and grip her knees while her mind went drifting off to Grandfather in the empty house, or Grandfather in the field with his weed cutter, or Grandfather drunk in the street and fighting with neighbors.

Stuart would cry sometimes. He would rage and cry but always he would come back to her. "I could put it in you," he would tell her eventually. "I could put it in you right now."

Miwa gripped her knees.

"Would you like that? Does it scare you? Are you doing it with someone else? I bet you are."

Then, always, he was sorry again. He would grow sorrier and drunker, and Miwa would wait for the peak of it, when she felt safest, and then she would carefully, slowly, shoulder her rucksack, cross behind him and mount her scooter, get her kendo stick anchored between her legs, everything quietly in order, and then she would turn the key on her scooter—"Hey!" He would cry out, stumble up, and she would rush home to Grandfather.

It was during a thunderstorm in August that Grandfather must have seen them. Miwa had dozed on the train home from Takata, and again she had seen the dream: Grandfather liked to cut weeds during a rain. The stems were easiest then, he said. Fat with water, they cut instead of bent. And she had dreamed again of his accident. He would slip on mud. He would fall, his spinning saw would slash him, and he would bleed to death in his rice field—all this while she gave her attention to Stuart.

She went straight from the train station to the bus stop that day. She skipped her English class. Stuart could live without her one day, she told herself. But there he came, down the sidewalk toward the bus stop. He must have left Miki Ebana and the others sitting in the classroom. He must have walked right past Noriko.

"Where are you going?"

"Home."

"Why?"

"Because I am worried about my grandfather."

"What about me?"

"About you? I'm sorry."

"Yeah. Sure."

He got on the bus behind her.

"You know what bothers me, Miwa? It bothers me that you think I'm really like this. You think this is really me. You think I'm something terrible. Don't you?"

"I don't know."

"You don't know?" He was tightly shrill at her ear. "After all I've told you, you don't know?"

He sat back with a gasp. The same old farm wife with the warty face had been on the bus. Once again she had begun with, "Cute! Isn't he? So cute. And so healthy. Look at the color in his cheeks. And so full of spunk. Lucky girl to catch him, isn't she? Isn't she?"

Miwa had lurched off a stop too early but Stuart came out after her. Panic had seized her. She could not go home. She had not seen Grandfather in his rice field and so he must have been inside, waiting for her. She had put up her umbrella and crossed in front of the bus, suddenly thinking the strangest thought as Stuart followed her, saying in her mind to the bus driver, *Hit him!*

But Stuart had trailed her into the West Mountain Village shrine garden. Thunder clapped as she hurried past the ancient jizo with their eyeless faces. Then the ragged sky had opened a patch of blue over them, a stunning shaft of sunlight knifing down between the thunderheads and lighting up the pond. The hungry carp knew Miwa, and from a dozen points they whirled on gauzy fins and cruised behind as she hurried along the pond-side trail. More appeared from nowhere, and more, soon a hundred multi-colored carp finning and trailing in the sun-lit pond water, thrashing and begging with puckered lips until Miwa felt angry and stopped. "Shoo!" She spoke so sharply that sparrows fled the pond-side bushes. Her voice echoed into the village, "Shoo! Go away!" She stomped.

The ball of carp burst and spread. Stuart was laughing. It was raining again. In a moment more he had his bony fingers on her shoulders. He was pushing her toward the shrine, its wide, dry steps, its dark interior. And in the moment before Miwa had fallen she had seen the bent old man turning, squinting in his undershirt before his ancient straw-roofed house: Grandfather.

Now as the old bus climbed West Mountain through the heavy November snow Miwa thought about her dream. It had come true, nearly. The night of Stuart's sayonara party, Grandfather had slipped in the typhoon and cut himself. Her dream had happened, she had cursed Grandfather with it, and he had survived. She should feel lucky, Miwa thought, but she didn't.

When she stepped off the bus in West Mountain Village the snow had paused. The sky had become silvery and frigid, the air still as ice. She crossed the street to her shaggy-roofed home. Her possessions had not been tossed out on the street, nor had Father's, Mother's, or Brother's. The heavy door was unlocked, as always. Grandfather, as always, sat at the kotatsu with his sake, his cigarette, the tv blaring.

But he did not move. He did not turn to snap at her. Nothing. Miwa saw at once that she was all wrong in her dreams. He would not die a glorious, bloody death among conquered weeds. He would die this way, alone before the fuzzing tv while Chef Takahasi diced leeks and quartered potatoes, Grandfather's dead legs baking under the kotatsu while she daydreamed about her troubles with Stuart.

"Grandfather!"

She slid to her knees beside him. His hand was cold. His last cigarette had burned down and tipped the wrong way out of the ashtray. She slapped him under the chin.

"Grandfather!"

He awakened. He made a strange noise in his throat and glared at her fearfully. His eyes had changed color. They were paler, as though someone had poured milk into black coffee.

"It's Miwa, Grandfather."

"I know who it is," he growled.

"You need to move, Grandfather. You need air."

She made him drink tea. She stood him up. He wobbled, and the leg he had gashed with his weed cutter would not unbend. She moved herself beneath his shoulder and took him outside.

"Cold air, Grandfather. Can you feel it?"

They hobbled through wet snow, across the road and through the red shrine gate. The fish, Miwa thought. Show him the greedy, swarming, beautiful fish, and along the pond trail the fish followed man and girl, smacking the water with their big lips until Grandfather muttered curses. "Whores," he called them. Miwa could feel him regenerating. Phlegm rose. He spat. Then he stopped and pushed her away.

"Lying whore," he accused her. "Right here, the hakujin touched you."

Miwa hung her head. She had not known what to do at first. Stuart had been behind her, steering her, and then he had lunged in and crushed his body against hers. She had felt bones and shirt buttons and the rattle-crash bottom of the universe. She had gasped. A sour curse had squeezed from Stuart's mouth, and she had fallen.

"Right here," spat Grandfather. "He trapped you in his arms. He pressed against you. Don't lie to me. I saw it."

"Yes, Grandfather. I'm sorry."

"You love hakujin then? You love this raping Golden Hair?"

"No, Grandfather. It was only a hug. It's an American custom. Basketball players do it. Parents and children. Teachers always—" she looked away, sparrows whirling "—teachers always hug their students."

As the snow resumed she could feel Grandfather shaking beside her, smoldering in his ignorance. She could lie and he could not dispute her. What did he know? The world had changed and left him behind. Father would sell his land. Kitayama would build an airport now, eat California rice, speak English.

"Grandfather—"

"If you touch a hakujin again I will cut you down like a weed."

"Grandfather—"

"Like a weed," he raged. "I have nothing left but that."

Miwa closed her eyes then. Harsh colors raced across her eyelids. She would faint, she thought. She had to balance.

She said, "I love you, Grandfather."

But when she opened her eyes, Grandfather had left her. Still he stood beside her, but he was gone, muttering softly, staring out at the twisting flakes of snow.

Chapter 14

Noriko sat in her truck until the snow, flake by flake, closed her in. *It's not you,* Tommy had told her. But who else was there? In Kitayama, now, who else was there, for Tommy, but her? Or did he mean that like poor Stuart he was too haunted by his American troubles? There was an idea that made her gut burn. An American, rich and free, with *troubles.* She parked in the alley behind Shinmei Street, behind Prince School, and let the big flakes fall, flakes the size of ten-yen coins, stacking up on the windshield until she shivered, furious, in a murky little snow cave.

Then she ate. First tuna rice balls and broiled squid, bites of each, alternating until the chewy squid became an impediment to her hunger and she dropped it on the truck seat. Then, within a minute, she had eaten all four rice balls. She hesitated, stunned, picking rice kernels from her cold fingers. But she wanted more. She peeled back the plastic top, split a fresh pair of chopsticks and picked the ginger pork shreds from the potatoes. Then she ate the potatoes, her share and Tommy's. That left the wild fern fiddleheads, gray and curled like sleeping grubs at the bottom of the container. She ate them. She lifted the ketchup-rice-and-spinach omelet with her fingers, folding it and devouring it, catching juice in her free palm and then licking her palm. She was done then, she hoped. She needed to be done. But there was still the squid, dusty from the truck seat. She ate it.

Then she shoved out into the snow, plowing with her sandals to the back door of Crazy Ono's Big Play Pachinko Center. She felt dazed, groggy, almost drunk but in a numb, unhappy way. As she pushed inside, the riot of sound seemed muted and distant. The lights assaulted her eyes through a filmy haze. She touched her lids, expecting tears, but they were dry. Then, afraid she might fall, she took the nearest stool. She plugged what coins she had, lost immediately, and then she sat there, smoking and staring at the machine. *It's not you.* How that phrase had twisted, she thought. Those were the words her mother had taught her—*it's not you they want, Nori-chan*—and the words that Noriko had run through her head whenever men had pawed and pulled her, flattered and proposed to her and launched their petty drunken extortions. It's not you they want, she told herself. They want a whore. They want a wife. They want a housekeeper. Anything but the true Noriko. So she had resisted. She had turned down a dozen serious men, a hundred jokers. And what had it done for her? Where was she now?

She stood woozily on a fresh burst of anger. Her stomach felt enormous. It pushed at the back of her mouth. Her feet felt small and her head seemed to float up into the racing, stabbing lights. Passing the counter, she slipped a ballpoint pen into her smock pocket. The women's toilet stank, a porcelain slot in the piss-spattered floor, but she bent over it. She guided the pen into the back of her mouth, found the spot and pushed. In one terrible moment it was over. She was empty again. She was sharp. She was ready to play. And she was broke.

She dried her eyes and rinsed her mouth and went to Ono's office. He was in.

He was happily surprised.

"You've decided!" he exclaimed. "So soon!" he celebrated, and he opened a desk drawer. He lifted out a cloth bag, and, from that, a handful of thousand yen bills. He beamed at her, his gold teeth ashine, and began to count.

"Ten, twenty, thirty. . . ."

"No," she told him. "I don't have the plans. I can't get them."

Now his grin inverted itself. Brow and mouth went down, teeth disappeared. He made like he was about to cry. That morning, as Noriko had worked up the courage to visit Mister Tommy, Ono stood behind, watching her money wane, and he had offered her fifty thousand yen to make a photocopy of the committee's secret plans for a new city-run hotel, and Noriko had thought about it. But she had decided she couldn't.

"But Sister," Ono pleaded. "They plan to ruin me. They plan to take my business. There are not enough tourists in Kitayama for two hotels. What can I do?"

Noriko dropped her head. "Ono-san," she explained, "the plans are big, on sheets of drafting paper an arm's length wide. To copy them would be a huge and clumsy chore. It would be puzzle work, slow and noisy. I can't risk it."

Ono sighed and lit a cigarette. He looked truly worried.

"Anyway," she told him, "you are right. The committee plans to ruin you. What more do you need to know? As big as your bath is, they will build a bigger one. As large as your rooms are, theirs will be larger. They will have better food, plusher towels, faster staff, more and better of everything. That is the plan."

But he was shaking his head now, squinting through his own smoke. "No, Sister. Not everything. No one ever thinks of everything. I want the plans because I will find out the one thing they don't plan for." He grinned. "And I will provide."

Noriko stared into her lap for a long moment. Her stomach squealed. Her throat burned. She had forty minutes left before Mother would be done at the Cut and Perm.

"So," said Ono at last. "You're not going to play the machines, Nori-chan?"

She reached into her smock pocket. She put a key on Ono's desk.

"It's a lost key to the police box. They keep the plans there in the cabinet behind Mayor's desk. Maybe you can get them yourself."

Now Ono squirmed, as a fabulous temptation collided with an incalculable risk. He looked tormented. He looked happy. He muttered a quick and ancient prayer—to Kappa, she imagined. Then he split his stack of cash and offered half.

Yes, she was going to play. She took it.

But when Noriko stepped from Ono's office *he* was there: Mister Tommy Morrison. He stood there, out of place, decked in melting snow and holding a crushed donut box. He spoke in a rush of English.

"I'm sorry. What?"

"I found Stuart's suitcase."

"What do you mean? You found a big, blue suitcase?"

Snow melted from his hair down across his bent nose. He wiped the back of his hand across his face. Something shifted inside the donut box.

"Yes," he puffed. "Under the floor of the apartment."

Noriko felt dizzy again. She pulled Tommy away from Ono's door. "Shh," she told him, tugging at the heavy body and glancing back. The moment they left earshot, Ono appeared in the doorway.

"I was looking under—"

"No," she told Tommy. "Don't talk now."

She steered Tommy outside and found herself surprised by a small crowd of snow-decked umbrellas at the Prince School door. She glanced at her wristwatch. These were the women from Tommy's two o'clock class. It was two-ten.

"I'm sorry," she told them. "Class is cancelled today."

She closed her mind against the general protest.

"I'm sorry," she repeated as her mind scrambled for the right excuse. "I've lost my key. I'll have to find Mister Endo and have a new one made and by then—"

"Then we'll hold class at my house," insisted Hidemi Ebana, the police chief's wife, and she giggled happily. She patted her purple-streaked hair and hooked her arm though Tommy's.

"I'm sorry, Missus Ebana, but Mister Tommy is ill as well. He ran out of heater gas last night, and he caught cold. I'm very sorry. Class is cancelled."

This worked. The women advised Tommy, donated tissues from their handbags, padded off under their umbrellas. All except Hidemi Ebana, who had dressed herself in heels and a tight skirt, with a trashy little faux-fur jacket on top. She pouted now. She shivered and stamped her heels in the snow. "You've been so careless, Noriko. You should see to his warmth. And as for my expense for this lesson, what will you do about it? Shouldn't you take care of it?"

Noriko shivered and looked down, dully outraged. "Ne?" the woman complained to Tommy. He stood stiffly in her grip, the donut box in both hands. "You should take care of it, Noriko."

"Okay, Missus Ebana. Would you take a private lesson?"

Yes, the chief's wife supposed she would take that. Noriko calculated numbly.

"Ten o'clock Saturday morning?"

Yes, the Stuart-hunter supposed she could work that in. Then at last Noriko and Tommy were alone. They huddled in the Prince School doorway as wet snow plunged through pink-and-blue neon.

"I was looking under my tatami mats," he continued, "trying to stop the cold draft. It was shoved under the floor."

"Yes," she said, "yes," trying to think.

He held the donut box in front of her, turning its side into the light so she could read the Japanese on the side.

"Where is this box from?"

"Takata," answered Noriko.

And Tommy said: "Miwa."

A minute later he stood in the dark Prince School office and watched her fumble at the phone. Finally she got her call through. Tommy understood her first words of Japanese.

"Wada? Can you keep a secret? Uncle, can you?"

She talked excitedly, angrily it seemed, rejecting what must have been Officer Wada's suggestions on the other end. *Baka oijisan*, she called him. Crazy uncle. But gradually she calmed and listened, her spine softening until her elbows were on the desk and one hand picked forlornly at the rough skin below her hairline. Tommy made himself breathe deeply. There had been no point in running, but he had jogged and skidded through the slippery alleys to the pachinko parlor, and now his knee hurt. He had asked his way through the parlor, tapping players on the shoulder and asking, "Noriko? Noriko? Is Noriko here?" The players had stirred, eyed him glassily, and mumbled in a dialect he could not follow. The sensation had been vaguely familiar: it had felt like a Tri-County Tech moment, like asking a group of stoned nineteen-year-olds for an arc-tangent of a line. Finally a red-wigged old woman had spared a thumb to point him toward the back . . . but now Tommy was thinking of Gus, of his own stoned and math-resistant teen. *Pottery camp*, he was seething suddenly. *She sends him to pottery camp.* Their spastic-fingered boy, who could not sit still through his own favorite tv show. *Learn the craft of the ancient Anasazi. Wilderness survival. Spiritual counseling.* Elaine had sent Tommy the brochure. She had clipped off the address and phone number. So there went Gus, who broke his own toys because he liked them so much, who whined and wheezed about a ten-minute walk to school. *White water rafting!*

Noriko hung up the phone and turned it toward him. She wrote the number on a scrap of paper. Tommy glanced at his watch. It was four a.m. in Utah. He put the phone to his ear and punched numbers. He listened to satellite signals bounce around a terrain he had only seen in pictures, orange and wrinkled, dry as old bread, a place mysterious to hockey players. But now as he waited it became detailed by his imagination: he saw a long vista, a black stripe of highway, a road house, a U-Pump, and then Gus, plump and clumsy Gus Red Cloud Morrison, on his way to pottery camp, heaving down from the Greyhound a stop too early, stumbling down into a chilly night and squeezing his Dr Pepper, a helpless child left behind like somebody's bag lunch.

The phone hissed and popped, then played a fast digital tune as though Stuart's number were being poured into a more distant electronic watershed.

Or worse yet, Tommy thought, boy got off at the right bus stop, made it to Black Mesa Pottery camp and was beset by Hopi wanna-be's named Arroyo and Juniper and Steven, the white kids Elaine despised for their 1/64 Indian blood ever-so-faintly colored by some distant rape. And Gus would smoke weed with Steven and impregnate Juniper and all bloody shit would break loose. What the hell was Elaine thinking?

A harsh *blaaat!* brought him to task. *Blaaat!*—like the onset of a flat tire, and then the static stress of technology stretched to the limit.

Blaaat! The sound created Stuart Norton's house around itself, a big and severe wood frame, thin runners over pine floors, a scarcity of places to sit, men and women moving in different dry spheres.

Blaaat!

And now a pick-up: "Yes?"

It was a woman's voice, thin and suspicious. Tommy's words came out roughly.

"Is Stuart there?"

A pause.

"No. No, he's not. Who's calling?"

He tried to clear the snag from his throat. He hadn't planned to start this way. He had planned to simply say what had happened. A man began to cough.

"This is a friend of his from Japan. I just wondered if you'd heard—"

Shifting static told him the phone had changed hands.

"Sturt's in Japan," barked a man's voice with peremptory vehemence. He said *Sturt*. "He set out on his own for a bit. Now who's this calling in the middle of the night?"

Out on his own for a bit. Tommy hesitated, off balance. He had pried up the apartment's central tatami mat, leaned it against the window. As cold air sank around him he had knelt and reached and then stopped, staring at the big blue suitcase until the certainty of trouble had claimed his mind.

"A friend of his. I'm trying to reach him."

The man's voice came out in shrill bursts.

"You with the Latter Days, friend?"

"No."

"Because we're broke from them. You got business with Sturt?"

"No, sir, I—"

"Well, he's out on his own for a bit. Like I said. He and the Lord are getting things squared away. Now can I get a name?"

Tommy couldn't speak. He was aware of Noriko's eyes on him. He closed his eyes. He had reached between the broken floor staves and hauled the suitcase up, then lowered his head through the shattered sub-floor to look for what else might be there. He struck his stove flint and opened his eyes. Nothing. Bits of trash. Nails. Dirt. Vending machine coffee cans.

"Mister Norton? Nobody's seen Stuart around here since August. He left his suitcase."

"Now friend, all ours run off at some point and acted like darn fools. We say fine. We say, Don't you come back until you're good and ready to serve the Lord. Momma," the man was coughing again, "get a name."

And now the phone came back to her. She waited for Tommy to speak.

"I found his suitcase. He hid it under the floor of his apartment."

The woman said nothing for a long time. Then she replied, "If you'll give me your name we'll send you some information on the Latter Days in Japan—"

The old man pushed his voice in: "We're broke from them, Mother. Never mind about it."

"His inhaler." Tommy took his own shallow breath. "His toothbrush, everything."

A fine, cold dust had worked its way through the plastic halves of the suitcase, soiling the toes of socks and the neat folds of underpants. Sunken into Stuart's slacks was the Book of Mormon, a cold brick so un-studied its pages clung with the attraction of newness. Laid carefully between sport shirts were a blue comb, a toothbrush with a rubber nipple, a razor. In the elastic side-pouch Tommy found a student ID from Utah State, a video rental card, a few dollars in U.S. cash, Stuart's driving license. He was not twenty-one, as everyone thought, but twenty-three. Tommy had dug deeper. Near the bottom he found a stack of pornographic magazines, lewd comics like the ones Ono had given him, and photo-galleries too, page after page of uniformed, white-pantied school girls in hungry poses, cuter and bolder than . . . and suddenly Tommy's shy and troubled student had come to his mind. Miwa. Then, in a paper sack at the very bottom of the suitcase Tommy had found a crushed Mister Donut box, one left, dried hard.

"Missus Norton—"

She droned into his ear. Tommy twisted the phone cord.

"Missus Norton—"

She wouldn't shut up.

"Missus Norton, listen. We're going to have to tell someone here. Nobody's seen your son."

"All ours run off," she repeated. "We don't worry."

In the dry pause that followed, Tommy thought about the magazines: if Stuart was done with them, they were trash. If he meant to stay in Japan, there were more magazines, everywhere. But he had packed them. He had planned to open them another time, another place.

"Missus Norton, please. Something's not right. I'm almost sure Stuart meant to come home."

"He'll do that when he's ready," she said. "Just like his brothers will some day."

Then the woman hung up. Tommy stared at the telephone. Noriko had risen from her desk. She shivered at the door with the donut box. Tommy spoke to her.

"Wada's just a deputy. Shouldn't we tell Ebana, and your father-in-law?"

She shook her head no. She was waiting for him, her key hanging from the door.

"Noriko, we can't hide this. There could have been crime. Stuart could be in trouble somewhere."

She shook her head again.

"Noriko, why?"

She shuddered from the cold. Her frail knees bent with impatience. Then her eyes blazed at him. "They will lie about it. Don't you see?" She rattled the door shut behind him and turned the key. "Any trouble with gaijin is a big threat to their plans. They will hide it."

At the sidewalk she turned and grabbed his hand. "Don't be a fool anymore," she said hotly, and hurried off.

Tommy checked his watch again in the international phone booth. Six a.m., her time. With raw fingers, he punched the numbers. She picked up, a muffled reply.

"Elaine?"

"Yes." She set something down. "Where are you? What's that noise?"

"A snow plow."

"Snow?"

"Snow."

It swooped at the booth, slid down the glass. Dusk had settled in the valley already, and along the sidewalks, store lights colored the plow piles, casting craggy shadows that crisscrossed at mid-street. The plow rumbled to the end of Shinmei, slammed a wave of snow over the river rocks, turned around. From the phone Tommy heard liquid. The bath.

He asked, "You got my message?"

And a flip top.

"Elaine."

"I finished a grant proposal at about five o'clock this morning," she said. "Though it's none of your business."

"Okay," he said. "I'll get to the point of my call. You want to hear it?"

"Yes."

"The address and phone of that pottery camp. You clipped them off the brochure."

Hot water slapped the tub. The plow ground back toward Tommy. "You can't have them," Elaine said, and she set her beer can on tub side.

"Why not?"

"You don't call home on a vision quest," she told him. "You don't call Mommy and Daddy. And Mommy and Daddy don't call you."

"A vision quest?" Tommy was stunned. "You send a fourteen-year-old drop out to some high-priced pottery camp and call it a vision quest?"

"He sent himself. He chose it."

"He—" Tommy's breath failed him. *Sent himself.* Meaning, Stop me, Mother. Protect me. I'm a child. But she hadn't.

"You don't call him?" Tommy wanted to know. "You don't write him?"

"I told you."

"But he's not some traditional Indian kid, Elaine. You sealed that when you married me. What the hell are you thinking?"

"I was dumb then."

"And now, too."

A splash. The beer can came down on the tub rim. She said, "Call over?"

"Elaine."

"What?"

"We can't just send him off to a strange place completely alone."

Water splashed again. The can fell empty on the tiles. Then the snowplow rumbled forward past the shoe store and thundered upon Tommy. He ducked as a breaking wave of snow rocked the booth, washed over it, settled head-high . . . and she was gone.

By the time Tommy pushed from the booth the plow was on another street. A few flakes twirled through the blue-red air around the pachinko marquee, and then the snow stopped too.

Chapter 15

Noriko parked her truck in a shadow alongside Kitayama Station and felt for coins across the dark and dusty dashboard. Yawning high school kids stumbled through floodlight into the station, where they huddled and stomped against the cold. Noriko found a one hundred yen coin and two tens. She sparked her lighter and looked on the truck floor. For a moment, in the dark space between the pedals, she worried that she had forgotten to start the rice cooker. She had lit the heaters, she recalled, and she had plugged in the electric carpet. She had boiled water and filled the thermos. She had whipped green onions, mustard, and soy into the natto, and she had grilled salmon and turned the broiler off. Meanwhile she had started a simple miso soup—potatoes, kelp, and clams—and that's when she had become distracted. Mama Yama had coughed from the bedroom. The old woman was rousing herself.

Noriko had rushed then. She had chopped eggplant pickles. She had cut up strips of dried seaweed. She had rinsed out Father's and Husband's bento boxes, dried them, and laid them out beside the old tub sink. And then, because no act of Noriko's in the kitchen could go unanalyzed, not even in the frigid dark at five-thirty in the morning, Mama Yama had scuffed in and said, "Noriko. What is in your head? Not beside the sink. It's dirty there. Set the lunch boxes out on the table." She coughed and spat into a tissue, tucked the tissue back in her sleeve. "And you've sliced the pickles too thick again. Father likes them thin." She peered into the soup pot. "Clams? On a cold day? Clams are a cold food in the body. With potatoes they slow the blood down. You're going to kill us."

"Yes, Mother. I'm sorry, Mother."

"Why are you cooking so early, making all this noise?"

"I'm sorry, Mother. I couldn't sleep."

"A-ra-ra." She waved her hand, shuffling off toward the toilet. "She couldn't sleep. Without a child, no worries, and still she can't sleep. So she wakes up and makes noises in the kitchen. A-ra-ra-ra."

Mama Yama shut herself in the toilet and voided noisily. Noriko searched for the moment after that, as she rushed into her coat and shoes, when she would have clicked the button on the rice cooker. But she hadn't. She had rushed out, coaxed her little truck to life, and driven to the station. So still the rice sat there, she imagined, hard little pebbles in ice-cold water. She would be responsible, now, for the starvation of Father.

She found another hundred yen coin beneath the passenger seat. She took a last deep breath from the warm tip of her cigarette and ran through the cold into the station. She bought two hot milk teas at the vending machine. On the way back, the train lights went on and the students began to shuffle en masse toward it. When Noriko saw the little Sato truck, one just like hers, she rolled her window down. Yasuyuki Sato, the brother, stepped out groggily and headed for the train. Then came Miwa, hauling out her heavy rucksack, rattling out her kendo stick, setting them both down in the snow as her father continued to the parking lot. Then, isolated within the swarm of her classmates, she picked them up, one at time, and got them situated on her back.

"Miwa!"

The girl startled. She turned. Hair fell about her eyes. Classmates jarred her rucksack. "To Takata," blared the speaker above her, "Six-fifty train to Takata."

"Miwa!" Noriko motioned: *come here, come on, hurry.*

The girl moved in a syrup of trepidation to Noriko's window. "Miwa-chan, I'm driving to Takata this morning. Father needs medication. So wouldn't you like to ride with me?"

Miwa turned toward the tracks. "Father and Brother—"

"Instead of that crowded old train," Noriko broke in. "How I hated that every day. Ne? Wouldn't you like a ride instead?"

"But Father and Brother—"

"Have they got their lunches?"

"Yes."

Noriko made a bright smile. "Then they won't miss you, ne? And I've got hot drinks. Don't you like milk tea?"

Still the girl hesitated. She turned, trance-like, and raised her face toward the train. It was packed now. All that Kitayama meant to her—neighbors, enemies, family—stared back from the windows in sudden, leering interest.

"Ne?" said Noriko. "Quickly, Miwa. Shall we go?"

She turned the truck around with Miwa aboard at last, eased it down the snow-packed road. A kilometer below, she turned left at the police box, shifted up into the eerie pink light of South Tunnel. As they emerged, the train appeared above them, its yellow windows flashing through breaks in the forest. The girl shivered, hugging her rucksack.

"So, ne, Miwa-chan." This is how Noriko made herself begin. "You didn't go to school yesterday?"

No answer. A half-frozen shrug.

"I looked for you getting off the last train. You stayed home sick?"

"I left school early. I was worried about Grandfather."

"How is your Grandfather?"

"He's fine."

"He's healthy?"

"Yes, of course."

"I may surprise you, Miwa, to say this, but I hope your grandfather lives forever. I hope the committee never gets his land."

Miwa did not reply. She stared ahead at the snow swept intersection of Minami-Kitayama. A small and final valley opened here: two crumbling storehouses, a flashing signal light, a sheet-plastic lean-to with two children, red and yellow blurs, waiting inside for the bus. The girl could not begin to speak of family troubles, Noriko imagined. She could not at her age know who was right, who was wrong, who was crazy and who was sane, and so she tried to make herself numb. Noriko knew. Her father had been a pachinko and Mah Jong gambler of incapacitating proportions. To Noriko's eyes, in high school, he had been a crushing embarrassment, a hapless, raging doormat, and yet everyone had instructed her on what a fine man he was. She knew the confusion, the pressure of classmates, the urge for silence.

When she glanced at Miwa, Noriko could recall herself feeling just like that, every day, shivering in that stupid sailor suit, white blouse and knee socks, the rucksack full of homework, the yawns and darkly clouded brow, all the way to Takata and home again. But she hadn't been truly numb, she recalled. She had only acted that way. And she had not changed anything with silence. She had only made herself a dying vegetable, like a winter radish, top shriveled, mouth and ears disused, still rooted in the same earth. She should have said something, done something.

But Noriko allowed the girl a stretch of silence. She held the wheel hard against the slippery road and drove on. She felt milk tea descend her throat and strike her empty stomach. She felt the caffeine swirl her head. At the edge of the valley, the highway split from the train route and carried them on a span bridge across a steaming chasm. She looked over: Hot Water River twisted far below, blue-green beneath clouds of vapor. Then another creepy tunnel, seven long kilometers, and by the next town, Kuroishi, the sun had cleared the eastern peaks and become too bright against the snow. Miwa stared through her bangs at the train across the canyon. Noriko slipped on her sunglasses.

Her father had been a troubled man, an absent parent, a monstrous husband, and yet he had been loyal to his employer and somehow in Kitayama that was all that counted. He had worked forty years for Yamaguchi Stone. He had breathed forty years of stone dust for them. He had lost a finger, crushed an elbow, and gone nearly deaf for them. He had showed up in his cheap black suit for every Yamaguchi function, every funeral, wedding, rock shack dedication, every blessing of every new car at the shrine, every hospitalization and every drinking party. Hence, and therefore, and forever, Shin Gotoh was a good man, and Noriko was never allowed to forget it.

Now Miwa had closed her eyes against the sun. Noriko recalled the news of her father's cancer. It was a great shock, she recalled, a great and much-remarked tragedy that such a good man would die so young, before his precious little girl was even married. Noriko recalled herself at the bathroom mirror in the old house on the mountain. Mother, soaping her back, had probed, "Nori-chan, there is much talk suddenly. Have you thought about marriage?"

"No, Mother!"

"You're twenty-three years old. You know what they say about Christmas cakes."

"Yes, Mother. Grandmother told me many times. After the twenty-fifth, they're no good. But I don't believe in that old idea. It's silly."

Her mother was quiet a long time, until they were both washed and had slipped into the bath, Noriko spooned inside her mother's legs as they had always done it.

"Your father is very ill, Nori-chan. Still, he has high hopes for you."

"I know, Mother."

"Do you love someone?"

"No, mother."

"Could you?"

It was such a question that Noriko still wondered about it. Could she? But now she turned her thoughts back to purpose. The girl was falling asleep.

"Have you heard from him, Miwa?"

"Eh?"

"Have you heard from Stuart?"

Miwa roused herself, hugged her rucksack.

"I haven't."

"Would he write to you?"

"I don't know."

Miwa looked away, watching the train cross the chasm toward them. Kids laughed and waved. Miwa lowered her head. Then the truck plunged into a long tunnel with green lights.

"Did he promise to write you?"

"I don't remember."

"Miwa."

"I don't remember."

Huge fans hung like jet engines from the tunnel's round ceiling. The hole in the mountain carved on and on, through rock, covered by earth, covered by brush and trees and snow and winter sky.

The girl turned suddenly. "Did he love you?" she asked.

Noriko was startled. It seemed she had heard a strange echo of her mother's voice. "Eh?"

"Did you love him?"

"Who?"

Miwa didn't answer, as if names escaped her.

"Who?" Noriko repeated. "You mean my Father? Stuart? My husband?"

Miwa closed her eyes against the flashing tunnel, hugged her book bag. She answered, "Anyone at all?"

When the truck broke from the tunnel, the train was exactly beside it, slipping forward and back. Around the tracks and the highway collected the pachinko parlors and apartment houses that formed the outskirts of Takata. Then, in another kilometer, a vortex of tracks and wires sucked away the train. It slid down a sooty channel and disappeared among freight cars.

"I need to talk to you, Miwa."

The girl was silent. Noriko turned the truck. She left the main road that led to department stores and movie theaters, to Takata Station and Takata Girls High, and she pushed the truck through slush along the mangled edge of farm and city. Farm houses, tattered greenhouses, bulldozers invading rice paddies, the scene was familiar. It was Kitayama, ten years ahead.

"I need to ask you if you know what happened to Stuart."

The girl drew a breath but didn't reply. Noriko felt her own breath shrink. She steered dizzily onto the empty street of a new-town, losing them among snow-decked skeletal houses.

"I'll be late for school," Miwa murmured.

"Yes. I'm sorry. But Mister Tommy found Stuart's suitcase, underneath the tatami in his apartment. I just wondered if you knew where he was."

"Kyoto," the girl replied quickly.

Noriko started. "Kyoto? Are you sure?"

Miwa stared through her bangs at the dashboard. "He went to Kyoto," she said. "He's teaching there."

"Are you sure?"

"So," she confirmed. "He was unhappy. He tried to love me, but I was too slow. My legs were too short and I was too ugly."

The girl paused as if the words felt strange.

"He went to Kyoto," she continued awkwardly. "He has a new job, a new apartment. All the old women chase him, just like Kitayama, but he has a pretty new girlfriend. She has long legs, high nose, good eyes. . . ."

"Miwa-chan."

"She takes him to Golden Temple, Water Temple, everything. She even shows him how to catch dragonflies. He loves her. Isn't that wonderful?"

Now the truck ground along in first gear. In three days now Noriko had kept down no food, and there came waves like this when all seemed weightless. The sounds around her seemed disembodied, the earth became not earth but scenery in a drama she could not follow. *Isn't that wonderful?* the girl had said. Wasn't *what* wonderful? Only a cigarette could start her thoughts again.

"Miwa-chan," she said finally, "that's not true about Kyoto."

The girl stared after a backhoe, suspended with its claw raised above a rice paddy. "Yes," she whispered at last. "Yes. It's true."

Noriko pushed the clutch down. She steered around a cul-de-sac and stopped the truck. They faced the same backhoe in the same snow field that led into the long, wind-swept Takata valley that ended in the mountains around Kitayama. She pulled back the parking brake. Then she felt through her bag. She lifted out a stiff, two-ply government paper with Stuart's picture, signature stamp, and fingerprint.

"Kyoto is an *Exotic Friend* story," she told Miwa. "I know he's not working in another school. I have his work permit right here. I kept it at my desk."

Noriko waited. She inhaled her cigarette deeply. *New Town California Heights*, read the sign before her. Two-story my-houses, American style, with garages, ovens, grass, and picket fences. Twenty million yen.

"He's working illegally," Miwa claimed.

"That doesn't sound like Stuart."

"He's changed."

"You know all this, but he doesn't write you?"

Again Noriko waited. There came the shriek of a carpenter's saw somewhere inside plastic sheeting. Miwa hugged her rucksack, staring toward the distant mountains.

"He calls me," she said finally.

The girl talked on then, lying about telephone calls. But Noriko's cigarette had pulled her into focus and then suddenly beyond it. Suddenly her mouth felt dry and her neck ached. At age twenty-four she had cut her hair, dyed it orange, and sung Beatles songs in a rock and roll band that died in a month. That summer she lost five kilograms and three jobs. She bought an old motorcycle and wrecked it on Three Cedar Curve, losing a tooth and a patch of skin on her back. She worked for six months as a hostess at Karaoke Happy. She had just enrolled in women's college in Takata when her mother confronted her.

"Nori-chan, your father is dying. He will be gone before the year. He is a proud man, but you shame him. He wants to see you married."

"I love no one, Mother."

"No one?"

"No one at all."

"But you love your father?"

"Yes, Mother."

"And you wish him to die happy?"

"Mother . . . yes."

And so the Gotoh family had hired a matchmaker. The memory made Noriko glance at Miwa. The girl had slumped toward the door, her hair making a curtain around her face. She seemed to shrink from Noriko, as if she understood the shape of fate beside her. As if she understood exactly how life had closed in when the matchmaker had finally called the Gotoh house with his miracle.

"Yasunosuke Yamaguchi!" Noriko's mother had reported breathlessly.

"Mother, I puke at the thought of him."

"But our luck, Nori-chan! A miracle! The best family in Kitayama! Wealthy, respectable! Your father's employer all these many years!"

"He is five feet tall, Mother. He never brushes his teeth and his hands stink like fish. They can find no other woman for such a stupid man. They are desperate. That is why they will take me."

"Nori-chan."

"I am the last woman in Kitayama."

"Nonsense, Daughter. You shouldn't think like that. He is the kind of man who can take care of you. That is why your father is willing to give you to—"

"To *give*, Mother. Don't you hear yourself? To *give* me, to settle an obligation, like a crate of cucumbers."

"Nori-chan, it's not like that."

"No. It's more like a cow. A breeding animal. He wants a child, I'm sure. A son, of course. Am I such a terrible woman?"

"Nori-chan, listen. All these years, through all his difficulties, the Yamaguchi family has kept your father on at the quarry. Even today, when he hardly breathes, they pay him! They are like family to him. And now your father, on his deathbed, is so delighted. . . ."

"Mother, I refuse to look at the toad! At the shrine last New Year, he pinched me, here, and here, and he stuck his tongue in my ear and he said—"

Mother had put hands to ears.

"Stop," she said quietly. "Daughter, stop this now. Always you are thinking of yourself. But now your father is dying, and it is time for your selfishness to end."

Then they were quiet. That day, like this one with Miwa, had been the aftermath of first snow. The roofs and trees were loaded. The steep roadside gurgled melt water. Far across the valley, tiny yellow dozers peeled white from the ancient Takahashi paddies, leaving the first brown scars of the business park. Father would die. Mother would go to Brother in Gifu. Noriko had pictured herself fleeing Kitayama then. She had pictured Takata, Niigata, Tokyo. She had seen herself in trains and subways, bars and ramen shops. But the pictures were stark and frightening, and she had closed her eyes rather than cry.

"What about love, Mother? Am I so bad to be denied that?"

She felt broken at last. She felt she knew nothing.

"You have only loyalty, Mother, don't you? You do only as Father tells you. You don't enjoy him. You don't love him."

Mother hadn't answered right away. In such a short time, with mountains around, darkness could descend. From up the mountain, the Yamaguchi Stone saws ground back and forth. Horiuchi's boar dog yelped and rattled its chain. Noriko listened to the rush of water down the roadside gutter and the panting laughter of school kids hiking up from the station. Then the five o'clock signal crackled forth from its ancient speaker: "Yesterday," in wavering digital tones, a Beatles song, Noriko's favorite once, one she could still sing in perfect English, though no one knew or cared.

Then Mother's tiny hand had arrived stiff and cold in Noriko's lap and squeezed hard twice, like wringing out a dishrag.

"Loyalty *is* love," Mother had said, and then she had opened the car door, cut down a length of dried burdock from the eaves, and gone inside to fix supper.

Now Miwa stared through her bangs across the dashboard. Beyond the blunt nose of the truck crept a farm cat through soft snow, shaking a paw with each step. Then the power saw shrieked again, and the cat darted away. A carpenter thrashed his way out through plastic, tossed a board end, a cigarette, an empty can. These disappeared into snow.

"Miwa-chan."

The girl made no reply. Once more Noriko reached into her bag. She lifted out the donut box.

"Miwa, look at this."

Miwa stared out toward the backhoe. Noriko lit another cigarette. Then she reached across the gear box and lifted Miwa's hair from her face. She trapped thick black strands behind the girl's small ear. She laid the donut box upon Miwa's rucksack. "You saw him that night, Miwa. You may have been the last one to see him."

She held the girl's hand.

"Now tell me," Noriko said. "Tell me what happened."

Then she too stared out at the muddy claw of the backhoe—hooked out in motion, then suddenly frozen above the stubbled white field.

Chapter 16

Grandfather.

With Stuart's hands pinching her shoulders and his body slamming into her from behind, Miwa, in that long and terrible moment before she fell to the West Mountain shrine ground, had recognized the old man far across the pond, his grizzled head just visible above the hydrangeas, squinting from the road beyond the red gate: it was Grandfather.

Then she was on her knees and palms in the mud. Her umbrella was beneath her, crushed, its spokes sticking up into her chest and face. Her rucksack had been thrown over her head and hung upside down, like an anchor, from her shoulders. Her kendo stick had flown . . . she didn't know where. Her dress was up, she realized, and she had heaved herself back on her heels, and then the trailing momentum of the rucksack sat her down hard in the mud.

Grandfather was gone from view. She struggled to her feet. Grandfather was hobbling toward home—for his eyeglasses, for his musket, Miwa didn't dare think. "Nan de?" she cried as she turned on Stuart.

"I'm sorry," he puffed. "I stumbled."

"You didn't stumble."

His cheeks were blotched pink and his hair was wet. He said, "Give me a break, Miwa."

It was raining on them. Miwa had stared at him, uncomprehending. She didn't know the phrase. He was stepping toward her, his hands out. "Give me a break," he repeated. "I'm not some kind of love god. I don't even know how to do it."

Do what? she had wondered, backing away, stumbling on her ruined umbrella. She had to hurry home. It was all she could think. She had to calm Grandfather. But when she turned to go, Stuart was suddenly enraged.

He seethed after her, "Don't you dare walk away. I said I was sorry."

She kept walking. Then he was in front of her.

"What the hell do you want from me, Miwa?"

She stared at her muddy knees. "Nothing," she said.

Stuart puffed. He touched her chin and tried to push it up. She let it fall back. He grabbed her shirt collar and gave it a hard tug. A single white button dropped upon the brown mud.

"That's a lie," he said. "You want me to put it in. You know you do."

Miwa's voice had barely functioned. Rain dripped from her bangs. "Please don't touch me," she whispered.

This seemed to dissolve Stuart, and he had begun one of his long, anguished talks, his English flooding her ears, overwhelming her brain. She picked out topics but not connections. He was sorry about many things. He didn't want many things. He didn't want himself. Something about his soul, his father, his church. Disappear, he said. Become nothing. Really. Never bother anyone again. Then hate. Kitayama. Utah. Bullshit. Wait for marriage. More bullshit. And whores. Everywhere. So what did he care?

Miwa waited and waited, her legs trembling with the urge to run, and when Stuart stopped at last and seemed calmer she spoke. "I really am sorry," she said. "About everything in Kitayama. I am sorry."

Stuart let out a long, foul breath.

"I'm sorry too."

"Please," she murmured, "pick me the most beautiful flower in the garden."

He grinned at that. She waited. When he had crossed the bridge and reached the hydrangea at the edge of the pond, she ran. "Hey!" he cried, and she heard his footsteps on the bridge.

Noriko had gasped when Miwa told her this. But, slow as she was with her bowed legs and her heavy pack slamming her back, Miwa had started with a good lead, and she knew the trail as it climbed steeply over stones and pine roots, then leveled and cut horizontally across the mountain, through sumac and wild grape.

She hit this flat stretch and looked back. Her legs ached. But Stuart had both hands on a tree trunk, his head sagging between his shoulders. He looked up. He was gasping for air.

"You!" he howled at her. "You bitch!"

She ran the flat stretch. Then, where the trail bent upward, she plunged down, pushing through the stubborn sumac and then a patch of slick tall grass, then finally beneath pines and then through the fragrant hydrangeas around the shrine pond. She had completed her circle, recovered her umbrella and her kendo stick, and she had hurried home.

Grandfather was in the genkan with his eyeglasses and his musket. It had taken him that long to locate them.

"Grandfather!" Miwa had exclaimed. "What are you doing? You can't go out into the street waving your musket. Grandfather, what's wrong?"

He explained that he had seen a hakujin, attacking a Japanese girl, and he was going out to kill the trespasser.

"Grandfather!" Miwa made a laugh. "No, Grandfather. That was me. That was my English teacher, Mister Stuart. I was showing him our West Mountain shrine, because he asked me, and I fell."

And this had worked. She had changed Grandfather's angle of attack. No pissing white men allowed in the shrine, he had raged at her. Never go with him again, he had commanded. Grandfather had forgotten what he saw, Miwa thought. He had forgotten her fall. And Stuart, she guessed, would chase her all the way to the top, to Kappa's shrine. "Never again!" Grandfather thundered. Never again, Miwa agreed, closing the door, bolting it, soothing the old man with strokes on his thin, knobby neck. Never again.

She served him tea and sweetened bean paste. She turned his television on. In an hour, when thumps came at the door, she hurried from the kitchen and said brightly, "Grandfather, would you like to see my kendo strokes?" And she had jumped about the sitting room, wielding her stick with all her precision and might, shouting from the depth of her worried gut *"Men!"*—a blow to the head; and *"Do!"*—a blow to the gut; and *"Ko-te!"*—a blow that broke the wrists.

The thumps at the door had ended. Grandfather had liked her stick work. He had smiled.

She avoided Stuart then. He had one month left in Kitayama. Miwa kept the English class money Mother gave her and used it for taxis straight from Kitayama Station to West Mountain Village. But one night, about a week after the shrine ground incident, the phone rang during supper. Miwa's brother answered. There was such a moment of confusion—Brother repeating bizarre Japanese phrases, while the whole family stared and listened—that Miwa knew it was Stuart. She was trembling, blushing hard when she touched the phone. Grandfather put down his chopsticks.

"Miwa," Stuart said, "I'm sorry."

"Thank you," she replied.

"I need you to forgive me. I mean, you're my friend, right?"

"What do you mean?"

Grandfather began to mutter. He had never heard English in his house before. Into her other ear, Stuart began a long and rapid story that she could not follow. Her dictionary was in her rucksack, across the room at the genkan. He was on Shinmei, she could tell. She could hear "Scarborough Fair" leaking from Karaoke Happy.

"Can you come down to my place, Miwa? I think I'm sick. I need you."

She had stammered, her mind locked with fear and indecision.

"Miwa!" barked Grandfather. "Is that the hakujin? Is that Golden Hair?"

"Please, Miwa—"

"I can't come down."

"Do you forgive me, Miwa? Can you come down and tell me that?"

" I can't."

"I'm sick, Miwa. I'm very frightened. I think I'm imagining things."

Brother was shaking his head. Mother had reached out to put her hand on Miwa's. Father was shoveling rice into mouth. Then Miwa had thought of something to say. "Missus Tezuka lives near you. So does Missus Ebana. They are both in love with you, and they are both mothers. They will know what to do. Why don't you call them?"

She quickly hung up. She hurried back to the table and poured sake for Grandfather.

"I don't know," she said quickly, before anyone could ask.

"Hakujin lover," muttered Grandfather.

Brother stared. He leered. Miwa kicked his outstretched foot.

"I don't know," she told him through clenched teeth.

Grandfather had eyed her with unrelenting suspicion after that. And his worries about his paddy land becoming airport gnawed at him. Every night at supper he disowned them, and they retreated to fan themselves in hot rooms while Grandfather sipped sake on the veranda and hectored neighbors.

"International city!" he would curse from his post beneath the eaves. "Ha! There'll be South Yamaguchi Tunnel on the south end, North Yamaguchi Tunnel on the north end, and between them nothing but hamburger shops and filth!"

He would scold, "Long grain rice! Ha!"

Then with one week remaining in Stuart's contract, on one still and sweltering July night, ancient Great-Second-Aunt Wada, the fat policeman's grandmother, came scraping and puffing by, bent double like a speed skater, one hand slung atop her back and the other swinging side to side. She was headed for the public bath to wash her thin hair. A bar of soap weighted her apron pocket and a small white towel hung over her neck. As the deaf old woman inched past, Grandfather raised up, steadied himself against a hewn post, filled his shallow lungs with night air and howled for the whole village to hear. "Now your grandson is working for Police Chief Ebana, eh? That's what you trade your ancestors' land for? A nothing job for fat Grandboy?"

Great-Second-Aunt Wada toiled on toward the bath, oblivious.

"Eh? You know, don't you, that Ebana's a biological bastard? Eh? Old woman? Fat Grandboy working for a traitor and a biological bastard? That's what you trade your land for?"

The old woman had traveled perhaps two meters in all this time. But she had traveled ninety-seven years to reach this point and she meant to wash her hair, and so when Grandfather plunged off the veranda into his wooden sandals and hobbled across her path, thundering accusations, she was sorely unamused. Yet being a respectable woman, she quietly adjusted her route toward the bath. When Grandfather jumped in front, she adjusted once more. The third time Grandfather blocked her she became blind as well as deaf and she lowered her head and bore straight into him.

Miwa had rushed to the veranda by this time. The old woman's head struck the old man's chest. Her arm swung to and fro and she drove him back, out of his sandals. Then Grandfather dug in, wheeling his arms, howling embarrassments. For a long and terrible moment they locked in static combat, like beetles in the dust.

Then Miwa pulled Grandfather away. She apologized to Great-Second-Aunt Wada, collected Grandfather's sandals. She hauled him back to the veranda.

"Grandfather," she panted, "your bath is ready."

He glared at her wildly. "Hakujin lover," he accused.

"I don't know what you mean, Grandfather."

"You are his lover."

"I'm not, Grandfather."

"He was here today. He was at this door, looking for you, speaking some kind of ridiculous Japanese. He said he loved you. I told him, leave or die. He wouldn't leave. I pulled the door shut in his face."

Miwa had collected her breath. Sweat had trickled over her lips and into her mouth. She remembered that Mother had claimed to hear something, the night before, beneath her bedroom window. Something breathing, Mother had said.

"Thank you, Grandfather."

He eyed her. "Traitor."

"Your bath, Grandfather. Look—you've soiled your feet."

That night the phone rang at eleven-thirty. Miwa jumped up quickly and beat Mother to it.

"Yes?" she whispered.

Stuart was on Shinmei Street at the phone booth. She could hear karaoke, a drunken man singing "Love Me Tender."

"Miwa?"

"Yes. Why do you call?"

A long pause. She heard laughter outside the phone booth. Mother sat up.

"You're my friend," he told her finally.

"Why do you say so?"

Another long pause stood between them. The singer finished his turn to hoots of disapproval. Some drunken woman began to warble an old minyo tune.

"I can't sleep, Miwa. Lately, I can't sleep at all. Are you there?"

"Yes."

"As soon as I lie down and come near sleep, I hear something. I hear somebody breathing. I feel like somebody's after me."

Pause again. What could she say? "Is that English?" yawned Mother.

"Huh?" said Stuart.

"It's very late," Miwa told him.

"I hear chewing sometimes," he told her. "Like something is after me."

Miwa snuck a look behind her. Mother was turning over, trying to sleep.

"Did you hear me, Miwa?"

"Yes."

"Something is out there in the alley behind my window."

"Perhaps," she whispered, "it's Missus Tezuka."

He was silent.

"Or maybe Missus Ebana. Maybe both."

"Miwa, do you believe in Kappa? I mean, I've seen that shrine. I guess it freaked me out, and I—"

He stopped. She heard him move in the phone booth. Someone said hello to him, and he answered. The person wanted to talk, try out some English, ask Stuart how tall he was, how many fingers he had, who was his girlfriend, and Miwa waited. Mother stirred and Miwa touched her. Then Grandfather grumbled in his sleep, his voice carrying through the paper door to the next room, and Miwa had come up with a strange idea. She had wanted nothing more, she told Noriko, than to stop his phone calls.

"Yes," she whispered. "I do believe in Kappa. Kappa loves me. He protects me. He is like my crazy mountain father."

She had spooked herself. Stuart made an odd little cough. A group of drinkers passed the booth, pounded on its sides, called his name.

Then he said, "Miwa, can't you just forgive me? Please? I told you I'm sick. I told you I'm sorry. I don't know why I'm doing this to you. Couldn't you just come down?"

There was a rustling behind her. Mother had sat up again.

"What's going on?" she yawned, now irritated. Then a thump in the next room: Grandfather, stirring.

"No," Miwa said. "I cannot come."

"I love you," Stuart countered, and she quickly hung up.

"What's going on?" whined Mother.

"Nothing," whispered Miwa. "It's over."

She sang to Grandfather strongly, happily, that final morning in August. Stuart was leaving and she felt relieved. But Grandfather waved her away, preferring the prattle of the tv. A typhoon bore down on Kitayama. He cursed the weatherman. He disowned Miwa five times before the others even arose.

"You'll marry a hakujin."

"I won't, Grandfather."

"You'll go with that Golden Hair."

"He's leaving Japan, Grandfather. Today."

"Go with him then," said Grandfather. "You're no longer my child. Do what you want."

"Your tea, Grandfather."

At Takata Girls High that day, Miwa had thought of what she would do. It was right to forgive, she told herself, and if that is what Stuart wanted, she would give him that gift on his final day, plus donuts. And then she had begun to feel sentimental for what might have been. She felt sad that love was such a twisted thing, that the simple pattern of *Exotic Friend* couldn't have worked for Stuart. She had been willing. She could have helped him. She could have loved him. And then she felt confused and guilty: *why?* Why had he chosen her? Why did she make him feel that way? What did he want? All afternoon, Miwa had struggled with this and hid within her bangs while her Kitayama classmates indulged their final gossip and stories and fantasies. And then, at the start of Calculus class, she had smelled the typhoon and she had moved her thoughts to Grandfather, in the house alone, his old bent neck uncovered, the tv droning, rice cooker puffing, Grandfather getting half-drunk and hobbling out in the heavy, whirling air to start his weed cutter and slash down grass along a paddy rim.

Lovely, ancient Grandfather—the true one who protected her!

And so, her stomach twisting, she had skipped Kendo Club and bought donuts. *Dear Stuart,* she wrote in trembling hand, *I forgive you.* She rode the train, she drove her scooter, she walked the steps to Stuart's apartment door and tapped on it. She had heard water running inside.

"I'm not home," Stuart had rasped at the other side of the door. Then he said it again in his strange Japanese. "Watashi . . . wa . . . imasen."

Miwa had leaned her kendo stick beside the door. She felt suddenly unsure why she had come. She lifted one sweaty palm from the crushed donut box and knocked again.

"I'm Miwa," she called.

When Stuart answered the door he was flushed and scowling. He wore his tan teaching slacks, hacked off at the knee. He wore a sweat-soaked blue t-shirt that said *Utah—World's Best Snow!* He carried a blue sponge and leaned against the wall with the sponge in hand. Soiled soapy water ran down the wall. He smelled like alcohol.

"I brought this for you," she said.

"Thanks," he said.

Behind him she saw his futon spread open, his big blue suitcase packed and strapped shut. His long fingers reached for the smashed donuts.

"The new teacher fell on me. I'm sorry."

"I don't mind."

He unstrapped the big blue suitcase. It sprang open. He pushed the leaking box beneath white shirts on the right half, closed the suitcase, cinched the strap, and stood it up. He looked over his shoulder.

"So you forgive me, huh?"

"Yes."

"Good," he said. "Because I'll tell you what I don't like. All that bullshit about Kappa. That was a bunch of crap and you got away with it."

She glanced up into the grimace-grin. The sponge was dripping on the mat floor.

"I'm sorry."

"There's only one God, Miwa. So don't give me that crap."

"Yes. I'm sorry."

Once more she had felt unsure why she had come. She should have just sent a letter to Utah, she thought suddenly. But now she was here, in this awkward moment, as Kitayama slipped toward darkness and Stuart came sloppily across the tatami to reach for her. He caught her wrist and pulled her in.

"Miwa," he was puffing suddenly, "I said I loved you. Didn't you hear that?"

"Yes."

"Don't you know what that means?"

She hung her head. She stared at his bare feet. His toes were incredibly long, as long as her fingers, like the digits of some kind of monster.

"Don't you love me too, Miwa?"

"I forgive you," she whispered. "And I do love you, as one human to another."

At this, Stuart had clacked his teeth and seethed. He had dropped her wrist and swatted his overhead light. It swung crazily, sending waves of light and shadow up and down the walls. Outside the typhoon sky rumbled.

"You don't love me as a man? You wouldn't marry me?"

She kept her head down. She gave the Japanese no: silence.

"So you're a flirting bitch then," he said, his voice cracking. "Just like the others. Aren't you? Aren't you just a little flirting bitch who wants to fuck?"

"No," she whispered. "I am not."

Again he grabbed her shirt collar. This time he yanked her shirt all the way open. She had worn her Mickey Mouse bra and Stuart laughed. "Jesus, Miwa. You're pathetic."

Then he reached for her, his jaw clenching, and he tried to unhook the bra. He fumbled. He couldn't. "Please don't touch me."

"What?"

"Please don't touch me."

"I'll do what I want," he answered. "You people did it to me. On my last day in this stupid country, in this stupid little town, I'll do what I want."

"Please don't."

"For once," he huffed, "I'm going to do it. And don't try to pretend you didn't ask for it. You all did."

A typhoon gust had slammed the door and raised the curtains into the room. Miwa had closed her eyes and pictured her grandfather then, in his straw hat and rubber boots, heading out with his weed cutter. She saw him limping slowly under the dark sky, under the thatched roofs, heading into his ritual before the last light was gone.

"Mister Stuart," she murmured to him, as another lie formed. "I need sake. Like you," she said, "I want to be drunk."

Stuart let go of her then. His strange blue eyes had widened in surprise. "Well then," he said, his voice trembling, weakening, "then . . . okay. I'm not like this, Miwa. Really I'm not. Normally. But okay then. If you want it."

As he went into his kitchen, Miwa had stepped silently back into the genkan, into her shoes. The door eased open under a clap of thunder and he didn't hear it. She slipped her kendo stick from its cotton sheath. She stood back, at the side of the door, her feet spread before and behind, the stick cocked behind her head. In that moment, lightning smashed above her, splitting the sky, and the rain cut loose against rooftops and car tops, splattering up the smell of earth. This is what she had come for, Miwa understood suddenly.

"Hey!" Stuart cried, his bare feet slapping fast toward the doorway. "You sneaky little—"

She brought the stick down squarely on the top of his golden head. Her voice burst in a fierce shriek—"*Men!*"—as the stick connected with his skull. A glass of sake flew out and shattered as he crumpled. Then Stuart writhed and gripped his head, cursing her.

But she hardly heard him. She hardly knew him. He was a terrible stranger, now sobbing at her feet. "*Ko-te!*" she had cried as brought the stick down again . . . and stopped it a centimeter short of his flailing wrists.

"Shut your windows," she told him, "before the rain ruins your mats."

And she had gone at once to Grandfather.

Chapter 17

Rennard Dombrowski was a stubborn bastard, even in a coma. He hung around. On the ice, he was one of those lead-footed goons who brought the whole game down to his level. He liked to tie up the puck in the corners, grab-assing quick kids like Tommy Morrison, leering through plexiglass at the puck-fuckers in the front row. Or he liked to ice the puck, blast it to the other end of the rink, voiding the more nuanced options. Then, when the game moved too fast, he would park his huge ass in front of the net, raise his stick, and cudgel anyone attempting real hockey in the slot. And of course he was ruthless in the mix-ups, pure homicidal rage, always taking a younger, better player out with him. He was a godawful drain on the game. He was everything that Tommy, post-knee, 30-year-old, trouble-at-home Tommy, had seen himself becoming.

When he hit Dombrowski, he was spooked by the way the big guy crumpled: sat down sharply on the ice, as if obeying something, with only a fistful of Tommy's jersey to keep him from keeling back. It was more in fear than anger that Tommy struck the second time—a downward blow with his fist, the butt of his stick cocked inside—more in a primal terror that said *strike now! again!—as* if to obliterate the awful glint in Dombrowski's eyes. He was hurt good.

Tommy had skated away, around the net, pulling off his gloves and helmet. The Thunder Bay crowd went crazy for revenge. A beer splattered him as he passed the face-off circle, and then a pint vodka bottle struck his shoulder and spun away on the ice. When he sat down in the penalty box, his teammate, Norm Briske, already there on a minor, screamed Canadian in his face: "You did it, Morrison! You took the fucker out! He can't get off his fucking bum! You're goin' up to the big club now!"

This had quickly come true. The big club. The Detroit Red Wings. Tommy was a gate draw, an igniter. "Combustible," the program said. He was ordered to fight, stitched up by real doctors and paid real money. Suddenly, Elaine could buy whatever she wanted, which turned out to be a subdivision colonial home that stuck up fresh as a baby's butt from bulldozed earth. Since he was sure it wouldn't, this newness had appealed to Elaine, the Elaine who then told him she had never liked their creaky, lived-in, campus apartments, never even liked their first real house with its red brick and stalwart arbor vitae, the changing Elaine who now said she wanted something without history, where she wouldn't have to think about the people gone before. This new house was hers.

She bought it with blood money, her aluminum wigwam on Lancelot Lane. And meanwhile Dombrowski made a long, dull mess out of getting better. It was of a piece to Tommy that in his coma the big brute managed to hog-tie and annoy the doctors. He was hurt, but not that badly, they assured Tommy, but it seemed as if some impulse in Dombrowski kept whacking the puck clear down the ice, kept grinding good ideas against the boards and shoving clever solutions out of his jut-jawed, slow-breathing zone.

"He'll be fine," the doctors said.

The new Red Cloud-Morrison house had misled everyone, too. Tommy's parents had believed Elaine was finally coming around. Bailey and Donna had bestowed on the new house a stream of knick-knacks and yard ornaments, Irish Catholic prayer plaques and sports paraphernalia, all of which Elaine hauled directly to her new burn pile. And then at Christmas, Elaine's father, Grandpa Rupert, thinking he must be welcome again in his daughter's life, loaded up the Winnebago—Grandpa Rupe found this funny, a Winnebago driving a Winnebago—and trekked south for an extended visit with his new wife, Bernice, a divorced white woman who nipped jerky sticks and Seagram's minis out of her purse and fought with Gus over tv channels. Mostly Tommy was gone, starting fights in Toronto, Pittsburgh, Chicago, spending his nights hanging off hotel beds to stretch his aching back while he tried to solve problems over the phone. He tried to advise Elaine, calm her, help her laugh things off, but her father wouldn't go home. He was so delighted, this trailer dweller, to be in a white man's castle. Then, while Tommy was on the ice in Boston, the old man resolved Gus and Bernice's tv conflict by massive appeasement: he scored a bingo prize from the Potawotami Casino down the road and bought the kid a big-screen tv and Nintendo set for his bedroom.

And here Elaine had lost her mind with frustration. She shut off the power: the furnace, the hot water heater, the lights, stove, phone, everything. Tommy had come home for Christmas and was greeted by Lady Bernice at the door, unwashed and wrapped in a Green Bay Packers blanket.

"Oh thank God," this strange woman uttered as he stepped inside. "Oh thank holy God."

They were all wrapped in blankets. Gus huddled on the hearth before a small fire, his hands venturing out to toss playing cards on a pile. Elaine sat cross-legged in a streak of sunlight near the porch door, reading.

"We rode around in the trailer all night," Bernice whispered, "but now it's out of gas. Rupert said if he's going to be cold he might as well be ice fishing. So he bought wax worms and he's over to the golf pond."

Tommy sat down beside Elaine. He recalled the book title: *The Countess of Pembroke's Arcadia*. He stared down at a page and his eyes crossed. That fall, she had declared intent to take her Ph.D. in Indian literature, to which the English department responded that there was no such program at the university. As she continued to study for her Master's exam, she simultaneously constructed a lawsuit. That day, Tommy beside her, she turned pages with a frightening snap.

"Good book," she told him.

"Sure."

"No really. I always thought Anglo culture went to hell in America. But this goes way back."

He stared at his hands, fuzzy blond in the sunlight. He was never sure exactly what she meant anymore. Outside it was a stinger: cold and crystal clear, with a steady north breeze. Gus looked blue, stunned.

She looked up, inspecting Tommy's face without a trace of affection. He told her, "I didn't think we could hold out much longer, so I talked to Bailey and Donna from the hotel last night and they're coming over."

"Today?"

"It's Christmas, Elaine. They're my parents."

"Fine."

"You know," he coaxed, "Rupert and Bernice are here, they could meet Bernice. They would like Bernice."

"I said fine."

"Then could we start the house back up?"

This was "fine" too. But in the basement, with his fingers on the breakers, Tommy felt each power switch starting up some separate anger in his wife, until the whole house had seemed to tremble and crackle with all that made her crazy.

He was afraid to let in his parents when they arrived an hour later. This fear became dread when in their wake—*holiday surprise!!*—trailed Tommy's eldest brother, Big Dog, with wife and starch-white kids. A minute later, while Elaine stared bug-eyed, middle brother Mad Dog arrived, pulling a hung over girlfriend with more blonde bedroom hair than Tommy had seen on anything short of . . . short of a yak, he whispered in the kitchen, trying to contain Elaine with humor.

But his only contribution that day, aside from general, global wrongness, was to mistakenly take Elaine's control away. Wanting nothing so much as to escape the slowly warming house, Tommy had rallied the Morrison men for their traditional Christmas Day hockey game.

"No," Elaine said.

"We'll be back soon," Tommy had told her, and they were, almost instantly, because Grandpa Rupert had drilled the golf pond full of ice fishing holes. They lost their only puck. Mad Dog fought with Bailey. Big Dog sprained his knee and they were back in a hot half hour with Gus all burnt-cheeked, foul-mouthed, and agitated. He couldn't settle.

"Gaawiin ganabach!" Elaine ordered him at the door. Her Ojibwa mother's phrase: *I think not!* But he blew past, slinging his skates to the floor, banging his stick along the wall: "Bullshit!" he hooted. "Bullshit!"

She commanded, "Gus!"

"Bullshit!"

"Gus, come back here!"

"Kiss my ass!"

He went to his room. Elaine turned to the families. Her father stood at the front doorway with a stringer of frozen bluegill and one small northern pike, stiff like a boomerang.

She said, "I want you all to leave. Period. Forever."

Grandfather Rupert's hand went straight down his pocket to his car keys and then he remembered he had no gasoline. Bernice rooted for snacks in her purse. Then Bailey broke the silence: "Well . . . Merry Christmas to you too, Pocahontas."

Tommy struck. He yooped his father with flat hands in the chest and knocked him back into Big Dog. Of a thousand blows delivered in icy combat he still felt this one in his bones, still saw through time his father's raging struggle for revenge while Big Dog smothered him in long arms and huge hands. And then came the scream from Gus' bedroom.

Everyone stopped.

A crash and a second scream—and then the girlfriend wobbled out gasping, a fat hank of yak hair soaked in blood and dripping. Gus followed, panting his explanation, some kind of heavy robot toy brandished in his fist, and as the girl collapsed and bled on the tiles, he said, "She was . . . she was watching . . . Mom, she was watching my tv. . . ."

He was eleven that March. He grew a mouse-brown ponytail and tied it with buckskin. He was tall, like Elaine's brothers. His eyes were gray, his skin dough-white and bruisy. He saw a youth counselor. He wouldn't say what they discussed. He wouldn't talk when Tommy called. "Yup," he would say.

Or, "Nope."

Elaine enrolled him in Aikido class, but the gym was in a strip mall and when she dropped him off he would eat sub sandwiches and play arcade games until she came back. She restricted his money, but Grandpa Rupert always sent more. He wrote on his skin with ballpoint pen. He made swastikas, skulls, dripping daggers. Somehow, on the small of his back, he got a real tattoo: the Tasmanian Devil, flipping the bird. Then he caught mono, spent April in his bedroom. Elaine ground herbal cures, coneflower and goldenseal and burdock root, but they didn't work. He got well on antibiotics, Dr Pepper, and pizza. When Tommy came home at season's end, the two of them, mother and son, were utterly estranged, and Tommy made three. Indian woman, half-breed boy, hockey hero: they moved about the huge house in separate orbits, as if cursed by the blood spilled to get it, and no doubt—this would be Elaine's point—cursed by the blood on the land itself.

And then on the first of June, Rennard Dombrowski abruptly died. The day the news came, their lives had lunged apart with sickening finality. Tommy was putting in sod in the front yard when he had taken a simple call from the Dombrowski family attorney: Rennard was dead. He had awakened in the night, disconnected himself, and died. There would be no suit. They wished him well.

Tommy had dirt on his hands and a need to vomit. The lawyer told him to avoid the funeral in case the Mounties made good on their felony charge. He stopped working, sat down in a lawn chair, swallowed warm beer that tasted like copper in his throat. Gus' Nintendo racket blared from the window behind him.

He remembered watching Elaine step off the bus at the end of the street. Her beautiful long stride shortened as she saw him. For annulment of her lawsuit, the university had offered her a fellowship to continue in the doctoral program, and he wondered—he assumed—that she had told them to shove it.

She stopped at the edge of the yard and regarded Tommy's slumped form, his bushy white calves burning pink in the sun.

"Where's Gus?"

"Playing videos."

She was panting slightly. She tossed her hair and the sun caught its faint redness.

"Well, I took it. I dropped the lawsuit, which I can't afford, and I took their money."

When Tommy stood and hugged her she was trembling. She pulled away and went into the house. Through the screen door Tommy heard her raised voice: "What?"

Gus, over the roar of Mortal Kombat: "That guy died."

"What guy?"

"Dad's guy."

Tommy heard, "Oh, shit . . . ." and then the shower started. She came back out an hour later, with car keys and fragrant hair, on her way somewhere. He couldn't ask where. Each life had twisted now and become painful in new and private ways. Gus banged around behind them, looking for something, calling, "Mom? *Mom!*"

"I feel like . . . Elaine . . . in your eyes, everything I've ever done is wrong," Tommy finally said, but this was old news to her, understatement. His lousy can of beer was somehow empty, as if to punctuate.

She didn't answer. She stood slightly behind him, watching Ted Caputo hose his driveway, Ted Caputo with his generous views on spear fishing and bingo. By then she hated any chimook who spoke out for Indians, as well as all those who didn't. Taking their scholarship would be the last favor she would ever do a white man.

Tommy tried for her attention: "What do I do, Elaine? I'm at a loss here. I'm done with hockey. I need to rebuild something. I need meaning."

Both stared at his ankles, shaved for taping: now that the season was over, they were growing back in thick stubble so that his feet looked like mutant bald eagles, aimed out toward the mud puddle Ted Caputo was making in the road.

Then Elaine looked up at Tommy. She was smiling faintly, coldly. "You've got a friend in Jesus," she said, and she turned back toward the driveway.

"*Mom!*" Gus screamed through the screen door. "Why don't you answer me?"

He raised his leg then, a clumsy, mixed-up boy whose ass was getting fat, and drove his foot through the screen. "Hey! Somebody help me! Fuckers! Help me!"

Morning: the stairwell blown full of snow. Two nights now, and Tommy had not slept. He stood outside his door, unsure where the steps began. The cars in the lot looked like driftwood submerged in blowing ice.

He plunged down into a world of outlines and ridges. He hiked leeward drifts and underhangs. At Shinmei, he borrowed a shovel from the post office to dig out the phone booth. Inside the plexiglass igloo, AT&T's Sherrona told him she had no town of Black Mesa, she had no entry under pottery camps, camps, youth camps, or pottery. If he could pick himself up a map of Arizona/New Mexico. . . .

"I'm in Japan."

"Oh. Interesting."

"I'm trying to track down my son."

"I hope you find him, sir."

He felt absurdly close. "Thank you, Sherrona."

"Have a good day, sir."

When he stepped from the phone booth, his tracks were snow-filled and Noriko was there. Her Yamaguchi Stone truck roared grill-high in a drift. She rolled down the window. Garfunkel's voice swirled out past him.

"I have news," she said, and he climbed in.

She spun down his alley, passing his apartment without a word except of Richard Cory, who once more put a bullet through his head. Then Noriko turned into the scuddy fetch of the river road, where wind and snow tumbled at them across the long plain of the south valley. They forded drifts past the sake brewery, then fishtailed suddenly left into the love hotel garage.

"We've been through this," Tommy said weakly.

"They have a good bath," was her answer.

She nosed the truck through frozen rubber flaps, stall five. Her jaw seemed set, ready to fight. She was dressed for Prince School: her navy blue secretarial ensemble, nylon stockings, black pumps, sad gear for a snowstorm. Her whole body tensed and shivered.

"Can you just tell me the news?"

She shut down wipers, lights, Garfunkel. She lit a Salem Menthol. She thumbed her dictionary.

"Stuart stalked her."

"Stalked her?"

"Don't you say? He followed? Bothered?"

"Yes."

"He said bad things. He tore her shirt."

But Miwa? Tommy meant to ask, except a quicker route through his brain found it perversely sensible. Of course Miwa. And of course, Stuart had said he loved her.

"He said he loved her."

Tommy rubbed his brow, hot skin under cold fingers. "Okay." He tried a deep breath. "Then what?"

"I think he went crazy here," Noriko said, sucking hard on her cigarette. "I think Kitayama made him crazy." Tommy waited. They were under the hotel, he realized, in a tight, dark stall, rubber flaps in back to hide the car, a narrow stairwell leading up. "She hit him," Noriko said. She checked her dictionary again.

"She . . . clobbered? . . . him with her kendo stick."

"And then?"

Noriko shrugged. She shivered. "Miwa went home."

Tommy twisted. The rubber flaps flopped in the wind. Wisps of snow blew in and swirled about the truck.

"Shall I call the embassy?"

"No. We should say nothing. Any kind of news will make Kitayama people into panic. I've told Wada. He is checking taxi, other English schools. He is talking to train workers in Takata."

"He won't alarm people?"

"Wada is actually very smart," she sighed, making a face. "He is sometimes stupid, if you know him, but only because he is too smart. Did you know yesterday he followed you all day? You called your wife three times in the midnight. You said a prayer at Shinmei shrine. He says you are innocent."

"Me? Of what?"

"Ne?" she said. "Stupid. But yes. He confirms you found the suitcase as you said. And now, if he can find Stuart quietly, perhaps there is no problem." She paused. She twisted a knob on her dusty dash. Though the fan spewed air, no heat remained in the truck. She said, "Any bad news is a problem for Kitayama. Any bad story is a big threat to the committee and they will fight to hide it."

Tommy nodded. He made fists to warm his fingers.

"And also," she said, her head lowered, "there would be much bad criticism of Miwa. I'm sure most Kitayama people will believe she has done a terrible thing. They will think she was cruel to Stuart."

"So we keep it a secret?"

"Yes. For now."

"And what else do we do?"

Now Noriko's eyes flared, as if daring him to refuse her again. She squeezed his cold fist.

"We survive," she said.

She killed the engine, crushed her cigarette and got out.

The bath was as good as she had promised. It was wide and deep and hot. Sunken within it, Tommy watched her in the other room, moving quickly between the vending machines and the bed. She chunked in coins. A microwave whirred. Plastic shredded. Then somewhere out of sight, beneath the low din of the tv and the roar of the wind, she ate.

"Whiskey?" she called. "They have whiskey."

He closed his eyes. "I'm fine." He laid his head against the rim of the tub. Hot water lapped his chin. *Survive*, he thought. But wasn't there some small chance that the suitcase, the inhaler, the passport, were the shucks of a life transformed? Couldn't Stuart be anywhere? Without his baggage and his name, wickedly free?

When Tommy opened his eyes Noriko had set a little Styrofoam boat, filled with sticky noodles, on the tub edge. "Fried noodles," she called, out of sight in the other room. He ate. When he stepped from the tub, she rushed in past him, wrapped in a towel.

"My turn," she said, and slipped into the water.

He lay naked beneath the quilt in the wide bed. For a long, strange moment he recognized his immense and trackless distance from anything familiar, anything he could truly understand or control. He was lost now. And he wondered again about Stuart. And about Gus. About all of them, gone too far but somehow not far enough. Had they all three driven themselves to a dead end, a place where their demons could slowly close the deal?

Tommy turned off the television then. He listened to wind rattle the old windows, to Noriko's purposeful splashing. In five minutes more she was naked and rubbery hot beside him, climbing over. And then they were finished. At ten minutes to noon on a December morning, Tommy finally slept.

He awoke a short time later with the bed empty beside him. He had forgotten where he was—the wide, high bed, the mirrors all around, the vending machines, the wind rattling windows. "Noriko?"

"Hai."

"What are you doing?"

"Hmm?"

"Where are you?"

Now a splash. "I'm in the bath again. Come in here."

Tommy hobbled from the bed and into the steamy bath room. Noriko lay beneath the green-tinted mountain water. Her cheeks were bath-flushed, sweat on her lip, her face free of make-up. Tommy had imagined her body, and now here it was fully before him. Her face and neck, hands and shins were dark as old bamboo. Her tiny breasts were white, blue-veined, black-tipped. He took her hand and stepped into the searing water. He sat behind her, sifted her hair, ran his palms along her hips and up the curve of her ribs.

Then suddenly, "Shh," she said, sitting up. She made him wait in silence. After a moment there came a soft thump and a rattle at the window by the bed.

"Nan de . . .?" she whispered. But nothing followed. Tommy tried to re-start his embrace. But she was stiff now, waiting. "Somebody," she said. Then again, the soft thump and rattle.

"Nan de?" Noriko cried. Now she splashed out, wrapping in a towel. Tommy followed, and they stepped as close to the window as they dared. Then, as they watched, a snowball rose, bent deliberately, and burst against the glass. Somehow Noriko understood its source.

"Baka," she cursed. "Stupid uncle."

Then she was all action. She pulled stockings over her legs, yanked up the navy skirt without untwisting it. Her breasts took a wild ride as she collected her shoes and blouse from the floor, stuffed her brassiere in the skirt band. She hung her purse on her shoulder and dug for money. Another snowball smacked the window.

She cursed again, livid and hoarse, then translated herself. "Uncle," she cursed. "Hole of ass. Why he follows me, too? Why he ruins my good time? Stupid uncle!"

She tilted into her shoes, glanced at Tommy.

"You must disappear," she puffed. "Go out the end, over wall, away from where cars come in. I will come out in five minutes. I will say I was just here taking a bath, because at home my turn is last and the water is always cold."

Tommy found his underwear. He tugged clothes onto his wet body. He stuffed socks into his coat pocket and stepped into his boots. Then leaned to the window, looked below. Snow blew from the valley across the river road. All he could make out, parked and snow-covered down by the sake brewery, was a little black-and-white patrol car.

Noriko shoved him.

"Go!" she cried. "It's Wada!"

Tommy paused in the dark hallway, unsure how he had come in. He stumbled with flapping belt and trailing laces down a stairwell into a stall that wasn't theirs—a white car, newly arrived, heads ducking behind tinted glass—then found the wall she meant and plunged over it into an alley.

The wind walloped him. It blinded him. It slammed snow up his nose, nearly blew the coat off his shoulders. He turned his back to it. At a slippery, knee-jarring trot, he took the alley toward Shinmei Street. In two hundred meters he crossed the main street and labored up an unplowed lane to the old castle ground. Enough, he thought then. He was clear, he thought, and he stopped.

But a siren turned him, and somehow the patrol car was now exactly behind him. The car surged up the snow-plugged castle lane, lights spinning, and Tommy cut on a sprint for the sunken ramparts, pounded across a red-railed bridge. Ducks exploded from the moat. He charged beneath loaded pines, then across the wide, deep snowfield where his gait became a wild plunging and then a slow and helpless thrash until he hobbled on the busted knee and once more stopped.

He bent, panting, looking back. As the patrol car backed off the castle ground, Tommy finally understood it was a different car. This car was larger, newer, more powerful. It was Police Chief Ebana's car. The vehicle surged again, around the moat, down an alley, and met him easily on the other side.

Ebana stepped out warily, his club drawn as if Tommy might attack. He unlatched the patrol car door, kicked it wide. Then he spoke two words of English, each one as if the taste made him sick.

"Telephone," he said.

When he had secured Tommy inside, he thrust out the committee's big red dictionary. His hand shook. His thumbnail marked the word. He spat it out: "Wife."

"Tommy, is it you?" The edge of panic in Elaine's voice choked his first response. Of course it was him. But he was unable to speak. Ebana's German lunged about him, sniffing.

"Tommy? Is that you? Tommy?"

"Yes. Yes, of course it's me. What is it?"

There was a commotion around her, someone else in the house, distracting her. The tv was on too loud.

"Have you heard from him?" Elaine rushed. "Have you heard from Gus?"

"Have I heard from Gus?"

The question stunned him. How would he? How could she ask this? He glanced up: Ebana scowled, heeled the dog.

"What do you mean have I heard from Gus?"

"He's gone!"

"What do you mean, gone?"

"From the . . . whatever . . . the camp! They called!"

"He ran away?"

Now Tommy stared at his feet. His untied boots were clogged with snow. After a conflict at the camp, Elaine gasped into his ear, Gus had left at night. A rancher saw him climbing fences, a trucker saw him hitchhiking on the interstate ramp. Tommy's mind opened again to the dry southwest. They were sure he had gone west, she said, on US 15 toward Vegas and L.A. After that, nothing.

Tommy looked around for a chair. Ebana kicked one under him and retreated. He lit a cigarette.

"Elaine? Do you want me to come home?"

He glanced at his watch. Her kitchen clock would say midnight.

"No. God no. I don't know why I called. There's nothing you can do."

"Would it help for me to be there?"

"I just wanted to tell you," she said. He heard the tea kettle whistle. Then she seemed to find herself. "I just wanted you to suffer too."

"Elaine." He took a gulp of Ebana's smoke. "I'm about to puke on the floor here. Will that work for you?"

"That would be nice."

She poured her tea. They listened to one another's breathing for a long time. The dog wanted to sniff Tommy again. He heard it gag, heeled sharply behind a desk. Then his eyes followed Ebana. The police chief strode outside to the trunk of his patrol car.

"You should see it snow here," he said finally.

"Really?"

"It comes down like—" He hadn't ever thought to compare it to anything, and nothing came to mind. He didn't talk this way to Elaine anymore. It came down like *snow,* like the word itself had finally been defined.

"Elaine?"

"Yes?"

"It's strange. I can hardly speak English anymore. I say the same simple words over and over until they lose meaning. Do you remember that? Do you remember when Gus used to say apple *a-pull* until it drove us both crazy?"

Tea came to her lips. The cup clicked the receiver. Tommy stared outside at Ebana. The patrol car's trunk lid flew up and the police chief lifted out Stuart's big blue suitcase. He carried it in, set it on the desk before Tommy. He unsnapped the latches, slammed it open.

Tommy told Elaine, "I think I'm in some kind of trouble here."

"I'm not going to feel sorry for you, Tommy. Not for a second."

"That's fine."

She took a slow breath. A door shut on her end. Then he felt the silence of the house, the silence of the police box. He looked outside again. Through the pitching snow, he watched Wada lead in Noriko. Her arm ripped free of his as they approached the door. She shrieked something at Wada, pointed inside, at the suitcase, and Wada retreated.

"I'll call you," Tommy told Elaine, "in the morning."

He was frightened by her silence. "Elaine?"

"Um?"

"Put yourself to sleep, okay? I'll call in the morning."

"Whose morning?"

"Yours. You'll see. He'll be all right."

Then at 12:10 a.m. Wisconsin time Tommy heard the frail, gauzy goodbye that was Elaine's battle with tears. She put the phone back on the kitchen wall. With the *click*, his picture went dark. Into that darkness, Noriko translated for Ebana, "You will stay here."

Tommy could say nothing. Ebana spoke again.

"You will wait," Noriko translated, "in this police box while Mister Ebana investigates the reason you have this Mister Stuart's suitcase under your tatami, why you tell no one, and why you run from police. You will wait here, with lock, so that you cannot run again."

She left then, commanded to go. She hesitated in her thin dress and high shoes, her truck a long way off. Wada flashed his patrol car lights at her, opened the passenger door. But she went to his window, berated him again. Then she slipped away down the road to town.

At sundown, Ebana fed the dog and locked the door. Tommy arced chairs around the heater. He lay bent, rolling front to back to balance the heat. Snowfall surged beyond the window. Tiny shadows flooded the floor and walls. At eight p.m. he called from the police box phone but Elaine didn't answer. She had gone somewhere, he imagined, to meet police, to pay a ransom, to identify a body. Dead end, he thought again. Demons. The dog growled, barked twice. Tommy closed his eyes and heard the soft tat of snow against the glass.

Chapter 18

Her private lesson, fumed the police chief of Kitayama town.

That was all his wife could talk about. How the Yamaguchi whore had cancelled classes, making a bunch of stupid excuses, but *she* hadn't taken it lying down, and now *she* had a private lesson. She told everybody. She would take a private lesson, she said, on Saturday, with Mister Tommy, who was actually, and here she whispered, *more exciting than Mister Stuart.* While she was confiding this to a friend over the phone, at supper, Police Chief Yosuke Ebana had felt like throwing up.

Instead he had pushed his bowl away and lit a cigarette. Her damned private lesson. He poured himself a whiskey and water. It was the night the blizzard started and he was raw about it all. He hated snow, all the ridiculous accidents. The stupid Tezuka wife, gawking at the gaijin on Shinmei Street, had slid and rear-ended Abe-san, who crushed a row of bicycles beneath the shoe store awning, the whole mess requiring three hours of paper work in the cold police box, one form for each mangled bike. And meanwhile, warm at home, his wife chattered on the phone about her damned private lesson. And now a lousy, tasteless supper. Ebana liked salt. He liked kim chee, pickles, and smoked fish on rice, but Madame Private Lesson had served him macaroni salad, exactly the kind of sweet and sloppy American food that expressed the direction of her brain since Mister Stuart had arrived a year-and-a-half ago.

Then Daughter had come home, whining about the snow and pitching her things about the genkan.

"Guess what, Miki-chan."

"What, Mother?"

Ebana closed his bloodshot eyes. *Private lesson. Mister Tommy.* He listened to his daughter's neigh of disbelief, her slide into envy, then her joyful recovery at the sight of fat tasteless noodles floating in mayonnaise. It was a kind of celebration dinner, he had realized.

It was all more than the police chief could understand or bear, and he had stomped out. He drank hard that night as the snow rushed down. He lost a small fortune at Mah Jong. After midnight, he stalked home past the gaijin's apartment. He had a strange and sudden desire to kill the man, to breach the door and club the big ape in his sleep. But the apartment light was on. Ebana stood concealed in snowy darkness, smoking, watching the massive jerk stomp around, hanging laundry, washing dishes, drinking a beer. Then the gaijin did push-ups, bent his knee in a strange way, and turned out the light.

Ebana stalked home. His wife slept. He slapped her fat ass. He yanked her stupid purple hair. "Wake up," he commanded. "I'm home."

But she only yawned a curse at him and moved over a bit. She knew who he was.

All night long while his wife snored and passed gas and mumbled in her sleep, Police Chief Ebana had stewed about it, his whole sordid and unfair history. His miserable secret. Who he was, the son of a son of a bastard, and those he blamed.

A poor girl had tempted a rich man. So whose fault was that? According to Ebana's long-dead grandmother, it was the work of the scheming Yamaguchi clan. The girl had seduced the old man as she carried lunches to her father and brothers in the quarry. She smiled at wealthy old Nobutaka Ono. Her kimono, Grandmother claimed, was loose at the throat.

Ebana tossed and shoved his wife. The year was 1916, and he wished to travel back, undo his destiny. Dynamite had just reached Japan, Grandmother had told him. The forests were full of moon bears and monkeys and wild pigs. Hot Water River was thick with char. Beneath it all, the black Ono granite bore flecks of gold. Mined from the mountain by the girl's father, cut and polished by her slaving brothers, Ono granite was a luxury known far and wide across the prefectures of Honshu Island. The Ono family was rich. The Yamaguchi family was hungry. And so one day, in her best kimono, with her hair put up, Ushiko Yamaguchi, fifteen, made her trip up the mountain with a bento box for Ono-sama, who was eighty and five times a grandfather. The old man savored the food and then turned to the girl.

The mountain boomed and shook. Monkeys screeched. Wild pigs scuttled through the underbrush. In a month of this, the girl was pregnant.

Ebana rose to piss. Something hurt as his water passed. He stumbled out of the toilet. In his absence, his daughter had crawled into his futon, taken his spot. She was curled up next to Madame Private Lesson, the two of them farting out their macaroni salad.

Ebana limped to the front room and sat under a blanket before the dead television. When the child first showed beneath the girl's rags, the Yamaguchi family met their employer with demands: half his land for their silence, half his stone, half his machinery, his dynamite, his workers. And so Ono Stone became Ono-Yamaguchi Stone. The girl was banished to Niigata. The bastard child was sold to a couple who kept an illegal pinball house in Sendai, and the petty gangsters raised her bastard son poorly, first in Sendai, then Takata. They slaved Ebana's grandfather in rickshaws and soap houses, and they bought their Takata pachinko parlor too late—the market was glutted. And then, just as they were about to move on, their ball dropped. The Takata newspapers reported that a Yamaguchi, their little bastard's true uncle, had become mayor in Kitayama, a small town two hours north into the mountains. Kitayama had no pachinko parlor, they found out, and the power of their secret suddenly possessed them.

Ebana fell to coughing at the thought of it. He turned on the television. Static. He turned it off. He poured himself a cup full of whiskey. Grandmother had been pained to tell the rest. The couple had set out for Kitayama with their eight-year-old meal ticket, her future husband, in tow. By that same evening, by the subtle arts of implication and extortion, the Ebana family had acquired from the Yamaguchi mayor a permit to run a pachinko parlor on Shinmei Street, plus the land and loan to build it. But the position of the Ebana family in Kitayama grew only as a root grows in darkness: darker, deeper, more alone. In this way, perversely, Grandfather's power sank as it grew. The old man and the girl, the bastard and the pachinko deals, the Ono-Yamaguchi-Ebana tangle, these grew into secrets ten times their original size. They became knots, fungi, run-away cancers, and they killed Grandfather cold dead of a stroke at forty-five, left Grandmother alone and bitter. But still the secrets and lies branched and magnified. They burrowed and grasped into the next generation until both the past and future felt like an illness that came from the earth itself and that filled the body with retching and the soul with rage. Ebana stared into the darkness of his cold house. This was his life.

He had done what he could to escape. He had ruined the parlors, sold the land, demanded of Yamaguchis a respectable job, but he could not be at peace. He smoked and drank and gambled too much. He fished with a stiff back and a jealous eye on other fishermen. He resented his wife and daughter, who knew of his darkness only how to use it against him, who wore expensive clothes, ate sweets, studied English. He resented anyone who gained respect honestly, anyone whose life was simpler than his, anyone who expressed happiness or pride or love. In his police uniform, he felt unworthy, untrusted. Without it, he felt naked and deformed. He craved the cover of the fisherman, the hunter, the kendo warrior. He hated to bathe. At night he hated to go home. He sat in taverns behind veils of smoke, snapping down Mah Jong tiles. He stalked the town in drunken darkness, growling at dogs, pissing in gutters, and every night he fell on his futon sick from a whole life polluted by secret and scandal, and he lay awake hating Yamaguchis, young and old, male and female, hating the rock in the mountain, knowing that no matter what, his life would continue to be about car wrecks and snowplow supervision, a cheap and drafty police box, and beyond that, secrets alone, debts and lies, arm-twistings, a tissue. He sat awake in the cold front room the night of the blizzard, drinking himself back toward sleep, knowing it would go on and on, knowing that to break out, to break the silence and the lie, would make him a pachinko gangster bastard again.

And all she could worry about was her damned private lesson.

In the morning Ebana rose from a bent and troubled sleep and started a cigarette. His daughter had gone to school. But he heard water. The bathroom door, marbled glass, made a flesh smear of his wife.

Suspicious by nature, and now by the need to find some wrong that could be righted in the full fury of his miserable soul, Ebana stepped outside. He pushed snow off the genkan step. He coughed and spat. He kicked through a drift along the side of the house. His wife had cracked the window to let out steam. He blew his smoke the other way, kept his shadow off the window. She stood nude in front of the mirror. She stood sideways, her hips cocked. She pinched the fat on her belly. She straightened her spine.

"Hello," she said to the mirror in English. "Nice to meet you."

She turned the other way: "Do you like macaroni salad?"

It was all more than Police Chief Yosuke Ebana could understand or bear, and that afternoon the urge to strike someone had overcome him. As fat Wada sauntered past his desk with yet another soda, Ebana rose suddenly and slammed a fist into the back of the young man's neck.

Wada did not so much as stagger. He stopped walking. He turned slowly, his face bearing a quizzical look.

"Why?"

"Always drinking soda," Ebana fumed, "shuffling around here drinking soda. Why don't you do something?"

"For that you hit me?"

The stupid kid seemed truly confused. Hit me? Clever me? He had been forced on Ebana, a Yamaguchi deal with the Wada family for airport land, this giant, grinning fruitcake with nothing to do but swill soda.

"For that I could kill you," Ebana said.

And Wada smiled!

"I've been hit harder," he said. "At the National High School Sumo Championships in Kawasaki there was a guy there who is pro now—"

"Shut up," Ebana told him.

"Okay."

Wada shrugged. He waddled on toward his desk.

"Shut up and do something."

"Alright," he said. Smirking. Always smirking. "I will do something."

The snow had paused and the roads were clear. Wada worked a while, though on what, Ebana could not figure. Then the fat boy went out, came back, made phone calls. Later that afternoon, the young Yamaguchi wife came by and they spoke outside, under resuming snow. Ebana's suspicion turned. He called out the door, "Wada!"

"Yes, sir."

"If you're just going to flirt with girls all day, why don't you go home."

"Flirt?" said Wada. "With her?"

"Go home."

Then Ebana searched the fat boy's desk. He found suspicious phone numbers: English schools, train stations, police departments. He found a fax from Narita Airport passport control about Mister Stuart. He found a photograph. He found taxi calls, bank records. Golden Hair had saved a million yen in a Toho Bank account, then withdrawn it. But he had not taken his flight home. He was not at any English school, not in any jail, not in any morgue. No cab or train had carried him. What any of this meant, or why Wada was asking, Police Chief Ebana had no clue. But he had found a focus for his suspicion, and when the Mister Tommy's wife had called the next day and Wada had gone to retrieve him, Ebana had seized the chance to search the apartment.

In five minutes he had laid the place bare, leaving only the tatami unturned. Then he pried up the tatami and found it: Mister Stuart's big, blue suitcase. He smiled. He didn't know why. But suddenly he felt better.

Driving back to the police box, he had been blessed with the luck to spot Mister Tommy, vaulting over the love hotel wall, the shaggy-haired, despicable, fornicating donkey. Ebana had followed. The gaijin had looked over his shoulder on the castle ground, seen a police car, and run like a criminal.

Now, closing up for the evening, Police Chief Ebana took a final, satisfied look at the gaijin as he huddled around the heater. He laughed to himself. The Yamaguchi bitch had tried to argue with him, her bra hanging out of her pocket. She had claimed she was bathing alone. He had laughed in her stringy-haired, rough-skinned, no-tit face. He had laughed at the gaijin too, hair all over him like a fungus. In his mind, he had seen them fucking in the love hotel, seen his wife fucking Golden Hair, seen Golden Hair fucking his daughter, and he had seen himself, boot raised, kicking them apart like animals. Now, at the door of his squad car, he looked back through the police box window purely to appreciate himself, the way he might check his stringer, lift it from the river once more to admire the big fish on it.

He thought this as he locked Mister Tommy inside the police box: *so much for private lessons.*

Chapter 19

Tommy was shoving the dog away, funneling more kerosene into the heater when Ebana returned in the morning. The police chief scowled, spewing smoke. He slipped on the snow, flung an arm out to catch the squad car door, and then limped to the police box, fumbling through a huge ring of keys. Ebana didn't dress for the cold, Tommy observed. Back in Wisconsin he had known guys like that. One layer. No hat. Cotton socks. Not much of a jacket. They smoked just like Ebana did: as if the burning cigarette were the core of their being. Then, fifty times a day, they threw their life source on the ground and crushed it.

Ebana opened the police box door. He grunted and pointed, kicked the dog away. He wanted Tommy to come out, to get in the car. Five minutes later he delivered Tommy to Noriko's Prince School desk. He spoke harshly. She bowed and murmured, "Hai . . . hai . . . wakarimashita . . ." *Yes, yes, I understand.* Then she rose from her desk and held the door for the police chief, bowing until he had disappeared down the steps.

"Why am I here?" Tommy asked her.

Her voice was barely audible. "Private lesson."

Tommy frowned. "Missus Ebana." Noriko pointed toward the classroom.

"You are to wait here when the lesson is finished," she told him. "Mister Ebana will pick you up and return you to the police box for question."

Tommy studied Noriko a moment. She wore slippers and an apron, wet in the center. Her hair was stiff and her skin looked bad. She swept an arm toward the room. "Please?"

Tommy sat down across from Mrs. Ebana. Between them on the table she had set out a bottle of sake, a hand-knit stocking cap, an electric blanket, and something in a clear plastic bowl that smelled sweet as the lid came off.

He blinked at the woman. "My son is missing."

She put a hand to her purple-streaked hair. She reached across and touched his arm. Then she was stammering hard: "Do . . . you . . . like . . . macaroni . . . salad?"

When it was over, Tommy retreated to the teacher's office and quietly popped the fire escape door. He waded down the snow-clogged steps and east two blocks to the Nippon Telephone and Telegraph office. He paged through his pocket dictionary, then stepped to the counter and composed a Japanese sentence: "I would like a telephone installed in my apartment, please."

It didn't take. The young woman blushed. She put her hand in front of her mouth. She looked behind at her co-workers, all of whom were suddenly too busy to notice customers at the counter. Tommy broke the words down, reassembled them, and tried again.

"As for me. In my apartment. A telephone. Install. If you please."

The woman burst into happy compliance. She came around the counter, fast feet in high heels, sturdy body in tight company uniform, and led him to a pay phone in the lobby. She bowed proudly. Now her co-workers were watching. She smiled and directed his attention to the telephone. "Dozo." She bowed again. Tommy bowed back. "Thank you," he said.

He picked up the receiver to make her happy. He dropped in ten-yen coins. He punched random numbers and turned away while the phone rang in some stranger's house. His eyes were suddenly blurry and his hands trembled. There was no bigger fool, he told himself, than a man who would leave his son. No bigger fool, anywhere on the planet.

He walked home, ran a scorching bath, drank beer at the tub rim, waiting. It was only forty minutes before Ebana pounded on the door. Tommy dried and dressed and answered. Behind the chief in the doorway huddled Noriko, and behind her, Wada. Snow decked their heads and shoulders. Only Wada spoke as they stepped in.

"Ojamashimasu," he said, brushing his shoulders. "Excuse please."

He passed a foil pack to Tommy. "My wife," he whispered. "Japanese rice dumplings. Please enjoy."

Then they stood in sock feet on cold tatami while Ebana started a cigarette and made a long and grim announcement. With his shoes off he was a size smaller. He wore a tiny service pistol and kept his hand on its case. He looked hung over. Tommy moved his eyes to Noriko. She wore no jacket. Snow melted in her tangled hair. She kept her head down and spoke softly.

"Mister Ebana has many important questions, which he advises you to answer with true statement. First, he asks this. When did you find the suitcase?"

Tommy answered in Japanese: two days ago.

Ebana grunted. Noriko shrank further as she spoke his words.

"Mister Ebana tells you to speak your own language. And he demands you not to lie. Didn't you find the suitcase in August?"

"No."

"You first found it when?"

"Thursday," Tommy said. "November twenty, in the evening."

The chief wheeled at this, ordered Wada to stop gaping. The big man began to unpack a camera case.

"Mister Ebana says that your neighbor, Mister Motoki, saw the mat raised at two p.m. So you found the suitcase then or before. Not evening. And since you have lied so quickly, Mister Ebana therefore believes the date of November is not accurate. He believes you found it before, much before."

Tommy stared at Ebana. "I found it then."

"Speak your own language, he tells you. He tells you that foreign people cannot speak proper Japanese. They should not try."

Now Wada fit a lens and flash on his camera. He pulled on the overhead light and stepped back as far as the tiny room would allow. "Cheese!" he said and his camera clicked.

"Mister Ebana demands you to answer this question. Yesterday, when he followed in his car, why did you run?"

Tommy stared at the chief. "He knows we were in the love hotel?"

"Yes."

"Then he already has his answer."

"Yes."

Still she waited.

"Tell him to go to hell," Tommy said.

Whatever she made of this, Ebana snorted. He blew smoke out his nose and said something to Wada.

"On yesterday, Mister Ebana says, you sent forty thousand yen in postal order of money to Elaine Red Cloud."

"Yes. That's my wife."

The chief smiled faintly at *wife*, his cigarette slipping between his thin lips. "Omoshiroi," he said. *Interesting.*

Tommy said back in Japanese, "What's interesting about it?"

"He warns you. Speak your own language. Your Japanese makes him sick. And now he asks you this. Did you open the suitcase?"

"Does he know that I did?"

"Yes. I think so."

"Then, yes."

"Did you take something?"

Tommy began to answer, but suddenly she looked up at him. She appeared sleepless and half-crazed behind her snarled hair. "Please," she said, "We can not tell about Miwa and the donuts. Kitayama people will blame her. Her life will become very difficult. We have to protect her."

"But she's part of whatever happened."

"Maybe," Noriko said. "Only maybe. But anyway she will suffer. Any Kitayama man like this—" she meant Ebana "—will make her suffer."

The police chief was watching them. He shook his head in disgust. Then he ordered Wada to photograph the tatami, the window. Tommy coughed. The chief had filled his room with smoke. Now Ebana knelt to raise the stained tatami. He heaved the mat against the window. Cold air spread around their feet. The police chief barked commands. Wada's camera whirred and snapped. His flash popped. Inside, outside, a hundred shots. Then they were finished.

Ebana seemed more composed as he stepped into his shoes. He made a speech, but Noriko's translation was barely audible, her face half-concealed behind a curtain of wet hair.

"He says it is big disaster for Kitayama, if Mister Stuart had some trouble here. He says my father-in-law has worked ten years to make Kitayama an international city. If we cannot take care our foreign guests, all of Japan will laugh at Kitayama. Therefore, he is now prepared to hear the truth. He believes you took something from the suitcase. He threatens me ten times already. He will tell Husband about our visit in the love hotel if he does not hear the truth."

Tommy watched her step numbly into her sandals, slender feet into battered plastic. He hadn't noticed yesterday: her toenails were neatly painted red.

He said, "So it's you or Miwa in this? One of you gets ruined?"

She shook her head. "No," she said softly. "It's no choice. I am already ruined."

Then, repeating the question for Ebana, she asked him: "Didn't you take something from the suitcase?"

"No," Tommy answered. He looked the chief in the eye. He said it in Japanese: "Nothing."

Ebana made an ugly smile and stepped out into the snow. Noriko scuffed after him. Then, with a smooth power that shocked Tommy, Wada grabbed Tommy's arm and politely steered him out.

At the police box, Ebana fed the dog and locked the door. He returned once, shoved a jug of kerosene through the door, and re-locked it. Tommy stood at a leaky window, watching the snowstorm slow at last, watching the sky clear to a pale blue and then darken as sun left the valley. The clouds and snow had been like a blanket over Kitayama, and now, at dusk, warmth leapt up from the valley, sucking heat so strongly from the police box that the walls rattled and the gas stove quickly lost ground. Gus, Tommy pleaded suddenly, stay warm. Then he was struck by the simplicity of his thoughts. Dread, he might have guessed, would unleash a great storm of feeling, great poetries of grief, but like the new sky he now felt empty, black, and cold.

He dialed the phone. Somehow he knew what to expect: no answer.

He funneled in kerosene and paced, his mind stuck on *stay warm*. The police box was small, cramped with the trappings of old paper bureaucracy. He circled once between the stuffed file cabinets and the boxes of forms, the old kanji typing machine, all the scrolls and proclamations and legal documents, the spindles with citations impaled. Then he turned out the lights and pulled down the phone and sat cross-legged in the blue glow of the heater. He found a new thought. *Gus*, he prayed, *stay safe*. Again: no answer.

It was sometime after midnight when the door rattled and the dog growled and Ono's moon face appeared beyond the glass, clearly astonished by what he saw inside. The door rattled a bit more, then the knob turned, and, behind a knot of squid jerky that the dog nipped and carried beneath a desk, Ono stepped in.

"Mister Tommy?" He seemed delighted. "Verily?"

"Yes, it's me."

Ono made a little dance of joy. He put his thumb and forefinger a centimeter apart. "A little bit wait," he said. "Thou shalt chotto matte." Then he backed out, carefully locked the door behind him, and disappeared. Tommy waited dully. He watched the town darken below, and then he remembered hitchhiking in Canada. He was just out of high school, playing Junior A hockey. He had been knocked out in a fight in Regina, and in the middle of the night he had awakened in a hospital surrounded by wheat fields. A combine droned outside, cutting wheat by spotlight, and Tommy realized he was still wearing his skates and his uniform. He had walked out barefoot onto the moonlit highway, his skates over his shoulder. He was still loopy from the blow to the head. He stuck out his thumb at the first truck. "So," the driver had asked him, once Tommy had settled inside, "Like to score, do ya?"

He shuddered now, stood and paced the memory away. In a half hour Ono was back, opening the police box again and this time, trailing the shank bone of a cow, grinning hugely, he tiptoed in with beer, squid jerky, nuts, cigars. He showed Tommy his key before he slipped it back in his pocket.

"Ne?" he said, his teeth gleaming in the blue light. "Miss Noriko, ne? She is a good girl. She is very good to me." He urged Tommy to sit beside the heater. "Ne?" he said. "First, to having the party."

They toasted. The dog gnawed. As the beer hit Tommy's stomach he felt abruptly sick with grief. He dialed—nothing—then stared at the blue flame while Ono went on cheerfully, incoherently, and then suddenly rose to some greater task.

"Chotto," he said. "Ne? Chotto investigate."

Tommy watched him turn on a small flashlight and search a file cabinet behind Ebana's desk. Soon he gave up there and tried a second cabinet. No. Then he opened a standing metal closet and finally found what he wanted. He danced back to the heater with a roll of white papers. He spread them on the floor, cupping his light, murmuring as his finger ran over some kind of multi-layered blueprint.

About ten minutes of this brought him to an apparently painful conclusion. He sat back on his heels, wringing his hands.

"Chotto," he said. "Ne? Chotto try to pox me, ne? Chotto try to ruin my business!"

Tommy didn't follow. He didn't want to. But Ono slapped his leg.

"No!" Ono cried. "Not do! Ne? Survive!" As he began to pack up their picnic, he began to explain something, making a wild word salad about a phone call, about how some thing was like a chain, how it could happen quickly, how chains worked, linked, and then his Cadillac, a train, a boat, and—he said *voila!*—he could un-pox himself. No one else would have what he did. Ne? Then he paused. He spent a long moment in suspension, eyes popping, struck by some fantastic idea.

"You come," he told Tommy.

"Come where?"

"I must go to Sado Island," he said. He blew his cheeks out. "Yamaguchi," he puffed, "tries," he managed, and he made a smashing motion, then an exploding motion, "to smite my hotel. Ne? So I must to survive my business."

Ono slapped him on the knee.

"You come. Ne?"

"Where?"

The old man made a grand gesture, his small shiny hands snatching at the air. "Unto the waters." He grinned. He slapped Tommy a third time. "Chotto exodus, ne? I must to telephone. Then I must go west coast Japan, Japan Sea. Pick up cargo to survive my hotel, ne? Unto the waters."

It didn't matter where, Tommy decided. There would be phones. He stood. Ono opened the door to the frigid night. The whole town yawned before them, under starlight. The old man danced out and motioned for Tommy to follow.

"Ne?" he said. "Chotto exodus," he said, and he carefully locked the door.

Chapter 20

The first morning train out of Takata followed the route Tommy recalled from August, hammering south through tunnels and patchwork rice fields, then curving west toward the sea through valley towns where snow reached half-way to the roofs.

They changed trains in a local blizzard at Shinjo, and the new track settled in above the wide, slow Mogami River. Wind blew snow against the current, turning the water nappy and gray-green. Beside Tommy, Ono happily narrated their progress, opening beers and bags of dried squid. At Amarume, near the coast, they boarded a bullet train and reached Niigata before they could find seats.

Tommy felt stunned. The entire journey had taken only three hours. As he followed Ono through busy Niigata Station, Kitayama clung to him. He moved too slowly, with a self-consciousness that was entirely vestigial. No one knew him, or cared to know him. No one shouted, "Gaijin!" Mormon boys hawked salvation at the turnstiles. English teachers, younger versions of himself, laughed behind the window of a noodle shop. A troop of pre-schoolers in yellow rain caps split and moved around him, hardly looking back. Ono pulled him to a snack stand, bought him ice cream, another beer.

"No thank you," Tommy said.

"You are welcome!" Ono replied.

Shakily, Tommy trailed his guide to the taxi line and then beyond it. "We walk to boat," Ono said happily. He slapped himself below the ribs. "For liver, walk is good, ne?"

A half hour later Tommy stood puffing on the steps of the ferry terminal. He gazed back at the city. It looked like East Saint Louis on a bad day. Smokestacks and fences, cranes and tugs, barges and oil depots, a grease-green river. Scarcely any snow survived here, though it was cold enough. Across the river along the bulwarked shore, a helicopter beat down through swirling mist. Then a tour bus swung into the harbor lot, parked fastidiously, and discharged a group of elderly tourists. They inched under umbrellas like bright barnacles toward the ferry office.

Tommy stared until his eyes blurred. He found a pay phone: busy. Two a.m. in Wisconsin and now the line was busy. He let the tone pulse in his ear, and he started a memory of camping, years ago, with Elaine and Gus. But then a jostle stopped him: Ono at his elbow. The old man grinned, wall-eyed and perspiring. He extended a slice of Japanese pizza: sweet corn, soybeans, cheese sliding over the fatbread crust.

"Ne?" he said. "Ne?"

The air grew warmer as the ferry pushed out to sea. The huge craft pitched faintly through long blue swells. Tommy listened to the engines and the rain on the steel deck, and he remembered there was rain on the tent that night, the night he wanted to remember, hard rain and thunder booming in the sky, but he had awakened the next morning to dove-song and sunshine on the dewy flank of Castle Rock Creek. Gus was missing from the tent.

But Tommy hadn't worried. Where would the kid go? Where would he want to go? He had stretched in his bag and listened. Doves, a kingfisher, milk cows bawling in the distance. He remembered smelling the wood smoke in Elaine's long black hair. He remembered the sting in his bladder, the rattle of empty beer cans at the foot of his bag. Elaine was just feeling Indian then, excited to share it. He had rustled up camping gear from the Morrison basement: a white man's wealth of multi-colored nylon and canvas, lawn chairs and lanterns and coolers. They even had an air mattress, and a radio that softly hissed the tune of empty sky. He remembered turning and finding Elaine's eyes, wide and ready, their light already risen. He sat up, excited suddenly that Gus was gone.

Elaine whispered, "He's outside!"

They had not made love right away. The greater pleasure had been the sounds of their ten-year-old boy astir outside the tent, thunking firewood with Bailey's ax, then pausing—Elaine whispered he was moved by the dove's call—then thunking again, setting sticks and newspaper, striking matches, arranging the stumps, taking a long piss against a tree trunk and then softly calling, "Mom?"

She did not answer. They smelled fresh smoke. She peeled Tommy from his bag, crawled over him, pulled her bag on top. She raised her shirt and his, connecting flesh. Into his ear she murmured, "Hey . . . I remember you."

"Mmm."

But then ice rattled in the cooler. A flip top fizzed. She sat up.

"It's Sprite," Tommy promised, pulling at her.

"How do you know?"

"He's okay."

"I won't have him drinking."

"He's not."

"How do you know?"

"I'll check."

But she sat on him. Her shirttail snagged on her brown-tipped breasts, then fell. She gathered hair from her face.

"I'm going to quit," she whispered. "Really, Tommy, I'm going to quit. Including beer. You can do what you want, but I have to quit." She whispered, "I started at his age, I never told you, at ten years old."

He remembered stretching beneath her and lifting his knees, puffing out the fusty warmth of the bag. He held her hips and pushed her over. He knelt and peeked through the tent door.

"Sprite."

She looked at him.

"Sprite, Elaine. Really."

She scooted from her underpants, balled them under the mattress. Then man and woman took their places again. The fire popped and the sun rose, the air turned hot and green inside the tent and the cows came down swishing and munching and Tommy Morrison and Elaine Red Cloud Morrison gripped each other, locking eyes for silence, grinding into slow collapse. It was the last he could remember love. And he had lied for it. Now he remembered. The can was beer.

Three hours later, from a starboard window, he watched a large, mountainous island solidify in the watery air. As the ferry docked in Ryotsu, it was snowing calmly, huge flakes disappearing as they touched ropes and railings and the slick black landing.

"Now is cargo," grinned Ono. "Ne? Little bit upgrade, survive my hotel."

The old man led Tommy onto a bus that snaked around the island rim, between mountain and sea, to the cliffs of the northern shore. Here a north sea wind jostled the bus. The driver paused, seeming to collect his courage. Then he turned down a steep and narrow road. On the corners, while the driver cranked the wheel, chunks of the bus hung out over the sea. Ono seemed delighted by this, chattering about the sea's various foods and how best to prepare them, soy or miso, grill or broil. Then at last the bus leveled and rolled into a small harbor town of wooden houses, glazed in smooth white ice.

They stepped from the bus beside tossing boats. Ono breathed deeply of the fishy air, spread his short arms. "Ahh," he celebrated. "Squid!"

The bus pulled away. Tommy looked about for cargo. But there were only the fishing boats, the frothing sea, the heaps of iced nets.

Ono shouted into the wind, "Mister Tommy, you must partake squid of Sado Island!"

"Ono-san, no thank you."

He was undampened.

"Ja, then," he said cheerily, setting off along the slippery quay toward a boat house. "Partake after we boat ride. Ne?"

"No."

Ono stopped his feet but he kept sliding. He slipped and flailed ten feet, far enough that Tommy saw him from a new distance: a frail and ancient child, a scamp dressed in a thin black suit as if for a business meeting, half drunk and going for a boat ride.

"Gomen nasai, Ono-san. No boats for me. Phone call. Ne?"

"Ah! Phone call!"

He struggled back, fumbling at his wallet. He produced a telephone card.

"I'm fine," said Tommy. "Take your boat ride."

The soba shop was dingy and empty but had a phone on the wall between chest high stacks of comic books. Tommy checked his watch. Five a.m. He dialed: no answer.

He didn't have the strength to walk out. He sat in a dim corner, ordered soba and a large Super Dry beer.

"Arigato."

Elaine was sleeping, he told himself. A long night on the phone, and now she had it turned off. She was getting some rest. He poured and drank, his eyes fixed on the flash of the master's knife through a fistful of green onions. When he heard the chuff and jingle of nylon packs, the dull thud of English in the soba shop doorway, he cringed and sank to his corner.

"Irrashai!" shouted the soba master.

Tommy didn't look. His mind had skipped from bliss to agony, from the old Elaine to the newer, angrier one who wouldn't touch him, couldn't speak to him kindly. White European men, she had come to think, were the "advancing pricks of civilization." Americans were their grasping, spoiled, and twisted children. They ruined everything they touched, she said—and Tommy, after the course of his life, had been powerless to disagree. Now, in this isolated soba shop, at the end of the world, it seemed, he could stand nothing so potent now as the sight of his own culture. Nothing so raw as the blush of gaijin tourists.

"Irrashai!"

But there they were. Into the shop stumbled a monstrously large young couple in jeans and parkas and hiking boots. Their hulking packs scraped the ceiling beams as they peered into the shadowy room.

"Can we just sit down?" the woman asked her partner.

"Look," he said. "A fire pit. I wonder if they make the soba right here."

"Peter," she whispered. "What do we do? Do we just sit down?"

"Irrashai!"

"I don't know. I don't know what he's saying."

She moved around behind him, zipped open his pack. "Where's the book?"

She waggled his pack as she searched. They were both tall and handsome, apple-cheeked from a cold walk. The young man was thin and loose-limbed, a little stooped, with a wispy beard and gentle eyes. She was robustly built, the kind of woman who rowed the Charles at four-thirty in the morning.

"Peter. The book."

"I said I don't know."

His irritation was pure and simple, as if she were his sister and he could fight her ten times a day and never doubt himself for a second.

"Let's find another place," she said abruptly, with a huff that blew chestnut bangs from her brow. "This place looks cheesy anyway."

Peter let himself be wagged about as she closed the zippers. "Sure," he said. "Whatever."

But then the master shouted "Irrashai!" once more and they froze.

"What's he yelling for?" she asked no one in particular. "Are we doing something wrong?"

Tommy felt himself smiling. Maybe he was drunk and lonesome, but their need was so simple. His mood lightened a shade, his befuddlement clarifying a bit as a tiny claw of adrenaline raked his fatigue. His voice felt clear and strong, his math teacher voice, and he sent it across the room: "He's saying welcome. You can just sit down. In fact there's room right here."

They made their humpbacked way across the shop, clinking and jangling, towering over the hustling waitress. Tommy stood and pulled out chairs for them.

Kristie was her name. They were from Ann Arbor, graduate students in history, engaged to be married in two years, just starting English teaching contracts in Nagoya.

"Beer?" Kristie exclaimed when she had settled in, turning Tommy's bottle around. His Super Dry was half over. "You're drinking beer alone, in the middle of the afternoon?"

Somehow Tommy didn't mind the intrusion. She leaned close to him, her straight chestnut hair tangled from having pulled a sweater over her head. She regarded him with a blend of suspicion and glee. He was lost for a moment in her face, stunned by how easily he could read the components of her mood. Meanwhile Peter twisted in his chair, popping his spine. "Forgive her," he said. "She's Catholic." He pulled off his stocking cap, scratched his entire head until his thin brown hair stood on end. Then he sank in his chair, relaxing. "You want some beer, Sister Kristine?"

She grinned wider. Her teeth were white and perfect. "Okay. Let's."

Tommy ordered more beer in Japanese. He felt their keen attention.

"Wow," Kristie said at last. Peter scratched his head again.

"No," Tommy said. "I'm lousy. Considering I've been here six months."

Kristie blurted, "No shit!" She finished her first glass excitedly. Foam stuck to her lip. Peter said slowly, gravely, sinking lower in his chair, "Right now, from our point of view, that sounds incredible. You must be having a great time."

No, Tommy thought. He fumbled for a way to express how wounded he felt, how bitter, how sick with worry. But for the moment these sensations seemed to have vanished, leaving behind nothing concrete he could tell them.

Finally he said, by way of approximation, "I live in the snow country."

Kristie leaned closer, Peter farther. "Our Japan book has the most incredible pictures," she said, and Peter asked, "Do you know Kawabata's novel about the snow country? We just bought it in Nagoya. Kristie's been reading it."

"Snow everywhere," she reported. "Hot baths. Sake. This guy from Tokyo goes there to see a woman. They move around in snow tunnels."

She put down her second empty glass. "End of first chapter." She laughed. "It's very strange writing. I'm not sure I'm getting it. But it's very beautiful somehow. Very lonely."

She looked into her glass. "Peter? Peter the fink? Are you letting me get drunk by myself?"

Peter drained his glass and with a flick of his long fingers sent it scooting over the rough-hewn table for her to fill. Then he scratched his head all over again and sank deeper in his chair. He grinned at Tommy. "Glad we met you."

"You saved us from a fight," Kristie said. "We get so yanked off at each other when we can't decide where to eat. I swear someday we're going to starve to death, fighting. You'd do us a big favor if you ordered for us."

She poured Tommy a beer too. Then she looked around the soba shop. It was grimy, unadorned except for the smoldering fire pit and curling wall placards announcing inflated prices.

"So," she said, "we don't know these things. Is this place cheesy or not?"

Tommy laughed. Cheesy. How a word like that could sum things up. A burden seemed to float up from his shoulders. His tongue loosened.

"Cheesy," he said, "and a rip-off. I was about to do an about-face myself. But it's probably our only choice, and here we are."

He extended his glass.

"Kampai."

They touched glasses over the table.

Kristie asked, "So is it really lonely?"

Tommy turned his glass. Kitayama seemed to have left him now. He could hardly feel it. An idea floated up. Had he read this? He shrugged and said, "Loneliness leaves no footprint."

Kristie blurted, "Wow!"

Embarrassed, Tommy kept his head down, peeling at the beer label. "I mean once you stop feeling it, you can't remember. But yes, it is lonely. I think I felt crushed by it, like buried under snow."

He stopped. Kristie wanted to hear more, but he wasn't sure about Peter. What *was* the rest? That he felt much better now, with them? That his son was missing, maybe even dead, but he felt okay now that they were here?

Then Peter sat up. He tried to paste down his hair. "Kristie says in the Kawabata novel the tunnels clog with snow and the trains can't get through."

"No," Tommy replied. "Maybe in the past."

"So, in theory, I mean, we could just ferry back to Niigata, and tunnel through the mountains from there into snow country?"

"Sure."

"Maybe pay you a visit?"

"Absolutely," Tommy said, and then he looked up, hoping their food was on the way. It was: a platter of soba and tempura, steamed pork dumplings, miso soup, pickles and three more tall Super Dry.

"Oh my god!" Kristie cried. "A feast!"

"Absolutely," Tommy told them again. He refilled glasses, feeling the flush of that precious instant before hunger is answered. He reached out and touched their hands, stopped them for an instant. They both looked at him. But he had nothing to say.

"Hot," he warned finally. "Very, very hot."

After eating, they stepped out into sunlight. The wind had calmed. Ice glittered on the masts and lanterns of the squid boats while the sea still churned beneath them. Kristie darted ahead, skidding on the ice with the strong legs and sure balance of a skater. She spun to yell at them, "Slowpokes!"

Peter was a loper, a dawdler. But in a way, with his guide book, he was leading them. At the north end of the fishing village, a stone wall stretched along between beach and mountain, the broad top of it making a walkway. Trailing Tommy, Peter took one slick slab at a time, considerately, as if each deserved its own calibration. He spoke the same way.

"This place is called Sai No Kawara," he said. "Our book says the shrine is known all over Japan."

There was no shrine in sight, though. Beach and wall and mountain curved north and merged at the sea in a jumble of huge stones pounded by waves and rimed with milky ice. Kristie had reached this point. She looked back and Peter waved, murmured, "I guess." She went on, disappearing amidst the spray.

"It's a shrine for lost children," he said. "Still births and early deaths, accidents, suicides, runaways."

Tommy kept walking. He could have been surprised, or moved to collapse, but somehow this wasn't so. Instead he felt surrender, an odd release, as though by this bizarre chance, and in the care of his two friends, he had slipped through the entanglements of hope into pure grief and was free to mourn.

"My son is a runaway," he said. His voice was weak with pain but not forsaken. He was only saying what was, only asking Peter to go in earnest. The young man stopped. He moved a hand through the squiggles of his beard and blinked.

"He's been missing nearly a week."

"Wow. I'm sorry, man."

"And in the town where I work, an American teacher disappeared. We don't know what happened."

"Wow. I'm really sorry."

Peter put his hand on Tommy's shoulder and they began to walk again. Together they bore this mood along the rock wall. Then, among the tumbled stones at the point, the trail dropped through a slippery crevasse, beneath a massive rope. After a half dozen steps it bent sharply upward into the mouth of a cave and Tommy's breath left him. Five hundred pink pinwheels spun in the sea breeze, their plastic stems planted in cracks and piles of pebbles at the grotto mouth, planted between the shoulders of a thousand small stone Buddha that dwelt in shells of ice on every surface of the cave.

He could not walk further. Peter stopped with him. Inside the grotto, Kristie's big frame lunged about.

"Peter! Look at this!"

Tommy turned away. Down to the seashore went the neat little stacks of pebbles, the tiny Buddha, the pinwheels, occupying every niche that nature made, right into the surf.

"Peter!"

Incense burned inside. Here some of the Buddha wore hats and tiny jackets, red cloaks, kimono, and some stood bare, eroded, eyeless. Among them were arranged mementos: teddy bears and matchbox cars, cookie boxes, origami.

"Peter!" Kristie begged. "Please!"

She was crying. Not weeping or sniffling, just crying silently beneath her excitement. At her feet spread a heap of toys that must have fallen from their places. Naked, molding dolls. Rubber animals. An-Pan Man, UltraMan, and Godzilla. Dumbo and Dopey. Stuffed rabbits. Rattles and Nuks, trucks and guns and robots. A horn. A motorcycle. A cup.

"It's so sad," she whispered.

She took the book from Peter and began to read. Tommy felt the impulse to pray. He stepped back to the sand pit where the incense burned and by old instinct dropped to his knees. He had nothing to say. That was just it, wasn't it? Another thing Elaine had been telling him? That he was so comfortable, so privileged, so hell bent on motion and control that he had made no bonds with spirit? That he had nothing to believe? When his self failed, she asked him, where would he be?

Then Kristie blurted loudly, "Oh, now wait a minute!" The guide book flopped open in her big hand. "I'm sorry," she said, "but this is not right."

She dragged a coat cuff across her cheeks, done crying.

"I am sorry, but abortion is not the same as kidnapping, or murder, or. . . ."

Peter put his hands up. "Stop."

"No way. It mixes in abortion with all these other disasters and its not the same thing. It's a separate thing—"

"Goddamn it, Kristie."

"—than a dead real child."

"Stop."

She flared at him. A huff, a toss of the book. She stormed out amidst the pinwheels. Peter followed at his slow pace. She turned before he reached her.

"I know, Peter. I'm not here to crusade for Western values."

He took her hand, but then Tommy rose and Peter's voice rose angrily with him.

"You see?" he fumed. "The spell is broken. You put your Western context on it and it's ruined. We can't be part of it anymore. We're critics now, outsiders. We're jerks."

She hung her head as Tommy joined them.

"I just think abortion is a separate thing," she answered glumly.

They stood there in silence a long time, facing the sea. A large trawler chugged away to the west. A squid boat motored toward the harbor. Tommy wanted to touch them both, pull them together around him like a blanket.

"I know," said Peter finally. "I know."

Back in the village they strolled together. To ease them toward cheer again, Tommy talked of Kitayama. He told of heatless houses and meters of snow, dwindling classes and the failing school, the impossible beauty of sagging cedars and a steaming, sparkling, snow-flanked river. That was enough water for him, he chattered on, just one river, with its small beauties. This ocean before him was overkill. Too vast. Too frightening. He explained how he secretly hated boats, bobbing around, and hated recreational sailors all wind-chapped and thirsty for champagne. And real men of the sea, he claimed, were a brutal, insensate breed. Now *freeze* the ocean, he told Kristie and Peter, and I'll happily skate from here to the Strait of Magellan.

He could have talked on and on, but then the putt-putting squid boat blew its horn inside the jetty, and Tommy hushed. He could make out bare-headed, black-suited Yoichi Ono, waving upon the deck.

The old man raised his arms, hollered, "Oy!" Then from the cabin a crewman shooed out two black-haired young women. They huddled behind Ono beneath the lamps and hooks on the starboard rail. As the boat drew up to the dock, the crew burst around these awkward figures, throwing ropes.

Grinning, Ono raised his arms again. "Oyyyy!" he celebrated, and he tottered down the plank toward them. Behind, shivering shoulder to shoulder, trailed the two young women. Ono turned, urged them to keep up. He spoke neither Japanese nor English.

"Peter," Kristie said. "It's that weird guy again."

Tommy murmured, "You know him?"

"Before we met you," Kristie said, "he was out here yelling at a fisherman. Chewing his butt real good."

Ono skated between the three Americans and grinned up.

"Hungry, ne? Everybody hungry. Now to eat."

He turned to the young women. He spoke their language again in a harsh way. As if he were channeling the sarcastic Elaine, he seemed to say, *Smile. These are important people. These are Americans.*

Tommy looked at them more closely. Only one managed the smile: a short girl with a stiff curl above her forehead and frightened eyes beneath. The other girl was tall and thin and plainly fierce-looking. She glared back at Tommy. Their clothing was new but dirty and not right for the weather. The tall one carried a small gym bag, woefully cheap. She put her arm around the other girl and said something harsh to Ono. When she finished, they could hear the trawler putt-putting out to sea.

Tommy felt Kristie and Peter staring at him. He turned his hands out. "I don't know," he said. "I'm not involved in this."

But Ono took his arm. "Okay now, Mister Tommy? We partake famous squid of Sado Island?"

Tommy looked from Kristie to Peter. She was chewing her lip. Peter seemed to be nodding faintly. He reached up slowly beneath her hair and touched her neck.

"So . . . you two are together?"

"We came together," Tommy said. "From Kitayama. He has a hotel there. But I'm not involved in this. Whatever this is."

Peter's eyes fluttered, trying to rest somewhere. Tommy looked at the girls once more. The shorter one with the giant bang curl was trying her smile every which way. She had odd, heavy legs that seemed to be collapsing beneath her. The taller one coughed hard. At last Ono detected the awkwardness. He threw a nod at the girls.

"They exodus Thailand," he said happily, as if that explained everything. "Dancers, ne? Survive my hotel. New hotel, no dancers." He winked at Tommy. "You like dancers, ne?" He tried to direct them toward the village. "Now, to eat the squid?"

Peter said slowly, "Ah, I think we're going to head back to the ferry."

"Ah!" said Ono. "Yes! Ferry! We go ferry! I pay taxi!"

Nobody answered exactly. But they were stuck together. There was no return bus for hours, and just one taxi, and soon all of them were crowded inside it, with Ono making his Old Testament chatter, the girls smelling like fish and smoke and engine oil, all of them stuck together all the way to the ferry terminal. At the ticket machines, Peter and Kristie listened without expression while Ono extolled the virtues of the high-speed hydrofoil. Producing cash, he bought tickets for all. Then they watched him work a vending machine for a supply of beer and sake. Kristie whispered in Peter's ear. Peter slipped away, bought two tickets for the slower ferry. "We'll think about that snow country trip sometime," he said to Tommy. "We'll be here all year."

He shook Tommy's hand. "I'm not part of this," Tommy claimed once more. Kristie gave him a mixed-up smile and they were gone.

It was not until the four of them, Tommy, Ono, and his smuggled cargo of two Thai girls, traveled through the winter darkness of the mainland mountains that Tommy spoke again.

"Ono-san."

The old man slept, rocking with the train's motion. "Ono-san, what is this? You can't involve me in it, you know. I'm not going to watch them for you."

But Ono had spent himself and he would not wake up. His head drummed the train window. Tommy eased the slopping beer can from his grip and threw it away.

"Ono-san, can you speak to them? I think they're going to bolt. Chotto exodus, ne?"

For an hour he had been watching them argue quietly. The short girl with the bang flip had grown agitated and weepy while the tall one grew rigid and furtive. The train was packed and slow, groaning upgrade into the spine of snow country. It stopped every few minutes, dropping a soul or two into knee-deep snow at some remote village, letting on another. Each time the old conductor wobbled through for tickets, the tall girl had fled into the toilet, taking her little bag. Then, feeling alone, Bang-Flip Girl made urgent goo-goo eyes at Tommy, the conductor, anyone she might soften.

"Ono-san—"

Tommy gave up.

In a half-hour more, a fair-sized town gutted the train of passengers and the girls began to whisper loudly. The tall one urged some action upon the shorter one, who quickly lost the debate and dissolved into sobbing. Then the train emerged from a tunnel and slowed at the zenith of dark obscurity. The tall girl looked about wildly as the train stopped and opened its doors onto snow and cedars. It was a lightless stop, some kind of shuttered hiking outpost, and still the train paused there as if in a yawn, its boarding bells ringing. Bang-Flip Girl made a teary smile at

Tommy. Then the bells stopped and the doors hissed. "Yaa!" the tall girl cried. She tugged the other, and they jumped out.

Tommy yelled, "Ono!"

Nothing. The doors shuddered, half-closed. The brakes let go.

"Damn it!" Tommy took half the car in two strides. "Ono!" He bulled his way through the pinching doors, leapt free into a drift to his shoulders. "Goddamn it!" he yelled at Ono's head as the train pulled away. "I'm not part of this!"

Then the snow shocked him into silence. It stung his ears and fingers, melted down his neck. His knee hurt where the door clipped him.

"You'll die out here!" he hollered at the tall girl as she pulled the other toward the road.

They were decked in snow, phosphorescent in the moonlight. Tommy's voice rang. The train had vanished into a tunnel. Then he found solid ground and started after them.

Chapter 21

Something woke Noriko suddenly. She sat up beneath her quilt and waited, her pulse quickened. What was it?

She rose with the quilt around her. Husband snored beside in his futon, fully dressed, stinking like sake, and by this she knew that she had been spared. She shoved her window screen. It snowed still. There was nothing else outside.

She stepped across Husband and slid the door open. Into her slippers, she huddled down the squeaky planks past Father and Mother's room, past the scents of sake and tobacco from the meeting room, past the kitchen to the genkan. They must have all been very drunk in the end. Mayor had left his umbrella. Police Chief Ebana had dropped his Kents among the boots. But these things had not awakened her.

She rattled back the heavy front door. It was the same view. She lit one of Ebana's cigarettes and stood a moment in the cold draft, then shoved the door shut and carried the cigarette into the kitchen. The old house was cold as a shed at night and she didn't need the refrigerator anymore. She could leave food out anywhere. She lifted the lid on a pot of pumpkin dumpling soup. The soup was frozen on the top. All the burners were off. Rice soaked for morning.

So what awakened her? She thought a moment. Maybe a better question was this: how had she ever slept? She must have been exhausted. She must have given up.

"Why," Father had raged at Ebana, early in the meeting, "why, why, why was I not notified instantly when the suitcase was found?"

"Because your daughter and the gaijin—" began Ebana, but the police chief stopped himself. He could have hurt her then, could have told them about the love hotel, but releasing this secret would get him nothing. He had cast a cold eye on Noriko. He was saving it.

"Anyway," Mayor put in, "that is past. Now, what shall we do?"

Noriko threw her cigarette out the back window. It died in a small hiss. She wondered if hunger had awakened her, and she began to eat the frigid gummy dumplings and stewed pumpkin in their salty soup. Poor Mayor, she remembered. He had wanted to stop the finger-pointing and pointless tirades. He had wanted to find a proper action. But Husband had jumped on him.

"What do you mean, what shall we do? What *can* we do? Idiot! We're ruined!"

Then Mama Yama had rubbed Husband's shoulders and said to Noriko, "Your dumplings are too small. Men do not like small dumplings. They like big dumplings. Now go in the kitchen and find some shiitake. They need shittake for their nerves."

Police Chief Ebana said, "We investigate. We see what that donkey-assed hakujin was up to. We arrest him."

Then Husband leaned across the table, pointing. Noriko knew the pose well. "Mister Stuart," he seethed, "did not have a donkey ass. He had a rabbit ass, like a queer."

Ebana snorted. Mayor made the correction for Husband. They were talking about the ass of Mister Tommy.

Husband sat back. "Stuart was a queer," he persisted, and emptied his sake cup. Then he looked at Noriko. "Don't just stand there," he snapped. "Get the shittake."

Mayor said, "But how does that help anything?"

"Mushrooms help the blood pressure." Husband scowled at him. "Most people know that."

"To arrest Mister Tommy," Mayor clarified. "For what?"

Perhaps that question had awakened her, Noriko thought. Or rather, the answer that Ebana had given. The chief had eyed her as he spoke, telling the committee that Stuart had saved a million yen, that the bank envelope and receipt for this were in the suitcase but the money was missing. Arrest Mister Tommy for theft, Ebana said, and then the whole lot of them had fallen silent, Father wheezing loudly and rubbing his chest.

Then finally Mayor had asked, "But what about Mister Stuart? Where is he? What do we do?"

Standing on the icy kitchen floor, Noriko ate pumpkin dumpling soup until the ladle scraped bottom and the pot was empty. Then she removed her quilt. Wrapping arms around herself, she shush-shushed down the hall to the toilet room. She knelt in her slippers and threw up everything. Then she went back to the kitchen and pulled the quilt around her.

"What do we do?" Mayor persisted.

No one could answer. But after a period of quiet, Noriko remembered, Father and Police Chief Ebana had somehow cut to the essence of an ancient conflict.

"I say Donkey-Ass killed Golden Hair," said Ebana. He sucked his cigarette hungrily. His eyes flickered over Noriko. "Donkey-Ass and Ono. They were up to something when we stopped them on the night of the party."

Mayor had taken his glasses off, sighed deeply, and rubbed his face. Husband had looked to Father. Noriko had set down a dish of shittake and bamboo shoots and Mama Yama made a dissatisfied face. "More sugar," she said.

"Leave it alone," Father decided finally.

Ebana snorted.

"For seven months now Mister Stuart has been somewhere." Father swallowed. "And that has apparently caused no conflict for anyone. Meanwhile, we have made progress here in Kitayama. Our first factory will open in the business park this spring. The newspapers will be here. Where is Mister Stuart? What should we do? Why should we do anything? Why should we ask the question? Leave it alone."

Ebana snorted again. "Sure. Pretend nothing is wrong. What is one more lie among the Yamaguchis?"

And then Husband was leaning over the table again, jabbing his finger at the police chief. "And what will you do, huh? Stirring everything up? Just because your wife loves gaijin."

The police chief had made a grimace of heartburn and disgust and put his cigarette out. Now he had a use for his information. "Yours too," he told Husband.

"You lie!"

Ebana laughed. Husband lunged. Noriko had been on the threshold of the room with the re-seasoned shittake dish, and she had stepped back quickly as the bodies thrashed. She had put the dish in the kitchen and run to her room. She had crawled beneath her blanket, trembling. Somehow, awaiting blows that never came, she had slept. In the end, Husband had been too drunk to hurt her.

And so why wake up now? Why else but to run, now, while she had the chance? She raked the outside door back once more and stared out into the snow, thinking as she had three years ago, before the wedding, that she should leave now, go to Takata, Niigata, Tokyo, be a bar hostess, tour guide, office lady. She would go now, she told herself. But the snowflakes curled in the yard light and flung themselves against her, saying no, no, no. . . .

Somehow no. It was not the urge to flee that had awakened her. And then finally, feeling air rush past her into the yard, she knew: it was too warm in the house.

Sure enough, a blue glow and a faint hissing came from the meeting room. Noriko shuffled back down the plank hallway and saw it: the men had left the heater on. This was it. Danger had awakened her. This was how houses burned and death came in Kitayama: men drinking on winter nights after the women had gone to bed. Heaters burning, walls and tatami bursting into silent flames, whole houses becoming roaring bonfires.

Staring at the blue flame, Noriko inhaled deeply from another of Ebana's Kents. Then she stepped out of her slippers and into the meeting room. She crossed the tatami and knelt before the heater. They had left the screen open too. She looked out at the same winter view: the stone display shed across the road with its lanterns and gravestones buried in snow to their tips, the saw shacks gathering in snow beneath their cones of light, the mountain paths erased, her truck drifted in, the road buried in a half-meter of new snow.

She rose then. Her head spun from the cigarette. Again her eyes were caught in the heater's ring of blue flame. Had it come to this, she wondered, for Stuart too? Had it come to a moment where control was gone and inspiration stormed the soul and life could change forever?

She reached down through her own blurred view. The handle on the heater's top burned her, but she needed only an instant to jerk it off base. It tipped toward her, its fall arrested at knee-height by the kotatsu.

She backed away. The flame spit and smoked, then flared orange. Its angry light leapt upon the walls. Life could change, she thought, or end.

She hooked her foot around the far leg of the kotatsu and pulled it back. As she ran toward her bed, the heater fell.

Chapter 22

Tommy stood still. His shout died quickly among snow-robed cedars. The train became a faint cold squeal in the rails. His knee screws stung. He watched the taller girl retrieve her bag. She lurched away a few steps. Then she must have gone off the edge where the platform ended. She plunged in snow to her neck. She cursed, stumbling over things she couldn't see, while somehow the shorter one, seal-like, made her way back to the tracks. In a moment they were both there, clinging to one another and shaking.

"You'll die out here!" Tommy yelled again, "You'll freeze!"

He looked around. He could make out no trail of footsteps, no stairs leading off the platform, no benches or turnstiles or trash cans. These things, if they existed, were only contours in the snow, glazed and gleaming under a weak spotlight.

The larger geography was much more clear. Trackless mountains rose on all sides. Tunnels opened east and west. They were high in the range that walled in snow country.

As Tommy waded to the tracks, the tall one yelled something at him. Her voice was a spark of heat, quickly spent. She cradled her little gym bag and shivered.

"You got your toothbrush in there," he said back hoarsely, "or something else?"

He reached for the bag. The girl twisted away, spat back in English, "Leave alone shit man."

"You understand me then? If that's drugs, we're going to bury it right here."

She shook her head and glared. She shrank her hands inside her cuffs. Her partner snuggled in, crying quietly.

"You're going to freeze to death out here."

"Leave alone."

"You have to be kidding," Tommy said.

In the cold silence he begged himself for calm. He walked off a short distance. The tracks intersected a narrow road that was packed hard, scattered with frozen chain cleats. There were no signs of life in the valley below. Through the trees above, a single light shone. He looked back at the girls. Snow clung in bright clumps to their thin clothes. Move, he told himself. Any direction. Move or die.

"All right," he said. "Let's go. There's a light above us. Take turns in my coat and let's start walking."

The tall one grew roots and turned her face away. Tommy hung his coat on the short plump one and she raised her face. First the huge curl came up, glittering with snow crystals. Then wet, pleading eyes. Then she smiled.

"You like me?" she asked. "Okay sir?"

"Just move."

He herded them off at a fair pace behind the train platform and into a deep grove that echoed with the sound of trickling water. They made a kilometer along a low grade, but then the road turned uphill steeply, and the small one hadn't the strength or coordination for climbing. She moved only from the knees down, her feet swinging around in sideways arcs, driven it seemed by a single overworked muscle above the ankle. She grew tired immediately and began to sink toward the road. The other girl pulled her onward. But they were going nowhere fast. And the light above proved illusive, farther off than it seemed, then invisible between the snow-thickened trees. It had been switched off, Tommy thought, or it was never there at all. He turned.

"Names," he said. "What are your names?"

The slow one panted steam at him, smiling. A tree limb had dumped snow on her. "I name Sudra."

"Nice to meet you, Sudra."

"Nice too," she said. Her bang curl sailed away from her forehead three whole inches and then coiled back toward the top of her head, leaving off just before full circle. She thought it protected her, Tommy decided, a permanent, prosthetic cuteness. Her smile pulled him back. She pointed to the other girl. "She is May."

Tommy took his coat off Sudra and put in on May. "Nice to meet you, May." But May glowered at him and shivered, clutching her sad little bag. Now Sudra shivered too.

"Okay," Tommy said. He felt his stomach tighten, his body closing ranks against the cold. "I'm Tommy. Let's keep moving."

They hiked another half hour, and when they reached the light at last it shone down a spike road into the mountain, lighting a narrow tunnel of plowed snow marked by a peeling billboard. As Tommy read slowly, sounding out the katakana, the shivers caught him. His chest felt cold and he coughed. *Trout park,* the sign read.

Rainbow trout.

Yamame trout.

Char.

Three fish for one thousand yen.

Closed for the winter.

And then he whispered, "Fuck," and his word fell away, less than a snowflake. His cough fell away, his puffing breaths. Then abruptly into the ancient trees dissolved his life-long certainty that he was safe and could protect himself. He was nothing to these huge trees, these tons of rock and snow, this creeping cold. He was freezing now and his teeth hammered.

Trout park.

Open May to September.

He coughed again. The Thai girls huddled behind him, sharing the coat, waiting. But the rest of the sign meant nothing to Tommy. He could do nothing to understand, nothing to change where they were. He heard Elaine's voice again. *Maybe someday you'll feel powerless. Then you'll know.*

Okay, Elaine, he answered. His heart labored dangerously. *What is it I know? What can I do with it?*

He coughed a third time. His muscles had formed a tight case around his chest. He started to move then. He led Ono's cargo down the spike road, but the trout park was no more than an attendant's shack. From its snow-loaded eave, a single bulb pushed back darkness across two ponds and a flat bed truck with a vat chained in its bed. A hose fed the vat, and frozen overflow piled up like candle wax down the tailgate into the snow. *Steal it,* Tommy thought. *Steal this truck,* he commanded himself, and he suddenly recalled a day in Detroit five years ago when his rental car window had been smashed, his trip bag stolen. He had told Elaine he felt violated, afraid, and Elaine's laughing, taunting voice had come back through the wires, correcting him. "You feel violated? *You* feel afraid? Think about the poor guy who had to steal it!"

Tommy kicked the ice column against the truck's tailgate. He kicked it again, and again, his fear of freezing a momentary fury, and finally he broke free a piece as thick and heavy as a fire hydrant. He staggered with this great weight through a drift and staved in the shack door. Inside, he searched: a barrel of fish food, an empty till, a hundred squashed-out cigarette butts. In a drawer stuffed with pornographic comics he found a key, and the truck engine fired.

But higher on the mountain, after the road forked north, he could not feel saved. Instead, he felt haunted. He should have led them down the mountain, he worried. He should have kept them in the shack until daylight. At the fork, he should have turned south. He should have checked for gas in the truck, and now the dash was black. As these uncertainties scattered his thoughts, he saw headlights in his mirror, and then he didn't. He was followed, or he wasn't. It was help, or it was Kappa. He thought of Kappa. Why? He didn't know. He was afraid.

The road climbed and twisted deeper. Tommy drove the truck hard, his hands knotted on the wheel. Beside him, May sat in rigid protest, her angry eyes drawing a bead through the cracked windshield and across the rusty hood to the road's dim whiteness. Sudra chattered hopefully in Thai, her hands on May, her eyes desperately active.

"We'll be okay," Tommy croaked. He checked his mirror. He felt May's glare, Sudra's smile. But on the next turn the grade became too steep and the snow too deep. The truck began to shudder and slip. Tommy pumped the stiff clutch on corners to make the wheels dig. Sudra had risen to her knees on the seat. She was watching through the back window and now she cried out in Thai. She wanted May to look, but May refused. May cursed something and stared straight ahead. Then Sudra wanted Tommy to look. He spared a glance into his side mirror: a thin shape flashed and spun, turned briefly red, then vanished behind the truck. Then a large flicker, wriggling upward, plunging back through the tail lights. Trout. The trout were jumping ship.

"Stop!" said Sudra.

May cursed her.

"I can't stop," Tommy said. He gulped the clutch as the wheels slipped. On a wave from the vat, a dozen more trout hurled off into darkness. It seemed then that May told Sudra to shut up and turn around, not to concern herself with fish, but Sudra wouldn't. She seized May's arm and hung on while May thrashed and argued and then her foot shot out and kicked the gear stick from Tommy's hand. In that critical instant the truck flagged, bogged down, and Tommy cranked into a switchback with failing momentum, his tires slipping on the soft inside corner. The side of the road vanished beneath his door. The vat sloshed. A dozen rainbows vaulted out into the hole of the night.

"Stop!" wailed Sudra. "Fish!"

The truck lunged toward the road's edge, tires fizzing. Tommy felt his feet drive pedals down into nothing. He saw the snow-frosted tops of the trees beneath them. Then his right rear wheel struck something. From beneath Tommy came the dull clang of guardrail, and they were shuddering back into the road, gaining altitude at a crawl toward the summit.

Tommy's voice came out grim and frail. The spot where his breath came from had shrunk somehow. It was too tight to push air.

"Sit still," he managed, "both of you. And shut up."

"Shit man," muttered May.

"Try this without me," Tommy panted back.

The road leveled briefly at the summit. There was a turn out, a scenic overlook, and a hundred meters on, where the descent started, a boarded up snack stand, a tour bus stop, and a pay telephone. Tommy stopped the truck. He set the emergency brake and took the key.

Elaine's phone rang and rang. Then at last there came a click and a muffled voice said, "Yeah?"

"Elaine?"

A stranger's voice: "Who's this?"

"This is Tommy Morrison. You're in my house."

The line made thumping sounds, as if the phone were being tossed across a carpet.

"Tommy? Hey, where you at, man? China or something?" It was Robert Red Cloud, Elaine's big brother. "You got news, man? What's going on?"

Tommy stared off at the moonlit snowscape. There were valleys on both sides, then more mountains. Somehow the girls had turned on the dome light inside the truck.

"You tell me, Robert."

"We're just answering the phone, you know? We're watching cartoons on cable. You got no news?"

"Where's Elaine?"

"Oh, man. Little sister, she's out. She took something, man. She's sleeping."

Laughter rose in the background, then the Looney Tunes theme. "By the way," said Robert Red Cloud, who had run away a dozen times himself, "don't you guys have a can opener?"

Tommy hung the phone up. He ground his teeth and closed his eyes. When he opened them he knew what he would see: the trout truck, May at the wheel, rolling silently downgrade, engineless but picking up speed. And then, before he could leave the booth and clear the snow pile into the road, the truck was gone.

Chapter 23

He limped downhill all night, through tunnels and around switchbacks, building a grim admiration for May's skill and strength. Then he found the truck at last, at dawn, lodged in deep snow beyond a tight curve, a hundred feet from the road amidst the knobby trees of a pear orchard. The cab was empty.

Tommy sat inside and rested. Slowly, the sun escaped East Mountain and burst over the deeply shadowed gap of Kitayama valley. He was too far north, Tommy saw, but home. He started the truck and backed it out.

He found the girls about a mile down on the floor of the valley, huddled in the shack of a wooden sandal maker, surrounded by stacks of sandal blanks and shivering before a small fire. Scattered about the coals were the heads and bones of trout. May growled like a mad dog, but Sudra jumped up, took his hands and rubbed them. "Okay?" she wanted to know. "Okay?"

"Okay," Tommy said.

His jaws were numb. He sat on the sandal maker's stump. It was his feet that burned with cold. He removed his boots and sat on them, fearful that May would toss them on the fire. He held his sock feet above the coals. Sudra fed him morsels of roast trout, pinched between her long fingernails. She carried in handfuls of snow. She gripped his ears in her palms. All the while May sulked and scoffed. Finally Tommy said, slowly and carefully, "Escape later."

Sudra met his eyes.

"Do you understand? Escape later. Not now. Later."

Sudra turned to May and, for the first time, she spoke powerfully, as if this had been her point all along. May scowled at the fire.

"Later," Tommy said. He talked with his hands. "Go to the hotel with Mister Ono. Get money, food, clothing. Then think about escape. Later."

Sudra looked at him. Her large brown eyes glowed with comprehension. She nodded. "Later," she said.

Beyond the next corner, the truck rolled into a tiny village: lamps aglow beneath thatched roofs, the yellows and blues of school uniforms as children moved at the windows. As yet, not a soul had seen them. And May was quiet now, slumped against the door. Tommy let a breath out. Then another one. He thought they might make it.

It was dark yet as they rolled into the pit of the valley. But the sky had opened above them, blue and still. Tommy slowed within the thin cover of a mulberry grove. Ahead was the long, open decline between rice paddies to the Hot Water River. The fields were clean as vast sheets of white paper. Smoke curled from the clay chimneys of the scattered farmhouses. Above the river, the train line reached a vacant northern station.

"We'll leave the truck here," Tommy said as they reached a narrow bridge over the river. He backed down a tractor trail, set the brake and left the key. As they walked up to the bridge he felt Sudra's hand slip into his. He smiled inside. Then she pulled at him. She wanted him to stop, to look back. She pointed at the vat of trout, at the climbing sun, at the river so close. "Please?' she asked him. "Please, nice man?"

"No. We have to get to the station."

She tugged his hand. "Please? Fish?"

"Look, you're not even supposed to be here." He watched a frown collect beneath her impossible bang curl. "You get caught now, putting fish in the river, and you—"

But he didn't know. He glanced up behind them. The road appeared in vacant fragments, curving down. What would happen? Back to Thailand? Soapland? A Japanese jail?

"Please fish," begged Sudra, tugging him, and Tommy shrugged and climbed into the truck bed. For the next half hour, one eye on the tracks above, he shoveled rainbow trout with a broken-handled net, flipping them down into the sparkling current. Sudra spoke sharply to May. Then the two of them waded knee-deep into the icy water, urging the trout upstream, fighting the river with a torrent of Thai.

Then, on the train at last, May slumped into exhaustion. She slid down the seat as she lost consciousness, her jeans twisting up into her vulva and her small head bouncing on Sudra's shoulder. A large black gap showed at the canine when her lips split to breathe.

Sudra smiled. "May sleep," she said.

The sun shone down strongly. Tommy felt passably calm on the warm seat. He might have dozed himself had the train not stopped at every crossroad to let on puffy-eyed students. They stumbled on, breakfast on their lips.

"Gaijin!"

He closed his eyes to a thin line, leaned his head on the warm glass. As the train curved through North Tunnel, the junior high school kids began jostling toward the door to get out.

A moment later, the train wobbled into the bright morning edge of Kitayama, coasting on squealing brakes toward the station. The sun gave the three meters of snow a cloying, suffocating effect. It seemed to give off heat. Tommy glanced at May, still sleeping, and then at Sudra, but her soft smile had crumpled. Once more her eyes had gone round with fear.

He followed the path of her terror beyond the windows to the station. There, high school kids flooded the Kitayama platform, waiting to go to Takata. Amidst them like a stone in a river stood Officer Wada, his gaze solidly on the train.

Sudra gasped, shook May. The thin girl awoke quickly. She threw her hair back, squinted through the window at the huge policeman, then spoke wildly in Thai. Sudra collapsed in tears. May cursed her, pulled her to her feet. She said to Tommy, "Shit man."

"Just stay calm."

She eyed Tommy as if calculating something. Then suddenly all the other passengers were in motion. Tommy clawed a handful of bills from his pocket. He pushed the cash into May's hand.

"Take a taxi to Ono Hotel. Stay away from me. Don't cry. Don't yell. Don't speak Thai."

Then he was shoved back by a scrum of rowdy boys, incoming. He lingered, stalling, creating distance. After a moment, May and Sudra emerged on the platform, balky and shivering, utterly alien. Then May began to drag Sudra toward the taxi line. Wada rotated to watch them.

Tommy raised his arms, squeezed his way to the door. He would go straight to Wada, distract him. But as he stepped onto the platform a voice called him.

"Gaijin-san! Gaijin-san!"

A thin boy came at him full speed, then skidded to a cartoon stop while his mates laughed from the windows.

"Gaijin-san! Bag!"

The boy thrust forward May's pathetic little gym bag. Now it hung in Tommy's fingers. Clever May. He turned straight into the rushing bulk of Wada.

"Tommy-san!"

"Wada. Konnichi-wa."

The big man took in a big breath and held it. He held a dictionary in one hand. He looked excited and struggling to contain the feeling. He clapped a hand onto Tommy's shoulder.

"Nice travel?"

Tommy couldn't move. His heart felt hard and sore in a corner of his chest, like a cramped calf muscle. His tongue was thick and dry. Now the girls approached a taxi. Sudra wept again. May yelled at her in Thai. Every eye at the station had found them. Wada's too. Tommy's brain skipped, flashed to thirty years in Japanese jail, to Wisconsin in the twenty-first century, to Gus, alive or dead, settled, grown-up, gone.

"Mister Tommy. Is girlfriend?"

"I don't know them."

"Is girlfriend?"

"No."

His finger marked a page in the dictionary.

"I receive phone call," he managed. "You drive truck?"

"No."

"Fish truck?"

"No."

He made scooping motion. "Fish. In river?"

"No, Wada. I don't know what you're talking about."

Tommy broke the policeman's grip and walked ahead, clutching the little bag like a steam iron, thinking it was better this way, that he could smash with it, run, make something happen.

But Wada kept up easily. He returned his hand to Tommy's shoulder. He still seemed happy. Maybe he couldn't believe his luck. He lifted an arm and aimed it past the girls, out beyond the taxi line toward his patrol car.

"Mister Tommy, please to police box?"

At least Police Chief Ebana was absent, Tommy thought as Wada led him in. But the dog in proxy stirred from beside the heater and jumped in suspicion at Tommy's legs. He sat in surrender, letting it growl and sniff. Wada reached for the bag, set it on the chief's desk. Then the officer pushed the dog aside and brought a phone to Tommy's lap. Tommy stared at it. A lawyer? The embassy?

"Mister Tommy, please. Call to wife."

Slowly understanding, Tommy's fingers moved over the buttons. As he listened to the phone ring in Elaine's kitchen, his body felt right there with her: midnight, exhaustion, their nervous anticipations colliding. This was it.

"Jesus, Elaine."

He let her hear the tension in his voice, the readiness.

"Jesus. Do you have to call the damn police station?"

Her voice had an edge, too. "They always find you."

Tommy took a deep breath. He glanced at Wada. Wada grinned.

"Okay. Tell me."

"The cop didn't tell you?"

"I don't think he could."

"Gus is in L.A."

Tommy's pulse jumped and he smiled. He felt a strange pride.

"He got that far, huh?"

"No. He got to Barstow. But the hospital there didn't know what to do with him."

"What happened?"

"What didn't happen?"

He took a deep breath. Wada held the gagging dog.

"Come on, Elaine."

She said nothing.

"Elaine, what happened?"

She let out a breath, cleared her throat. "He's okay. He was dehydrated, sunburned. He ate something somebody gave him. He was robbed, maybe beaten. He won't tell me anything. It's a great country, isn't it? Real advanced civilization."

Tommy was distracted suddenly. The dog had escaped Wada and begun to jump at the bag, whining. Wada grabbed at it.

"But he's okay? Are you going out to L.A.?"

"Grandpa Rupert's on the way already. That's who he said he belonged to."

"Grandpa Rupert?" Tommy tried to picture it, the stiff old Winnebago in L.A., without his Winnebago, thinking he was still in Wisconsin, trying to hoof it from the airport to the hospital, across on-ramps and God knew what neighborhoods. And then the two of them together, Gus convincing the daft old man he needed to see a dozen movies to get well, needed lifetime Dr Pepper, needed an apartment, a car, sanctuary from his awful parents. Grandpa Rupert would do anything.

"Jesus, Elaine."

"I know."

The dog began to bark loudly. "What's that?" she asked.

Now Tommy felt his full game sweat. His thoughts narrowed quickly to a dark tunnel into which he took a small careful step: "I helped these two Thai women. I think they're prostitutes. Now there's a police dog barking at a bag I ended up carrying."

"Is there something in it?"

"I'm not involved in this, Elaine. Really."

She was silent. He guessed what she was holding back.

"Is there something in the bag, Tommy?"

"Well, maybe." He stood. He was sure Elaine could hear the tremor in his voice. "Yes. I guess there is."

She was quiet a moment. Then she said, "Oh shit, Tommy," like she was honestly afraid for him. "Oh holy shit. What have you done? Are you going to be okay?"

"Maybe." He watched Wada throw the dog away and scold it. "If I leave right now."

There was a moment of heavy silence between them where Tommy felt they had embraced. Then Elaine said, "So go."

"The boy is lucky," he told her. She didn't answer. "Elaine? Have you told him that? He's lucky."

Wada saluted Tommy as he stepped free from the police box. He started quickly toward downtown. At the first alley he dodged in, tossed the bag into a flaming burn barrel. Then he stopped, overwhelmed by the clear warmth of the air, by the full, embracing plumpness of melting snow. He breathed in deeply and held it, wanting to feel himself solid again, wanting to stop the rubbery tremors that had seized his heart.

Lucky!

Chapter 24

The flames first followed the splash of gas across the tatami as Noriko dodged away. They flashed high and hot, making the screens rattle in the window frames. Then they drew down quickly and smoldered like a grass fire, spreading across the old straw mats. The smoke was fragrant. It streamed through the old house's cracks and fissures, through its paper doors and warped windows, smelling like burnt straw cured by a century of bare feet and salty food, tobacco and spilled sake, old straw cured just so and set afire as if in sacrament to the past.

The old house went up. The paper doors at the entrance to the meeting room lifted flame to the beams and sent it along a line of dry laundry to the kitchen. While in one direction it gnawed at the spine of the building, in the other it scorched through bags of onions and rice and dried seaweed, through Noriko's aprons and towels and slippers, fizzed across the sweet bean dumplings on the table, then backed up and took the table itself. The windows whistled as air rushed in. The rice cooker exploded. Tracers of wet rice hissed through flames.

It was the fast collapse of the genkan that finally roused Mama Yama. The flames had turned back around the tipped kotatsu and burned through Father's newspapers and over the shelves of masks and wooden dolls and old photographs. It scorched across these, then quickly popped the thin mud-and-straw wall and feasted on boots and umbrellas in the genkan. In moments, the heavy tile roof crashed in, waking the old woman.

Like any Japanese her age, Mama Yama was drilled in earthquakes and bomb raids, both of which led to fire. She knew what was happening and exactly what to do. Noriko heard her cough twice, then slap Father. "Fire," she told him, then fell to a fit of coughing. Within seconds their window rattled open and the two old people thrashed through waist-deep snow in their pajamas. It was a long way around the back of the house to the side where Noriko slept with Husband, and while she waited she wondered if they would truly come. But of course they would. Husband was with her. She raised up. No smoke had reached them yet but the whole house was beating its windows and trembling as air forced its way in to satisfy the flames. Still Husband snored on. Perhaps he felt it was an earthquake. But more likely he felt nothing, heard nothing. She slapped him.

"Husband. Fire."

"Huh?"

As he settled back to sleep, the window rattled. The old woman shouted.

"Yasunosuke!"

This was his name. Not Husband. Not Vice Mayor, as he had just been appointed. Yasunosuke. He sat up sharply at his mother's voice.

"Huh? Mother?"

Noriko lay back, feigned sleep.

"Fire!"

He must have heard the blaze then and felt the supernatural chill of the room. He stumbled to his feet, stepping on Noriko's ankles as he rushed to the window and flung it back.

"Fire, is it?"

"In the front of the house! The genkan's collapsed! Get out!"

"Where's Father?"

"Get out! He's at the saw sheds!"

Would they leave her? Noriko wondered. Was she so bad that she would be left to burn? With the window open she lay directly in a frigid wind that cut through her quilt. Husband jumped out into the snow. He paused a long time. "Come on," he said at last, and yanked her covers off. She sat up. "Eh?"

"Fire," he told her, and they were gone.

The massive tile roof steamed and rattled like a lid on a pot. Flames jumped around it, lighting the sky. No snow fell in this circle of heat. Noriko stood in bare feet on the icy road, watching her crime evolve into she knew not what, but feared, most of all, into nothing. Up the road hurried neighbors to clothe and comfort the family. Mama Yama began to wail and rush the house until a circle of old women closed on her and held her still. And meanwhile Father, who knew this would happen someday, had fixed hoses to his saw-flushing system, and within ten minutes a team of quarry workers unfurled whipping canvas snakes. Soon the entire mountain stream Father diverted to cool his blades was splashing over the house. With a massive, hour-long hiss of steam, the blaze went out.

By morning it was clear that the kitchen was gone, and with it all traces of food and laundry. Charred and broken dishes littered the freezing ash pit of the floor. The meeting room had become an open pavilion under matchstick-black timbers. Somehow the roof over it had not collapsed. Every onlooker praised the massive central beams, which remained stalwart like singed tree trunks after a forest fire.

Through the next day, as the thaw ensued, Noriko absorbed the blame as well as the gossip. She and Mister Tommy were lovers, the story went. Husband, of course, had taught her the proper lesson, and she had cowered in her room. Nevertheless, continued the gossips, she should have never gone to sleep before the men. No son's wife should ever do that, and so in any case the fire was her fault. She had failed at love, at family, at duty. Noriko kept her head down, knowing this talk. She had succeeded, she knew, only in elevating Mama Yama, who perfected a grandly wounded air as she led keening sympathizers through the remains.

But plenty remained. The old house was so massive that an entire generation of rooms survived untouched on the up-mountain side, the rooms of the first Ono household, abandoned in late Meiji as wealth grew, dusty and plain rooms, shut off for a century, and inside them curious still-lifes of old documents and stuffed pheasants, ancient moth-shredded kimono, ceramic pillows, high-pronged geta for walking in mud before the road was paved, a fire pit for roasting and a hole in the straw roof, and in the very back a dim kitchen that was only a floor, a charcoal brazier, and a free-standing bamboo cabinet packed with old dishes and dull knives.

And so Noriko's deed plunged her backward in time. All the next week she cleaned ancient objects and aired old rooms. Like a wife of the bygone century she squatted over the kitchen floor and chopped and diced and mixed. She crawled back and forth. She sharpened knives and blew on coals. Meanwhile, Mama Yama led tours through. Old women chattered as they passed her: *yes, yes, now she knows how it was for us. Chop the leeks more thinly, dear. Yes, sad, but this is what a young woman deserves who cannot take care of her easy life with a fine husband and generous mother in a nice new house. Yes, yes. A shame. Yes.*

The thaw went on through the week, making such a noise at the eaves and puddles that Noriko could not sleep. Up mountain, huge slabs of snow slipped from the saw shed roofs and fell with muffled thumps.

She rose one midnight. It was hard to move around without detection. The old doors stuck, the old floor squeaked and groaned. And the family slept upstairs now, needing to climb up and down a half-timber staircase that rattled windows with each step.

Still, Noriko went downstairs. She had hardly eaten since the fire, but she passed the kitchen without a thought of food. She wrapped herself in an old Ono Stone jacket and went outside, crossing the wet road to the display shed.

Inside, she turned on the one-bulb light. She used to play here, she recalled. On summer afternoons the bus stopped here, across from the Yamaguchi house. The Yamaguchi kids simply crossed the street and they were home, while the rest of the mountain kids walked up or down. But she and her brother Yuji would hang around, waiting for their father to finish in the quarry. It was always cool in the shed, even with the wide doors raised to the sunstruck road. Rarely did anyone come to look or buy. The stone cutting business must have worked another way, by catalog or something. Even now, Noriko didn't really know. But in those days, she and Yuji could play in the shed unbothered and still keep an eye out for Father. The stones were so impressive to her then, their weight so incomprehensible, their surfaces so excitingly cool. Even the smallest of the stone Buddha could not be moved, and this solidity, when Noriko was eight or ten, had become her understanding of Buddha spirit: density, timelessness, a smile of stone. Her brother liked to climb up and walk on their heads, jumping from one brow to another as upon safe stones across an invisible river. The Buddha didn't mind. They smiled on, unbudged. She had followed Yuji once and felt the giddy thrill of his dare, tilting with her head near the steel rafters, always another solid Buddha wherever her wild feet came down.

She looked at them now: little Buddha on the wet floor, stored here with uncarved gravestones and cold lanterns, merchandise. So much had changed. It seemed now that she stood fast on this mountainside in the stream of time. She had survived something, and she felt solid. Yet the little idols seemed insubstantial now. She could tip them aside with one hand. What she could not escape now was her own sudden weight.

Chapter 25

In the morning, as an exercise, she hanged herself. Between breakfast and the time she would need to open Prince School, Noriko unplugged the fat black extension wire from the rice cooker and followed it out of the powerless old house and across the slick road into the stone display shed, pulling the cord in after and disconnecting its other end.

The cord's heavy plugs were easy to throw up through the bare steel rafters. They hung stiffly. She pushed up from below; and they returned to her hands. She made a knot with the male end that slipped back up to the rafter and held fast. Then she tried to make a noose of the other end. She could hear Mama Yama yelling for her, something about how the pit fire wasn't banked right. But what did Noriko know about a pit fire? The old women knew a lot, she admitted that now. They had lived much more difficult lives. They had worked harder than she had ever guessed. Their Husbands were rarely more useful than Husband. They never drove cars or wore pants or studied English. And they could never be young again, in her time. They could never understand her. It was impossible, so impossible that the thought of it made her smile.

Noriko's fingers fumbled with the fat cord. She was unsure what a noose was, except for neat pictures in her mind that could not be reproduced. Then at last a knot held, with a big enough loop at the end.

She climbed as she and her brother had long ago, upon the heads of the little granite Buddha, and then onto just one, both feet crowded onto one small stone pate, and then she kicked it over and swung there, not her head but her strong hands in the noose, thinking yes. Yes, this could be done. Even Stuart could have done this.

She rolled the cord up and took it back inside. She walked next door and knocked. "Please," she asked old Mrs. Ameda. "May I use your phone?"

Down the mountain that same morning, in Officer Wada's tiny apartment, while his wife did laundry and his small boy and girl watched Alf re-runs, the huge young policeman padded out of the bedroom in his Snoopy long underwear and his monogrammed, five-toed socks. He took Noriko's phone call, grunted twice in agreement.

Yes, he would think about places where Stuart could have hanged himself.

"But Gotoh," he laughed. "You're late as usual. I've begun already."

Then he laid out photo albums on the kotatsu, all his proof sheets from a decade of picture taking, since high school and through the abortive sumo period, through the odd jobs and no jobs, the position at City Hall, the valley bus driver stint, the soba roller stint. He was always taking photographs. Through all the stops and starts that drove his family and then his wife crazy, these photographs were the core of Wada that none of them understood.

He poured tea. His children grinned at him, turned back to the television. His wife gasped. Too much soap in the washer!

Wada focused on the hundreds of tiny pictures, quickly lost in them. Through his photographs, he found out the souls of things. Not in the pictures themselves but in the taking of them, the choosing of light and angle and distance and moment. Such an idea was as simple to the huge young man as it was impossible for others to understand. It required a delicacy of character that none would permit him and a gumption that he had long since been judged to lack. Of course his critics, wife and family among them, left him alone now that he was a police officer, as if this were somehow more appropriate for him than a bus driver or a soba maker. Perhaps they were comfortable that size meant power after all. Perhaps this excited them the way sumo did. When he took pictures now, people wanted to think there was a purpose to it, that he was on an investigation, that he was collecting evidence against people, that he was about to pounce and crush, and somehow these fantasies had begun to satisfy in Kitayama people the emptiness he had left by failing them at sumo.

But Wada put these thoughts aside. This time, he *was* on an investigation. He was looking for buildings. Pole shacks. Tractor sheds. Abandoned places. Road crew sag houses. Fishing huts. Places a person could hide and hang.

He looked for an hour, letting the possibilities fill his subconscious. Then he put on his uniform, kissed his wife as she passed his lunch, hugged his children, and drove to the police box. The thaw had reversed, locking water in vast ice sheets everywhere, and now a light snow dusted the ice until it could not be seen. No sooner had Wada entered the box than Chief Ebana snapped at him, sent him back to clear a three-car wreck on Shinmei.

Pole shacks, he thought. Like the one far down south valley, where the rice paddies climbed the mountain until the last was the size of his futon, a meal's worth of rice. Or the sheds at the quarry where stones and explosives were kept. Or there was an abandoned pump station at the bend in the river where the airport project was now.

He honked and waved, seeing Mister Tommy in the phone booth. The white man scowled out, looking for the noise, sick of being honked at, perhaps. It would make a good picture, Wada thought, a white man scowling through a Japanese phone booth. Or a window. Anything with Japanese characters on the glass, the white man framed in anguish within them. He had a picture like this of Mister Stuart.

Hadn't he? Or was it dozens?

"They *what?*" Tommy said back to Elaine.

He knew he was too loud. His voice had escaped the booth. A honk turned him. Officer Wada.

Now Elaine let him live with his shrillness a moment. His aggression. As if he hadn't changed. Not that she was calm, of course. No. Instead of coming home from L.A., Gus and Grandpa Rupert had been camped out at the Anaheim Holiday Inn for the last week and a half. They had been to Disneyland three times, Universal Studios twice, and Gus had been raving to her on the phone about the Terminator set, the Matterhorn, a fist fight on the freeway. Their only limits were Grandpa Rupert's many credit cards—he never turned one down—and the old man's sense of responsibility, in which department, Elaine had stormed in different times, he was pure Indian, substantial as a sparrow.

Tommy asked again, "They what?"

"They're in the air. They're in a plane right now."

Time, space, money, these meant nothing to Grandpa Rupert. He just floated. Now he floated toward Japan.

"Jesus. They won't last five minutes. They won't get out of the airport. Anywhere in particular, Elaine?"

"They land in Narita in the morning. Then they want to see Hiroshima."

"You talked them into it."

"They wanted to see the A-bomb stuff."

"You wanted them to see the A-bomb stuff. With me."

She took a deep breath. "Okay," she said. "I did."

Chapter 26

Ebana watched him now, cruised his alley a dozen times a day, but Tommy slipped away from Kitayama again. Out his apartment's kitchen window just before midnight, along alleys to Shinmei, three hundred dollars for a cab all the way to Takata . . . and six hours and four trains later, at dawn, he was riding the long escalators up into Narita Airport. He called Prince School and left a message for Noriko. He was sorry. He wouldn't be in.

When he met them at the customs exit, Gus was blue and shivering from the plane ride. Grandpa Rupert was hatless and bewildered, hanging on to his big silver belt buckle. They wandered out to a stream-edge of rushing Japanese and stood as if on the banks of the Mississippi River, a long way from a bridge.

Tommy waded across.

"They took his fucking hat," Gus complained.

Grandpa Rupert's oily white hair was dented where a hat had been. His cracked palm felt across the top of his head. His vague eyes followed the Japanese rushing by.

"What hat did they take, Grandpa Rupe?"

"The feathers!" yowled Gus, as if Tommy should have known. "They said he couldn't have the feathers!"

Tommy tried to look back through the customs gates. Fish trap. You didn't go back.

"Shall I ask about your hat, Grandpa Rupe?"

Tommy wondered how Elaine's father could have aged that much in a half year. Maybe the trip had been hard on him. The old man seemed to hear him through the baffles of some deep confusion. And he didn't look well. Like Elaine in a slow burn, his jaw was set and his skin was pale brown like putty. But he wasn't focused. He wet his lips.

"I picked up that hat. . . ." he began and stopped.

Gus shivered sullenly, kicking at his bag. "Jesus." He clawed at his arms. "What is this shitty weather?"

"You're dressed for L.A.," Tommy told him sharply. "This is Japan. In winter."

He found them a bench. As he stepped away into the crowd, he felt Gus' eyes on his back. His own voice echoed. *This is Japan. In winter.* He had bitten the boy already. He moved on with a twinge of despair. Time and place made no boundaries against anger, he thought. And no one helped him with Grandpa's hat. When he returned, the boy was asleep across the entire bench, sprawled like a corpse, with Rupert camped uncomfortably atop the suitcases, his naked old head nodding between his legs. Tommy was reminded: Grandpa Rupert never got mad at the boy.

He began to move them toward Hiroshima then, another three trains and six hours. Their bodies and bags seemed inert and misshapen among the streamlined Japanese. He herded them like some strange lumpen-zombie flock to the airport train. At Ueno Station, he woke them, drove them through the midday insanity to the subway. From there, the travel sequence ground on and on like an epic nightmare: Tommy reading schedules, asking questions, getting lost, muscling the helpless pair down the subway to Tokyo Station, onto a bullet train to Osaka, another to Hiroshima, a bus to Tourist Information, a taxi to the Hiroshima International Hotel, and finally up an elevator, down a hall to a door where the key fit and the last of his patience fell away with a sweep of the arm.

"Lie down," he told them. "Just keep sleeping."

His own sleep was thin-skinned, gnawed by a persistent, unwelcome anger. Then, as his exhaustion finally prevailed, Gus and Grandpa Rupert sat up, one after the other, abruptly wide awake. Gus began to hammer through the television channels, around and around as if Star Trek would eventually shuffle up among the midnight talk shows and sumo replays. Grandpa Rupert tried to open the windows. He tested the toilet's industrial flush several times, and after that he seemed to be committing himself to some kind of phone call.

Tommy sat up, dry-mouthed and jittery with fatigue.

"Are you hungry, Grandpa Rupe? You want room service?"

"I picked up that hat at a forty-nine in Eau Claire back when Lainy was a little girl."

Tommy stared over Gus' slumped shoulder at some kind of cooking show. A hefty Japanese woman dribbled canned corn across a pizza.

"What's wrong with Grandpa?" he asked the boy.

Gus shrugged. His thumb drove at the remote. He found a samurai drama and stretched out across the end of the bed. Rupe replaced the phone and leaned back, centering his head on a stiff white pillow. A strange, numb patch of time spread out between them, and then Gus and Grandpa Rupert were asleep again, leaving Tommy with the samurai drama.

After some feudal trespass was avenged, he at last drifted off, only to be jolted awake before dawn as Gus reamed through the channels again. Each channel made a noisy rip of static through the fragile hour. Tommy felt his son's weight on the end of the bed. He had put on a growth spurt, it seemed. He seemed longer, stronger, about ten pounds heavier than last August.

"You were lucky," Tommy rasped at his back, yanking himself upright. "You survived, but you were lucky. Goddamn stupid and goddamn lucky to be alive. Did anybody tell you that?"

Gus slumped deeper.

"I knew you were going to say that shit."

Tommy squinted. The boy's face, crawling with static, hung in the small mirror behind the tv.

"You were lucky."

Gus pounded the bed. His voice cracked. "I knew what I was doing!"

They stared with uncertain fury at each other's mirror self. A few slow minutes later, as morning news aligned the static, they were asleep again, the boy flopped back and curled snoring against his father's legs.

In the full of morning, the sun high, something about Hiroshima surprised Tommy. They sat in McDonald's, at a Formica table by the window. The city looked clean and strong, with wide streets and space between the buildings. Beyond the modest skyline were round bluffs, still green. And the pace in the streets seemed calmer. Instead of Tokyo's lemming surges or Kitayama's festering knottedness, people here moved by internal clocks, pleasing themselves.

This made Tommy look at Grandpa Rupert. He still hadn't spoken, except in grunts, and he hadn't touched his coffee. He looked around with the indefinite focus of a baby.

"What's wrong, Grandpa Rupe? You feeling sick?"

"Just fine," the old man said. "Happy to be here."

"He's gonna need a hat," Gus put in. He unwrapped an Egg McMuffin and looked at it suspiciously. "That's not ham," he pronounced. He made a puffed face and pushed it away. "Grandpa, you eat it. It's not ham."

"Why should Grandpa eat it?"

"He doesn't care. It's meat. He eats any meat."

The old man took off the top muffin and removed the disk of meat. He carefully folded it in half and put it in his mouth. He coughed several times before he could swallow.

"Is he sick?"

Tommy was determined Gus would answer. "I've never seen him like this. The Grandpa Rupe I know talks and smiles. Is there something wrong with him? Gus? Is he sick?"

The boy thrashed in his plastic seat. "No!"

"Then what's wrong?"

"He's fine! Christ, Dad! Get off my back!"

Grandpa Rupert's hand slid across the table to knock knuckles with Tommy. For a moment his eyes focused and there was a flicker of a sickly smile.

"I'm fine," he said. "You lead on. Daughter sent us to learn about the A-bomb."

But they wouldn't quite be led. At Tourist Information Tommy acquired maps and brochures and tickets, but then Gus walked ahead with blind impatience, pausing only to inspect the alcohol vending machines, and Grandpa Rupert shuffled behind, gazing into the windows of camera shops and drug stores. Then Gus wiggled through the crowd out of sight. When Tommy and Grandpa Rupert caught up, the boy was doe-eyed and guilty, smelling of beer.

"Dad," he said. "You better get Grandpa a hat."

At the A-bomb dome, Tommy stopped Gus, read to him that the initial explosion had been exactly overhead, that the twisted wire frame of the conservatory dome before them was all that remained standing within a square mile.

"Nobody knew what happened," he read, feeling the boy's attention drift away. "People thought a plane dropped phosphorous that exploded as it touched the electric tram lines. Or they thought the city had been drenched in gasoline and set on fire."

Gus burped. "Cool." He was looking ahead at the wide open space of Peace Park. "Dad, will you buy me a skateboard?" He didn't wait for an answer. He loped off, tried to balance his sloppy feet on the curb around a flower garden.

"This was the center of it," Tommy mentioned again as Grandpa Rupert caught up. "It spread from here."

They both looked up into the vacant blue sky. The Japanese tourists around them were doing the same. Tommy wondered if they all felt his strange impulse to imagine the bomb falling, to see it up there in the blue, rocking softly, cradled in this sweet air, and then to imagine the moment, the ecstatic millisecond when the world turned inside-out, when the history of molecules reversed and chaos leapt out from where they stood.

"Are you taking something?" he asked Grandpa Rupert. "Did the doctor give you something to make the trip easier?"

Grandpa Rupert answered, "When I heard about this bomb I was in the Philippines with Uncle Sam. I was on my way to the mainland here, but that was that. I went home and got married to a Chippewa and that's how you got your wife."

Tommy led him away, bought a red Hiroshima Carp baseball cap and put it on his head. It was too big. Rupe pushed the bill up for vision. Peace Park spread out before them: a wide promenade and parade ground, cherry groves, a reflecting pool, the tomb of the A-bomb victims, and in the distance, with an odd gap of air beneath it, as if jarred from the ground, the famous A-bomb museum. It was the most wide-open space Tommy had ever seen in Japan.

"What is this place?" Grandpa Rupert seemed suddenly confused.

"It's a kind of shrine," Tommy told him. "Like Wounded Knee."

The old man took off the cap, inspected it, made it tighter, put it back on.

"I never went for all the Ghost Dancing and AIM stuff," he declared. "I thought those people were just a bunch of showboats."

Tommy felt Elaine's anger toward him. Maybe he dissented with reason, maybe he saw a more pragmatic path. Or maybe he had just selfishly closed his mind to the past. But in the next moment he gave Tommy a loopy glance and a smile out of nowhere.

He said, "Ha!"

"You're sick," Tommy said, taking his arm. "I don't know what you're not telling me, but you're sick."

Gus was circling back to berate them, his newly big legs stomping and scattering pigeons across the wide concrete panels of the promenade.

"This is bullshit," he whined. "It's all like peace and love and forgiveness. And origami. What the fuck does origami have to do with anything?"

Tommy watched him pause to gather a phrase, like a bad skater turning around to go backwards.

"Racist imperialism," Gus huffed at them. "That's what it's all about. Racist imperialist warmongering—" He hit a crack in the ice. "Whatever."

He spun clumsily away, marching off toward the museum at the far end of the park. "White *men!*" he finished, but forlornly so, as if the vastness of the park had suddenly overwhelmed him. The groups of yellow-hatted school children barely figured on its surface. A hundred Japanese men playing chess and Go under the budding cherry trees could not define an edge or suggest any limit to the monument. Red-faced, Gus wheeled back to them.

"Grandpa, come on!"

The old man hurried after his grandson, his head swallowed in the red baseball cap. Tommy sat on a bench beneath a black-limbed cherry tree and let them go. Gus *had* put on a spurt, he saw. The swaddling of tallow he wore as a child had broken apart and now hung in clumps above his hips, between his thighs, under the braided tail of hair twitching between his shoulders. But the frame beneath, the flat butt, long legs, broad shoulders, the frame was Elaine's and Elaine's mother's. And then he saw Elaine in Grandpa Rupert too, the way the old man lifted his feet in quick, sharp steps, what Elaine always called his "white man's walk" except that she had it too. On Elaine the "white man's walk" made her hair come alive, made her breasts bounce, made you look to see where she was going.

The Elaine who sat down then beneath the cherry tree with Tommy seemed as fresh as fifteen years ago, as much his friend as she had once been. He thought back, sifting memories, attempting to find the moment in their past from which this sensation of closeness sprang. They had been close, sometime, hadn't they? They must have been, he reasoned, if he could feel this way now, watching their son walk away. He thought when Gus was an infant, perhaps, when he had worn them out, when they had collapsed together. But no, they had done shifts so Elaine could study. The boy knew them separately, and Tommy recalled only his own exhaustion, the stiffness of his legs as he swung them over the bed and went for the crib. There was the marriage party at Nig's in the Dells, when they cried together back by the dumpsters. But that was alcohol, so much was alcohol, and Elaine had disavowed it all, claiming later that she wasn't even there. But maybe, maybe they were sober the evening a month before the wedding when she had taken him to the farmette outside Baraboo to meet Rupert and one of his white ladies. Tommy could recall clearly what Elaine wore: fresh blue jeans and his pale yellow shirt with thin red lines, her brown skin so strong in the twilight he kept touching it while she laughed nervously. The house was small and trim, with whirligigs and a birdbath, and as they approached, the lady's tiny dog leapt onto the back of the sofa and yapped berserkly into the glass. Hadn't they shared the same web of feelings, the hope and fear and sly arrogance, the lust driven crazy by the presence of yard ornaments and parents?

No. He hadn't known her. They hadn't known each other or themselves. That whole bit. He had heard this disclaimer from Elaine a hundred times. And it was true.

No, Tommy thought. It was *now* that they were close, at this moment. In the eye of destruction, in the eye of spring, their boy storming away again, again. It was *now* that he felt Elaine with him. He loved her now. She was right here beside him.

The thought came to him as naturally as the blossom-scented breath he drew and then held in sudden pain. She would sit here and brace herself with this horror as large as her own. With the image of the blasted dome, the vision of flame rolling out, she would fortify herself, and then she would turn to him, seeing him at last, and tell him to leave her life forever.

He could not rise from the bench. The school kids trooped disinterestedly past. They had seen gaijin before, more than they wanted. Tommy watched them fasten origami to the tomb. And then Gus had cycled his grandpa through the museum and was coming back at Tommy, demanding with bug-eyed fervor that they find a place called Asano Park. His fingers spindled out with excitement. He spoke in the rapid monotone Tommy identified with video game obsession.

"Slow down."

"In there," Gus said, "they got maps of how it happened. And they got kids' lunch boxes and shoes and buttons and the kids are just vaporized, and a black shadow of this guy who was like sitting on some steps, and so Asano Park is this place where hundreds of people went to escape the fire, they swam across a river, or on some guy's row boat, only they died anyway from radiation."

He seemed disappointed, when they arrived at the park, to find the bodies removed. Or maybe that was too harsh. Tommy tried to put a hand on the boy's shoulder, to steady him, but Gus wrenched away and stood off in a puffing sulk, chopping a hand through the lobe of a bonsai tree. The park scrolled out around him, an exquisite garden of raked paths and ponds with gliding carp. The precise foliage was just lush.

"It's fifty years later," Tommy told him. "It's a work of art now. I think the point is to focus on feeling better. Forget, maybe. Or forgive."

Gus split a branch from the bonsai.

"Whatever."

Tommy saw him trembling.

"Are you hungry or something?"

"I hate it, the way they have to make everything pretty."

"Why do you hate it?"

Gus turned away and walked off bitterly. "Because it's a bunch of shit, that's why!" He slapped the head off a lily and disappeared around a hedge thick with tiny green buds.

Grandpa Rupert had started off the other way, around the central pond. From Tommy's distance he looked, with his weathered brown face and small springy steps, like an elderly Japanese gentleman, come to soothe his memory. Tommy watched his hands fall like hooks to his side, then relax, then lift slowly to brush the tendrils of a vined bower he passed beneath. He stumbled on the other side but kept on, drawn deeper into the oasis of beauty.

Tommy crossed the pond on a central bridge, carp trailing him in a vee. The park, he saw from this vantage, was a closely manicured microcosm of Japan itself: shoreline and forest, volcanic ridge and plain. He stepped off the bridge into a kind of miniature mountain biome. Manicured pine trees made the air fragrant. A tiny stream, a hand's width, trickled down toward the pond, its voice rich and elegant in the quiet. Thrushes flitted in low branches. This was Kitayama perhaps, the idea of it, its essence and the peace beneath its turmoil. He remembered his initiation by Ono last fall, the old man's rapture at simple things, the smell of the mountain as the sun faded, the old stone steps at the heel of the plateau, the windswept silence of Kappa's shrine. He remembered the air from there, cold and sweet, and the shiver he had felt as Kappa's windshield cracked.

But this seemed like years ago. Slowly, trying to gauge his place now, Tommy climbed atop an earth mound carpeted in pine needles. From there, he could see an old woman in a red scarf sweeping the trail where Grandpa Rupert had gone. She was bent at the waist, her straw broom whisking to and fro. The trail beneath Tommy was grooved by her strokes. He touched it: a cool, delicate rawness, a place to lie down in heat and turmoil.

Then the old woman looked up at a sudden splash. Tommy turned. Gus had climbed the park's fence and was at the riverbank, reaching for something as it floated by.

"Gus!"

The boy intently paddled the water with his hands, trying to draw the object in, but the sluggish current was too strong. Gus followed along the steep shoreline, his feet stumbling in the high grass.

"Gus, get back inside the fence."

As Tommy neared, he could identify the boy's focus: it was a *manga*, a Japanese comic book, pink and bloated like a jellyfish as it floated in the green water. Among the sprung pages Tommy could make out a woman's cartoon breasts mashed together by powerful hands.

"Gus, goddamn it! Leave it!"

But Gus tore his shoes off. His first step into the soupy green was uncertain, and the second was a lunge for balance that brought him down on something sharp. He cried out and plunged forward, knee deep and thrashing unsteadily. He sank his fingers into the magazine as it bobbed away from him. Then his eyes widened in fear as he slipped down some underwater hole. He was dunked to his forehead once, then swept downstream, the filthy water slapping his face.

"Dad!" he sputtered. "Shit, Dad! Help me!"

But by the time Tommy had cleared the fence, his son had found the bottom again and was struggling for shore. Tommy reached out and felt his son's angry hand sink like a claw into his forearm. Then Gus pulled himself ashore and threw Tommy's arm away. He was gasping, coated to the knees with black mud. It was a moment before he realized the bulk of the magazine had torn loose from the pages in his hand.

"Shit!"

He flung his handful of pink wet pulp to the ground.

"Son of a bitch!" he wailed.

He kinked forward on his fat bare feet and took a wild swing at Tommy.

"Son of a fucking bitch!"

He swung again, his soft wet fist smacking the bone behind Tommy's ear. Tommy pushed him away, held him at arm's length. The boy wrenched away again, then fell and began to sob in shrieks like an infant, tearing at the earth as if to injure it. He put his shoes on. Then he sprawled over the low fence, squished through Grandpa Rupert's grasp, and ran.

It was a strange kind of fatherhood that played out then, a purely physical role for which Tommy felt glumly he had trained all his life. He chased the boy. He dogged him like some young hot-shot winger. He stayed close, rode the boy, boxed him and steered him, allowing flashy but harmless breakaways while he circled back to round up Grandpa Rupert.

The old man had slipped further into some wry-eyed dither, had taken to chatting up bewildered Japanese on the street. But he too could be steered. Tommy got him heading south on a fairly vacant straightaway, then swung back to contain Gus. Far ahead, the boy had gotten cocky enough to stop and work a vending machine. Tommy saw the flash of a giant Super Dry. Then Gus fled with his beer, slowing soon to a heaving walk, holding the can to his face. Tommy watched, squatting on the curb to pull a cramp out of his back. Then he rose to finish it.

At a grim trot, he threaded down his side of the street, deep beyond the boy, then sliced back hard in his face, showing him from a block away the kind of dead-on angle every defenseman saved in his heart for Gretzky.

Gus stopped on the stones of a shrine entrance, his rhythm broken. He looked around lamely. The rich geometry of his flight pattern had collapsed into the single awesome vector of his father bearing down. Tommy sensed this absolute between them, the frightening power of it, and stopped too.

The boy hung his head, his jellied hips heaving inside his sopping clothes. When he looked up again, the anger seemed ebbed from his face. He looked sheepish. Tommy felt the same surge of embarrassment. It was as though one of the crudest questions of love had been answered. *I will not let you go.*

It was on the train to Kitayama that Tommy found his way through the labyrinth of things he could have said. Passing back through Ueno Station in

Tokyo, the boy had been unable to cope with the shoving crowd. A pair of buff-cut Mormon boys stopped commuters outside the narrow upper entrance, creating a bottleneck, and Gus, stepped on from behind, had turned and pushed a salaryman. Tommy had felt his anger rise.

But all he said finally was the boy's name. "Gustav Red Cloud Morrison," he said, and he flipped the boy's hair-tail aside and put a cool hand on the hot skin beneath.

Five hours later, in Kitayama valley, snow fell lazily, rounding everything. Far below, along the curve of Hot Water River, the rip-rap looked like giant cinnamon buns. It was this deep, long winter, Tommy thought, that made it hard to know how much had happened. But once upon a time, here, there were weeds and rice, dragonflies in hot wind, and into the eye of that late-summer typhoon another lost young man must have fled in fear of himself across this grid of valley roads, his soul in flames, seeking the resolution of fate. *What am I doing, alive?* Stuart must have wondered. And there had been no one to answer him.

Tommy's gaze withdrew slowly from West Mountain. He looked across the train seat at his son and his father-in-law. Grandpa Rupert had puked at Ueno, then stopped the concessions girl and asked for egg salad and juice. Now he looked like his old self again, patiently absorbing the scenery, thinking about a gift for Bernice, maybe, or a long walk he would like to take.

"Gus."

The boy looked up groggily.

"What happened to Grandpa?"

Gus frowned. "I didn't mean to, Dad. Okay?"

"Okay."

"But you know how Grandpa is, right?"

"Right."

"He drives Mom nuts."

"I know. He took you to Disneyland three times."

"Five."

Gus glanced at his grandfather as if to reconfirm his recovery.

"We were in the Tokyo airport, Dad. And like, when I was in L.A. I bought some stuff from this guy."

"Stuff?"

"Weed, Dad. Okay? No big deal. Just something to relax. But then we got in the line where they were checking everybody's suitcase and suddenly I'm scared. Okay?"

Tommy nodded. He anchored his mind to the train's empty clacking out of the last tunnel, its slow swing and wobble up to the station.

"Dad, I was scared. I took out the bag and it's like, Grandpa, what do I do with this? It's weed. He doesn't even know what weed is. He doesn't know it's illegal. So I try to explain while we're moving up in the line. We're getting real close. . . ."

Now Grandpa Rupert was laughing and talking into the window. Gus sighed, trying for world-weariness.

"He's not sick anymore, but he's got like a major buzz on, Dad. He ate the whole bag."

Tommy stared at the boy. Gus turned away, watching the other passengers prepare for Kitayama.

Tommy said, "Gus."

The kid's eyes were angry again as he stared off into the aisle.

"Gus."

"What?"

"You're lucky. We all are."

His guests were asleep in the apartment by mid-afternoon. Tommy was kneeling over them at the window, trimming the heater, when a Kitayama patrol car swung in. He stood. Behind the patrol car surged a long, black Nissan Cedric with curtains in the windows. Tommy stepped back. He put on pants, kicked aside the mess from Gus' bag.

In a moment, Police Chief Ebana rapped on the door. Tommy looked behind him. Not Noriko and Wada this time, but the committee: Husband, Father, Mayor, the big red dictionary.

Tommy let them in. His new guests stared in suspicion at the two sleeping on the floor. Then at last Mayor flopped dictionary pages. He put his finger under a word and Ebana demanded, "Who is?"

Tommy explained: son, son's grandfather, visiting Japan. Ebana said, "Speak your own language." So he went deeper into the story, using English, but of course they didn't understand. Gus flopped out a long arm, struck the wall. "Kiss my ass," he whined in a dream.

Then Ebana pointed at the two sleepers and demanded, "Passport."

Tommy found them in Rupert's fanny pack. They were Winnebago Nation passports. Rupert Red Cloud, Gus Red Cloud. United Tribes of the Winnebago. No other nationality. No way to explain. Tommy watched the men stiffen and grunt to one another: the plot thickened. Tommy shook his head and walked away into the kitchen. He had rice on.

Ebana followed him. "Ruggage," the chief demanded.

"Sorry?"

Under Mayor's thumbnail the word *luggage*, then *small . . . black . . . bag*. As Father Yamaguchi puffed and muttered heavily, Ebana shaped May's little gym bag and jabbed a finger at Tommy. "Train," he said. Husband, red-faced, clarified. "Train ruggage," he said.

"I don't have it."

"Where?"

"Not," Tommy said. "No. Don't have."

"Ruggage where?"

"Nowhere. Don't have."

Ebana made his suspicious bag shape again, his cigarette trapped between two fingers, burning the chilly air. Tommy shrugged. He said in Japanese, "I don't know. Please search."

They conferred. Mayor was for leaving now, for re-grouping, but Ebana and Husband searched: his cabinets, his toilet tank, beneath the tatami again. Tommy spooned rice into a bowl. He squeezed on honey, shook sesame seeds and seaweed flakes, stirred with chopsticks. He stepped around them. It was funny, he thought, to see a policeman in sock feet, to see angry men in grim black suits, like funeral suits, slipping around on a cold floor in threadbare socks, their dirty, crooked toes poking out.

They searched in vain, of course, and then Ebana turned on him in full fury. He stood over Tommy as he sat on the floor beyond Gus' twitching feet, eating rice. Ebana read prepared statements written inside the dictionary cover.

"Escape police box!"

"Ono let me out."

"Carry strange bag!"

"What bag?"

"Steal truck of Yamato Trout Park!"

Tommy nodded. Now they had something. "And-o," continued Ebana, but Husband cut him off. He sputtered and fumed in Japanese, the rage of a cuckold, Tommy worried, and he rose to get his skates beneath him. But in the end it was something else.

"Poison river!" he accused. He waved his arms. "American rainbow trout!"

This left them silent for a long moment. Then Father Yamaguchi cursed his son. Ebana glanced furtively about the apartment and Mayor said, "Please, Mister Tommy. Give passport and alien card."

Tommy handed over the documents. Then Mayor said, "Sorry." He had another finger in the dictionary. He flopped over the pages: *house arrest.*

"Not," said Ebana, "leave Kitayama town."

Then Grandpa Rupert sat up. "Are you fellas game wardens?" he asked. And he reached over Gus as if to find the white man's fishing license he always bought just to be amenable. He found an old pair of moccasins instead, and turned to give them as a gift, but the committee was gone.

Tommy left Gus a note: *I'm taking a walk. Don't let Grandpa outside.* As he crossed Kitayama Bridge on foot, he wondered where Noriko and Wada could be, why they hadn't come with the committee. But no sooner had he made boot prints across the first farm road than Noriko's truck pulled up behind him.

She tapped the horn. Wada piled out nimbly, camera swinging from his neck. He made room for Tommy in the middle. They were looking for Stuart, Noriko told him. They had looked inside every shack in the valley.

"Doko deshoo?" Wada wondered.

Where, do you think?

"The one place no one dares to look," Tommy mused.

And at once, all of them knew.

The climb to Kappa's shrine took an hour. The trail was buried in snow, its roots and stones invisible. Wada slipped and puffed, his camera wild about his neck. Noriko shivered and coughed but would take no help. Tommy led them. Only Tommy and Ono, Wada panted, had been to the top in twenty years.

They climbed high among the mountain's dense cedars to the windswept pine summit. Wada's camera flashed here and there, recording their approach. Untouched drifts encircled Kappa's shrine. Deep snow smothered Ono's decades of gifts, filled the Cadillac through its missing windshield.

They rested until cold moved them to their task.

Then they pushed open the weathered shrine doors. A figure slumped there, beneath the empty chain that hung from the rafter. Wrapped in winter clothes, under a broad fur hat, surrounded by bottles and candles and statues, canned foods and gifts of every kind . . . a slumped human figure in yellow farmer boots . . . and when Tommy opened the coat and tipped the hat back the head fell off. Noriko screamed and lunged away. Then up from the heap of clothing rose the faint departing stench of Stuart Norton.

Chapter 27

It was as though the snow had paused in shock for the moment and then resumed. And when it resumed it came down with new intensity, a warm yet thinly frozen typhoon where each raindrop bloomed into a lacy crystal that spun and fluttered and stayed where it landed and took up space. Snow blocked the roads again, again over a skin of ice. Even the trains were slow, and so it happened that the coroner was four hours late coming from Takata.

In the Kitayama police box, Father Yamaguchi kept chest pains to himself. If he died today, it seemed, it would be from waiting one more moment to know just how and why his dreams for Kitayama had slipped away. He sat in Ebana's wooden swivel chair, forgetting his cigarette. Mayor snicked ash into the same ashtray, blinked behind his huge glasses. He listened to Police Chief Ebana and Vice Mayor Yamaguchi divert their energies with long, redundant rages over the rainbow trout in Hot Water River. They would crowd out the char, Ebana said. They would take up space and food and eat the char eggs and fry, Vice Mayor said. He glared. They would eat the food and crowd out the eggs and fry and take up space, Ebana said.

Mayor blinked and coned his ash and worried for a split second about the flush on Father Yamaguchi's face and said, "Couldn't you just catch rainbow trout then?"

"Stupid American fish," replied Ebana. He paced, the dog trotting at his heels.

"All they do is breed," said Vice Mayor.

Father Yamaguchi said, "Hun!" and slammed a fist against his sternum and they all glanced at him fearfully and sucked their cigarettes. Beside him on the desk was Stuart's body in a zippered blue plastic bag. The men looked away.

Only Wada was calm. His calm was obvious and irritating, and they sneaked angry glances at him. Without permission, and using his patrol car, he had driven Mister Tommy's guests back to Tokyo, and now, despite a fearsome scolding from the chief, he remained relaxed. *Click, click, snap* went the camera parts in his fat hands. *Click, click, snap.* He sat on a stool that looked tiny beneath him, beside the door, apart from them, irritating. *Click, click, snap.* Moving pieces around, lenses, rings and screws and filters, whatever cameras were made of. A massive fat boy who should have been rich at sumo, should have been wrestling on tv, should have been bouncing Tokyo glamour girls on his fat lap, instead he lifts his little black toy and aims it around.

"Don't point that thing at me," Ebana snapped.

"I wasn't," said Wada.

"Don't talk back," said Vice Mayor.

"I was only reading my light meter." Wada had a faint smile. "There's not enough light."

Now Father Yamaguchi looked up as if from a deep hole. He panted fiercely, tossed a mangled hand at Wada.

"There's plenty of light," he squeaked. "There's plenty of everything. This is a good town."

They all waited to see if he would die then, but he didn't. He found his cigarette and touched it to his lips. "Bastards," the old man muttered. Ebana looked up. "Takata bastards. They used to let us have our own coroner." Then he said to Wada, "Turn that thing the other way."

Wada did so slowly, without apology or resentment. He just smiled and turned his huge bulk on the stool and aimed his camera over the low counter out the window into the blurring snowfall. He leaned on the counter and aimed out, panning, stopping and becoming still, his giant rump blooming backward into the police box. He wound the film and became perfectly still, his trigger finger poised. The four men waited, waited, waited, and then Wada lowered the camera and turned around and sat back down on his stool.

"Fat clown," cursed Police Chief Ebana. "I ought to kick his ass."

"It's been kicked already," said Vice Mayor.

Mayor said, "Easy on him. He's just not a fighter."

"Woman," cursed Ebana.

But Wada could not be aroused. These were old insults, poorly delivered. He had been born big and had grown bigger without effort. It seemed that in a race of generally small people a few were chosen to be giants for some purpose that sumo only approximated. Small people needed big ones. Wada was at peace with this. It was a mystery, but he let it be. Insults slid off him like snowflakes off glass.

But he had been good at sumo, as a matter of fact. He had been very good. He was big, strong, clever, and, above all, patient. He was Tohoku champion in high school, and after that he had carried the hopes of Kitayama to Umiyama's Nagoya stable and trained there four years. Never did he flinch at the hazing. Not when his senpai spat on him and dragged him by his long hair across the dirt ring. Not when they called him runt or snake or tadpole or even insect. Not when he bathed his huge bulk dead last, in an inch of filthy lukewarm water, and not even, finally, when they called him a quitter.

He wasn't made for sumo. His fires burned elsewhere. He wasn't sure where, but elsewhere. He had risen steadily in sumo only because he was good at anything he did, because he was clever and patient, but sumo could have just as well been hole digging or ticket taking or bus driving because he simply didn't like it much, or dislike it much, and he saw himself retiring someday with bent ears and torn knees, at a middling level, maybe sandanme, coming back to Kitayama where he would be expected to open a chanko-nabe restaurant, drink beer, tell stories . . . and his fires burned elsewhere.

But burned where? Kitayama people found this irritating. Parents, friends, well-wishers, sumo fans: what was he doing with his life? He was only twenty-one when he came back. He weighed four hundred and fifteen pounds and could push a train car off its tracks. But he didn't want to. He drifted and puttered and through sheer cleverness and patience married a girl he had always loved and then drifted and puttered some more until his father in exasperation traded him a job for land with the Yamaguchi clan. Suddenly Kitayama, a town with scarcely enough work for one police officer, had a whopping second.

Wada showed no disgrace at this. He was implacable, steady, cheerful. He did what he was told, as well as what he was not told. He reorganized files, bought a computer and a coffee maker, photographed flood damage, car crashes, and fist-bruised women. He never said I'm grateful or I'm sorry. He never said why he quit sumo. To all those jilted sumo fans in Kitayama, four of whom glared now across the police box, Wada was supremely annoying in his refusal to hustle and worry, to wince and duck and dissemble in a proper display of the shame he had brought upon himself and his town. He didn't feel it. He was numb in some slight way, nearly amused. *Click, click, snap.* His big hands toyed with the camera.

He turned back to the window. He aimed the camera and spun the lens, focusing through the depth of snowflakes. His fires burned at the mountaintop now, in the fourteen frames of film he had taken, still in the camera. He could see each frame in his mind, perfectly. He never had to look at his pictures. He developed them almost reluctantly, stored them on proof sheets, in a box, in a closet, like an adjunct to his brain, but the pictures, these especially, remained vivid.

He had taken six by flash that evening with Gotoh and Mister Tommy. The first pop of light had blown deep grain into the ancient wood of the shrine walls and made spider webs snap like lightning. From a roof beam hung a chain with loop in it, golden hair stuck in the links, then the inside-out darkness after the flash.

Picture two: the body had pulled loose from the head and Ono must have reassembled the pieces against the wall. Then the winter coat and hat, the offerings, the desperate attempt to make it right by his Kappa. All of it dusty and stiff, lurid, empty-looking.

Picture three: the neck stump rotten black, then frozen, a cap of sparkling crystals. The hands, perfect bone.

Picture four: the wider angle took in chain and body and deep wood grain, lightning webs and frost, Tommy on haunches with his face covered and the white blur of Noriko's hand flying past the camera as she gripped the door frame and threw up.

Picture five: again.

Picture six: again.

He hadn't known what else to do.

On the recovery mission the next morning, while Chief Ebana and Vice Mayor Yamaguchi struggled with a stretcher sled on the trail behind him, Wada had arrived at the summit to take five more shots. In daylight, the colors were less lurid and the scene seemed much older and smaller. It seemed that time had moved on from this moment. The tragedy seemed simple and complete to Wada. He couldn't say why yet, but he understood. He had backed up with his camera as far as the small plateau would allow, until twisted pine branches touched the edges of the frame and gray sky filled the top. In the center of this, mid-distant, Kappa's shrine was weather-beaten and small, littered and slumping. Beside it in the snow were rubber gloves, blue zippered bag, sled, and inside the shrine's shadow, two abstract shapes of a dead young man, head and body, and then through this tableau tore

Chief Ebana and Vice Mayor Yamaguchi, waving and screaming at Wada to point that thing the other way.

He did. His fourteenth picture caught the yellow sun sharp on the fulcrum of East Mountain, prying the heavy pewter lid off the sky for an instant before it slammed back down.

Now Noriko's husband, Vice Mayor Yamaguchi, cursed rainbow trout again but no one answered. Ebana was phoning Takata, complaining about the coroner. They couldn't wait forever. Why couldn't they have their own coroner? This was a big town now, a modern town, looking to the future. He was standing right here, was he not, with the very committee in charge of internationalization? They had business park, an airstrip, plans for a new bridge. They had an English school. What? Of course they had deaths under unclear circumstances. Last year they had an insecticide poisoning, had they not? And what was this here, this severed gaijin mess in a bag? What was this if not suspicious? "I'll tell you what it is," Ebana raged. "It's a murder."

A taxi stopped in front of the police box and Ebana hung up. The men all stood except Wada, who sat down. It was not the coroner. The committee sat back down, their cigarettes confused.

"I'll say it's a murder," muttered Ebana. "I'll go ahead and say that."

Mayor said, "Now, Ebana-san, let's just wait a bit longer."

"Where's the money, then?" snapped Ebana. "Someone has a million yen. You tell me who."

Mayor removed his glasses, rubbed his face.

"They took the perfect hiding place," Ebana went on. "They had perfect reason."

"But Ebana-san," protested Mayor, "Ono has no need of money. He could hardly care about a million yen."

"No. But Ono wants to destroy our plans. That gives him plenty of reason to embarrass us like this. It was his idea, no doubt. But it's the gaijin who wanted money. Every week, every week, Japanese money to his American bank. He and Ono had the time that night, they were together—"

"But Ebana-san—"

"They've destroyed Hot Water River," interrupted Vice Mayor. "Now it is full of fat foreign whore fish. Today I caught five rainbow trout in one hour. I left the river in disgust."

Mayor replaced his glasses and aimed a small, curt bow at Vice Mayor. "I was about to suggest to Police Chief Ebana," he said, "that if Mister Tommy helped Ono kill Mister Stuart, he would not then lead us to the body."

"Aha!" Ebana jabbed a finger triumphantly. "And how did he know where the body was?"

Mayor could not answer this. Vice Mayor began to enumerate the fishing holes from which he had extracted enemy trout. Wada's camera parts went *click, click, snap*. Lens on, lens off. "One trout from the big rock below the bridge," said Vice Mayor, "one from the pool just below the waterfall, two from the tail of Three Cedar Corner—"

Then old man Yamaguchi slammed a hand down on the desk. He followed this with a fused silence, as if laying dynamite to his thoughts. At last he erupted, "Kappa!"

"Kappa has done this!"

He wheezed, lowered his jumpsuit zipper and worked a bent hand inside. He massaged his heart. "Always this town has terrible luck. We are cursed. Some force works against us and I say now that it is Kappa who is our enemy. We are beset by a fiend who resists our efforts and laughs in our faces."

He rose into his pain, an old salmon nearly home, and tipped his face to the ceiling, the sky, the mountain.

"Kappa!" he thundered. "Cursed Kappa! You possess this town! I blame you! Fiend!"

He did not die then. He missed his chair a bit sitting down, but his heart still beat and his breath clawed in and out. After a moment, Mayor replied thoughtfully.

"However," he said, "I think, perhaps, Father Yamaguchi, that it is not in the best interest of Kitayama to phrase the problem as such. I mean to speak of fiends and demons and bad luck and such. In respect, I mean, to the goals of tourism and development."

Then cigarettes burned out. Snow fell. The clock dragged its hand around. And then a deep voice came calmly from beside the window.

"Suicide," said Wada.

The four men glared.

"This is foolish," Wada said, "this talk of Kappa and murder and stolen money. If you want to benefit Kitayama, these lies only make the town look ridiculous. The truth is that Mister Stuart was unhappy here and he killed himself."

"He was not unhappy."

Vice Mayor tried a pitying look on Wada.

"He was always smiling, many girlfriends, wonderful food. We have many photographs."

"So do I," said Wada. "I photographed him many times. He was living in a nightmare. Something went wrong inside him."

"We gave him everything."

"He was sick."

"Sick?" Old man Yamaguchi rose as if to attack Wada. "Sick?" he snarled. "Who isn't sick? That's nothing to kill yourself over. Doesn't Mayor here have just one lung? Look at his hands shake. He doesn't hang himself. My old friend Sakamoto just had his nuts cut off and he doesn't complain."

"Sakamoto still catches fish," supported Vice Mayor. "He caught a one kilo char just yesterday at—"

"Shut up," Father Yamaguchi snapped at his son. "One more word about fish and you'll be sweeping rock dust again."

A miracle then. Vice Mayor shut up. For a moment anyway, while he paced and hid his face. Then he wheeled. "You big queer," he cursed at Wada.

Wada shrugged.

"My deputy will not speak again," promised Chief Ebana, and then he put on a stare that Wada had seen ten thousand times in the sumo ring, just before the opposing wrestler tossed the salt, slapped himself in the butt, and dug in to fight. The big cop just shrugged.

"I say the truth is best for Kitayama," he said. "That's all I mean."

He turned away then, focused his camera once more into the plunging snow. There was hardly any light left. He put a wool band around his ears. He put on a traffic jacket. Before Ebana could have the pleasure of commanding him, he grabbed his snow shovel and pushed the door.

Outside, headlights reflected the green tape on his jacket, like a sketchy, partial x-ray of his huge frame. He shoveled a minute, then faced them through the window.

And now he took the picture: four men in a box of light, darkness descending. Behind him, the coroner's taxi swung in from the highway.

Chapter 28

For Husband, Father, and Noriko, the ritual of atonement over Stuart's suicide was a pure and endless torment, a panorama of shame and physical torture that spanned the whole of mid-December, across the New Year, and into the first inklings of spring. From house to house went Kitayama's first family, stooping and bowing, kneeling on hard floors, apologizing, taking responsibility, eating stale packaged snacks and filling their bladders with tea, then moving on through the snow and cold to the next house. For Noriko, Husband and Father this was pure and endless torment. But for Mama Yama, the end of Stuart's life had begun a social event of the grandest kind.

By no other means could a person see inside so many houses, see the dust or the cleanliness, see the quality of the flower arrangements and how well the ancestor shrines were kept up, see how mothers and ill-mannered daughters got on. Thrilled by the prospect, Mama Yama rose early each morning and wound herself in her best red kimono. And then, from the first visit at mid-morning to the last call well beyond the supper hour, she remained sharp-eyed, talkative, and gay. If life as a Yamaguchi wife had once, years ago, turned the old woman alone up a steep and narrow trail, it seemed that now her journey had crested, broken into giddy sunlight, and pitched her breathlessly downhill.

She began with a deep bow just inside the genkan. No ordinary courtesy bow for such a great occasion, but a bow of high drama: knees on the hard floor, palms flat before the knees, and then the body bent low, lower, until the forehead touched the floor and the nose detected cleaning fluids, or the lack thereof. Then she rose resplendent in red kimono, all eyes upon her. "We are so sorry," she said, in barely a whisper.

"We take responsibility," the men said in stiff and humble grunts.

"Oh no, not at all," said host after host.

"Yes," said Mama Yama. "Mister Stuart was our responsibility."

"We take our burden," recited the men. "We ask that you hold us responsible for life of Mister Stuart and the great damage done to our town."

"We will do no such thing," replied the hosts politely. "You couldn't have helped it. You are good people. You would never hurt anyone."

And then came tea and snacks, the eager ears, and Mama Yama could talk. So many were the splendid things to say that the old woman enjoyed complete attention for perhaps the first time since she was a little girl in the stone cutters' hamlet, seventy years ago.

"Of course we don't know exactly what happened," she liked to begin, while beside her Noriko and the men settled in grimly. "But the coroner says. . . ."

And the whole town listened, open-mouthed and silent, while clumsy daughters-in-law came and went with snacks and tea. "Mother, please," Noriko always interfered. "Mother, please not again."

"Nonsense, Noriko. They deserve to know."

"Then excuse me, Mother. I will use the toilet."

"Such a rude girl, ne? Only thinking of herself at a time like this."

"Yes, mine is the same."

"Always the same."

"Yes."

"But the coroner says," Mama Yama continued, day after day, house after house, snack after snack, "that he died by hanging. The brain lost oxygen. He says Mister Stuart took the chain off the car up there. The Cadillac. Yes. You've heard of it? Something of crazy Ono's. But Mister Stuart took the chain off the car and simply put the hook through its own link and hung the chain in the rafters. He must have climbed up the wall, you see. Then he jumped. His neck broke."

She sipped her tea. The snack at the Endo home was soba, a bit overcooked and cold. They ate, then off went Noriko to the bathroom again. Mama Yama let out a sigh. "So rude," she said. In this pause, young Ritsuko Endo stood too and went to the kitchen, leaving two mothers-in-law face-to-face with the men silent beside them, perhaps sleeping with eyes open.

"You see," Mama Yama sighed, "how rude she can be?"

"Of course, dear."

Old Mrs. Endo touched Mama Yama's hand. Then Ritsuko brought more soba. The bowl banged the table a bit hard. She returned to the kitchen. The old women exchanged glances. *How heartlessly she puts it down!*

"And even so," sighed Mama Yama, "we're not so much as allowed in the kitchen."

"Yes, dear. Yes."

"Mister Stuart was quite sick, of course. The coroner says that normally a body rots from the inside out because of the food, the bacteria. But the boy was empty, nothing inside him. So the body hung there rotting very slowly until it. . . ." Here the story paused her. "Until it separated. From the weight, you see. And so the face was gone, the meat from the hands and neck. And then it froze, which makes the time of death too hard to guess. But it was suicide. No question. The coroner is very clear about that."

"And what about the money, Mother Yamaguchi? I've heard there was a million yen. Has that become clear?"

Noriko came back, her hands wet, her mouth clamped shut. She knelt on her cushion. Old Mrs. Endo pushed the soba bowl toward her.

"Eat, dear. You need more strength."

"Chief Ebana will see about the money," said Mama Yama. "There is an investigation, of course. Arrests will be made."

Ritsuko returned with more dipping broth for the soba. She set the bowl down quietly, but still the old women exchanged glances.

With one hand she sets it down! And not a word! Looking off beyond them, as if her mind were elsewhere!

On and on this went while the snow thinned and seeped and the river filled its channel, while the body was burned and the funeral arrangements were made, while Stuart's parents were at long last contacted and summoned, on and on until finally, through a kind of inner staleness and social fatigue, Mama Yama began to listen to what she was saying.

The boy's stomach was empty, she had been reciting. His intestine was empty, his colon was blank. His teeth were corroded. He had been busy and lonely and crazy with despair and self-torment. She had come to say these things. He had hanged himself and rotted and froze and now he was a pot of ash waiting for his parents to pick him up. This was the story she was telling. It became surreal to

Mama Yama, as does a single word repeated too often, and then it had become abruptly, shockingly real.

Stuart had killed himself.

In Kitayama.

Amidst them. In spite of them. And she wondered: because of them? What could she have done? What had she done that she shouldn't? The young man had looked so unnaturally fragile. So empty. So in need of . . . what? Of *her*, she had imagined. In need of *me*, every Kitayama woman must have thought. But who were they now, Mama Yama began to wonder, these Kitayama women? Who were they, who had failed to see and failed to help? Some, she knew, were only teenage girls who had assaulted Stuart with healthy curiosity. But some were grasping girls, unhappy young women who had grown into discontent and lust. Some were young wives whose husbands went elsewhere and nowhere, whose babies shrieked and whose dreams had collapsed around them. Some were women in middle age who loved Kitayama too much, or hated it too much, or loved themselves too much, or hated themselves. And some, finally, were lonely old women, mothers-in-law who had lost their way to love. Every one of these was a woman she had been sometime in her life, Mama Yama saw, every single one.

"Ne?" she said by reflex as Noriko started once more for the toilet. "So rude. And she's run me out of the kitchen, of course."

"Yes, Dear," answered another old one. "Yes."

"And always too much salt in her food. Or not enough. Always drying out the fish."

"Yes, Dear. Yes."

But she felt strange saying it, and she began to reflect. She had done her best, she felt, to fill the void after Noriko had claimed her kitchen. After Dear Son's marriage she had studied flower arrangement and gained considerable skill. But of course men didn't care about flowers like they did about food. Flowers didn't feed them. She could not see a flower arrangement disappearing into her men's mouths. She could not feel a flower arrangement moving through their guts and bowels. And thus, at the advent of her daughter-in-law, though she hadn't know it then, Mama Yama had lost her way to love. And she had hated Noriko for it.

She began to see this now. It began to seem so simple, house after house. Her sad, busy old women friends. Their distant men. Their exquisite flowers. Their daughters-in-law looking thin and haunted, or fat and haunted, staying out of sight, their food not right. And then soon enough these girls would have their own sons and get their own daughters-in-law, and soon enough they too would become annoying rubbish.

What Mister Stuart meant to Kitayama, Mama Yama saw, was a break in this loop. He was a beautiful young man with no past, no future, no wife, no mother. And so naturally Kitayama women had loved Stuart, Mama Yama thought. She and the rest had been in love with him. Fifty women, one hundred, two hundred hungry breasts and lips, a thousand rice balls and dumplings, ten thousand smiles and winks and pinches, the very air thick with yearnings, and not an ounce of it what the poor boy needed!

Then, as the atonements mounted, Mama Yama began to feel sad and guilty and cheated for herself. House to house, instead of reciting the gory details of Stuart's death, she silently began to turn over the details of her own love story. Her face grew stiff as the men's. She made what grunts and bows were required. But her mind recollected the first boy who touched her *there!* She recollected handsome Takayuki Suga, his wavy hair and tall nose, his pledges, and how he vanished. And how Husband spent a lifetime concealing his failure to love her as promised. And Dear Son . . . well, a son always turned his back, didn't he? But always, until Noriko, there was food as her way to touch them.

"Ne?" said Mama Yama to the woman beside her. "You will feel this pain too, when your son marries."

But where was she? Whose house? And who was beside her?

She looked about for a dizzy moment. It was a huge old farmhouse, as primitive as her ancient home below the quarry. This was how they all used to live, wasn't it? The tatami around her cushion was brown and shiny, like old leather. The table at her sore knees was a burnished slab of pine wood, ten centimeters thick. Above her head loomed the massive, smoke-candied beams and fret work of an old straw roof, the spider webs and dust, moth pupae and crusts of old sap, the settled black grime of a century. And then the ancient brown photographs of kamikaze boys, the dust-fuzzed daruma with one eye still blank, the shrine for family dead with its shadow-feast of tangerines and rice cups and steaming tea, incense still smoldering. It was morning yet, she realized, and they were in West Mountain Village.

"Ne?" she said to the woman beside her. It was Yukiko Sato.

"Off she goes again to the bathroom. All day long, back and forth. Like a three-year-old child. I'm so sorry, ne?"

Beside the Sato mother with head bowed knelt the daughter, clumsy Miwa. Around the table were the sulking son and father, the skeletal grandfather, and then

Mama Yama's own exhausted men, Dear Son and Husband, then Noriko's embarrassing empty cushion. The snack was green tea and, once more, for perhaps the twentieth time in a week, a store-bought bean aspic. And Yukiko Sato was offering more.

"Thank you," said Mama Yama.

But inwardly, today, she groaned at the sight of the glistening brown jelly. One must eat a gift, of course. But her guts were stuck, and for a moment she felt nausea at the thought of filling herself once more with all the bean jellies and rice crackers that lay ahead.

"No reason to do such a terrible thing like that to yourself," she said mechanically, hiding her new and branching pain. "But of course we still take responsibility."

"Please don't blame yourself," murmured the mother.

The girl trembled.

Noriko returned from the bathroom and knelt on her cushion. Yukiko Sato warmed her tea and pushed her bean aspic forward.

"You're so thin. Please eat more."

"Thank you."

Mama Yama felt a cramp in her bowel and suffered it quietly. She would like to go to the toilet herself, throw up the cheap food. But she was caught in the glare of the girl's ancient grandfather. Then her mouth popped open.

"There is still the money, of course. No one knows where that is. But Chief Ebana will make arrests soon, I suspect."

Still the grandfather stared. He had narrow, ruined, farmer's eyes, like her bygone father's. Any light was too bright. And above these were bushy white eyebrows, a hairless, spotted skull, and giant ears for which no noise was loud enough. He drank sake and ignored his bean aspic. He was hibernating through winter, the way old farmers did. But his eyes burned upon her.

"Of course he took it from the suitcase," Mama Yama said, "and sent it home to his bank."

The mother wondered dimly, "Who? Who took the money?"

The grandfather shifted his glare to Miwa. He swallowed the last of his sake from its small clay cup. His eyes came back to Mama Yama.

"Mister Tommy, of course. You knew, I suppose, that Chief Ebana has discovered that Mister Tommy is a wanted felon in Canada."

This was her newest story, how Mister Tommy had killed a man at ice hockey, which meant that naturally he. . . . But she felt uncertain suddenly, sick to her stomach and chilled by the way the old man and his granddaughter traded looks.

Then the old man rose. His gait as he hobbled away might have been hard to watch except that a whole generation of men walked like him, and to Mama Yama the drama was not the impossible stiffness of his hips or the bent angle of his back but the question of where such an old man might think he had to go at a moment like this.

She watched him inch his way to a cabinet beneath the ancestor shrine, where the incense had now burned out. He opened a drawer, pushed papers aside with one arthritic hand while he supported himself on the drawer edge with the other. Then he lifted out an envelope. Painfully, with a full minute's work, he pushed the drawer back in. He hobbled back to the table. He set the envelope before him, inside his knobby hands.

"I was cutting weeds that day," he began. His voice was at once too loud from deafness and too soft from a lifetime of smoking. "Tea," he commanded, and the trembling girl, Miwa, poured.

"There was a typhoon coming to knock the weeds all down and make it so I couldn't get at them. So I made up my mind to cut them all before the rain started."

He sipped. Both hands moved in to touch the envelope, then apart.

"But the rain came. It beat me. Miwa came to stop me but I sent her home. I said I would slash her in half if she bothered me. I kept cutting anyway and then up through the tambo on a bicycle comes this hakujin, white shirt and white head, all white in the rain like a ghost. He comes straight at me, up the wet levee that I'm standing on. So I step down into the tambo. But its deeper than I remember. I don't go in there anymore. Legs too are weak. Let the younger men do it."

He sipped again.

"I didn't turn the saw off. I tried to jump up and hack him with it. But he moves back out of my reach, and he says to me, 'Grandfather Sato?' He shouts it into the rain."

Miwa broke in now with sobs. The mother put an arm around her. The old man spoke straight at Mama Yama.

"It's raining hard now and still I can't hear much. I'm coming around to the plank so I can get out, cut him down, but the hakujin doesn't even notice. He goes on and on in some half Japanese, bawling, but I can't understand a word except for I love Miwa-chan, I love Miwa-chan. I'm sorry, I'm sorry. Here, here. Please, please."

The girl gasped and laid her head on her Mother's arm.

"I swung my cutter at him and I slipped. I fell on it, it slashed my leg and I had to stop it with my palm. I'm bleeding everywhere and the hakujin is still standing there. I spat at him. Many times until my mouth was dry. Then he left."

With shaking hands, the old man turned the envelope over. He cut the flap with a sharp, filthy thumbnail. He dumped out fifty-thousand-yen bills and counted twenty of them. A million yen.

"The hakujin went off up the mountain," he concluded, washing his hands of the story.

Then he pushed the money toward Miwa.

"I took it for her. She will go away from Kitayama. She cannot marry here. No decent man would have her now, and she cannot be happy."

Now he shifted his eyes to the Yamaguchi men. He stared a long time.

"This is the work of your committee," he said.

He reached to his sake bottle then, filled his tiny clay cup. His eyes clouded. He felt the table for a cigarette and Miwa, breathless in her grief, helped him.

"When you take the ancient Sato land for your airport," he told the men, "pay with your conscience, for I have given that too to my poor granddaughter."

There was no sound then but the girl's quiet sobbing. Then the trickle of tea into cups already full. Then the old man rose and shuffled into the next room. He lay down on cushions before a heater. After a very long time, the girl rose and followed. She pulled a blanket over him, placed a ceramic pillow beneath his neck. Then she passed them into the kitchen and returned with a basket of wet clothes. On a pole just beyond her grandfather, she began to hang long underwear. Her voice carried faintly to Mama Yama, raising old, lost tears as she sang.

Red sky, red dragonfly
I chased you with my net . . . when was that?

Mountain field, mulberries
Into my basket I picked . . . was it a dream?

"Miwa," called the girl's mother, "hush." But she didn't seem to hear. Over and over she sang the words, until at last the basket was empty and the old man snored. Then she passed them into the kitchen. A door slid shut. She did not return.

"Please," whispered the girl's mother at last. "Eat more bean jelly."

She pushed it out, sliced, served.

"Thank you," whispered Noriko.

They ate once more. But Mama Yama's throat closed to gag now and her heart ached. Her head hung heavily. She could not speak now, could not face the eyes of anyone. The bean jelly spread its dull, grainy taste as if to smother her. It was the taste of indifference, of empty manners, of bitter and pointless old age. Oh, she despaired, what an awful woman she was, and in a week more, at supper in her own house, she was finally able to act. She looked up from her bowl. She swallowed her bite of rice and candied squash. She took more from the serving bowl.

"Nori-chan," she said, and she made herself smile. "It's delicious."

Husband frowned, grunted. But the smile wouldn't leave her face.

"Thank you, Nori-chan," she said. "Thank you."

Chapter 29

On the Friday when the last of the snow melted away, the sun stayed trapped in the valley until suppertime. Tommy finished a bowl of ramen with dumplings at Great Big Delicious Dumpling House and stepped outside. The junior high boys had their navy blue jackets off, the sleeves of their white shirts rolled up. The girls wore skirts above the knee. Light poles and bike seats were warm to the touch, and the air smelled like earth.

Tommy stood in line at the new Toho Bank automatic teller, disoriented for a moment because here it was nearly spring and he had no idea who was contending for the Stanley Cup. He laughed at himself then, punching the numbers, withdrawing sixty thousand yen for Elaine, a hockey-free spring in the air and he didn't care. He was turning, intending to cross the street to the post office and wire a money order, when he heard the Cadillac's horn. *Toot! Toot!*

Ono had the top down. He wore a sweatband around his bald head, and as he sprang from the Caddy he looked like an elderly Slick Watts, about to do amazing things with a plastic sack. In fact he withdrew from the sack a liter of sake that, when he shook it, displayed a storm of gold flecks. Then Tommy absorbed a full minute of chop-talk, mixing and matching subjects and verbs, untangling biblical English from Kitayama Japanese, applying his own dawning comprehension of the language, until at last he was able to say, "Sure. I'll be there."

"Chotto translate, ne?" Ono beamed. That afternoon two Americans had appeared at his hotel. "Mister Tommy join. Chotto big party," he said, "ne?"

"Okay, Ono-san. I'll be there after my last class."

At dusk he peddled up East Mountain on a bike he had been given by the niece of Wada's wife. It was a shopper, low slung, girl's bar, baskets on the front and back, vinyl mittens factory-attached to the handle bars. It was pink. It said "Love, Love" on the chain guard. It was beautiful.

About halfway up, he stood on the pedals to apply more force and the chain broke. But Tommy pressed on cheerfully, pushing the bike, imagining that Peter and Kristie, the pair from Sado Island, had surmounted their strange encounter and decided to give Kitayama a try. He shoved Love, Love up the darkening road, smelling tree buds, listening to the frantic nocturnes of mating song birds.

But soon he saw the Americans down the long hotel driveway, and they were not what he had hoped. They were two young white men, passing a football across Ono's carp pond.

"Greg Torkelson," announced the tall one, reaching for Tommy's hand when Tommy wanted to bow. For a moment their body languages clashed. The American seemed alien, at once eager and sloppy and somehow careless with the idea of first meetings. "This is my new partner, Todd Jeffries. He of the ubiquitous pigskin."

Tommy stared, his spine bending for another bow. But Todd wanted his hand, wanted to demonstrate the results of some post-adolescent iron pumping.

"Hey," Todd grunted. "How you doing?"

"Fine, thanks. How about you guys?"

"Us?" said Greg Torkelson. "We're having a big old time. We're doing this place up real good."

Meanwhile Ono had appeared on the hotel steps with the gold-flecked sake. He wore a stained apron and swirled the bottle. He surprised Tommy, spoke to him in straight Japanese.

"Dinner is served," Tommy told the guests. "He wants us to go inside."

"See?" said Greg to Todd. "I knew that. I told you I could handle this language."

Ono had roped off the best corner of his dining room, the spot by the window where you could look down on Kitayama as its lights came on for night, or across to the last rays of red sky spraying past the top of West Mountain. Their host poured gold-flecked sake. Todd marveled at the tiny fortune in his cup, but Greg seemed unimpressed.

"I've had this before," he announced. "I've had this in Osaka."
Ono touched Tommy's arm. "What? What did the guest say?"

"He's had this before."

"He likes it?"

"It's decent," Greg said. "It's not bad sake. But I prefer Hana Haru."

"Yeah," said Todd. "That's the best. Hana Haru."

Tommy watched Ono, who was nothing if not a delicate antenna of pleasure or its lack. The old man winced, squirmed, then recovered a grin. He bowed and hurried away.

Tommy said, "You guys must be important."

Greg waved a pale, freckled hand. "Naw. We're just Americans. We always get this."

"We're with Japan KFC," supplied Todd.

Tommy's look was blank. "I'm sorry?"

"Japan Kentucky Fried," explained Greg. "Quality control consultants. Make sure the taste stays the same, all over the world."

"Like," said Todd, downing his sake, "the breading. They always want to change the breading. Now the sauce, that's okay. Soy, for example. We permit that. That's a cultural prerogative. But the breading is who we are and we kick butt on that."

"Big time," said Greg, and they shared a laugh.

Then in came the Hana Haru. Ono poured huge portions into beer glasses. He passed out Cuban cigars. "Ne?" he said. "Ne?"

"Oishii," Greg assured him. Ono beamed and rushed away. "Oishii, Toddster. That's one you gotta learn. Always makes them happy."

Tommy disconnected from the ensuing language lesson. He stared out at the darkening valley, trying to picture Greg and Todd at their work, kicking butt over fried chicken breading. He stared until reflections claimed the window. He had lost something in all these months, he thought. He had lost his sense that anything American was normal. A bucket of chicken, standardized, seemed bizarre and dangerous, a kind of imperial weapon. He had lost his way of ignoring things like that. Then he looked at his new dish. Horse meat. Ono had brought them raw horse meat, with a dip of hot pepper oil.

"They've had this before too," he translated for Ono. "Mister Greg several times. He likes it, but he prefers raw clam."

Ono's eyes spun oddly, as if searching for clams in the back of his head.

"Don't worry," Tommy told him, but the old man hurried away.

"Since I got here," Todd began on a new topic, pausing for a big gulp of sake, "we like to get out on weekends, see the country. We've done, what, seven prefectures?"

"Eight."

And Todd tried to list them, mixing up prefectures and cities, thus opening himself to a geography lesson. Tommy slumped, picked at his horse meat. "These are quail eggs," he translated as Ono returned. "He has no clams, but Mister Ono gathered these eggs himself, this morning, from the mountain behind the hotel. They're boiled in soup broth. Very good with sake."

"Ask him," said Greg, popping in an egg without comment, "if he's ever had clam so raw it was still moving. That's the best."

"Damn," said Todd. He drained his Hana Haru.

"What?" Ono begged. "What is he saying?"

"Raw clam," Tommy struggled. "Still walking? I can't say it. But you've eaten it, of course."

"Hasn't he got any rice?" Greg wanted to know suddenly. His voice sounded imperious, that idea again, like he was expecting even more consideration than Ono was providing. "And ketchup? Todd likes rice and ketchup."

But Ono, clamless, watching his precious quail eggs go down like popcorn, had moved desperately on. He splashed around more sake and suddenly he was singing something, dancing for them, rolling his eyes and wiggling his fingers as he tottered back and forth beyond the table. Tommy's heart sank as Ono urged him to translate.

"He has dancers. Two young women from Thailand. He'd like to give you a private show."

Greg shrugged. He pushed his plates to the center of the table and lit his cigar. "Works for me."

"No problem," said Todd. Suddenly he was sitting up very straight. "You mean, right now?"

Tommy rubbed his face. He hadn't started his sake yet. He took a sip while Ono chattered in his ear.

"Right now, he says. He'll tell them to get ready. Then after the show you can take a bath, and after that they will come to drink with you in your room."

"Ne?" probed Ono. "You like dance?"

"Watashi wa," said Greg, releasing a puff of cigar smoke, "tsuki desu."

Ono bent, cocked his ear. "Eh?"

"Watashi wa tsuki desu."

Ono looked at Tommy, his brow puckered in confusion. Tommy took another swallow. But the cheap Hana Haru stalled in his throat, dusty-sickly-sweet, bad alcohol. He told Greg, "You mean 'I like it.' But you're saying, 'I am the moon.'" Greg scowled at his cigar. "But listen," Tommy went on, "there's a couple other things you might want to see while you're here."

Todd stretched his chest muscles. "I might want to see Thai dancers, I know that much."

"But the river is pretty at night, reflecting the lights as it flows through the town. Or, we could take a cab ride into the valley and listen to the frogs peep. It's stunning. Really it is. And it's so dark out there in the valley that you can see the stars like you've never seen them—"

Greg puffed. He was still scowling. "I'll take Door Number One. Dancers."

"You like?" Ono jumped in. "You like dance?"

Tommy closed his eyes. *I am the moon*, Greg said stubbornly.

What played out then, in a small, mildewed auditorium behind the dining room, became for Tommy the equivalent of open-soul surgery without anesthetic. Ono sat them at a round table an arm's length from the stage. He disappeared behind the curtain, and after a moment techno-funk began thumping from the speakers overhead. Then the lights dimmed. After an awkwardly long time, May emerged, not so much dancing into their presence as stamping and twitching with furious precision. She was all elbows and kneecaps, performing her steps inside tall heels and some kind of wrapped-on neon-orange bathing suit, a big, rabbity bow on top of her head. She stared at Tommy for a moment, then at nothing. She turned at the far side of the stage, showed them her tiny rear end, and marched back.

Then Sudra seal-walked out. Her wrap was neon blue, and because of her weak ankles she wore ballet slippers instead of heels. Thank God, Tommy thought, looking at the floor, grinding his palms against his temples. But a moment later he looked up again. Sudra's movements were warmer, more real, and she smiled at him, waved at the guests, began to lift objects from a table at the rear of the stage. It was a magic act, Tommy realized. It was a dancing magic act, he realized, and in the next few minutes the show pulled at his eyes like a car wreck crossed with a porn movie. It was impossible to watch, impossible to look away. May pulled a sparkling blue scarf from Sudra's ear; Sudra pulled an orange one from May's; then they acted indignant, each demanding the proper-colored scarf from the other. Then suddenly both scarves passed through pulsing thighs and disappeared, except that the tip of May's hadn't quite made it beneath the band of her suit. Greg beat his hands and woofed approval. Next, Sudra targeted Todd with a card trick while May gyrated in the background, and meanwhile everything rotten thing about being male began to well up in Tommy. He could leave, he knew, but something stopped him. May's movements had become like porn film backstory, the disaffected cheerleader in need of a wake-up call, a dramatic phallic rescue. She was the one you wanted, Tommy thought, but Sudra, fumbling cards, then working cheerfully through the rest of the tricks, was the one you could have. The tension was unbearable. And then suddenly, emptily, it ended.

The two young women bowed, hand in hand. Greg whistled. Todd pounded the table. Then May tried to leave, but Sudra hung on to her, dragged her along as she passed a basket for tips.

"Man," said Todd, dropping in a handful of coins, "we gotta tell Moto-san about this place."

"How about Nozawa? Nozawa-kun would go nuts."

Tommy, his hand in his pocket, discovered sixty thousand yen. He slipped the whole wad into the basket. "Come on," he said to Todd and Greg. "Let's go take a bath."

Ono peeked in on them as they soaked in the scalding water. He set more sake on the edge of the bath. Did they desire more of anything else, he wanted to know. Tommy asked the two Americans, who reminded Ono of his promise that the girls would come to their room. Tommy changed this a bit in translation. "Yes," he said. "They would like more quail eggs."

Ono was delighted. But it would take time, he said as he hurried out. From the bath window Tommy could see the old man, in his yellow farm boots, with a bucket, scuffing off into the woods with a flashlight.

In the room Tommy turned on baseball—Giants versus Swallows—and poured more sake. Now the two guests were red and limp, sprawling sloppily on the floor in their Ono Hotel bath kimonos.

"Drink up," Tommy told them. "By Kitayama standards, you guys are just getting started."

At nine-ten exactly the baseball game went off the air, replaced by a samurai drama.

"Huh?" Todd sat up irritated. "What the hell?"

"That's the schedule," Tommy said. "The broadcast is over."

"But how the hell do I know who won?"

"I guess that's not so important."

"Man, that's crazy. What the—"

"Good workers, though," Greg put in. He yawned, burped. "Toddster, you gotta give them that. Damn good workers."

Tommy poured more sake.

"Man," said Todd after a long pause, "where *are* those Thai girls?"

Tommy heard a car door shut. He rose stiffly out of crossed legs and hobbled to the window. He had only hoped, and vaguely, for what he saw. He didn't really think it could happen so smoothly. But *there* were those Thai girls. They were dressed in jeans and sweatshirts now. They were tossing bags over the side of Ono's Cadillac. Then they were in the car, May behind the wheel. In a moment more the engine was running and the headlights were on.

The Cadillac rolled out. Then Sudra was looking back, looking back, her wide-eyed gaze turning red in the brake lights at the corner of the drive, and they were gone.

Tommy tried to wipe his smile off as he turned.

"Gentlemen," he said, "I think I'm done here."

Chapter 30

Tommy let the little bike go, coasting down the black mountain road with his big feet held clear of the dangerously wheeling pedals, baskets rattling and brakes screeching, cold air streaming past the smile that wouldn't leave his face. He felt unburdened.

And his final weeks in Kitayama then opened before him as a kind of slowly blooming reverie. The rough hide of memory had split and fallen off to a mental distance where he could touch it, rub it between the thumb and forefinger of astonishment, grasp its alien thickness. He felt lightened as Police Chief Ebana's judgments came down against him. He had lied. He had obstructed justice. He had staved in a shed door and stolen a truck. He had tossed a strange bag into Mrs. Nakamura's burn pile. He had lain with the wife of the Vice Mayor. He had spoiled the fishing.

All of this was true. He was guilty. But the version of Tommy Morrison that rose to play Kitayama's rogue gaijin was clear-eyed and calm, a gentle dreamer yoked bemusedly into the traces of the damned. Somehow, so far from home, he recalled high school, when he was clean-skinned, fast, and free. Anything was his, nothing was stronger than the sweet muscle of his will.

Perhaps it was the completion of Stuart's death that made him feel this way: the exhilaration of a life lost that was not his own, and yet somehow was his own, as if he had been allowed both to die and to live, or to lose Gus and to have him, or more simply to be swallowed in a strange land and emerge whole.

And a wonderful thing happened after the funeral. First, Stuart's body was ashed and stored in a small grey urn. Then, since the deceased had no home in Kitayama, Tommy's apartment was used for the week-long wake. Giant paper-and-tinsel flowers were leaned outside. A small shrine was stationed inside. Kitayama people came and went, kindling incense, leaving food and prayers. Tommy dutifully worked the crowd, and at last he welcomed onto his tatami the parents of Stuart Norton.

The old man was tall and thin, bent-necked and bald like a vulture. He didn't know enough about Japan to take his shoes off. When Tommy told him, he blinked down at his long brown oxfords and still did nothing. The mother took a long time getting through the genkan, arriving finally as a vast, punctured blimp of a woman, her eyes sunk deep as the holes in a bowling ball. Tommy did not ask her to remove her shoes.

They prayed with their backs to the shrine. Incense made the woman wheeze and cough. For perhaps two minutes after, they made austere, suspicious small talk. "We thought you all'd have them swords on," the woman said to Tommy. Her small eyes were bluer than Stuart's. "Come to find out, there's liquor for sale on the street corners." Then they took their pot of ashes and returned to the taxi.

But they left behind the million yen that Miwa's family had returned to them. On a sheet of photocopied church letterhead, some breakaway Mormon branch, with the old man as pastor, Stuart's Mother had scrawled instructions for a Stuart Norton English Scholarship Fund, and this is how, only two weeks beyond the funeral, Tommy found himself in front of his first real English class, teaching practical conversation to engineers at the new Endo Fiber plant in the business park.

"Hello!" he called out to them.

"Hello!" they called back.

"How are you?"

"I am fine thank you!"

"What is your name?"

"My name is Kennichi Sato!"

"My name is Shuichi Ozawa!"

"My name is Koi Shibukawa!"

"My name is Kenzo Funada!"

For nearly a month this went on, and went on wonderfully, and then it abruptly ended. Tommy was standing in the factory classroom, noticing that farmers had begun to till their paddies. All the way across the valley, on East Mountain, he saw upon the chestnuts and wild plum trees a thin film of green. In a month's time, his engineers had graduated to *when* questions, and he had just asked them *When is our next class?* At that moment, beyond the window, Noriko's Yamaguchi Stone truck pulled up beside the guard box.

The engineers checked their watches, scratched their heads. They twirled mechanical pencils on acrobatic thumbs. They saw the truck too. They knew more than Tommy did. He felt strangely touched by their discomfort. "Or are we finished for good?" he asked them in Japanese. He took the dropped heads for his answer.

So he said good-bye to his engineers, changed slippers for shoes at the entrance, and walked through warm-cold air to the truck. Inside, Noriko was all mewling Garfunkel and Salem Menthols. She was all shifty eyes, gear-grinding and expressive bursts of speed. She was angry. "They're making you leave Japan," she blurted at last.

But at the Kitayama bridge she didn't turn toward town. She kept driving north. She sped them in silence past a river-bottom gravel quarry and then through a familiar pear orchard where the trees were pruned to small black knots. She turned onto an up-grade dirt road that split a pine forest, then slowed for deep ruts. The day's thin warmth lay trapped among scaly trunks. Early flies lumbered dizzily. She turned into a pitted lane, and amidst a litter of old campfires and beer cans, she stopped.

It was here that Tommy began to set himself up with fond memories. The turn-out was a spot for teenagers, for lovers, a spot where a small flame in a dark stolen hour was a thrill beyond comparison. The place was so like the turnout behind Castle Rock, in Bear County, five miles from the high school, seven thousand miles from Kitayama, that Tommy had felt abruptly relaxed and happy, even as Noriko slipped from her pumps, spun on the seat, and drove her toes beneath his thigh. Her skirt rode up to show the hourglass cotton panel of her panty hose. She didn't care. She turned down Garfunkel, blew menthol smoke at a fly braining itself on the windshield.

"This is your sayonara party," she said.

Tommy laughed. He touched her ankle and felt the blood tunneling beneath coarse nylon. He scratched his finger on the fabric. He stared out and thought he saw Wisconsin red pines and Blackpoll warblers flitting in arced limbs of sumac. A gray crust of snow cracked around a tussock of saw grass. Hockey season was just ending. The hair was growing back on his ankles. Soon his feet would no longer look nude and raw at the ends. Elaine had a pick-up truck, stolen from Grandpa Rupert, who would allow her anything. They smoked together, some off-brand, Cambridge or Merit Low Tar, whatever Rupert and his lady were buying, but the smoke smelled fine spreading out in the clean spring air. They liked Miller High

Life shorties, in eight-packs. They were seniors and nobody could tell them anything. Elaine was the smartest girl in the school. Not even her string of book-dumb Red Cloud brothers could take that away from her. Not even more class skips than a flat stone on flat water could hurt her grades. She was the best. And Tommy was all-state, easy. He had legs that could pull the ice apart. He was going to gain weight, get meaner, play a little college, and then the world would be his.

In the turnout behind Castle Rock, the earth was always damp. Maybe there was a seep there. Maybe so much beer was spilled it never dried out. Nothing soaked into the ground. Elaine would squat chastely below her door and Tommy could look out the passenger window and smile as her pee wandered out foamy and yellow from beneath the truck, pushing through pine needles and paper matches and meandering into the grass at the edge of the turn-out. He remembered this as knowing that he loved her. He remembered the nights growing dark and chilly, and them emptying their bladders again together, spreading Rupert's old wool camp blanket along the seat, and struggling, always, to find just the angle that made that clumsy space comfortable for lovemaking.

Tommy's finger circled Noriko's ankle. His other hand toyed with the wing window. What he remembered was that long instant in man-child time when he was perfect, when he had done no wrong. The instant before Gus was conceived on the pickup seat, before the Morrisons pushed marriage and Rupert said go ahead, before Elaine learned she couldn't afford college, wasn't enough of any one tribe, before Tommy had swaggered off to the minor leagues like her chivalrous white knight and everything had begun its slow collapse into ancient rage and confusion. He felt the lightness of ozone before a storm.

"Why do you smile?" Noriko asked him. "Do you laugh at me?"

Tommy said, "No," and straightened his face.

But he had come full circle. His life had come around, spiraled, and stopped for him to feel a beautiful moment over again. Noriko was under his skin. She was familiar, real, the ankle in his fingers an exact weight, a map, a road into her. His will to follow was buried, and he knew right where, but he stayed with the hard bone, the bumps atop the foot.

He said, "So who's watching the office?"

"Miwa-chan. She's my assistant now."

After a moment, she reached over him to the glove box and brought out an envelope that she balanced on his thigh. Inside was a snapshot of the two of them, coincidentally side-by-side, smiling different ways under a tangle of crepe that first day long ago at Stuart's sayonara party when the world was different. Tommy looked into his own eyes and saw fear and hunger, so plain he might as well have been beating himself and screaming. He looked from Noriko's eyes that night to her eyes now and saw them softened, browner, hanging back in the steerage of some milder spot in her brain.

But then she gripped his hand and pulled them together, studying his face.

"What happened on your lip?"

"You know."

He pulled back. She was teasing him now. Everybody knew what happened. Drunk like everyone at Stuart's funeral party, he had challenged Wada to sumo. The monster had slapped his thighs and hunkered down, grinning. Tommy had followed. Someone hollered *hakuyoi!* and Wada had exploded forward with such speed that Tommy thought he had been hit by a planet. Wada's forehead mashed Tommy's whole face and drove a tooth into his lip. He bled, laughed, drank more.

Noriko teased him, "Maybe you kissed some hungry girl?"

"No."

"Maybe she was dangerous?"

"I don't do that anymore."

"Anymore, ne?"

"Ne."

"By the way, do you know my replacement yet?"

Noriko was blowing smoke and now she bent the angle to show frustration.

"Smith," she said.

"Smith, huh?"

"So." She looked away. She picked up Tommy's hand once more and dropped it. He chased her hand and brought it back in his.

"So be careful with Mister Smith."

She scowled, said nothing. They stared at each other a moment and then their lips came together. She opened her teeth, slowly probing the welted lip with her tongue. Then her teeth felt the swollen spot. At first her grip was tender and exploratory, then playfully firm. Then some resolve within her burst. She bit down hard.

Tommy felt his flesh pop. He squirmed. His outcry hit the back of her throat. His eyes rolled as the lip tore. Then the truck roof, the windshield, the pines and sunshine all slid around her twisting head. He pushed her chest, tasting blood, grabbed the hair at the base of her skull, yanked, and at last she let go.

"Don't forget," she panted. "Don't forget . . . that I hurt you too."

Then her face clouded and tears came to her eyes. Tommy put a hand beneath his chin to stop a thin trickle of blood. She brought a tissue to it. She would not cry. Her eyes filled to the brim and stopped, bulging with anguish.

And then, dropping her head, she said quietly, "*Miss* Smith."

A day later Tommy was packed and climbing into Wada's tiny patrol car. On the way to Kitayama Station, the big man stopped at his own apartment, excitedly leading Tommy into the genkan and calling out the names of his children.

"Miya-chan!" he called. "Jo-kun!"

But they weren't home. They were out with their mother. Upset, Wada raced about the tiny apartment looking for a photograph. Tommy felt no pain other than his lip, which he milked for its bracing soreness. He admired the huge man's sweet footwork with the slippers as he raced on and off tatami, in and out of the genkan.

Then at last Wada found a picture: himself and a frail young woman with bent teeth and permed hair, two grinning tykes, all of them posing in Mickey Mouse ears before a mini-castle at Tokyo Disneyland.

Wada puffed up with the stress of saying something in English.

"Walt Disney," he managed, and began to point to his head, drawing a circle as if to make it larger. He grew frustrated. Tommy unpacked his dictionary. By now he could thumb it in a flash.

"Genius?"

Wada smiled. "So!"

He made Tommy promise to write his children a letter. Then he strapped on a small, holstered pistol. "Very sorry, Mister Tommy," he said.

"That's okay."

"Please no trouble, ne? My job, ne?"

And they were back in the patrol car on their way to Kitayama Station.

Why Noriko came along on this final journey was never clear, and perhaps she wasn't supposed to, but at first Tommy was glad. Still, the seed of his sudden mood swing was planted as the train wobbled out of Kitayama. Tommy had sat between the two old high school friends, telling Noriko in the secrecy of English that his lip was fine and that he wasn't angry. Then Wada spotted something out the window and rose suddenly. It seemed as if he would jump off the train. Then he sat heavily, rocking the train and cursing some bad luck.

Noriko told Tommy, "He saw a washing machine beside the road for garbage. He wants to take home to fix. He says he can sell it."

She reached across Tommy and shoved Wada's big leg. "Garbage man," she teased.

Wada retaliated by calling her a rich girl. He called her Princess Yamaguchi, and for a while they argued across Tommy in Japanese he could not understand. But he had never thought of Noriko as a rich girl. This bothered him somehow. He could still hear her ramshackle house rattling as his heels struck the hallway. He could feel the draft around the loose windows. He remembered, one fall evening, on a walk up East Mountain, seeing Princess Yamaguchi appear shivering along a treacherous bamboo catwalk outside the second floor, taking in a sad chandelier of men's underwear that hadn't dried. And then he recalled Wada and his nifty footwork, his sideways walking, a big man in a tiny trailer.

When he was called back into the conversation it was to arbitrate a dispute. Who was the bigger genius, Wada demanded. Walt Disney or Simon and Garfunkel?

Noriko snorted derisively, sitting back as if the answer were obvious. Wada scolded her. He was sweating. He exposed his pistol trying to find his handkerchief. He wiped his face all over and left two tufts of stiff black hair sticking up, like tattered mouse ears.

"Walt Disney, ne? Of course, ne?"

"It's stupid question," Noriko complained. But as Tommy was about to agree with her, she added, "Disney is just cartoon. It's for children. Simon and Garfunkel is about real life. Together they are a great genius."

Wada slapped his forehead, and some insult Noriko flung for good measure made him laugh. The debate continued. It was clear to Tommy that they knew vastly more he than about the candidates for genius of the western world, and when they needed him again, his good mood had somehow frozen, become stiff and breakable. They were chugging out of snow country toward the Japan Sea and the bullet train. The topic had shifted inexplicably, and yet inevitably. Wada wanted to know how big Tommy's house was. Noriko had become his eager translator.

"Is it bigger," she asked, "than this train car?"

Tommy shrugged. "Sure."

"Two cars? How many cars?"

Tommy chewed the lip but didn't feel much. Everyone within earshot seemed to be staring. He wondered if they had taken sides on the Disney question.

He said, "I guess fifteen cars or so."

Wada made a grunt of astonishment and began to laugh.

"Really?" Noriko insisted. "And you heat everything, ne?"

"Yes."

She hooked her arms around his and teased, "I will come home with you, ne?"

Wada was stammering, his big chest inflated. He was making a square with his hands.

"Grasses?"

"Lawn? Yes."

"You have a garden?" Noriko asked. "And a swimming pool?"

"A small one."

She translated, and Wada did a mental belly flop that would have splashed the highway and knocked down Elaine's grape trellis.

"Mister Tommy," he hastened. "I visit, ne?"

"It's not mine any more," Tommy protested.

"But you can get a new one," Noriko reminded him. Her mind seemed to be flipping through the pages of Life or Cosmo or another of the magazines she kept stacked beneath her desk.

"Ne?" She assured Wada, "It's no problem for him to get more."

On the bullet train, down the coast and across the center of Honshu, they continued like this. Tommy's breathing became shorter and shallower and his calm balanced on what thin pain he could squeeze from his lip. They were supposed to be taking him, he began to think. But it seemed he was taking them. Or it seemed that long ago they had given themselves up to him, long before he ever met them, and now they were confirming the details of a relationship he had never foreseen. They began to seem emptier with each question, with each English word, each gasp of astonishment. As Tommy watched the urban grotesque of Tokyo slide into view, he gripped his bags and hung on to a facade of good cheer, as much for them as for himself.

And he had nearly made it. But they stopped to rest at Ueno Park. There, the far-famed cherry trees bloomed. Tarps and blankets covered every inch of the park's vast ground, and upon these, half of Tokyo had crowded to drink and sing and snooze beneath the pink-and-white petals. The best train to the airport was an hour away and Tommy volunteered to unload his yen at the soba shop. Noriko and Wada seemed so thrilled to be with him. Wada was getting drunk, warning Noriko with every sip to tell no one back in Kitayama, a promise that Noriko, drunk herself, gayly refused to make. He was a lousy cop anyway, she said. He ought to give it up and just take photographs. He was good at that. She kept pushing the jacket away from his hip, showing everyone the tiny service pistol and calling it cute. Did Tommy have rifles? Shotguns? A boat? A motorcycle?

Wada just shook his head in amazement.

"It's all junk," Tommy protested. "I don't even know where it all is right now. And I don't care."

Had he ever *seen* Simon and Garfunkel?

Tommy wanted to lie, but Noriko was too sharp.

"Nan de?" she cried. She grabbed at his hands. "What? You've seen them?"

Wada rubbed his face and stared off with a bewildered smile at the vast party under the cherry trees.

"Fantastic," he said. "Fantastic."

Then they were out of beer. Tommy rose, his mood balanced on the open palms of his soul like a thin sheet of ice. He moved through the crowd to the soba stand. He ordered all the beer his money could buy. Then, waiting, he turned, and a drunken woman under the cherry trees spotted his head of sandy, graying curls and began to call him, whistling with her fingers in her teeth.

"Gaijin-san! Come! Come here! I love you!"

She staggered on her knees in a tight skirt, waving for him to join her party.

"Gaijin-san!" she cried. "I love you!"

Wada and Noriko looked on laughing, wondering what he would do. As Tommy wondered himself, a warm gust drove limp pink petals from the boughs and across his face. Wada and Noriko had gone back to their conversation, and it was this precise moment that the last of Tommy's joy left him and sadness swept in. Then the crowd shifted to close this line of sight, and he slipped away.

He hurried down wide stone steps toward the airport train station. Arab men stared silently from the margins of the stairway, from the halls of the station. Their eyes followed his every step, the swing of his bags from the locker, the angle of his glance, the path of his flight.

At Narita Airport, the dense, shoving crowd rattled him and he became lost. Tunnels and corridors webbed everywhere. He stood panting, trapped. Then he struggled off in the wrong direction: some obscure loop through an upper corridor that took him out of Departures and around again, sticky with sweat and frustration, into some restricted area, spare and deathly quiet.

Detention and Quarantine, a sign said.

Tommy's collarbones stung from the rough bag straps. He set his bags down. Then he saw them through a door: two ragged, black-haired young women huddled on a bench behind a rope, one weeping, the other staring nowhere, an immigration officer standing guard over them. It was May and Sudra, Tommy thought. His throat thickened and his pulse rose. Or it was another two. Or it could be any two of a million, he realized. He couldn't tell in the moment before the door closed them in.

"Sir," said the efficient young Japanese man who had appeared behind him. He pointed with his open hand. "This is your way."

The American shouldered his bags then. He moved on, Tommy Morrison, heavy with the spirits of the dispossessed.